Melanin Mid

By

Katrina Chanice

For Colored Girls Who Have Considered Suicide / When the Rainbow Is Enuf

-Ntozake Shange-

I found God in myself
And I loved Her
I loved Her fiercely

THEIR EYES WERE WATCHING GOD

-Zora Neale Hurtson-

"All gods who receive homage are cruel. All gods dispense suffering without reason. Otherwise they would not be worshipped. Through indiscriminate suffering men know fear and fear is the most divine emotion. It is the stones for altars and the beginning of wisdom. Half gods are worshipped in wine and flowers. Real gods require blood."

Copyright 2023 Katrina Chanice All rights reserved.

The characters and events portrayed in this book are fictitious. Any similarity to real persons, living or dead, is coincidental and not intended by the author. No part of this book may be reproduced, or stored in a retrieval system, or transmitted in any form or by any means, electronic, mechanical, photocopying, recording, or otherwise, without express written permission of the publisher and author.

Table of Contents

PROLOGUE
A Southern Salute
ACT ONE
Drop Dead Gorgeous
The Life of the Rich & Famous
Don't Be A Tease
Travel Lite
Baggage
Date Night
History Always Repeats Itself
The Image of Perfection
Hog Nation
A Pimp Named Slickback
ACT TWO
Pretty Woman
Approved Overtime
Forbidden Romance
Bastard Out Of Mississippi
All Night Flight
Last Rites
Bad Business Moves
Baecation Vibez
A Fool In Love
Drunken Confessions
ACT THREE
Her Heart's Desire
The Invitation

Twisted Troubles
Epiphany of a Lost Love
Trapped in the Past
A Mother's Love
Sinister Sisters
Fraudulent Behavior
Divorce Party
The Masquerade Ball
ACT FOUR
No White Angels
His Favorite White Girl
Heaux Talez
Delusional Dreamer
Family Portrait
Blackjack
Breaker of Chains
A Low Down Dirty Shame
Jungle Fever
Baby Blues
ACT FIVE
Iyanla: Fix My Life
Tennessee Whiskey
Fatal Attraction
At Last
Celebrity Deathmatch
It's A Wrap!
Puppy Love
Dreams Do Come True
Insane Infatuation
Picture Perfect
EPILOGUE
Proverbs 31

Prologue

WHAT HAPPENS AT HOME STAYS AT HOME

"YOU CAN'T HEAL WHAT YOU NEVER REVEAL."
– JAY Z

A Southern Salute

"Grandma's hands...clapped in church on Sunday morning. Grandma's hands...played a tambourine so well. Grandma's hands...used to issue out a warning."
– Grandma's Hands by Bill Withers

Tylertown, Mississippi
1915 AD
-The Hidden King-

He walked in with sweat dripping on the rustic wooden floors that creaked an inch louder with each step that he took, in search of my hidden king. The bounty hunter was armed with a shotgun and orders from German soldiers of Brune to kill my child on sight. They believed that he was an abomination and would one day fulfill a prophecy, causing the world to end. There was talk of ancient scrolls and how one day, he would come in the last hour. Those scrolls went on to warn the people of the many impure spirits that were already roaming about the land. Word of the German soldiers had traveled fast to the nearby town of McComb, Mississippi and warned the village that was entrusted in guarding our future king that our God had appointed.

Quickly, I gathered him up in my arms as the bounty hunter drew closer, placing him in a small wooden box asleep and sliding it under our bed. I fell to my knees as the door swung open. There stood the bounty hunter, the sheriff, and the constable ready to take my child. Tears rolled down my cheeks as I prayed to my God in a language unknown to my trespassers. The sheriff yelled out, "WITCH!" and yet I continued to pray while listening to the cold calculated sounds of the bounty hunter's steel toe boots looking to devour my innocent black king. The constable snatched me up by my arm and screamed in my face, "Where's the Brunner boy?!"

Vigorously, I shook my head with fear consuming me, refusing to give them the answers they desperately wanted. He slapped me back down to the hard wooden floor with the back of his hand. The box cut ring on his middle finger, slashed the side of my face, causing blood to flow out freely in the mixture of my tears. I sobbed harder to my God as the bounty hunter, the sheriff, and the constable trashed this little shack of a house looking for anything that would lead them to my hidden king. When they believed that my child was elsewhere, they left, leaving the door wide open. I continued to sob on the floor, thankful that my sweet baby boy wasn't found.

After cleaning myself up as well as the shack, I fed and changed my little king. I slowly rocked him in my arms, as I hummed heavenly hymns to him. Life had been hell from the moment I took my first breath. I had prayed for better and yet better wasn't a word I even knew the definition of but looking into the beautiful brown eyes of my child, brought a warmth to me that transcended beyond space and time. Constantly, I wondered how I would protect him in this cruel world when I, myself, was on the run hiding out in this foreign country so far away from my home in Kingston, Jamaica. My only hope in this life was to see my son age up well despite him being the product of a secret love affair with a German Lord and if found alive, we'd both be killed.

*****

Jackson, Mississippi

2005 AD
- 90 YEARS LATER -
Chanice

In the middle of September, Linda had managed to get all seven of her living and jail free siblings together for a birthday celebration in honor of their mother, Myrtis Lee Rogers. She was turning seventy-eight years old and was the mother of eleven children, five girls and six boys. Having already lost two of her sons to death and one incarcerated for life, this celebration was one of many that we all hoped to cherish. Most of her children had gone on to get married and live their own lives except the two playboys in the family, Jonas and the baby of them all Keith. Didn't seem like they would ever find a sweet lady to settle down with. Two of her girls had left Mississippi in hopes of a better life with Margaret living in Nashville and Beverly living in Indianapolis. Myrtis wasn't at all an easy woman to impress as she sat with a frown watching her second oldest daughter parade around bragging about this salute that she cared nothing about.

Linda listed off the weekend's menu as she said, "Since it's Friday we're having fried fish. You know Mama, I think fish just don't taste the same any other day. Fried fish was just made for Fridays. Now on Saturday I might do some spaghetti. I know the kids love spaghetti and Sunday I'll do some collard greens with hamhocks, candied yams, mac and cheese, some cornbread, and some fried chicken. I already got your coconut cake and rainbow cake made and sitting on the cake stands on the table there. I know Beverly gone want me to help her preach and pray over the family. Oh yeah Mama this gone be the best salute ever!"

It's been said that if you want to make God laugh then tell him your plans so maybe Linda felt the need to try her hand at being a comedian because as soon as I got home from school, my great grandma Myrtis had already upset my grandma Linda and had her fidgeting the entire time. I called my grandma Meme and my great grandma, grandma though. It was weird to others, but it always made sense to me as I was the first great grandchild of Myrtis and yet adopted to my legally blind grandma Linda. Being legally blind didn't mean she couldn't see. It only meant she couldn't see as well as the rest of us. I learned over time that she seen what she wanted to see and one thing she loved to do was brag even if that meant over exaggerating the truth. Meme claims I was only two or three years old when she was leaving out of the room and I couldn't stand the thought of her leaving me, so I ran behind her screaming, "Me me me me me me me!" I don't recall ever asking about the nickname especially since my entire family loved to put emphasis on the fact that she was MY Meme. Never bothered me because she was MY Meme.

We had just moved to Jackson a few years ago, leaving the small town of Quitman, Mississippi in our rearview forever. I was young and didn't understand the fights a mother and daughter sometimes had but what I knew was that Meme was tired of taking care of her mother and she wanted to live her own life. For eleven years, I never seen Meme ever entertain a man and within six months of moving to Jackson, Meme had married Luther. As long as she was happy, then I was happy. She told me all about how they had known each other for years from working together at Mississippi Industries for the Blind and that they were always respectful of each other. Of all the daughters Myrtis had, it was my Meme that she had this overprotective nature with, and she wasn't at all happy with her marrying that man and showed contempt whenever she could. Meme simply ignored it and loved on her mother anyway.

This left Keith as Myrtis' caretaker for as much as she'd allow. She preferred for her baby girl Eunice to come from Jackson, Mississippi and see to her but she was too busy being a city girl with her husband to go back to being a country bumpkin in Clarke

County. Keith didn't mind it too much. Being married and having his own little family was something he believed would come along eventually and he wasn't rushing anything with anybody so taking care of his old, crippled mother wasn't too bad until he was ready to get out and find trouble like any playboy. Naturally, her loneliness caused her to lash out at people sometimes. Meme would tell me to look over her mother as she was just old and senile.

Whenever they came to visit, Myrtis would sit in the recliner beside the front door that faced the hallway. A lot of times, I'd think she was sleeping and so I'd never speak on my way out the door hoping not to disturb her rest but whenever I got home from school, I'd be in trouble for not speaking to my grandma before heading off to school. I'd constantly have to apologize for what I always thought was the right thing to do. This day was different. I spoke regardless. I was tired of being in trouble for trying to be nice. Sure, enough she was sleep but I still spoke when I came home from school as well. She at least smiled and I went on to my room. The second my room door closed, she was praying for understanding, believing that I was a troubled fourteen year old in need of help.

Instantly, she felt the emotions of a similar past pain that she once felt when she was only twelve years old. Her parents had died leaving her to raise all five of her siblings alone in 1939 in Tylertown, Mississippi. Four years later she had gotten married and at the age of nineteen she was giving birth to her first child, Ethel. Myrtis was a beautiful woman of light complexion with ginger colored hair while Cherokee and white ran through her veins. There wasn't a girl child from her line that didn't understand what she learned fast and that was that beauty was a blessing and a curse. She shared with Meme what she believed to be true as she spoke softly, "Lin, I need to tell you something about Niecy."

Whenever there was gossip, Meme was first in line but whenever there were words about me, she was quick to dismiss it. As far as Meme was concerned, I could do no wrong and even if I did do wrong, it wasn't as bad as what others had done. She knew that Myrtis had a temper on her, and she also knew that Myrtis was hardly ever wrong about the things she felt after she prayed for understanding. Myrtis and Linda were thick as thieves and stayed discussing the inner workings of the Brunner family. I'm sure Meme had this famous perplexed look on her face as she sat up straight and listened to what her mother had to say but ready to dismiss any and everything that wasn't for the good of her Niecy. Meme sighed and replied, "What is it mama?"

Myrtis looked down the hallway of the house and around to make sure no one heard what she was about to say before speaking low, "You need to talk to Niecy. She just came in and went straight to her room as if she's in trouble for something."

Meme quickly waved her hands in disregard to what her mother was saying as she replied, "Oh mama you know how teenagers can be. She's just on that computer or on the phone with her friends is all. She's not in trouble. The girl don't do nothing."

Myrtis shook her head understanding that Meme wouldn't be able to see this kind of pain if she's never felt it herself. She had protected her from as many dangers in the world as she could and even at seventy-eight years old, Myrtis still didn't mind protecting her, but she needed her daughter to understand so she spoke freely and said, "Lin, that child done been raped. You need to talk to her."

With a feeling of failure rushing over her, Meme refused to hear this bullshit coming from her mother's mouth, but she knew better than to disrespect her in any way, shape, or form. Myrtis stayed with a pistol in her purse, loaded, and ready at all times. It was a hard pill to swallow for any mother, but she stood up and with full confidence and lied to her mother's face as she said, "Don't worry I'll talk to her but let me get back to frying this fish. I think

Margaret and Beverly will be pulling in soon and I want everything done in time."

Myrtis wasn't a stranger to a lie. She herself had told a few and yet she looked at her daughter with disgust ready to take her crooked up right hand and bop her ditzy ass right in the head with her copper colored cane. She wanted to go express her love for me and understanding because she knew she wasn't wrong, but she knew Meme would make a scene. It took some time but during the visits that she made after the salute, Myrtis expressed her all of her love the best way that she could. She certainly wasn't wrong. I had been raped and for years I blamed myself trying to understand what I did to make this strange man look at me and take my innocence. At thirteen, I wasn't at all trying to dress like I was going to freaknik. I wasn't all in his face being grown. No matter how many times I replayed the scene in my head wondering what I could've done differently to prevent this, I found myself left with more questions than answers and the only conclusion I had was that it was my fault. Maybe if I hadn't gone outside to play. Maybe I should've stopped hanging with that seventeen year old girl like my Meme told me. Maybe I should've walked away sooner when I felt uncomfortable watching him and that girl talk and joke around. Those were the only maybes I had to stop him because within seconds he had turned around from that girl and ran up to me, lifting me in the air and over his shoulder. I kicked and punched his back, and it was as if he skipped happily into his house. Into his bedroom where he placed me on the floor. Still fighting. I fought as hard as I could to not even weigh a hundred pounds. My efforts to get him off of me were futile. I watched a smile creep across his face as he pushed my legs to my head and tugged my jeans off my bottom. I was balled up like a fucking pretzel unable to do anything but take it.

When he was done, he got up laughing as I pulled my jeans up and stormed out of his house directly into his gold car. He had wires hanging down and all I wanted was to hurt him like he had hurt me, and I had no idea how to hurt him so I just pulled the wires until they broke. Tweet and her little cousin laughed as she said, "Dang what took y'all so long? Were yall having sex?"

I hated myself. I hated being outside. The one place I used to love so much in Quitman. A true country girl at heart. Loving the animals. The grass. The trees. The cool breeze. Hearing the birds chirp and watching the flowers bloom. I was the weird one dancing in the rain on May 1st believing it would bring me good fortune. I found peace being outside and now all I wanted to do was disappear and be forgotten. I wanted to run away. I wanted to never exist. Secluding myself in my room was my only option and I happily took it every day while allowing the actions of a grown ass man to cause me to cast blame on myself.

This salute was already starting off on a bad foot, something Myrtis knew all about as well as she massaged the old incision scar on her left knee while humming, "Mmmmmhmmmm"

Despite the sour undertones, it was a beautiful sight seeing the Brunner family together. They may have had their differences, but you wouldn't have known as Keith was the ringleader of all trouble related activities. Enticing his older siblings to take a step on the bad side. Beverly had become a pastor, but she didn't mind a game of spades and a little wine on the side with her baby brother. As long as there was a case of Coca-Colas and a bottle of Jack, then Ethel and Eunice would be in attendance. Sweet Margaret and Meme's twin brother Joe just followed suit along with everybody else. There wasn't a show without the Mississippi Pimp himself, Jonas. His high yella self, sporting his Sunday's best on a Tuesday, donning his pimpalicious cane with a red feather in his hat always made him the man of the hour.

The children of the older siblings were now grown enough to partake in the Brunner Family shenanigans that they used to only hear about. Katrina and JohnJohn were the only ones to stop by and that's only because Katrina promised me that she would so that I could see my baby brother. My mom didn't get along with Meme and she certainly didn't care to get on Myrtis' bad side either, so she felt it was best to stay away. She wasn't everybody's cup of tea after shaking up with JohnJohn's father for the past fourteen years which was proving to had been about the worse decision she could've ever made but what was she to do. Blame it on drugs? Blame it on love? Blame it on lust? None of it mattered. She was in it for the long haul no matter how miserable she was on the inside. She was able to get away and spend time with her family without her warden breathing down her neck or causing a bunch of chaos. He was too busy at home in Battlefield with a crack pipe in one hand and a lighter in the other.

Her and Keith shared a doobie on the front porch and laughed about their teen years as they were only four years apart in age but so much had changed now that they were both parents. He took a hit and spoke freely, "KaTrina, Niecy is an amazing kid. You should spend more time with her. Get to know her more. She's your only daughter. She made you a mother."

As nonchalant as always, my mother shrugged as she sighed and said, "I want to but her Meme ain't gone let me and Niecy ain't nothing how I used to be. You know I was wild Uncle Keith! I stayed out shaking my ass somewhere getting into some of everything. Niecy is a good girl. She doesn't listen to the music I listen to. She doesn't like any of the stuff that I like. She may look like me but that's more Linda's daughter than she is mine."

Surely remembering my mother's wild days, Keith shook his head, exhaled, and replied, "Nah Katrina, she's more like you than you know. She just hides it better than you ever did. You got to really get her to open up to you and you'll see. I wish I could have a daughter as amazing as her."

My mother was a lot like Myrtis, always picking up on the not so obvious as she coughed and then replied, "What about baby girl? You don't think she's yours huh?"
Keith sighed as he said, "I know she's not, but I don't mind being a father to a fatherless child. Especially a little girl. They need to be protected at all costs." In that moment, I was walking up the stairs with a crisp ten dollar bill in my hands coming to hug my mom. Uncle Keith smiled and said, "Think fast" while attempting to rip the money out of my hand only for me to grip it harder and prepare for war over this ten dollar bill. I don't know what that man was thinking trying to make my little coins like that! All he did was laugh hard as ever as he said, "Smart kid."
It wasn't long before Keith left on a trouble run with the Mississippi Pimp and Meme's twin brother Joe. My cousins, Sheena, Janay, and Regine decided to go outside and play. Of course, I tagged along but as in any black neighborhood there was fresh meat on the playground and all the boys came out like sharks to chum. I wanted no parts of the fuckery because aside from the rumor mill saying I had given it up freely, Keith and Myrtis were in town and what Myrtis couldn't do, Keith would so I went back to the steps sat down on the porch. My cousins could do whatever they wanted to do. Sheena, however, followed closely behind because she too knew that Keith and Myrtis wasn't hearing shit about why they were talking to any boy.
For poor Regine, she had to make a decision and make it fast because Sheena and I were across the street as it was every man for themselves. Regine was the youngest at only ten years old and she didn't want to leave her sister alone with those boys, but her sister was the oldest of them all. Janay was sixteen years old with her foot propped up on the fence of the basketball court and about ten boys surrounding her. She had a smiled plastered across her face, enjoying every second of the attention these sharks were giving her

while Sheena and I watched from a distance as Regine yelled out, "Come on Janay!" before running across the street and leaving her sister to fend for herself.

All hell broke loose when Keith pulled back up from dropping off his brothers. He stormed into the house after running the boys off, demanding to beat every one of us because we all knew better than to be outside around those boys in the first fucking place. Everybody knew how angry Keith could get. Everybody knew that Keith was the protector of every girl in the Brunner family. From his mother down to his baby niece. If there was ever a problem, they knew to call Keith as they had done so many many times before. Eunice tried to calm him down as she said, "Well what done happened Keith? What did they do?"

He yelled, "All of them out there fucking off with those boys. It was about twenty of them trying to get them down! How the hell yall in this fucking house and they outside fucking with these boys and yall don't know shit?"

Eunice shook her head and said, "Oh I know not mine!" She yelled out, "Sheena!" Her light sugar biscuit colored daughter walked in, and she asked, "Were you out there fooling around with some boys and don't you lie?!"

Sheena shook her head and said, "No ma'am. That was Janay."

Fear fell on Margaret's face as she knew her niece wasn't lying. Janay was hot in the ass and the whole damn family knew it, but she couldn't stand to see her child get beat for it. Beverly noticed the strained look on her big sister's face, and she stood up to protest in righteousness as she spoke, "Now Keith, you need to calm down because these are teenage girls with hormones. They weren't doing nothing but talking."

Keith yelled out, "BULLSHIT!!! They were seconds away from fucking these girls outside and you want to preach about some fucking hormones. Ain't that how you ended up with LeShonda at sixteen?!"

The atmosphere had changed beyond repair, but Meme still had to try and calm down the situation as it was her house. She spoke softly, "But Keith it wasn't all the girls. It was just Janay and she do need her ass beat."

Keith shook his head and replied, "No, Lin! They all need their ass beat. They were all outside and they all knew better. Niecy, Sheena, and Regine just sat there and watched. Anything could've happened to Janay and y'all in this house not knowing a damn thing!"

Meme wasn't about to let anybody put their hands on me in our house, so she stood her ground and said, "I don't care who you beat but you ain't beating mine!"

He looked around as if he was Denzel Washington in 'Training Day', seeing all five sisters stand against him along with his mother sitting silently unable to utter a word in his defense. She too felt like he had taken it a little too far. Keith nodded his head in understanding as he said, "Don't call me when they all get pregnant and raped because you were too busy screaming 'Not Mine' because I damn sholl ain't gone answer."

Instantly Beverly remembered how she called Keith with tears in her eyes only some years ago. It was before she had moved out of Mississippi and most likely the very reason that she did. In the middle of the night, Keith had become irate and told my Meme to get the gun and put some clothes on. I remember everything so vividly as we all loaded into Myrtis' grey Cadillac. As I sat in the middle, Keith rushed to the back door and swung it open. He spoke soft but firm as he said, "Don't touch it Niecy." He slid a double barrel shotgun across my lap, and I surely did not fucking touch it.

We traveled from Quitman to Jackson at full speed to Beverly's house by Provine. Her second husband had her curled up in fetal position on the kitchen floor kicking her ribs in. That day, her baby brother saved her life, and it wasn't a day that he wouldn't do it all over again. She had a finalized divorce and a new outlook on life before packing up her life and moving to Indiana but in this moment, her past was her past. She was a pastor now and she was hurt to see her baby brother so eager to whoop on these babies as she said, "You need to calm down and see things from our point of view."

Keith looked her dead in her eyes and spoke firmly, "And you damn sholl bet not ever call me again."

With a belief that she would never need to ever again, her eyes filled up with tears as she shook her head. She pointed her index finger right in his face and boldly said, "You're dead to me Keith."

The salute was over. Beverly left out that same night heading back to Indianapolis while Margaret headed out the next day for Nashville. A riff had torn my family into shreds because of harsh words and unspoken hurts. In the car heading back to Quitman, Mississippi, Myrtis said to Keith, "Death is about to hit this family and it's coming in a set of three. I pray you find a woman to love you. I pray I get to see you, my baby boy, happily married before I leave this Earth."

Fear engulfed Keith as he knew some things just shouldn't be said.

ACT ONE

DENIAL

"Most men would rather deny a hard truth than face it."
-George R. R. Martin, A Game of Thrones-

PHYSICAL TOUCH

"Oh, I wanna dance with somebody
I wanna feel the heat with somebody"
-Whitney Houston-

Drop Dead Gorgeous

"I'm the type to count a million cash. Then grind like I'm broke."
– Dreams & Nightmares by Meek Mill

Imani

KNOCK!
KNOCK!
Without even checking the time or asking who it was, I jumped up from the couch and opened the door. Clearly still sleep and dreaming because I thought that I was looking at Channing Tatum rocking a brown FedEx fit asking for my signature. I rubbed my eyes trying to clear my vision only to be blinded by the sun even more. After I signed my name for the long rectangle box, I watched this fine white chocolate walk back to his truck giving me the sweetest view as I finally closed the door saving my eyes from the glaring sun. The box sat on the table taunting me. I hadn't ordered anything and the first thought that I had was to trash it without even opening it.

As soon as I started to open my mystery package, a black card fell out that read 'My Forever Love' which made me frown hard as ever believing that the sender could only be one person, my ex-Xavier. The man had some nerve to treat me like some random chick that he just met and knocked up. Immediately I got up and took the box to the trash. Any other time I could forgive and forget but this time I wanted him to understand that there was no coming back. He made it very clear that we were over and for once I needed it to stay that way. Despite me doing everything that I could to erase the past, I could never deny the love that I had for him and how he would always hold a place in my heart because he was my first love. I couldn't understand it myself but so much has changed in the last couple of months. It's hard trying to be the person that I was before walking into that clinic to get rid of what I believed was the biggest mistake of my life. From the moment the two lines on that pregnancy test appeared, I never stopped to think, to pray, or even question it. There were no other options to consider because I knew that I didn't have any other choice. Maybe everything shouldn't be attributed to that one moment and yet I'm left with so many what ifs. Dreams still haunt me of the most precious little baby girl that I wished I could've met. She had the biggest hazelnut eyes. The type of eyes that you could just get lost in. Her skin looked silky smooth with a head full of hair. She's all dressed up from head to toe wearing the prettiest red dress and matching socks with the ruffles on them.

When I looked at her, I could see myself and the man that I loved all wrapped into one with a beautiful red bow like a cherry on top of a sundae. Her smile shines so brightly making it obvious that she is a happy and loved baby. Seems like she was made just for me and yet no matter what or how I tried, I couldn't hold her. This pretty little baby would cry every single time as if she was being disturbed from her peaceful slumber. I simply wanted to comfort her and calm her down, but she rejected every effort that I made. That precious baby girl dissolved into a blob of blood in her crib. I started screaming at my loudest, still, no one came to the rescue. I woke up each time with fresh tears rolling down my face and regret filling my heart as I replayed those events in my mind of the day when I walked into that clinic.

My heart pounded with anxiety as I waited for my name to be called. I sat in the waiting room alone and scared after telling Xavier what I had decided to do with the pregnancy. Breaking my heart by cussing me out and ending our eleven year relationship without even taking the time to understand how the baby would've been affected if I had kept it. A nurse stepped out with a clipboard and called my name, "Imani Shelton."

Barely able to stand up from the crippling fear that had taken over, the nurse escorted me to the back where the pregnancy was confirmed with an ultrasound. A little later, a therapist went over my emotions and reasons for the abortion. For once in my life, I was honest with somebody other than my best friend and I could feel the judgement seeping from the therapist's pores. While trying to hide her disgust, the therapist referred me to Dr. Simone Julez for further counseling if I should start to experience Post-Abortion Syndrome.

I opted for the non-surgical route, hoping to avoid as much pain as possible. This seemed like it would've been easier. I needed to get this over with as quick as possible so that I could resume back to my classes at Jackson State University without anybody noticing anything was off with me. The nurse gave me the first pill to stop the growth of the fetus and at home is where I took the second pill which expels the fetus. It only took a few hours before the cramps started to roll in, getting stronger as the days grew longer. This debilitating pain caused me to bury myself under my covers away from the world. I couldn't walk, talk, or eat which caused me to lose a significant amount of weight as well as my grades dropping drastically. For the next thirty-six hours, I was crying in bed apologizing to my baby hoping it would understand that mommy was making the best choice for us both.

The Vicodin prescription for the pain sat on my nightstand waiting to be filled however I refused to get it filled, allowing myself to suffer alone. A decision that I later regretted. It was the most emotionally and physically draining event that I had ever experienced but seeing my unborn in clumps of blood is what truly broke me down into nothing. I wanted to be a mother. I wanted to love this baby, but I knew that was impossible to do. Now despite everything that I've done to forgive myself, that too seems to be impossible to do. I almost killed myself from the blood loss that was apparently all normal side effects from taking the abortion pill. Just once I wished that I could confide in my mama because she was my mama. I wanted her to hold me and tell me everything would be alright the way that I knew Vivian Banks or Harriette Winslow would've done to their daughters during a time like this, but that was something that my mama would never do. There was a time when my mama was an amazing mother but that's been many moons ago.

While pushing down the pain and regret that consistently consumed me, I called up my classmate so that we could study. My only mission this semester was to pull my grades back up and get back on track and yet here I was taking the time to smoke my first blunt with Ace. The scent of this green herb filled the air as I choked on the first few hits that also produced my first set of tears in front of somebody. My anxiety was slowly disappearing while a calming haze took over which only numbed the pain and made the worries of this world seem so very insignificant. If only I had started smoking sooner, I would've found more things to not care about but being in the national guard made smoking too scary for me. A dirty drug test would've cost me everything and in the end, I still didn't reenlist from dealing with the abortion.

All of my hopes and dreams were floating in the air and not an ounce of regret for losing a job that I hated. A bunch of snobby wannabe Instafame models acting like they were better than somebody because they attended basic training and had a quick two second glow up that they refused to maintain but thinking that they're securing a bag and yet stay in the most drama. There was never a time that there wasn't something new going on with my battle buddies that I never went to battle with unless it was on Call of Duty. I'd planned on quitting only after securing a better job with my degree since I only used the national guard to pay for school but looks like I had to etch up a new plan as soon as I got this degree. Ace was the one person that I trusted to not lace a blunt or spike a drink as well as the only one that I knew with the weed.

Ace broke my train of thought as he said, "So, are we pregnant or what?" I froze and said absolutely nothing.

He waved his hand in front of my face and I finally managed to say, "Ace, what are you talking about?"

He chuckled, "You think I haven't noticed how different you are. You're always in the bathroom and barely eating. You've become very cranky and emotional. You've even lost weight and my sister was the same way when she was pregnant with my nephew so what's up?"

I shook my head and said, "Okay, first of all why are you clocking my moves so hard and second of all who is we?!"

He seemed truly offended as he said, "Wow! You don't think this affects me too?"

I replied, "Uh no, I don't. Now stop being silly and pass me this study guide. I'm trying to finish so I can watch ShondaLand unless you want to be surrounded by study guides, study notes, and formulas all night long. I'm not missing out on Meredith, Olivia, and Annalise for you."

He handed me the study guide while saying, "Imani, not only would I have to deal with the cravings but the mood swings too. You're already crazy without being pregnant. I need to be prepared for this. Shonda and the rest of them won't be the ones dealing with these hormones. Do you want me to buy you a test or something because we need to know?"

We both just burst out laughing because we were high and something about the awkwardness of the moment was hilarious to both of us. Ace was a complete fool, but he wasn't completely wrong, so I said, "Okay, maybe you're my person and maybe you make a great point, so the answer is no we're not pregnant. Is that better?"

He sighed so hard that the papers flew up as he said, "Yes, it is! I don't think we're ready for a baby yet."

I giggled. "You sound more like the father rather than the would be uncle."

Without hesitation, he replied, "Well assuming the biological father is a figment of your imagination, then it's safe to say he'll be a deadbeat. Don't think for one second that I wouldn't take care of y'all, Imani."

The thought of Ace taking care of me, and my baby made me cringe. He was too much of a player for me to even picture him in the role of a father, then again, the thought of a man taking care of me, and that little baby also made me smile. Surely one day he'd make a great father, but I knew that it definitely wasn't going to be to any kids that I would have. The very reason Xavier broke up with me was because he wanted this baby and thinks that I didn't. Of course, I wanted him and the baby but sometimes you have to realize your wants can be bullshit and it's best to go with your needs. I replied, "Thanks Ace. That's real sweet of you but umm the fuck you mean a figment of my imagination. It's nice to know somebody cares but I don't think Xavier would walk away from his child like that. I'm pretty sure he'd be there."

Ace said in an aggravated tone, "Believe what you want Imani. The man didn't even want a commitment so how is he going to actually want a baby. You need to open your eyes. He just wanted some pussy and he got that."

I rolled my eyes and sighed. My first high and he was already blowing it with his asshole nature. Xavier may be a cheater but that doesn't mean he wouldn't have been a great father. Luckily, neither one of us will have to find out anytime soon as I replied, "You do realize you're a big ass man whore that doesn't want commitment either? What is so different between you and Xavier?"

He didn't have to say the difference. It was obvious. He wasn't married. Ace could be the biggest man whore he wanted to be. Xavier was the one stepping out on vows. I could clearly see that I had offended him. He already knew the difference and I was wrong to box him in with Xavier like that. He gathered his things in silence and when he was done he said, "You're going to believe what you want regardless. Congratulations I guess." He stormed out the door and I was left feeling angry and ashamed of myself.

After sending Ace a text saying, "Sorry friend. Exams just getting to me."

He quickly replied, "You good."

I wasn't but he wouldn't have understood. Him and his two sisters were adopted by pastors. His father is an ethics professor at Tougaloo College while his mom is the principal at Madison Central. Being the baby of five kids and all of them destined for greatness, excelling in any and everything that they touch. He came to Jackson State University so that his dad wouldn't be able to clock his moves, and everybody here thinks they know him but only they only know what he tells them. When he's with me, he's the most laid-back, goofy, pothead ever. On the outside, he's a standup guy. Truly, a completely innocent guy! We have a chill no judgement zone and here I was judging him like I didn't know anything about him. I'm the one that's scared of being judged in ways that I'm not ready for if anybody knew the truth about me and Xavier.

While checking social media, I stared at the package in the trashed wondering what it could've been. I pulled the long black rectangle box out and opened it. The contents were shocking and repulsive. I screamed and dropped the box on the floor. Inside was a dead rat laying on top of a dozen dead roses. There was another card on the inside saying....... *'DROP DEAD GORGEOUS'*

The Life of the Rich & Famous

"She is a stranger. You and I have history. Or don't you remember?"
– Rumour Has It by Adele

Chanice

Destiny said in a whisper, "I'm pregnant."
I laughed and said, "Girl stop lying."
With a sigh, she replied, "It's not a lie. I'm six weeks pregnant."
In full disbelief, I say, "Send proof."
Destiny quickly snapped a picture of the *'Confirmation of Pregnancy'* and sent it to me on Messenger while saying, "Did you get it?"
I stopped braiding to quickly examine the picture for the date and authenticity of it as I replied, "Oh damn. You really are pregnant."
She sighed and continued, "I told you. I stopped lying after we last talked about why I started lying."
Unbothered by the reason that she loved to lie, I replied, "Well congratulations."
While she popped the second pill in her mouth and guzzled down a glass of water she said, "I'm not keeping it. I can't let my mama know that I'm pregnant. She still ain't letting me live down getting pregnant at thirteen and fourteen."
Not knowing what to really say to anybody choosing abortion, I said what I thought was best, "Well that's your choice."
There was a sigh of relief from my words of approval as she replied, "I knew you wouldn't judge me. The doctors say I wasn't going

to be able to keep the baby anyway. Said that I was already miscarrying."

I shook my head at the lies that flew out of Destiny mouth while thinking to myself, *'Why get an abortion if you were already having a miscarriage?'* as I said, "I'm not here to judge. You gotta do what you think is best for you."

Her lies continued on, "Thank you! My mama wouldn't understand. She'd force me to have the baby. I already had to give up my first two. Now I barely see them anymore."

While finishing up one of my client's hair, I continued to give the best general statements that made Destiny feel as though we were connecting over the phone. She called me every single day about the same men and the same issues where I'd simply answered *'Un huh'* or *'Nah na'* while doing a million different things and tuning her completely out. It was seldom that I was actually ever paying attention to any conversation that we had but when she said that she was pregnant, that certainly got my attention. Destiny knew when I wasn't listening, but she never stopped calling to share the same story with a different name attached to it. Of all the stories she ever told, she never once told the ones that were true or that actually mattered. She kept those special stories tucked away under her bed of lies as she went out into the world causing confusion and chaos everywhere she went.

Once I finished this natural sew in slay, I told Destiny that I'd call her back later which was the lie of the century that everybody told in order to get off of the phone. I had a meeting with my Aunt Beverly that I had been dreading since I received the phone call from the nursing home where my grandma was living. My family hadn't come together in years for anything except death and despair. The only two left keeping the Brunner name alive was me and Beverly. In retrospect it was only Beverly on her third divorce since I was now finally married dropping the last name Brunner for good.

We were supposed to meet at Starbucks and chat over the next steps for what was left of the Brunner family. She walked in right on time wearing her finest as if she was a reincarnation of Lynn Whitfield which always made me side-eye her wondering what evil schemes, she kept tucked underneath that big ass church hat that she loved wearing. As soon as she made her way to me, she smiles big and says, "My darling niece! How are you?!"

I forced a smile and a warm greeting as I stood up to hug her and replied, "I'm okay auntie. How are you?"

We sat down together as she grinned harder and she spoke loudly, "Blessed and highly favored! Oh, niece where are my babies?"

The desire to roll my eyes was overwhelming. She said her babies as if she actually knew the names of my kids, their birthday, or even their age. Beverly never kept up with me but made sure that everybody kept up with her and her kids. We all knew about the dance show that her youngest won and still her contract was canceled before it even started as well as the dance show. The family couldn't help but hear about her touring with Taylor Swift only for her to act like a snobby rich bitch as if she was the one that put Taylor Swift on. Talk about fucking conceited! The girl tried her best to get her rock and roll music career going and never amounted to anything other than Beverly's daughter that won a dance show that nobody, but the network even knows the name to.

'Forgive me Father for not caring more but I ain't sorry about it.'

I smiled sweetly and replied, "Oh it's daddy daughter day so they're either playing video games or having tea parties. The sky's the limit."

With a nod, she said, "Oh good. You know niece I always thought you and Dustin would work things out. You two are meant for each other." She sighed as she continued with a low voice, "I just hate how we have to meet like this. We've got to do better at coming together as a family Niecy. We've both lost so much."

She wasn't wrong. It's something that I had certainly been praying for. I wanted my kids to know their family but the more I prayed, the further apart this family grew, and the more death followed. I replied with hope in my heart, "Maybe that's something we can start now."

That evil Lynn Whitfield smile grew tremendously as if I had just given her the answer to her schemes as she said, "Yes niece but first let's make sure that you and these babies are well taken care of. It's time to get you out of that little apartment and into a house so they can have a yard to play in."

Being a homeowner was obviously the goal, but I never wanted to put roots in Mississippi. I wanted to travel first before settling on a place to call home and now I had the means to possibly make that happen, so I said, "Absolutely but probably not in Mississippi. I've been looking though."

Seemed as if the conversation was suiting her just fine as she smiled even harder and suggested, "Have you thought about Tennessee?" I shook my head no and she continued, "Oh niece you've got to come and visit me. I just bought a huge house in Lebanon. I'm certain that you'd love it there." I smiled as she lightly tapped her manicured nails on the table and said, "Your Meme told me how you're saved now. You know I have my own church there and I could use another Associate Pastor." She sipped her venti mocha latte as she eyed me with dollar signs in her eyes and asked, "Can you sing?"

Singing was my favorite pastime at home with my kids but everything about Beverly screamed *'Hell No!'* so I lied, "Oh no music is Dustin's thing, but we will definitely have to set aside some time to come visit you."

It was time to test her luck as she pressed on and said, "Oh good. I certainly hope sooner rather than later. Especially since there's a pastor's convention happening in Atlanta this weekend. I'd love for you to come with me. The last time I went by myself, and do you know some other pastor was looking me up and down all because I was wearing red bottoms." She scoffed and took another sip as she kept on, "You have not because you ask not!" While sitting her venti mocha latte back down she says with a cute little shimmy of the shoulders, "You know niece I believe the Lord is going to give me a Rolls Royce one day."

I nodded and smiled thinking to myself, *'Who the hell does she think she's fooling? Is this the best she got? I'm not investing a red cent into nothing with this con artist!'* before calmly replying, "Well seeing is believing and I'll believe it when I see it."

There was nothing about my words that went over her head. Beverly perceived herself to be the smartest in the family as she held a PhD in theology and biblical studies. My words crushed any hope she had at a family reunion into my pockets as she said, "That kind of attitude will get you nowhere Niecy. You should really be careful of the things you say. Death has taken a lot from the both of us and yet it didn't take everything. Are you ready to lose everything for having a reckless mouth?"

I leaned forward and folded my hands together as I said, "All I've ever spoken is the truth and if the truth gets me killed then so be it."

She scoffed as she rolled her eyes, gathering her things as she looked me in my eyes and pointed her index finger in my face and spoke firmly, "Don't you ever call me again."

With a light chuckle, I replied, "Oh, don't worry about me cause I ain't worried about you."

Beverly got up and scurried away with her tail tucked between her legs. Within a week, I had received a call informing me that

Beverly had been beaten to death by her new millionaire husband. His anger issues had gotten the best of him as he lost control plummeting her face in until it wasn't unrecognizable leaving the funeral home with only two options, cremation or a closed casket. Since she had burned every bridge in her life, the best choice was cremation. No need for an over the top funeral when nobody was going to show up. Now all of Myrtis' children had died off leaving a slew of grandchildren that had no desire to ever even meet and get to know each other. As far as I was concerned, I was the last child standing since I was raised by her as well. I didn't mind carrying her legacy on by myself.

Destiny

In the middle of the night crippling pain shot through my abdomen causing me to walk slowly to the bathroom. I didn't want to wake up my fiancé and believed that eventually the pain would subside, and everything would be okay again. As the night grew longer, the pain became worse and after another trip to the bathroom, I slow stepped up to our bedroom door and spoke softly, "Baby, I think....."

I had passed out before completing my sentence with blood flowing freely down my legs causing Vincent to jump up to my rescue in a panic and rush me off to the hospital. When I came to, I was surrounded by family and friends doting on me in my time of need. I smiled at the multitude of affection that the people in my life were showing me while hoping the truth of my actions never made the light of day. After finally getting the life that I always wanted, satisfaction still was beyond my reach and having my cake and eating it too had become my new mission in life.

Vincent had already provided me with a beautiful two story house in Clinton, Mississippi and together we were happily awaiting the day that we said *'I do'* after planning every little detail together. Being the wife of an NFL player was a dream come true to a smalltown girl like myself but this new attention of the many men around me provided me with a sense of pleasure that I wasn't ready to let go of.

When Dr. Brown came in, my family and friends gave us privacy to talk as he said, "How are you feeling? Gave us all quite the scare there."

I nodded with a smile and replied, "I'm okay. Just ready to go home."

Dr. Brown held my hand as he said, "In due time. I assume that you're unaware that you were pregnant and suffered a significant amount of blood loss from a miscarriage. If Vincent hadn't brought you in sooner than you would've died."

While placing my head down into my hands to hide the tears that I knew wasn't going to fall as I acted in shock of that which I already knew and replied, "No! I didn't know."

Only a couple of weeks later and I was dressed in pure white ready to marry the one man that promised to give me the world. Both of our families smiled with joy waiting for the ceremony to start and as time ticked away, it was clear as day that no wedding was happening between Vincent and I as he never showed up to the church. Frantically I called him, and he didn't answer. I called again and again and still no answer. His whereabouts were my only concern. Everybody was blowing this man's phone up at my request and Vincent was sending everybody straight to voicemail. I ran to Niecy hoping that he'd answer her since they were such good friends and to my dismay he did. While snatching the phone from her hands, I screamed, "Where the fuck are you?"

Nonchalantly, he sighed and replied, "I'm at home."

With a puzzled look on my face and confusion in my voice, I asked, "Why are you at home when today is our wedding day? We're supposed to be getting married!"

His energy hadn't changed as he said, "I don't know nothing about that."

I stood frozen with my mouth wide open as the call ended and my dreams went up in smoke. I handed Niecy her phone back as I walked away in a daze saying, "Tell everybody to go home. There's no wedding."

I was forced to move back in with my mom which caused me to wild out in the worse way with absolutely no care. When asked what happened, I told everybody what I believed to be true which was that the man broke up with me because I had a miscarriage and didn't know I was pregnant. As everybody started to despise

Vincent for being so heartless, I relished in the attention that I received until my mama started to poke holes in my story thanks to Medicaid papers that she had received with my name on it. I can never get anything past this woman but if she was waiting on me to come clean about already knowing, then she'd die waiting because I had my story and I was sticking to it. I knew that she'd find out eventually because she always did find out the truth but if she was going to be the fool and believe my lies then I was certainly going to tell them. I don't mind running around town singing these bullshit lies to everybody that will listen because it's fucking fun to do. These dumbasses will believe I say if I put the right act on. The only one crying about me being a liar is my mama and everybody is too busy believing me over her making everything she says null and void.

At thirteen, I ended up pregnant and when I told her she didn't even care. Oh no it wasn't until she found out that the guy I had been fucking was twenty-one and in the army is when she got pissed off wanting to press charges and have me screaming rape. I was clueless then but now I understand that the bitch just wanted my man. Her antics ruined any chance I had with him because me lying about being seventeen didn't stop him from fucking when he found out the truth. Only a year later and I was pregnant again. She didn't even get the chance to meet this one, but it was another child support check. My life was good until I met Niecy's loud mouth ass. At first the bitch never said anything. She was just as clueless as everybody else hanging on to my every word until something between her and my mama. Now all of a sudden, all the bitch do is tell my fucking business to my mama while stealing every man I've ever liked.

I made it my mission to keep Niecy and my mama far away from each other because as long as nobody asked Niecy anything, then Niecy wasn't saying anything, however, my mama loved asking

Niecy all about me. It was as if she was more of her daughter than I was. It was after Niecy had some kind of panic attack when she was out of town that she came back acting completely fucking different. When she suggested a puff of the magic dragon, for the first time I actually was ready with multiple men on speed dial but once the three of us were all in my room to smoke, Niecy started tripping. She looked over to see him laid out on my bed with me running my hands up his gym shorts while he locked eyes with Niecy since she was supposed to join in but the bitch got angry and walked out. I don't know what the fuck made her think the shit was going to be free.

I knew my mom was going to drill her but I wasn't worried and sure enough while Niecy sat in the living room watching tv, my mama walked in and sat on the sectional couch and asked, "Where's Destiny?"

Without a second thought, Niecy sighed and replied, "In the room with some guy. I don't remember his name."

My mama nodded and continued to dig for answers as she said, "You know she was pregnant a couple of months ago?" Niecy tried her best not to reply as she remembered distinctively that I said that I didn't want my mama to know anything about this and yet here she was telling Niecy as if she knew everything and actually didn't know shit. My mama knew she had Niecy right where she wanted her as it had happened so many times before when she said, "She lying saying she didn't know but like I told her the motherfucking Medicaid papers came in the mail. What she getting Medicaid papers for?" Niecy shook her head while shrugging her shoulders hoping that movement would be enough to make my mama feel as though they were connecting in the conversation, but my mama wasn't no spring chicken. She refused to settle for the bare minimal and she wasn't about to have anybody play on her intelligence as she pointed to the tv stand and said, "There they are right there! I know she told you about that damn baby."

Truly annoyed and over it, Niecy replies, "Well she was getting an abortion if that makes you feel any better."

That indeed did not make my mama feel any better. In fact, that pissed my mama off even more but at the very least she had her so called motherfucking proof of a lying ass bitch living in her house. She kicked me out the next month as I was still holding on strong to my story of not knowing that I was pregnant. This was the proof I need to know that I couldn't trust Niecy with anything else.

Don't Be A Tease

*"I'll freak you right, I will. I'll stick my tongue.
I'll speak that language. Use my foreign skills.
My hands all in your hair."*
– To My Bed by Chris Brown

Imani

An American author, once said, *'The man that masters himself through self-discipline can never be mastered by others.'*
One quote that I have truly adored, especially since men these days lack self-discipline to the tenth power. The act of resisting temptation and pursing what they think is right despite the fears that try to stop them. Shouldn't be too hard to do with the right man in charge, however, he was a complete conman with amazing quotes from his self-help books. I used to believe that men could only master self-discipline in the boardroom leaving the bedroom a dull and boring place as they trampled off behind some loose hussy only good for sucking their stress away. Being wrong was an understatement. Just like that American author, mastering self-disciple was just fancy talk for a few coins and bragging rights with presidents and millionaires. Just like any other thug from the hood selling fake dreams with sweet talk.....
"BUZZZ"
My phone vibrated with a text from Marcus that said, "It's slow today. I almost fell asleep twice."

A devilish grin appeared across my face as I've been wondering for a while now about how deep was his attraction for me and how far could I take things with him. There was nothing unattractive about this golden brown, beautifully built, muscle bound, six foot two, chiseled God from the land of wherever the fuck they made the USO twins. Literally everything about this man made me dumb drool. Fuck self-discipline! I wanted to see him lose control the way I wanted to when he got my number at the gas station and gave me a hug, smelling like he needed me to throw it back a few times in a few different places.

Six months ago, at the Circle K on High St, I pulled up in my black 09' Chevy Tahoe. Marcus noticed me first but as always; I was in the biggest rush trying to get gassed up and on the road. I never cared about my dad's side because they never cared about me, but Niecy wanted me to meet everybody and know that I was a Brunner too. This particular weekend the family was laying Niecy's grandma to rest in Quitman, Mississippi. My cousin, Niecy was the only constant reminder of this side of my family, and this was her Meme, so I didn't mind showing face and being there for the only cousin that I knew in the Brunner family.

I dashed into the store, picked up a few items for the drive, paid for the gas, and was back out the door in no time. Just as I was passing by him, he spoke, "You need to let me drive that truck."

His comment had me whipping my head around so fast because of the audacity dripping from his words, that I almost gave myself whiplash. I was expecting to see some drunken gold tooth, scrawny ass, Monte Carlo driving bitch boy and instead, this MAN stood before me looking extra yummy in his black and red ClickTight Rydaz t-shirt and black jeans standing beside his chromed out Honda Shadow Phantom. It looked as if his shirt was painted on while even Helen Keller could see his print from ten miles away. The first thought that entered my head was, *'The fuck you been hiding?'* I smiled sweetly and replied, "Now you know I can't let you do that."

Baby licked his lips, smiled, and I melted instantly contemplating my commitment to my family. Thoughts running wild of, *'Did I really need to get ate up in the country by a bunch of mosquitoes? Could I skip the funeral and just drink a little at the repast?'* His voice interrupted my thoughts by saying, "Well how about you put your number in my phone?"

I nodded and with full confidence, I replied, "I can do that as long as you give me a hug." He held his phone out with that sexy smile plastered across his face. His close presence had me weak in the knees, but it was in the moment he wrapped his arms around me that I in return wanted to wrap my legs around him. I knew the moment I came back from Quitman, Mississippi that I was going to give him all the business. Yeah, that was six months ago though. Who doesn't love a hardworking man? He works in demolition or something like that and apparently never has time for much of anything. I've been trying to link up and put in some work on that hard dick. I realized that I had to apply pressure in ways that caused me to branch out of my comfort zone.

Instead of replying to his text message, I ran to the shower to massage my throbbing aches away with the pulsating speed on my detachable showerhead. Of course, it only made me want him even more. Images of him spinning me around and pinning me against the wall with the water beating onto our bodies kept flashing through my mind. I needed to make this fantasy a reality, but Marcus was a heavily guarded man and very much in control of his thoughts, actions, and words. As soon as I hopped out of the shower, I set the phone up and considered making a quick video of my fingers swirling inside of my honey pot. Certainly, that would wake him up but that wouldn't be enough for me. I was craving his touch and at the very least would've needed to see his reaction, so I Facetimed him instead.

It only took two rings before he answered with the biggest kool-aid smile across his face as he sat up leaning into the camera for a better view as if he could see through the towel that I was wearing. With water still glistening on my coffee brown skin from my hair dripping, I couldn't have been more aroused watching him look around for his supervisors and coworkers while trying to form the words to start a conversation, and yet all he could do was sit there on his phone biting his bottom lip and rubbing his forehead. He asked, "What's funny?" when he heard me giggling from seeing him constantly adjusting himself well over four times in the ten minutes that we were on the phone.

I spoke coyly and said, "Did I wake you up?"

While adjusting himself once more, he replied, "Yeah you woke up everything!"

Here I was, still unsatisfied with the reaction and yearning for so much more of him. He was clearly turned on, so I pushed my luck and asked him to come and give me a kiss after he got off work. A fucking mission impossible with this guy but he agreed and now all I needed to figure out was how to get more than just a kiss.

Hours later and excitement was written all over my body as I walked out the door to his pure white 2014 GMC Denali. When he jumped out of his truck and walked up to me, instantly I imagined him picking me up and carrying me to the bed. I shook my head as I grabbed his arm and walked towards the backdoor of his truck, knowing if things happened the way I wanted tonight, we weren't making it to my bed. Marcus looked me up and down with a light chuckle and that's when I knew that he understood the assignment.

After getting inside, I had to think fast on what my next move would be, but he was faster when he asked, "Where's my kiss?"

With a surprised look on my face, I replied, "Your kiss?"
He laughed as I moved to the center console and instructed him to sit in the middle of the backseat. This black sundress hugged my voluptuous body perfectly and underwear wasn't needed for what I had in mind. I slowly pulled the dress up as I leaned back slightly to give him the best view of my smooth waxed kitty. Once again, my actions were turning him on. It was obvious from the sexy way that he licked his lips, smiled, and raised his right eyebrow as if he was The Rock. I caressed my inner thighs until I could feel his hands slowly moving up my legs. While looking him seductively in the eyes, I spoke softly, "You can look but don't touch."
While pulling his hands back, he allowed me to continue my show of self-pleasure. My fingers slowly parting my outer lips, with the tips twirling in mini circles around my protruding pearl until an uncontrollable flow started to ooze out. As I began to moan, I could hear him unzipping his jeans and repositioning himself, so I darted in two fingers as I whispered, "Oooh Marcus."
Continuing this back and forth motion until I heard him matching my moans. Maybe I had given him the wrong impression. This wasn't a mutual masturbation show. I wasn't letting him get off and think that was it for the night. When we locked eyes, I pulled my fingers out and placed them into my mouth, licking my sweet juices off. I teasingly said, "Which set of lips would you like to kiss since they both taste the same?"
Without any hesitation, he ran his hands up my thighs to my waist, pulling me to his face and diving into my honey pot with no further instructions needed. My hips had a mind of their own, swaying to their own beat from the feeling of his tongue dipping in and out of my honey pot mixed with the gentle suction on my aching pearl. Slowly he twisted his head from side to side creating figure eights and then viciously devouring me while my hands scratched his cloth seats damn near ripping holes in them.

Continuing through my climax until my legs begin to tremble, signaling to him a job well done. While pulling me onto his lap, he begins to kiss me with one of his hands exploring up my back, lifting the sundress even higher and his other hand cupping the back of my neck. Unable to stop the beast that had emerged, he slipped the dress completely off and started suckling and palming my breasts.

His manhood had been at attention this entire time and I had been craving to taste him since the moment I seen him at the gas station. I climbed out of his lap and tooted my pretty plump ass up while getting face down to meet my new thick friend. As I rolled my tongue around the tip of his head, I lightly massaged his balls. Hearing him moan along with one of his hands combing through my soft passion twists had me inching his thickness deeper into my mouth which only gave me more reason to take all the time in the world enjoying him enjoying me. Bobbing in circles, making my own version of figure eights caused him to moan out, "Shit!" Music to my ears especially while feeling my thick friend pulsate in my mouth. Marcus went from combing through my hair to using both hands on my head, giving me the speed that he desired. It wasn't one moment I didn't love it and then he said those magical words, "Baby, I'm about to cum."

There was no need to stop so I continued, ready to slurp up every drop that blasted my way. Only slowing down as I felt him go limp in my mouth. I looked up at him and said, "I hope you don't think we're done."

As he smiled his manhood started jumping in my hand since I never stopped stroking him. I placed him back in my mouth and sucked him lightly until he was back up at full attention. Marcus looked confused when I came up but soon realized what was happening when I straddled him backwards with both hands on the middle console as I glided down onto his throbbing thickness.

He squeezed on my hips while I bounced up and down as if I was in my very own private twerk show. I leaned up straight when I felt one of his hands inching its way around to rub on my clit with the other one pleasantly cupping my breasts. His soft lips planting tender kisses down my back, sent euphoric sensations throughout my entire body. My breathing staggered and he knew I was reaching my peak once again, so he whispered in between kisses, "It's okay. Let go baby."

Before I knew it, I was screaming out, "Marcussssss!!!!!"

With my hands on the back of the seats for support, Marcus held my hips and commenced to drilling me without a care. The faces that I made were from the best pleasurable pain that I'd ever felt. Moments later he finally let off the sound of victory. We were both drenched in sweat and the truck smelled like nothing but puhdussy. The windows were fogged up like that scene in Titanic and it was hot as hell. I contemplated putting my sundress back on because I felt just fine walking back into the house with just my birthday suit on.

We looked at each other and he said while grinning with satisfaction, "You good."

I could feel tingling chills in the middle of my back thinking about the event that had just happened seconds ago, as I hopped out of the truck saying, "I'll live to fight another day." Marcus laughed as he hopped out behind me, grabbing me up and saying, "Don't be such a tease next time." If only he knew, I was already playing my next move and it was going to be a doozy, but I nodded and replied, "Lesson learned babe."

Travel Lite

"Bag lady you gone hurt yo back. Draggin' all'em bags like that. I guess nobody ever told you. All you must hold on to. Is you, is you, is you." - Bag Lady by Erykah Badu

Jackson, Mississippi
5/1/2006 AD
- Eight Months After The Salute -

Chanice

The Brunner family was certainly hit with death after death in a set of three just the way my grandma Myrtis had prophesized. Each lost more devasting than the last causing me to vow to never attend another funeral ever again. It didn't matter to me who had died. I couldn't bring myself to say goodbye to another family member, so I made sure to love them while they had breath in their bodies. They always said it's the little things that count so I made sure to pay close attention to the details. If I ever became a bother or a burden, then I knew to give a person their space. Being a loner was my favorite pastime so if space is what they needed, I knew how to give it without there being any drama.

The Mississippi Pimp was the first to fall as he literally dropped dead from a heart attack while trying to leave out of his house heading to refill his prescription. It was October, only a month after the salute and nobody understood how he could ignore the signs of his health as he wasn't mentally handicapped and knew very well to keep his affairs in order. I watched in horror as we pulled up to his house in the middle of the night where his body laid out in the cool of the night. The ambulance was nowhere in sight, but the coroner was apparently on the way.

Ethel was screamed and ran to the side of the house from shock scaring the literal piss out of her as she squatted on the side of the house with tears rolling down her face at the disbelief of her baby brother being dead and gone.

Meme was squalling in anger at how those no good summabitches had left her big brother on the ground without even taking the decency to cover him with a blanket before leaving. She made a great point. The man was laid out on the ground beside the porch in nothing but his underwear and socks with defibrillator tabs still stuck on his chest. His pretty green eyes were cold and glassy as Meme bent down and closed them for the final time. At the time, I wondered how she seemed so comfortable with a dead body. It made no sense to me how she could give him a goodbye kiss at the funeral. I simply watched not understanding anything because this was only the first of many deaths to come to this family. I simply wasn't comfortable yet.

One thing the Brunner family knew how to do was dress and this was the Mississippi Pimp, so it was mandatory that they wore their finest in his honor. During the repast, Ethel sat in the passenger seat of her son's car singing the blues with a bottle of E&J in her hands. She was a carbon copy of Myrtis with her light complexion and ginger colored hair. The sassiest one of all her siblings and she too stayed with a pistol loaded and ready for anything and anybody. I always said it was Ethel and Eunice that were my favorite aunts. Ethel was the fire while Eunice was the ice. They paired well together as the oldest girl and baby girl of Myrtis and were a force to be reckoned with at all times. Ethel looked out to me and with a drunken slur as she said, "My baby's gone. My baby's gone." Tears welled in her eyes as she patted the bottle and continued, "This my baby now."

While others seemed to cling to death in the most toxic of ways, it had become the only reason the family came together, and I had grown tired of meeting cousins that I never knew existed. I was never warned against anything other than how to act like a lady but these cousins of mine in Tylertown never got that memo and it wasn't long before I was labeled the *'mean'* cousin by Sheena. She felt like she was the *'nice'* cousin and it's only because I didn't mind fighting a couple of them. Not sure why that ever classified me as mean considering these cousins didn't care that we were cousins. One smacked my butt, and I spun around so fast I almost gave him whiplash as I hissed, "Touch me again and I'll cut your ass!"

He backed up and left me the fuck alone. I literally never seen him again and didn't want to. It was Janay that didn't mind batting her eyelashes and at a cute boy regardless of the bloodline. When the adults had all went to bed, Janay wanted me to come to the living room and hang out with her and another cousin. He was our age and seemed cool, but he was our cousin so I'm expecting video games and other cool things. Silly naive me. I walked to the front and there Janay was sitting on the floor in front of him as he sucked on her neck. I turned around and walked back to the room that I was sharing with Meme.

It wasn't long before Ethel lost her husband. They were separated but he was still family as they had been together for so many years. In the midst of them planning the funeral, I was sent to my aunt on my mom's dad's side of the family. It was supposed to had been a way of getting to know my family. I'm pretty sure they were just tired of me fighting my cousins. Beverly's grandson always caught the worse of it and it was always by accident. As if I meant to kick him in the nose! Total accident! If only he had moved when I told him to since I was swinging rather high on the swing. It was him that wanted to defy the laws of gravity. Punching him in the nose was a complete accident as well. He truly did walk into my swings. Then again, I certainly didn't have to throw the watermelon rein at Sheena's head making Eunice think I was a menace to the family. Sure, I had bitten a few others. I was biter but I always warned them beforehand, and they still continued on! I was also a tattletale. The worse cousin to have around when you're trying to do wrong because once Keith dotted the door, I was singing like a canary and hiding behind Meme for protection.

This funeral weekend was cut short after only twenty-four hours of me being there. It was about six of them crowded in a room kissing and rubbing on each other as the one lonely one looked at me and says, "Want to join in?"

Facial expressions got the best of me as a disgruntled look of disgust appeared on my face as I replied, "Nah, we're cousins."

"Bitch we ain't cousins!" His reply was stained in anger from my rejection. I simply turned around and walked out of the room back to the living room alone with my baby cousin that could do no harm. I was at peace until he stormed to the front hoping to poke the wrong fucking bear. He snatched away HIS baby cousin and sat down on the floor beside me. Crisscross applesauce. He used her wittle baby hands to 'punch' me in the face repeatedly. I took a deep breath. If there were words coming from his mouth, then I didn't hear not a one because I had punched the shit out of him and the damn baby. Poor thing crawled away screaming and confused while we both stood up in fight mode. He had the advantage as boys are naturally stronger than girls, but he slipped up when he pinned me in the chair, so I Mike Tysoned his ass and bit his ear. I had all intentions of ripping that motherfucker clean the fuck off as he yelled out in pain, "Help!!!! Auntie!!!! Get her off of me!!!"
I would've laughed but then I would've had to let go and I wasn't letting go until his ass was off of me! Our aunt stormed in, shocked at the drama I had created in her house. She pleaded, "Niecy, let him go!"
I purposefully shook my head no like the rabid Pitbull that I was, and he cried out some more, "Get this bitch off of me!"
When our aunt seen that he was going to be in misery until he got off of me, she helped ease him up. We lifted together out of the chair because I refused to let go until I knew for a fact that he wasn't about to jump on me again. When I did let go, he was being soothed like the little bitch that he was with sweat and tears mixing on his face. I was sent back to my mom's apartment, and I didn't mind not one bit if I never seen those fuckers again. Of course, I told my mom and Meme everything and as always, I could do no wrong. I left with Meme heading for Tylertown once again as that's where the family plot is. We'd stay at Myrtis' sister house which was simply the old family house.

A small little shack really. It was barely hanging on. Something you'd see in one of those movies with Cicely Tyson or Oprah as they picked cotton and dealt with the long-suffering of being a black woman in America. I was certain if the wind blew too hard, it would tip completely over. I only ever visited that little shack twice and over the years, the wind eventually did knock it down. Now it's just vacant land that the Brunners own.

In the hallway, my female cousins were playing a game that AJ had never heard of called *'Jigg A Low'* and it sounded fun as hell. They invited her to the circle and gave her the instructions. The chant started:

"Jigg a low, jigg jigg a low"
"Jigg a low, jigg jigg a low"

I pretended to mouth the words since I didn't know the game. One of my cousins jumped into the middle of the circle and started popping her back. Seemed fairly easy to do but I didn't have a clue on what I'd do when it landed on me. The chant started again and landed on a different girl. She jumped into the circle making her hips roll as if swinging a hoola hoop around her waist while all of the girls cheered her on. I was scared about my name getting called but I knew that I was going to pop and roll something too and as soon as they called my name, Uncle Keith popped out from around the corner saying, "Oh y'all got the wrong one. She can't dance." Whether I could or couldn't didn't matter anymore. If I had jumped my happy go lucky ass in that circle, then Uncle Keith was going to make sure that I never wanted to jigg a low, a high or a sideways ever again. I politely walked back to the living room and sat down on the floor beside Meme and Myrtis as I listened to a bunch of old folks share family secrets that I probably shouldn't have been hearing.

During the next funeral, which was only four months after the last, Ethel lost her husband in a way that I never understood. When

I asked my Meme said that he swallowed his tongue but when the topic came up with my mom, she gave a much more detailed version of how he dropped dead in the middle of the night falling off the toilet fighting demons and ghosts of his past. Both reasons were a bit too much for me and I learned to stop asking questions about the death of Ethel's husband. I'm pretty sure that my Aunt Beverly must have felt like it was her daughter's time to shine because at every funeral she belted out, *'His Eye Is On The Sparrow'* causing sorrow and confusion on who we were actually crying about. At this point it was both the Mississippi Pimp and Ethel's husband.

Days after this last funeral, I was in the hot seat standing in the need of prayer as my Pawpaw Henry had told his wife, Myrtis and Meme about how I was cussing out my cousins. In shock Meme yelled out, "Niecy come here!"

I walked into the living standing in the same spot as my Uncle Keith facing my own tribunal as I said, "Yes ma'am."

Meme asked, "Were you in Tylertown cussing with your cousins?"

Instantly, I was weak in the knees as I looked back and forth between Meme, Paw-paw, and Grandma. Without saying another word, I had silently chosen to plead the fifth of my actions when Pawpaw said with a smile, "Tell them how you told that boy you were going to cut his ass if he touched you again."

His smile did not warrant the release of my admission of guilt, and I continued to stand frozen in fear of what Myrtis and Meme was going to do when if I confessed to not only cussing these folks out but threatening to slice a motherfucker too. Myrtis leaned forward with all seriousness in her voice as she said, "It's okay baby. You told his ass right!" Her words were the key I needed to finally exhale and admit to the accusations that laid before me. When they dismissed me, I went back to my room to rejoice.

Within eight weeks, Uncle Keith had broken up with one woman named Lola and married the next named Theresa. I adored Lola because she was a woman that truly loved a man inside and out. Uncle Keith was a tough pill to swallow and as the only kid growing up in Quitman, I watched woman after woman barely last more than a few months as his woman. They all seemed to love him, but it was always something about them that was the red flag that always ended the relationship. Whether it was bad ass kids or being a simple minded hoe, Keith was going to chunk the deuces with the quickness. She witnessed in the heat of the moment during the Mississippi Pimp's funeral how hurt and fear caused Uncle Keith to lash out at Lola leaving her feeling embarrassed with tears in her eyes. Pride is a hell of a drug and Lola was a hell of a woman that he should've apologized to.

None of us knew a thing about Theresa until Myrtis came to visit with the biggest smile as her baby boy had finally settled down. Wasn't nothing fake about this marriage as Uncle Keith had gone so far as to start moving out of his mother's house and in with Theresa. He had even changed his voicemail so whenever somebody called and he didn't answer, you'd hear, 'Hi, you have reach Keith. Sorry I can't come to the phone right now but I'm a happily married man so all of you floozies stop calling my phone! Everybody laughed and adored how the playboy had fallen so deep in love with an older woman. They were all ready to meet her until they were all ready to kill her six weeks later.

Theresa drove eighteen wheeler trucks across the state and Keith had started traveling with her on the road until one night Lola called his phone and his new insecure wife lashed out, "Why this bitch still calling your phone Keith?!"

With an aggravated sigh he replied, "I don't know baby. Everybody knows we're married. Just leave it alone."

She refused not knowing the temper that Keith had as she continued, "The only reason that this bitch keeps calling is because you still want her! I told you to change your fucking number."

Anger was starting to set in as his voice grew louder when he said, "And I told you I'm not changing my fucking number." Through his clenched teeth he replied, "So leave it the fuck alone!"

She pulled the truck over to the side of the highway and turned the engine off as she screamed, "You lying son a bitch!!! If you want her so fucking bad, then go be with her!"

Keith had the right mind to jump out of the truck and do just that as regret had set in. Theresa wasn't wrong though. He was in love with Lola and wanted her bad. Although he wasn't talking to her, he was happy just to see her name pop up. She treated him like a king and even in her anger she was always so calm and loving. The laughs and jokes that they had shared were once in a lifetime and something he never wanted to forget. She was the woman he wanted to marry but he knew that he fucked that up and yet here she was calling him because she missed him and didn't want to believe that the one man, she loved more than anything in this world had moved on so soon. He got up, leaving his phone on the passenger seat, heading to the back of the truck as he said, "Think what you want. I'm going to sleep."

He laid in the bed hoping to dream of his lost love in peace as Theresa started the truck up to make it to her next drop on time, but she wasn't done and still had a lot more to say when he woke up. The truck jerked and she said with resentment dripping from each word, "Aight Keith we're here." His eyes opened to the reality that he needed to find an escape. She hopped out first and he followed only to be met with another argument as she said, "Why the fuck you won't get your number changed? If you don't want her or any other woman like you say you do, then what's so wrong with getting it changed? Can't you see that I'm unhappy about this?"

It was official. He was over it as he said, "If you're unhappy then that's on you. I'm not changing my gotdamn number for you or any other broad! You knew I had a past when you met me and as long as I'm being faithful then there shouldn't be any fucking problems. Keep this shit up and I'm gone leave yo ass right where the fuck you stand!"

Her insecurities had gotten the best of her. She knew she couldn't compete with these younger girls and yet she was giving it all she could because she looked amazing to be fifty years old, but she found keeping a man to be the hardest mission to accomplish. Everybody had flaws and still she couldn't find one man to love her, flaws and all. She hopped back in the truck with tears flowing because her husband couldn't reassure his love to her by simply changing his number to appease his wife. While he instructed her to back the truck up into the loading dock, his phone vibrated against the passenger seat and lit up again with the name Lola. Instantly, Theresa seen red as her foot slammed on the gas causing her to ram into the loading dock.

There was never a thought in her mind that she'd just killed her husband until she looked out her side mirror and didn't see him. Fear that'd he left her crept in as she hopped out the truck to see him lying dead on the ground with his face smashed in.

It was the biggest and coldest blow that death had brought to the Brunner family as the news traveled in a mist of confusion and disbelief. I was half sleep when Janay burst into my room saying, *'Uncle Keith been in a car accident. He's in the ICU.'* I dismissed the claims and went back to sleep and moments later, Janay was back saying, *'Uncle Keith is dead.'* Still refusing to believe the news, I sat up emotionless in my queen size bed trying to understand what was even happening. Days went by and the family poured in while I waited with his Oreos on standby. I knew when he came, he was going to want reading material for the bathroom as if he was Craig on *'Friday.'* I had a couple magazines sitting on my dresser waiting and ready. He was allergic to fish, so I was going to make sure that nobody served him any gotdamn fish on that Friday. Meme was just going to have to have that on another day. I waited for the only father that I knew to show up and say it's just a case of mistaken identity. I waited for a week until I was forced to walk into the funeral home and view the body, but it wasn't him and I was relieved with hope that he'd still show up and tell everybody it's okay. They had pumped some man's face out and dressed him up real nice, but it didn't matter to me because the man that laid in this casket wasn't Uncle Keith.

On the day of the funeral, I could feel my heart beating so hard because Uncle Keith still had shown up. The weather matched my mood as the raindrops hit the window of the black family car that drove us to the funeral home. At the time I didn't understand that I was lightheaded and unable to catch my breath because I was beginning to hyperventilate as I walked in beside Janay and sat down in the third pew behind my Meme who was behind Myrtis and Theresa. Behind me sat Janay's brother smiling with sorrow. It had been a long time since I had seen him and that's when the reality set in that Uncle Keith wasn't coming back. It wasn't a mistaken identity, and I couldn't remember if I ever told him I loved him. I was a kid that stayed to myself. I loved from a distance. I stayed in a child's place but now when it was my turn to partake in the Brunner shenanigans there would be no ringleader. I looked down at the obituary and there he was, his face smiling amongst the clouds. While shaking my head still in disbelief, I opened the obituary to see what felt like a thousand different pictures of him with everybody and except me. We never even got to take a picture with each other. I started breaking down in sobs at the death of the only man that I would've allowed to walk me down the aisle.

Baggage

"Holding me closer than we've ever been before. This ain't a dream. You're here with me. Boy, it don't get no better than you." - Every Kind Of Way by H.E.R.

Imani

The infamous walk of shame started at one that morning while Marcus was snoring from the twenty-minute session that we just had. A round second would've been too kind, but he was one of many needing to work on stamina instead of needing his sweaty nipples twisted as he roared like a lion casting for the naughty version of *The Wiz*.' I eased out from under his embrace and tiptoed out of the room while quietly slipping back into my black leggings and grey tank top. At least at this time of night the roads were clear, and I could enjoy the quick ten minute drive from back home. I thought I was tripping when I pulled up to my townhome because Xavier was pulling up beside me. I couldn't understand why he'd even be up at this time of night let alone pulling in behind me like some crazed stalker.

I watched him stagger up to my door and lean against the frame as if he was too drunk to even know where he was. Whether he was bearing gifts or not didn't mean anything to me because this certainly needed to be the last time that he popped up at my place like this. I took my sweet time to get to the door, just to hear lies pour out of his mouth in a river of cheap liquor as he said, "Hey baby. I've been missing you. I got you something special."

I chuckled and replied, "Oh, thanks."
A stank look emerged on his face trying to understand why I was being so nonchalant with him as his drunken lies poured out some more from him saying, "Don't be like that baby. Come on. Let me in and I can make it all up to you."
As tempting as that sounded, it wasn't enough. I'd rather have furry sex with Marcus than to succumb to Xavier again so I declined his offer and said, "I'm exhausted and I do believe you have a wife to get home to."
He took a step back almost falling on his ass before wobbling off to his car and saying,
"Wow. Okay Imani."
I didn't bother watching him walk away. There was nothing exciting about Xavier to me anymore. He was the oldest old news that I had. After entering inside of my house, I threw away the Victoria Secret's bag that he'd had given me but not before looking inside and seeing some green and black lingerie. Classic Xavier. I made my way inside to take a quick nap before getting the day started.
After waking up, I called my mama to wish her a Happy Mother's Day. She answered as if she was out of breath, "Hello!"
I replied with love, "Hey mama, Happy Mother's Day!"
With an aggravated voice, she replied, "Oh thanks." I attempted to show concern as I asked, "Are you okay?"
She sighed as she answered, "Yeah, just wondering where the fuck my Willie is."
I rolled my eyes not wanting to hear anything about the man while my phone's second line started ringing from an unknown number. I ignored it and said, "Do you want me to pick you up and go out to eat?"
Now slightly offended, she hissed, "Girl, I ain't got my mind on that. Your fat ass is always thinking about food at the wrong damn time. Can't you see I'm worried about my husband."

I replied, "I understand. I'll talk to you another day." and hung up. It wasn't my job to deal with an attitude that I didn't place there. My phone started ringing again and at this point I wasn't in the mood to talk to anybody especially since I had planned for me and Marcus to have a movie night at my place. It was a good thing that my mama disrespectfully declined because now I could cook for him the way I had been wanting to. He had a biker meeting at their clubhouse and said that he'd be here a little after seven but it was two in the afternoon and somebody was banging on my front door like the police in a drug bust.

I just threw my hands up as I went to look out of the peephole. It was Destiny popping some gum and screaming at some scrub, about why he can't get with her. I slung the door open and said, "Bring your country ass in here. Being all extra loud and shit."

I walked in giggling, "Oh my bad. I forgot you live by the wypipo. I'm surprised you're not working. I came by the other day, but you weren't here."

I rolled my eyes and shook my head as I said, "If you'd get a job, you wouldn't make wasted pop ups."

She smacked, "Oh it wasn't wasted. My boothang stay out this way but girl what kinda work you do? Do they drug test?"

I chuckled and lied, "Nah na and yes they do."

I was very particular about who I allowed to use my name when it came to my coins. Being an advertising manager for a real estate investment company was a job that I wasn't trying to lose over nonsense. Destiny dismissed the lie as she exclaimed, "I see you got that glow again!"

I glared at her and asked, "Bitch what glow?"

She started to bounce on the chair singing,

"That I just got some dick glow!"

We both laughed but I wasn't the type to tell everybody about my love life, especially not Destiny because of her track history. I had already forgiven Destiny for messing around with a few of my exs and crushes when we were young, dumb, and full of cum, however, Destiny has proven that she's a hoe through and through. There's no sugarcoating that and I didn't mind getting real feisty when it came to my man. My guard had already gone up and I was ready to smack her, if the next line out of her mouth called for such a response. I quickly changed the subject as I said, "Girl, I'm too busy with work."

She looked content with the answer as she replied, "Oh well bitch it must be that money making glow." I got up and headed towards the kitchen to check on what I had just started cooking. Destiny followed along saying, "Damn, girl you got it smelling good in here. I hope I can get a plate too!"

I quickly gave her that 'girl stop' look as I said, "You can get a plate tomorrow. This right here is for work."

She started to pout, then quickly realized she was getting nowhere and asked, "Have you heard from Niecy?"

I replied, "No not really. She's visiting her sorority sisters right now. She mentioned somebody about a new business idea. She wouldn't go into details, but she says it's big and wants to talk to me about it when she gets back."

Destiny said, "Oh, I heard she's opening a strip club somewhere in Jackson."

I said to Destiny, "Girl shut up! I know she ain't using her inheritance to open a fucking strip club?"

She shook her head with her hands raised and said, "That's what I heard boo. You know all that girl care about is some quick get rich scheme. That shit ain't gone last in Jackson anyway."

I agreed, "Yeah, you right. All she see is money. She should be thankful that she was able to receive an inheritance and put it towards those kids' future."

Destiny nodded and continued, "Some people don't deserve to be parents. She's always been the one to have to learn the hard way. Never wanted to listen. Even when I tried to tell her that Dustin was a hoe. Tried to tell her about Nate too."
I rolled my eyes as I never believed the wild and crazy fictious stories that came out of Destiny's mouth about Niecy. She was smart when she wanted to be but that didn't stop her from being a jealous hating ass hoe. We continued to talk for about three or four hours until Marcus sent me a text saying he was outside. I told Destiny that it was time for her to go while regretting not cutting it short sooner because now Destiny and Marcus would meet in passing. As Destiny walked out the door, Marcus was walking up. I noticed the weird look he gave Destiny and in my gut, I knew that he was one of Destiny's many men. They exchanged a few hellos and she switched her hips on to whoever was picking her up.
Marcus and I enjoyed our night together as we watched Netflix in my bed and that's it.
No sex. No fondling. Nothing. It was sweet kisses and laughs all night. I was so comfortable in his arms that I fell asleep for the first time in a man's arms. This was something I had longed for, to sleep while being held. So many nights I slept alone. So many times, I wanted to beg Xavier to stay and I knew he wouldn't. It was nice to have this moment. I felt wanted. Loved even. But of course, this didn't last long as we were both startled out of our sleep by a loud bang in the kitchen. Nobody was supposed to had been here but us. I started to get up, but Marcus placed his hand on my shoulder with a finger to his mouth instructing me to remain silent. He crept to the door and slowly opened it. I was right on his heels holding his arm, scared to death of what the noise could've been. Immediately after entering the kitchen, I snapped, "Ace, what the fuck are you doing?"

While standing at the kitchen counter, he replies, "Fixing a sandwich, what does it look like?"

Annoyingly I asked, "Ace, you know I only let you keep that spare key for emergencies only?"

As he made his way to the refrigerator putting everything up, he replied "And hunger isn't an emergency?"

I rolled my eyes, "Give me my damn key!"

He took his plate and went into the living room and sat down where his drink was waiting on the end table as he turned the TV on and said, "I've used it plenty of times and it wasn't a big deal then, plus I called a few times before I came, you didn't answer."

I shook my head realizing who was calling me back to back from a blocked num-ber. Marcus and I made our way into the living room, "Why did you call me from an unknown number and seriously give me my damn key back?!"

As I sat down on the sofa with Marcus standing by the kitchen entryway looking like he still wanted to fight, Ace wasn't even acknowledging the man's presence and continued relaxing in the recliner and watching TV while eating his sandwich. When he was finished, he placed the key on the table and he replied, "I made a copy anyway."

While I rolled my eyes, the vibe had become tense from the male egos sparring in the air. I gave a quick introduction as I said, "Well sir, this is Marcus. Marcus this is my best friend Ace."

Marcus walked up closer to Ace and extended his hand, but Ace got up and started walking to the front door saying, "Hey, I need to head on out. I was only here to make this bomb ass sandwich. I'll hit you up later and uh nice meeting you Mike!"

I bit my lip at the utter disrespect he just threw at Marcus. I knew Ace could be an ass-hole, but I didn't think he would've slammed the asshole card down so soon like that. Marcus wasted no time in getting his keys and heading out the door as well. He told me that he needed to get home and get some rest but that he'd hit me up tomorrow. I doubted that he would after what had just happened, but I kept a glimmer of hope that he would. I called Ace to tell him about himself. He answered as if he hadn't done a thing wrong, "What's up?"

I was firm as I said, "Did you really have to do Marcus like that?"

He pretended not to know who I was talking about as he replied, "Who?"

Annoyingly I said, "Marcus! The guy I literally just introduced you to!"

He sounded genuinely confused as he asked, "Oh! What did I do to him?"

I scoffed, "You were rude as fuck to him!" Still clueless, he inquired, "How? I don't see anything I did wrong."

While shaking my head in disbelief, I replied, "For starters, the man tried to shake your hand and you not only dismissed him, but you completely jacked up his name and called him Mike."

The audacity of him to burst out laughing on the phone let me know that the asshole in him couldn't be controlled. Ace was so deep in the pool of arrogance that he didn't even see the error of his ways. He replied, "Ahhh damn my bad. I ain't got no beef with the man. He must be ya new lil fuck buddy."

I rolled my eyes and sighed as I said, "It's not just sex. We're getting to know each other."

Ace replied, "I didn't ask about that."

I continued boldly, "Yeah, well I said it! Anywho have you been in my apartment like this before because I'm starting to notice a few things missing."

He chuckled and said, "Yeah I been stealing ya dirty drawls so I can smell them later."

With a cringed look, I replied, "What? Boy shut up!"

He laughed harder and said, "I only ever come by like that when I'm in the area and hungry."

Even though he couldn't see it, I was once again rolling my eyes so hard as I said, "Whatever. Just chill out a bit. Never know I might actually be having sex and I don't need the awkwardness that I experienced today to ever happened again. Cool?"

He replied, "No problem."

After getting off of the phone with Ace, I searched my apartment and couldn't find my MacBook. My hope was that I had left it at Niecy's but deep down I knew that I left it on the couch. It was clear to me that I've been a little too carefree in my life because I've lost an entire freaking laptop.

Date Night

"Shawty go jogging every morning, And she make me breakfast almost every morning, And she take a naked pic' before she leave the door, I be waking up to pics' before a nigga yawning."
- What You Know About Love by Pop Smoke

Chanice

I sat at the bar in M-Bar reading the apologetic text that my husband of only eight months had sent after thirty minutes of me waiting for him to show up. I sighed and placed the phone face down without a reply. He didn't deserve another slap on the wrist after I had gone out of my way to secure this date for us. The kids were at my mother-in-law's house for the next few hours, and I had gotten off early to get ready for the night that we agreed to have. At least for one night I wanted to let my hair down and be the woman I was before having kids since it seemed impossible because of the way we both worked all the time.

The sound of a bell went off in the party room where an annual speed dating event was taking place. The room looked as if Cupid himself had come and thrown up over everything. It was filled with red heart balloons, pink and white streamers, and roses at every table. The most seductive music was playing in the background. Whoever had planned this speed dating event definitely knew how to get a crowd in the mood.

I motioned for the bartender to bring me another Romeo and Juliet while silently observing the prospects as they entered into the event. I had no desire in letting the date I had planned go to waste because of Dustin and his constant state of forgetfulness, however, none of the men I seen seemed to be able to afford more than the entry fee to be part of the event. I rolled my eyes at the mere thought of entertaining any of them. Another sigh of frustration escaped as I reminded myself that I was a happily married woman and that my husband was a wonderful father to our kids. At the same time, maybe we were just too young for marriage and kids. We barely knew ourselves and here we were trying to be a family. Dustin was always a good friend to talk to when we were younger and then we had kids only to get married after the kids. Now we were facing adulthood completely and utterly clueless.

It wasn't long before a tall, dark, and handsome guy sat down at the bar beside me. I kept my attention fixated on my drink, but a whiff of the scent of his cologne caught me by surprise. A sucker for a nice smelling man, I glanced his way and there he sat, bold and beautiful in a grey cashmere sweater with black slacks on. I caught his eye and he turned and smiled at me in the sexiest way as he said, "Can I get you another drink?"

I knew I shouldn't have indulged but what else did I have going on? I replied with a smirk and a shrug, "Why not?"

The bartender came with another drink for me and a Love Martini for the gentleman as he continued, "You're too beautiful to be sitting here alone."

I sighed as I said, "Tell that to my husband."

He nodded and said, "He shouldn't be so careless. Any man could just come along and believe they might have a chance with beautiful woman like yourself."

I chuckled and spoke softly, "Do you think you have a chance with me?"

With a smile he stood up and straighten his sweater as he boldly replied, "I wouldn't have sat down beside you if I thought

otherwise." He stretched his hand out for mine and continued to say, "Come with me and let me turn your night around."
I was hesitant to place my hand in his. The bartender stared at us with discontentment, having heard the entire conversation from afar as he wiped the whiskey glasses. I was intrigued to see how far I'd let this man go. I wanted a carefree fun night and the moment I placed my hand in his, sealed the deal for whatever was to come next. A devilish smile appeared on his face and within seconds our night had begun. The chemistry wasn't so bad. We stopped by Applebee's for dinner where we shared laughs and small talk.
Thankful that the night wasn't ruined, and that this man had rescued me from a night of boredom and loneliness. After Applebee's, we made our way to a special spot that only he knew about by the Reservoir. The moonlight glistened on the water creating a vibe that I had yearned for countless of times over the last few years. The touch of his hand on my lower back and the words he spoke next sent chills down my spine when he softly whispered in my ear, "What do you want to do next?"
First, I replied with a deep passionate kiss. Next, I looked him in the eyes and spoke with confidence and seduction, "I know exactly what I want to do next."
Forty minutes later and I was entering the bedroom that I shared with Dustin while this perfect gentleman waited in the living room as requested. I went in the bathroom to freshen up and then went on to pull out her freak nasty lingerie while showering the bedroom with rose petals. He heard the door slowly open and was in awe as he watched me walk out wearing red heels, red lace stockings with a garter belt attached to my red leather corset that attenuated my red thongs. In one hand, I was carrying black furry handcuffs as I motioned for him to come join me in the bedroom. Happily, he obliged and followed me with the biggest grin on his face. I instructed him to sit in the chair that I placed in the middle

of the room. I handcuffed his hands behind the chair and started to do a sexy striptease in front of him to *"Earned It"* by The Weeknd. He bit his bottom lip in anticipation for the moment he'd be able to touch my curvaceous body. His breathing became more intense from seeing me sway perfectly to the beat of the music with my hands rubbing all over myself. It wasn't hard to see how ready he was. While I slipped out of my thongs, I squatted with my legs spread wide and bounced as I stoked my fingers in and out of my moist box as if I was riding his dick. The torture of being handcuffed made him groan in agony but he never took his eyes off of the nympho that was emerging from within while I grinned and laid back on the floor, continuing to finger fuck myself. My moans mixed in with the music causing him to lose even more control.

With an overwhelming urge to taste my sweet spot, he inched out of the chair, still handcuffed and made his way to me. As soon as I felt his touch, I laughed slightly and scooted away after he'd only gotten a quick taste. He was ready to devour me and yet I was being the biggest tease that he'd ever seen. I made him sit up with his back against the bed while I placed one leg on the baseboard and guided his head to his dessert. He dove in with no further objections. My hips rolling in circles of pleasure, making him want to caress my body but all in due time. As soon as those handcuffs were off, he was going to have to show me what he was really made of. My juices filled his mouth while my moans grew louder. He knew this was just the beginning because I stepped back with a grin, admiring the glazed donut effect that I had placed on his face.

My eyebrows quickly raised from the surprise of him getting up off the floor after breaking free of the handcuffs. He spoke, "Did you really think they would hold me?"

I giggled like a little schoolgirl watching him come out of his sweater, admiring the man before me as he pulled me closer to him and we kissed again. The more intense the moment became, the

more power it gave me to defy him control at every turn causing me to push him back on the bed where I had silk hand ties waiting on the bed posts of the bed. After tying up his hands and feet, I then placed a blindfold over his eyes as I replied, "You should've known I was prepared for you breaking the handcuffs."
With excitement in his voice, he replied, "Have your fun."
A trail of warm kisses and light nibbles went from his collarbone to my grand prize as I commenced to sucking his rod hoping to taste him. I could feel pulsations beginning so I increased my speed but soon his pulsations disappeared as he groaned with disappointment and said, "Baby, it's not you. I just don't like head."
Nothing is more of a mood killer than knowing you're not even pleasing your lover, so I switched it up and tried something different. After placing a vibrating ring on his erection, I slowly straddled, sitting upright and rode him like it was the Black Rodeo. Feeling those amazing vibrations on my pearl only made me ride him harder and faster with him trying his best to match my moves by gyrating his hips but failing miserably from his hands and feet being tied up. I spun around keeping his rod safely snug inside and untied his feet, ready to turn over the reins of this freak show and see what he had in store for her until he moaned loudly unable to control his release inside of me. With my head hung low, I eased off of him and untied him. His smile was victorious as he sat up ready to smoke a cigarette until he seen that my face didn't match how amazing he felt. He leaned forward and kissed my forehead as he said, "I'm sorry babe."
I rolled my eyes at the reality of how my night was ending. All of this planning only to have some chicken alfredo that I could've made better and five minutes of sex where I could've fucked myself longer and better all night long. We laid in bed watching a movie as I tried not to allow my emotions to get the best of me. I wanted more but before I could say anything, his phone started to ring.

He jumped up and answered it. I sat up and watched him get his clothes and head to the bathroom to freshen up. While shaking his head, he looked at me and said, "Aren't you going to get dressed?"
After a deep sigh, I shrugged and replied, "Do I have to?"
He chuckled while saying, "Yes, baby. We have to go get the kids from my mom's house."
While rolling off the bed onto my feet, I groaned loudly and replied in a whiny voice,
"Just one more round pleaseeeeee!"
Dustin walked up to me as he said, "How about we stop by Romantic Adventures and get you some toys before picking up the kids."
I sucked my teeth as I reluctantly got up and took a quick shower to pray to God for a better sex life. Toys are great but I didn't want no damn plastic. I wanted to get picked up and fucked all night long and as always Dustin was spent after only a few minutes.
He always said sorry when he was done which only made me feel like such a horrible person for not being satisfied with him sexually. We're married and I didn't want to cheat on my husband. I also didn't want to divorce him because of bad sex so I perked up and got ready to have my way in Romantic Adventures. Masturbation is fun. I just hate doing it as a married woman. I looked at my husband in a totally different light, remembering how I felt earlier that evening, believing that he had once again dismissed the need for romance and passion in our marriage. He surprised me when he showed up acting like a total stranger, but the reality came crashing down the moment sex entered the chat.
When I came out of the bathroom, Dustin was holding a card and three roses saying,
"Happy Valentine's Day baby."

I did what I did best and faked a smile as I walked over to my side of the bed, grabbing the gift bag I had for him. With a kiss, I said softly, "Happy Valentine's Day."

History Always Repeats Itself

"They say I'm crazy, I really don't care. That's my prerogative. They say I'm nasty but I don't give a damn." - My Prerogative by Bobby Brown

Imani

Niecy rolled her eyes because she knew where the conversation was going when she just wanted to relax as she said, "Don't call her a hoe. I wouldn't let her call you one and besides she's your godsister, you just won't give her a chance."
I slick spazzed out saying, "I don't give her a chance because I know what kind of lowdown nasty ass hoe she really is!"
Niecy laid back on the floor while I was getting ready to go in on this girl since she wasn't there to defend herself and Niecy had already given it her best shot at directing the conversation in another direction when she asked, "What has she done to you for her to be all of that?'
I sighed as I said, "The girl is a straight up hoe. Who she ain't fucked? All she do is fuck.
She traded the fucking pacifier for some dick and ain't been right since. Hell in sixth grade she walked in the classroom with nut on her shirt and everybody was making fun of her. It was so bad that she had to switch schools."
Niecy looked at me and said, "But maybe it wasn't nut. Could've been ranch dressing. There's literally like a million things it could've been Imani."

I sucked my teeth while saying, "All she do is eat dick. Baby what else could it have been?" That shit pissed Niecy off because she didn't understand why it mattered what Destiny did nor who she did it with. I continued, "I see that face you making. Don't look at me like that. You only looking like that because you don't know her like I do. You only know that fake ass woe is me version she gave you when y'all met in high school, but I know nasty ass Destiny from middle school. She changed a lot when she got the breast reduction. Couldn't tell her shit after that. You ain't got to believe me but it's true. The bitch is a hoe and will fuck any man that look her way."

Niecy shrugged her shoulders with the belief that everybody was a hoe in their own way. Nobody was waiting until marriage and sex felt damn good with the right person. She looked at me and said, "Imani, you still mad that she fucked that biker boy. That's really what this is about."

As I stood up, I declared, "No! No, that's not what this is about. Yeah, I liked Chaos and she knew that but she done fucked almost every guy that I've liked or been with so no that's not it. It's just facts and you don't want to see that. Just wait until she's fucking your man though. You'll see."

Niecy wasn't blind to the fact that Destiny had whorish behavior. She remembered all too well how she introduced her to an old friend named Fred. After she pleasured Fred, there was a guy ad his twin brother, and then her so called ex. The difference between Niecy and us was that Niecy had many *'boyfriends'* and sometimes many of them at the same time as she has always enjoyed the conversation of a cute boy while they always went on to claim her as their girlfriend. They were lucky if she even kissed them because sex was completely out of the question. It's funny how the guys never knew that they were just pawns collecting dust in a game she was never playing. We all knew that the boys only wanted sex but Niecy didn't mind passing them along in the direction where they could get it and like so many others she sent them Destiny's way.

Destiny

It's been said that what they don't know won't hurt them and yet for me, I really don't give a shit about who knows. That's why I had to be me when Imani went with Niecy to handle business in New Orleans while leaving her house key with me. Imani's single so no man to worry about me stealing and plus I needed a place to stay after my mama had kicked me out for being a lying ass hoe. I had only one mission in mind, and it was accomplished the moment Ace walked through the door looking for Imani as I said, "Oh she's out of town but I'm sure I can help you with whatever you need."
I was standing in the middle of the living room, butt ass naked, twirling my hair around while licking my lips with my leg slightly bent as my other hand ran up my thigh and up to my perfect brown breasts. I used one hand to massage my breasts as the other slid down from my hair to fondle my-self. As I moaned out in, please, he bit his bottom lip and frowned his eyebrows at the words that he uttered, "We can't do this in Imani's place like this."
I walked up to him and licked his neck up to his ear as I spoke softly, "I won't tell if you don't."
Ace shook his head trying to deny the urge to give in when I clasped my hand around his already rock hard dick causing him to exhale from the touch of my hand. He stood frozen as I started to unbuckle his pants while he tilted his head back to avoid looking at the girl, he knew he shouldn't have been with. He had taken the bait like I had hoped that he would and right there in the middle of my sister's living room is where we fucked like dirty dogs.

Although he was a man in love with Imani, he knew that he would never get the chance to truly be with Imani. Not even in his wildest dream would that ever come true. I enjoyed the satisfaction of a man being unable to say no to me. It gave me a sense of power that was unmatched by anything else in this cold and crazy world. Once I had my fill, I was over them. As long as I could say that I had them and ruin another woman's day then I could walk away smiling but I had no desire to ever tell Imani about this. Neither did Ace. This was something that we would take with us to our graves. The satisfaction for me was being able to have the secret not tell it. To watch Ace flirt so helplessly with a woman that he could never be with while knowing that I had the one bullet to kill all chances of his dreams coming true.

After a week, Imani was back and looking for me as I was hiding out in fear that Ace had spilled the beans when in reality, Imani was just concerned about me and wanted to make sure that everything was good. I couldn't chance it though. Niecy was a crazy enough, but I didn't feel like rumbling with Imani over a nothing ass dude like Ace. All she was going to do was give me a headache about something that her precious Ace could've said no to. Imani believed that I had nowhere else to go but that's why a bad bitch like me keeps sponsors on deck. I had no desire to stay at Imani's anymore because I'm a grown ass woman that's going to do whatever the fuck I wanted to do.

The Image of Perfection

"These are the tales, the freaky tales. These are the tales that I tell so well." - Too $hort

Imani

A few hours in bed and there goes my phone ringing loud as ever with Ace's name across the screen. It stopped ringing before I was able to ignore it and then started ringing again. I hadn't seen nor heard from him since our graduation and him doubling down on Terica while completely throwing me away. That Bachelor of Arts degree gave me the only real reason to dress up and feel good about myself. Our last interaction with each other were like two people forced to meet at a gathering because Terica was there, and nobody needed to catch a case based on stupidity. That awkward and tense feeling of please somebody save me from this conversation stained every word that uttered out of our mouths, however, he never stopped calling. I forced myself to answer the phone since I really wasn't trying to be up at seven in the morning unless I was making money and today was supposed to had been an extremely lazy day. My first off day from my new job and here he was blowing up my phone with nonsense. As soon as I answered, he said, "Open the door."

Groggy and confused, I replied, "Open what door?"

He sighed as he said, "Your front door."

I stumbled out of the bed and made my way to the front door. Destiny was dead to the world on the couch. WWIII could have been happening around her and she'd sleep peacefully through the gunfire and bombs going off. I wasn't worried about waking her up nor did I bother to put on a robe or house shoes. I had on clothes for the most part but a crop top, boy shorts, and long mix matched Spongebob socks isn't the idea attire to open front doors with. The man laughed as soon as the door swung open. I tried to slam the door closed and he caught it. I wasn't up for the games this early in the morning and was highly annoyed to have gotten up to be laughed at by a stranger. I swiftly spun around and headed back to the bed as I said,

"I don't have time for you today. I'm tired. I just want to sleep."

He continued to laugh as he said, "You look like you've been thrown away."

Sarcastically, I replied, "I have by you." I snuggled back in bed under my covers as I continued, "Where have you been stranger? Thought we weren't friends anymore?"

Ace shook his head and replied, "I didn't throw you away butt face and if I remember correctly you stopped answering my calls and text messages but fuck all that. You got some shit going on."

In mid yawn, I replied, "What do you mean?"

He handed me his phone and there I was butt ass naked across the screen. I laid in bed frozen stiff from the embarrassment until slowly I sat up and said, "What the fuck? Why do you have this on your phone? Where did you get this?!"

With a shrug, he replied, "It was sent to me last night on messenger. I knew it wasn't you, so I came over to see what was going on and who I needed to fuck up?"

Anger caused tears to form as I screamed, "If I knew who, you would be bailing me out of jail right now! I can't fucking believe this shit right now!" I was freaking completely out as I picked up my phone and seen that I had seventeen missed calls, twenty-eight text messages, four voicemails, and a bunch of other shit. They all read and said the same thing. My Facebook account had been hacked and everybody had all kinds of pictures and messages from me. I didn't answer nor call back anybody. When I finally logged into my page, my heart dropped. The nudes were sent in messenger, but so much more was on my page. Disgusting posts that I would've never posted and replies to the comments with shit that I would've never said. I quickly changed my information around and deleted the page. Fuck social media! If they didn't have my number, then they didn't need to contact me.

Ace asked, "Who did you piss off Imani?"

I shrugged with tears in my eyes as I answered, "Ace, I have not one idea who I could've made this fucking mad. I only sent those pictures to one person, and I don't even know how anybody else could have them right now."

He rubbed my back while continuing to question me, "Who did you send them to?"

With shame written across my face, I replied, "I don't want to say right now but believe me they were somebody I completely trusted."

While trying to give hope to a hopeless situation, Ace suggested, "Well maybe their phone was stolen or something. Maybe somebody hacked their accounts as well."

Still filled with guilt, I say, "Maybe so. Still, I don't know why this is happening. Just a couple of months ago I received a package with a dead rat and three dead roses. Can you believe that shit?"

Ace concluded, "Imani, this has to be somebody you know."

While nodding my head, I agreed, "I don't know anybody it could be though."

He inquired, "What about Xavier?"

With a frown I asked, "What about Xavier? Why would Xavier do this Ace? What does he have to gain from this?"

He raised his hands in defense as he said, "I don't know. It was just a suggestion."

I sighed as I said, "I'm sorry I'm not trying to lash out at you. I just don't know what to do right now."

Ace placed his arms around me and held me close and spoke softly, "No, it's okay. I'm here for you."

The tears flowed harder from the embarrassment of it all. Before heading down to the precinct to file a report, I tried calling Xavier to eliminate him as a suspect and of course he didn't answer. I was dumbfounded and hurt, and although Ace went with me to the police station, it didn't do me any good as they told me exactly what I already knew. It was nothing that they could do for me. There was no surefire way to find out who the hacker was since the person didn't physically harm me. Once again, I was defeated. I felt violated and hands down scared believing that this person was just watching me and waiting to snatch me up. Ace drove me back home to find Destiny had already started drinking and smoking again.

Ace rolled up a couple of blunts and as soon as I hit it, I was on the verge of coughing up both lungs. Ace just laughed and said, "I thought you were a pro by now since you've been smoking with us."

I took a sip of my screwdriver before I said, "Boy shut up! You know I'm a rookie."

While shaking his head with a chuckle, he replied, "That you are." With a serious face, he continued, "I missed your crazy ass. Aside from all of this stalker shit going on, how are you?"

I figured it was best to be honest with him this time. These creep sessions with Marcus hasn't helped me in accepting the bad along with the good and moving on with my life. I replied, "I've been okay. It's about to be a year now since I had an abortion. I'm feeling like I barely have a handle on my life now. I feel like I'm just now getting back to me." Destiny chimed in with an attitude, "I didn't know none of this."

Ace seemed stunned, "Oh damn. Maybe it'd be good if you found somebody to talk to. You look better than before. You got a whole glow on you. I should've been a better friend though. I didn't know you had so much going on."

Destiny continued, "You know Niecy is basically a pastor. I talk to her about every-thing."

Ace chuckled as he said, "Why haven't I met this girl yet?"

Destiny glared at Ace while I slapped his arm and said, "Boy! You know you're a hoe plus she's married!"

He waved his hand in the air and said, "Shid never stopped me before."

I laughed as I got up to cook something to eat. I replied, "I ain't got time for you Ace. I'm gone put your ass out!"

He got up and followed me into the kitchen while Destiny stayed in the living room trying to make my misery about her as Ace replied, "Nah, don't do that. I gotta keep you safe."

I smiled and replied, "I'm good. I'm sure it's just somebody playing pranks and shit."

He walked up close to me as he spoke in almost a whisper, "You know if I had known about the baby, I would've been here for you. I'm just a call away."

I lied, "I know Ace. I didn't want anybody to know. I thought I could handle it on my own and for the most part I did. I just didn't realize how hard it would be to forgive myself but I'm good now."

The menu consisted of an oven pizza with buffalo wings. Ace joked on the healthy eating since I had the pizza with the cauliflower crust, but I didn't care. It was still healthier than what Destiny wanted which was fried pork chops, rice with sugar, and mac and cheese. He was lucky to have a friend that loved to feed her friends. I was terrified to be alone and no matter how honest I had been with them. I still didn't really want to blurt that out as well. It was obvious in the same sense though.

It wasn't long before my mama started to blow my phone up as well. I walked outside to get away from Ace and Destiny. My mama clearly knew about the Facebook hack because she only called me when somebody died or was in jail. I answered with much hesitation dreading the conversation that was about to take place as I said, "Hey mama."

She screamed, "Have you lost your fucking mind? You need to take that shit off of Facebook. I don't need people looking at me crazy because of the dumb shit yo ass is doing? The fuck are you a prostitute now?!"

I thought about explaining how it wasn't me but it didn't matter to my mama. She was convinced that I was the one behind the Facebook posts and messages. I attempted to reply, "Mama, I've already deleted Facebook.

Nothing else to worry about."

She wasn't hearing a word that I had said as she continued to belittle her only child for something that I didn't do, "I don't give a fuck about you deleting Facebook. That shit gone stay on the internet forever. Do you know my Willie received that nasty ass shit? I should come beat your ass since you want to try my fucking husband!"

I shook my head in disbelief at the hate that my mama was spewing and hung the phone up without even replying. I didn't truly have the mental capacity to deal with the toxicity of my mama, but my phone started ringing again. Now that anger had filled inside of me, I quickly answered, "Look, the shit wasn't even me so back the fuck up off of me!"

A male voice spoke with compassion as they said, "Baby, I know you wouldn't do this. Do you need me to come over there?"

I glanced down at the phone in my hand and seen that it was 'Xavier' and not 'My Lady' going across the screen. He couldn't leave well enough alone. He couldn't possibly be this in love with me and still be a happily married man. With an annoyed voice, I replied, "No! How many times do I have to point you back in the direction of your fucking wife! Call me again and I will tell her every fucking little tidbit about us."

His tone quickly changed as he hissed, "Try me bitch! You'll be dead before you can utter a word!"

I laughed and replied with boldness, "Do your fucking worse you low life son of a bitch!"

If somebody had told me that I would be in this zone with Xavier, then it's a guarantee that I would've fought them for speaking negatively on us. They say it's a thin line between love and hate and I was learning just how true that was when it came to Xavier. Nothing in my life was making sense and it was probably time that I started to get some sage or something. Ace stepped outside and hugged me as he whispered, "Everything will be okay."

Although my mind was in disarray, I believed him and together we prayed for my strength to endure the turmoil until the culprit was captured. The benefits of being friends with a pastor's kid. They're definitely going to pray over you and with you.

Hog Nation

"Beware she's schemin, she'll make you think you're dreamin. You'll fall in love and you'll be screamin demon, ooh" - Posion by Bell Biv Devoe

Destiny

With my head glued to the phone, in full fangirl mode tweeting about how I was about to meet Ludacris, is how I ended up walking straight into Chaos. Initially, I was pissed at his audacity to be in the middle of the path that I was mindlessly creating. Disgust had my face frowned up as I looked down at my cute little pink and white short set which was now botched with wet spots from him wrapping his sweaty arms around me.
The first thing I screamed out was, "What the fuck?!"
He replied, "My bad. I wasn't trying to get you all wet. Just didn't want you to fall."
Immediately embarrassed after seeing Chaos in front of me with only his wet torn jean shorts and a dunking booth behind him that he'd just climbed out of. I turned my head to see the many drunkards staring at my stupid ass for not watching where I was going. While shaking my head, I said, "No, it's not your fault at all. I'm sorry for bumping into you."
He licked his lips while rubbing his hands together as his eyes looked her up and down, he replied with the sexiest smile, "You good. Just made my day." The man did indeed look like he knew how to properly blow my back out, but he wasn't my type as I

normally go for the high yella guys. He was slightly taller than me with locs that sat in the middle of his back and although I've had my fair share of chocolate covered stress, there was nothing wrong with adding one more chocolate chip to my roster but if I stayed any longer, I would've missed out on meeting Ludacris which was the only reason that I was even at Scrapin' the Coast. I cared nothing about motorcycles or tricked out cars and trucks.

While walking away, I said, "That's cute. I'll let you get back to ya swimming lessons."

The urge to look behind me as I walked away to see if he was watching me was rather consuming as I love being the center of attention, but 1 held my composure until I made it to the DJ booth and realized, I didn't even get the man's name no less his number. Slipping on my pimping but maybe it just wasn't meant to be, so I quickly let it go and enjoyed the ATL vibes from Ludacris' live performance. My dreams had come true when I ended up pussy popping all across the stage like she was auditioning for his next music video. Not a lick of rhythm in these bones but couldn't nobody tell me I wasn't doing the damn thing on this stage. I was even able to get a couple pictures with him after his performance.

Jeremy convinced me to stick around after the performance and I was happy that I did since Chaos was being awarded the grand prize for Best Burnout. This had me completely impressed. I noticed that he had changed into some black cowboy boots with ripped faded jeans and a black ClickTight Rydaz vest in reference to his motorcycle club. Chaos walked up to the DJ booth and shook hands with Jeremy while looking me dead in the eyes as he said, "I finished my swimming lessons."

Jeremy looked confused and asked, "How do you know this crazy ass girl?"

Quickly, I replied, "He doesn't but he's about to."

Jeremy shook his head while laughing and saying, "Good luck man. She's a handful!" After we finally learned each other's names, Jeremy went back to spinning as the after-party was starting while Chaos and Destiny walked towards the parking lot to his white and royal blue BMW R1250 RT. I knew only a man with money was riding on something as pretty as what I seen. Clearly, I hadn't been paying attention to anything that had been going on around me because I asked, "So did you win the contest on this bike?"

He chuckled and replied, "I used an' 85 Impala Cutlass that I've been building on."

I nodded while saying, "That's good. Looks way too nice to end up with bald tires."

His eyes never left her as I made a circle around the bike, admiring everything about it. He asked, "You ride?"

While shaking my head, I couldn't help but laugh and say, "No, I'm way too scary for this. I like to watch sometimes though."

His smile was intoxicating. All I wanted was maybe just one kiss from the man as I watched him talk about riding and zoning out from the thoughts of riding him. The second I clicked back into the conversation was when he said, "You'd look good on a bike."

I giggled innocently as I said, "Maybe an ATV but I just can't do this two wheel death trap. I am not Carey Hart."

Even the man's laugh was infectious as he said, "Shit neither am I!" For whatever reason, I could only imagine two types of bikes. They're either older guys in a bike club like Martin Lawrence in *'Wild Hogs'* or they're younger daredevils like Carey Hart doing backflips in a dirt bike race. Either way, I didn't mind watching at least once but you'd never find me peeling off on one of those things. My ability to even stand back and watch came from Xzibit's MTV show *'Pimp My Ride'* and that's only because of how nice everything looked after building up a hump of junk. I loved to

see the Cinderella transformation from shit to a winner. After we exchanged a few more words he asks, "How about we go for a ride?" Quickly I backed away and took some time to really weigh my options. It was certainly enticing and possibly on my bucket list at number 9,999 of things to do so I replied,
"Sure, what's the worst that could happen?"
The sun was beginning to set causing beautiful rays of orange, red, and yellow in the sky making the scene much more romantic than I could've ever imagined. My first time on the back of a Hayabusa did not at all disappoint. Time passed us by so effortlessly that it was only noticeable by the night sky above them. One of the most soothing escapes that I'd ever endure and at this point, it's safe to say I may have become slightly addicted to the ride. We pulled up to an office building for lease on Pass Rd. I slid off the back of the bike to stretch my legs, when I noticed how cloudy the night's sky was becoming. Just as Chaos asked, "Did you enjoy the ride?" lightening flashed across the sky with a roaring sound of thunder following closely behind.
I sighed and replied, "I did and was hoping we could keep this going but clearly I jinxed us when I said what's the worst that could happen."
After I walked up to him leaning on his bike, he gently placed his hands around my waist and said, "Nah, if anything you made it better."
With the palm of his hand resting on my cheek, Chaos pulled me in for the sweetest kiss I'd ever had. I wrapped my arms around his neck, and it was there that we made out with sprinkles of rain beginning to fall around us. *'How ironic?'* I thought to herself while enjoying his soft lips on mine. His hands crept down and under my shirt, slightly scratching my back causing my breathing to become heavy while making my kitty purr. At that very moment, I was ready to jump him and hop around the parking lot. After I bit his

bottom lip, my kisses found their way to his neck. When Chaos grabbed my ass is when I started to nibble on his earlobe. I pulled his shirt over his head with absolutely no care to the fact that we stood outside in the sprinkling rain of an empty parking lot. It was obvious he didn't care too much either since he was smiling so hard. While he allowed me to collect light raindrops that had fallen onto his chest, I massaged his dick through his shorts.

Suddenly, he spun me around and as I was holding on to his bike, I started to grind my hips on his pelvis as if it was a slow jam playing in the background. The feeling of his hands caressing my ass cheeks and gripping my thighs only made me grind my ass on him harder. His excitement indicated that he was very entertained. I didn't have the fattest ass and I couldn't dance but I knew how to work what my mama gave me. When he tugged on my shorts, I paused and allowed him to pull them down just enough to see my g string and the playboy bunny tattoo on my left ass cheek. Just as the sprinkles around us turned to a light drizzle, Chaos pushed up on me with his rod rock hard in his hand, tapping the head on my ass cheeks.

When he entered inside of me, I gasped from the monster size that I was feeling. Instead of winning Best Burn Out every year, he should've been winning the award for this trophy dick he was slow driving in and out of me. Chaos was going in deep causing me to dig into his leather seats. Trying not to scream out was the hardest thing I could do, so I snatched his shirt off of the handle and bit on it. It really didn't help when it was becoming very clear to me that he must have been a dancer for Chris Brown from the way he was rolling his body with these strokes.

When I felt his arms crossed, I shuddered realizing the mission that he was on. He was trying to blow my back out and I wasn't about to stop him. I had to put in a little work before my legs went completely out so I started swaying my hips in circles, trying to match up with his body rolls. I thought to herself, *'Why the fuck did I do that?'* This pornstar of a man switched up the rhythm and started pounding me so hard that my knees began to tremble.

It didn't stop Chaos show as he spun me around again and stood back to allow me a two second break. Seeing him stroking in the rain as I pulled my shorts and g string completely off, hanging them on the bike handle where his shirt once was, turned me on even more than I already was. It gave me a much needed energy boost and I was craving more within an instant causing me to rub on my clit, preparing myself for the rest of what he had to offer. Chaos walked up to me and whispered in my ear, "Hold on tight."

While holding on to his bike for dear life, he grabbed my ass and pulled me up to his pelvis. I wasn't expecting him to start going crazy in this kitty worse than he was from the back. It couldn't have felt more amazing. The rain started pouring down heavily only making the moment that much more intense. I wanted to take a rain check on this divine dick but just as the thought crossed my mind, Chaos had bent over slightly making me wrap my legs around his waist.

With my arms wrapped around his neck, he went into some powerful ass kangaroo hops around the parking lot. It's exactly what I wanted from him since the moment I met him at the dunking booth. As I moaned out in pleasure from another climax, he growled lowly in my ear and I hoped he was reaching his peak especially since I had reached mine a few times and more. Chaos slowly let me down as if he knew I would be walking like a newborn calf. I stumbled only slightly, and he chuckled.

I replied as I pulled up my g string and shorts, "Ain't shit funny."

With that sexy ass smile, he shrugged and said, "It was a little funny. Wet clothes look good on you Destiny."

The rain had settled down, but you knew it was bound to start up again with the mist that filled the air. I smirked and replied, "I guess next time I'll do the wet t-shirt con-test."

Chaos grabbed my waist pulling me close and with another sweet kiss he said, "Nah, that's just for me to see."
I nodded and replied, "Just tell me when."
Once I hopped on the back of the bike, we rode off again.

A Pimp Named Slickback

"Y'all should know me well enough. Bitch better have my money. Please don't call me on my bluff. Pay me what you owe me" - Bitch Better Have My Money by Rihanna

Chanice

The smell of success created a feeling of triumph as the club was packed once again while the audience waited for the show to begin. Everybody had come out to see the one and only Ri La Belle as she was the headliner of Femme Fatale, a French styled cabernet centered in the heart of Jackson, Mississippi which slightly mimicked the famous Moulin Rouge. The dancers mixed the styles of majorette along with the tasteful art of burlesque as well as the elegant pirouettes of ballet and the sexy thunder claps of a twerkaholic.

They sashayed around on stage with big fan feathers dressed in beautifully hand crafted corsets as they teased the audience one minute while playing out comical musical parodies the next. It was giving the men everything that they had ever hoped for as well as the women. Being that it was new and fancy with nice music and good food is what drew a crowd in no problem but what made them keep coming back was how different it was from anything that they had ever seen.

A few celebrities had entered the building, having attended a show at the famous caber-net in Paris and went on to report to others that Femme Fatale was indeed the Moulin Rouge of the South.

She had made a name for herself as the hottest club in the city of Jackson, Mississippi. Some wanted to say that Femme Fatale was a strip club because in the privately closed off VIP rooms were poles and plush couches for the entertainment of those willing to put the money down to touch the dancers however this wasn't a strip club as so many wanted to believe, and I wasn't about to explain that to the simpleminded folks in that country ass town. They could believe whatever they wanted as long as they paid the entry fee and didn't cause any problems in my establishment.

Vanjettia, the club manager, walked up to me and tapped me on the shoulder while pointing in the direction of two gentlemen waving at us, the darker one motioning for me to come over to him. I sighed with a smile and made my way to the dimly lit corner as both men stood up to greet me. The darker one smiled, pulling a Cuban cigar out of his mouth as he said, "Damn Niecy, you're still easy on the eyes."

I smiled as I lightly shook my head and replied, "How you been Freddy? Still wrecking 18 wheelers for the insurance money?"

He chuckled and said, "Maybe. The dog fights are keeping my pockets heavy right now. How are the ladies?"

My eyebrows raised slightly, knowing exactly what Fred wanted and as always I had exactly what he needed as I replied, "Sounds like you're trying to have some fun."

With a nod, he said, "Always." He placed his hand on the shoulder of the lighter gentleman clearly of Hispanic descent as he continued, "I want you to meet my new business partner. This is Javier Cortez. He's the owner of Cronix. Have you heard of it?"

I shook his hand as I replied, "Of course I have. It's the Fortune 500 company that's taking over Jackson and buying up every business that they can get their hands on."

Javier nodded with a smile and said, "Only the successful ones. I'd rather not deal with the ones destined to fail."

I looked back and forth between the men while keeping myself composed and continued, "So what brought you to my club? Business or pleasure?"

Javier eyed me seductively as he spoke boldly, "Both. I've heard some amazing things about how you do business and I can see for myself that you've created an amazing work of art with this club. I'm hoping to make even more money with you, if you're willing of course."

Fred stood by with the biggest smile on his face and a glass of whiskey in his hand while I contemplated the offer. One thing I never wanted to do was make a deal with the devil. I've had many opportunities to do just that as men have always thrown money at me. Drug dealers promising me houses and cars while others just wanted to take care of me by presenting wads of cash to entice me. I've heard all of the lines since the age of fifteen and each one went in one ear and out the other. Fred on the other hand was the only one that presented me with an opportunity to make money where I wasn't getting my shit busted in by the FBI or becoming the baby mama of a wannabe El Chapo.

I was a pretty girl that had pretty friends and all of my pretty friends were some pretty hoes. After he had smashed my entire circle of friends from the simple fact that I suggested that they do it, he advised me to pimp them out. Of course, I was hesitant at first and declined the offer. I didn't want to do my friends like that, so Fred decided to put me on in other illegal schemes as he revisited the idea later with the guys he knew that had the bands and didn't mind handing a few out.

At seventeen, I set up her first meet with Vanjettia and a wealthy land developer that flipped houses for the fun of it. Vanjettia came back gleaming at the fact that she had made two thousand dollars within an hour from doing something that she would've done for free and had done for free many times before. The next meet was a weekend in Cali with Brinae and a hedge fund manager with crazy jungle fever. I tagged along only to ensure that he didn't kill my friend or hurt her in any way or else we would've both been on the run for murder.

Luckily for him, he ate, he fucked, he came, and he left while leaving Brinae feeling like the richest girl in America with five bands all for herself. It was Fatima that made the big money making moves as she entertained five diplomats in one night, each donating three thousand dollars for their time with her. It was only supposed to be two, but she felt sorry for the other three and let them join in as well.

Fred made sure that every guy he introduced me to paid me upfront and I made sure that my friends got theirs as soon as service was rendered but Fred received nothing. He was a twenty-six year old man that had fallen in love with a seventeen year old girl and wanted nothing but for me to succeed in life. The time we spent together and the talks that we shared were worth more to him than anything else which was the very reason that he made sure to put me on and support me in any way that I needed. This didn't stop his multiple attempts at shooting his shot. Ten years later and all he could do was admire the woman that I had grown to become while respecting my marriage as much as was humanly possible for a man in love.

Now it was all about the connections and Javier Cortez was the guy that he knew would give me the keys to my own kingdom. He spoke honestly as he said, "Nobody is coming to buy you out. Javier has other Fortune 500 companies that's bigger than Cronix but since acquiring a lot of business and land here in Jackson, he needs a new CEO that knows how to keep the money flowing."

Javier added, "That knows how to keep it flowing and increase it as well. I'm willing to become a silent investor in you starting your own Fortune 500 company. I can't have just anybody running a billion dollar company."

My dream of becoming a successful business owner of an umbrella company sat before me on a silver platter and everything about it felt too good to be true as I replied, "Why don't we meet up tomorrow and talk about this over lunch? In the meantime, enjoy the show."

They both nodded in agreeance and sat back down with a smile at their corner table as they watched the sassy Ri La Belle sway her hips with two large purple fan feathers swirling around her to a comical rendition of *'But I Am A Good Girl'* by Christina Aguilera.

After handing Javier my business card, I went into my office to pray when Vanjettia barged in asking, "Please don't tell me you're selling the club!"

While shaking my head, I replied, "Ironically, no. I can't go into detail about it just yet but I'm definitely not selling the club. As a matter of fact, I'm about to head out. I'll see you tomorrow night."

Vanjettia still looked worried as she continued, "Okay, but Brinae needed to talk to you about the auditions this weekend. It's way more girls than she expected it to be and she needs you to help pick the right dancers for the show."

I nodded as I walked out of my office saying, "And we'll talk about it all tomorrow night. You have my word."

Before I could get out of the door good, God had already answered my prayers as Vanjettia stopped me dead in my tracks and said, "One more thing before you go." She pulled out her iPad and said, "Do you see this? We've gone viral in a matter of minutes. This TikTok video of us dancing as Femme Fatale IV already has over a million fucking views and counting. We need to celebrate this Niecy!"

So much was happening and so fast that all I could say was, "And we will but first I need to get home to my husband ma'am."

With a smile, she nodded and walked off singing, *'I'm on to see my husband. I'm happy.*

I'm happy!'

The drive home was filled with praise and worship as I blasted, *'I'm Getting Ready To See'* by Tasha Cobbs Leonard on repeat. The lyrics hit harder than ever as tears rolled down my face while I cried out, *'Beach house vibes, maneuver the jet ski. Cause I serve a God that parted the Red Sea. Multi-million dollar commercials for Pepsi. From food stamps to more ice than Gretzky. I don't gotta talk, the Lord defends me. I watch them all fall for goin against me. Cause me and all my angels shot the devil up. While you was trying to pull me down, I leveled up. I leveled up twice, I leveled up three times. He tapped them and told them she's mine. So even when I cried, I knew I'd be fine. Prepare for a miracle blessing in these times. Now praise Him, raise Him, name it, claim it. Every tongue that rises up against me, shame it. I breathe success in and out my lungs. I got the power of life ad death coming out my tongue!'*

All of my hard work was finally starting to pay off and the only thing on my mind was celebrating with my husband. I pulled up into my driveway and sat in the car for a few extra minutes before getting out and tackling the craziness of my family. A set of six year old twin girls ready to jump me as soon as I stepped across the threshold and a husband sitting back relaxing playing Call of Duty on his PlayStation.

After a few tickles and chases around the house with Tia and Tamara, I went into the bedroom to finally have a mini celebration with Dustin. As I started to undress as his phone went off. Normally, I wouldn't dare to check his phone. After eight years of being together off and on, I never had before but the name 'Alaysia' piqued my interest and I indulged, putting his passcode in and reading the messages. My husband had been doing what he did best, sexting other women and at this point I was becoming rather tired of the bullshit. Before they were married, all he ever did was cheat and get caught up.

Multiple women had sent me messages with screenshots and pictures, hell even videos, of his indiscretions in an attempt to break us up. It always worked and we always broke up only to get back together in the end. I believed the idea of him being faithful as a married man as I had certainly been faithful to him.

At the very least it wasn't intercourse, but I knew all too well that it was only the beginning of a meet up at an hour motel somewhere and if him and this Alaysia bitch were in a room together then nothing would've stopped them from making those fantasies a reality. I placed the phone back on his side of the bed just as he walked out of the bathroom with nothing on but a towel and little beads of sweat oh his chest.

I walked up to him and started kissing his chest as I glided my hands up his back. He firmly grabbed my shoulders and said, "Not tonight, Niecy."

Reeling from another rejection by my husband, I asked, "What's the problem Dustin?"

He shrugged his shoulders as he slipped on his boxers and got into bed saying, "You got a serious problem. All you want to do is have sex."

I scoffed watching him pick up his phone to most likely continue sexting Alaysia and multiple other bitches while I stood there hot and ready after months of not having sex with my husband. The switch to my humanity had been turned off as I stripped completely naked and laid down in the bed beside him and started to masturbate freely as if he didn't exist.

I could feel his eyes trailing my naked body watching my fingers massage my pearl. I dipped my index and middle fingers in and out, coating my heat with my sweetness as I heard his breathing adjust to the idea of finally pleasing his wife. This wasn't me putting on a show as I had no desire to please him. I simply wanted to feel a quick release and the moment my legs tensed up and a breath of pleasure escaped, he says, "I can help you with that."

I got up placing my clothes back on to head into my she shed and have a relaxing blunt to myself while calmly saying, "Bitch fuck you."

Dustin lashed out with offense, "What the fuck is wrong with you?"

Without backing down as I replied, "Bitch you! How you texting all of these bitches but got the nerve to deny your fucking wife?"

He rolled his eyes from the fact that we were having yet another argument over the lack of sex that I was getting as if we weren't still getting over the loss of our stillborn daughter from five months ago. It almost broke me when I lost that child, especially after experiencing the gruesomeness of hyperemesis gradvidarum for eight months rendering me completely incapable of doing anything for myself or my kids that needed their mother. I prayed desperately for it all to be over with as the doctors assured me that everything was fine with my baby girl. She was perfectly healthy and then randomly in the middle of the night I experienced a nagging pain that only slightly increased.

Believing it to be only gas pains, I asked Dustin to run me some warm water to sit in but after multiple trips to the ER and constant hospital stays because of dehydration, he had grown tired of me. I knew I had become a burden on him and yet it was nothing that I could. It wasn't like I gave myself hyperemesis gradvidarum. The only other person in the world that seemed to understand how miserable I felt was Princess Kate and it wasn't like I was going to call her up so we could have crumpets and tea and discuss how to keep it all down and not die from constantly puking our guts up.

I pushed through, handling it the best way that I could and when everything became unbearable, I went to the ER only to stay from being so close to death's door. Dustin's true colors showed as everything he did for me came with disgruntled looks and groans of misery. When the pain the didn't leave, I suggested another trip to the ER, and it was there that I faced death in the worse way.

Although I been avoiding funerals since my Uncle Keith's death, I sent my Meme off as if she was Queen Elizabeth herself. The only reason that I didn't have yet another panic attack was because I had just found out that I was pregnant, and I didn't want to stress myself out in the pregnancy only to lose my sweet angel five months later. Losing her broke everybody's hearts, from my in laws to the hospital staff.

The only thing I knew to do was be strong for my kids. During a final farewell in the hospital, I held my sweet angel and named her Jordan Danielle as I kissed her cold lifeless cheeks while remembering the kicks and the times in which she'd curled into a ball underneath my ribs and grieving the memories that I would never get of her playing with her sisters while wearing the prettiest colors I could find.

Death took a lot from me, but it didn't take everything and as soon as I made it home, I praised God and thanked him for being God because I know it could've been worse. It could've been us both. I didn't understand why I had to lose my sweet angel, but I knew just like Job that something good was going to come back to me. I knew that despite everything that I had lost, God was going to double it all up and give right back but bigger and better. I kept faith in that. In the fact that my life was not my own and that God could use me however he wanted. To the outside world, it seemed as if I had moved on fairly easy while Dustin spiraled out of control constantly replaying the doctor's words, *'I'm not sure when the baby died but there's no heartbeat'* and trying to find multiple ways to numb the pain without me finding out the truth.

He explained once again as he had plenty times before, "Niecy, I'm not fucking any of these women. It's just flirting and nothing else."

I squinted my eyes as I spoke, "You just asked that bitch when she was going to let you eat her out. Excuse me for not being a simple minded bitch and knowing the difference between a meet up and flirting because that ain't no motherfucking flirting that I know about!" Dustin got up to try and please me in order to shut me up when I stepped back as I threw my hands up and said, "Don't fucking touch me."

Ignoring my warning, he continued walking up to me when I punched the flat screen TV that sat on the chest dresser and snatched the PlayStation while heading for the front door. As soon as I opened the door, I slammed it against the concrete, and it shattered into smithereens. Anger instantly arose in Dustin as he rushed behind me yelling, "What the fuck Niecy?"

I went into the kitchen next as I was trying my best to avoid laying hands on my husband and started grabbing plates throwing them at the walls while yelling obscenities. Huge holes formed in the walls as some plates didn't manage to break whereas others had shattered on the floor. Dustin charges me while saying, "Think about the fucking kids!"

I screamed back, "Fuck them kids! If they're stupid enough to walk over here, then they deserve to get hit!" With only inches between us as we stared each other down. He knew not to lay one hand on his crazy ass wife for fear of how far it may actually go. Annoyed by his presence I grabbed the coffee pot and smashed it against the sink as if it was a beer bottle and said, "You gone move or what?"

Slowly he backed up while shaking his head with his hands up as he's trying not to cut the bottom of his feet on any glass retreating back into the bedroom. I took a deep breath and comforted my kids standing in the living room watching the horror scene take place. I helped them in bed and then went back into the kitchen to clean up. Tears freely flowing down my face turning into silent sobs from not understanding why I wasn't good enough for the man that I slept beside every night. The prayers that were supposed to had been for the finances became prayers to become a better wife and mother as I knew that I had taken things too far.

Act Two

ANGER

"Angry people are not always wise."
-Jane Austen, Pride and Prejudice-

WORDS OF AFFIRMATION
"I'm writing you a love letter tonight
You better keep watch cause the mailman's coming"
-Aaliyah-

***Pret*ty Woman**

"I charmed a king, a congressman and an occasional aristocrat. And then I got me a Georgia mansion and an elegant New York townhouse flat. And I ain't done bad" - Fancy by Reba

Destiny

Two years later and the dust had seemed to settle down between me and my mama which was good because my kids hated to see us fighting all of the time over things that they were too young to understand. While my mama was off handling business for the church, I was setting up plans for my first trip out of state. Niecy had stopped by preparing dinner for our kids and cleaning up while the kids ran around the house having the time of their life as I said, "I'm leaving town next week."

Niecy nodded and replied, "You never leave town. Where you going?"

I smiled and said, "Maryland. This doctor is flying me out. All expense paid."

With a face full of shock, Niecy said, "Oh damn. Okay na!"

I nodded as I watched her start to fix all four kids' plates and said, "Girl I'm so excited. He ain't all that cute but he's nice. Met him on TikTok."

Niecy shook her head with disappointment in my actions from not understanding how people really fell for the fake life that people posted on the internet. Social media was an amazing outlet for me to post a bunch of nonsense to laugh and joke with others, but Niecy only ever seen it as a business opportunity. It was never something for her to truly connect with people. She preferred to interact in person which had its ups and its downs because not

always did people enjoy her random pop up visits or how she'd abduct people and on a whim and go out of town.
Nobody ever told her no though. She always came with a good time and love which was hard to say no to. Once people started taking her posts serious, she pulled back and deleted her social media accounts. Some thought that was weird and crazy, but she ended up with stalkers and people thinking that they actually knew her when she was out and about while others reached out in their time of need believing the false image that they were real friends. It was too much for her but for me I didn't have all of those *'celebrity'* problems.
Phone conversations were enough for me as well. I know she really only came around so that the kids as she looked at them with a smile laughing and playing. The moment she looked back she noticed me chopping up pills and mixing it into one of my kids' plate of mashed potatoes and her overly righteous ass asks, "What are you doing?"
Without a second thought, I replied, "It's my mom's lupus medicine. It's going to knock them all out."
Suddenly Niecy was standing beside feeling like flames were radiating from her body as she spoke calmly, "Oh is that the first plate?"
I nodded and replied, "Yeah, don't worry I'm putting some in all of their plates."
One thing Niecy hated was giving her kids any kind of medicine for any reason. As off the wall as that may sound, she preferred natural remedies such as hot honey lemon tea or homemade chicken noodle soup with orange juice instead of filling her babies up with Robitussin for every sniffle or cough they made. She for damn sure wasn't giving them any other pill or medicine that wasn't prescribed to them and since melatonin was natural, she allowed her kids to run the energy off the same way that she did as a kid. It took every

fiber of in me not to drop a mickey in her fucking cranberry sprite to loosen her the fuck up. She spoke like an old school teacher holding a paddle as she stood looking over my shoulder saying, "Don't put that shit in my kids food!"

Quickly, I exclaimed, "Okay damn. I won't!"

It was only minutes to an hour before Niecy was leaving as both of my kids had fallen asleep while hers looked around bored and confused. I was content, happy, and at peace because of no loud ass kids running around. It wasn't the first time that I had done something that appeared so vile to Niecy but whenever she thought she was telling me about myself, we'd would get into it bad and not talk for months at a time while I went on telling everybody it was over some dick to hide the fact that she was probably going to tell everybody some fuck shit about me fucking over my kids. Already dealing with the aftermath of my mama taking them from me in the first place but when the cat's away, the mice will play.

The next day, my mama drove me to the airport as she said, "Are you sure about this Destiny because I don't want to have to come kill this man if you go missing?"

I rolled my eyes wishing that I could've avoided the encounter before boarding this plane for the first time as she lied, "Evan isn't some crazy stalker off the internet. Niecy introduced us years ago. He just moved a couple of months ago is all."

My mama sighed while accepting my answer because as always, she knew that she could trust Niecy. She never felt the need to question anything that I said if I stamped Niecy's name on it. Her one downfall was believing that I wouldn't throw my own child under the bus to save myself but believed this relationship between me and Niecy to be the purest. My mama loved herself some Niecy and hoped that one day I would get my life together as Niecy had done. Sometimes all you can have is hope. She watched as the airplane took off while praying for my safety.

Everything was cute the first day in Mary-land. Evan was the perfect gentleman. Our first date was to a steakhouse which was supposed to had been followed up by going to the winery. Somewhere down the road, Evan went from being the perfect gentleman to the perfect asshole and on the second day we laid in bed all day in the hotel room after he'd gotten his fill. All of the promises he made about loving me and moving me there flew out of the window when his best friend called and he answered the phone inviting him and some other girl to the room.

A sweet getaway turned into a hotel party within seconds of them entering in with bottles of liquor, laced blunts, and pills. I was in Rome and when in Rome, you must do as the Romans. For years, I swore a lot of things that I'd never do and that night was the night that I started lying to myself as I placed my head between the thighs of my first female and dipped into her lady pond while Evan rammed inside of my anal canal.

Tears formed as I pretended to enjoy the moment. We fucked and sucked all night until for the first time ever I was completely worn out not wanting to be touched. The next day, Evan's mood turned from sour to sweet as he watched my airplane takeoff. As soon as I landed back in Mississippi, he had blocked me on all of his social media accounts.

Days later, when my oldest daughter asked about my trip, I swallowed back my tears of rejection and smiled as I lied, "It was great. He wants me to come back next month for good, but I just can't be with him. I'd miss my kids too much." I ran the back of my hand down the side of my daughter's high yella face as I said, "You're not going to have any problems in life. You're so pretty. You'll be able to get any man you want." My oldest smiled while the youngest looked at the encounter like a ghost because although I tried, I never seen beauty in her the way I did with my oldest. Only a shade or two darker was too dark for these men and so I looked at my youngest, I told her the only truth that I knew to tell, "All you have to do is be nice to them and they'll be nice to you." They both listened to me and loved me while believing my insecurities and lies to be loving truths.

Later that night, I tried to confide in the one person that I knew wouldn't judge me until Niecy said nonchalantly, "Well I ain't gone say go to church but you definitely need to read your bible and pray more."

I sighed as I said, "Just feels like I'm talking to myself."

With a chuckle, Niecy replied, "Yeah that's exactly what it is though."

I dismissed her words and went on to say, "I'm meeting up with Chris tomorrow. He's been hitting me up and I need something to take my mind off Evan's gay ass."

Although I couldn't see it, I knew Niecy was rolling her eyes as she replied, "I thought he was married."

As I slightly perked up from the thought of the challenge, I replied, "Not my problem.

That's his wife's problem. He said vows to her not to me."

The moment Niecy opened her mouth, the words flew out stinging hard than a bee sting as she said, "Girl go get your husband!"

Before ending the call, I sucked my teeth and with the nastiest attitude, as I said, "Nobody asked you to be Jesus."

Approved Overtime

"I want you face down, ass up. On all fours. Girl, you can scream all night long. Girl, I want you to myself" - Face Down by Vedo

Chanice

The clock was ticking while Lester tried to finish the last of the blueprints for the city of Jackson, Mississippi's pipeline so that he could finally leave. He's literally the only one in the building after midnight. Everybody else had taken off early for the holiday break but not him. The worst thing he could have ever agreed to was doubling his workload but his partner and his ClickTight brother on this project, Marcus is a happily married man with young kids at home waiting on their Santa to arrive.

It's that time of the year when family should come together, and Lester couldn't be the reason that this new father wasn't at home in time for milk and cookies. Lester had been putting all of his time in at work trying to keep himself out of trouble as he was newly divorced and dealing with the mayhem of having a crazy ex wife that still wanted him.

The only thing on his mind was hitting the road by six for this seven hour drive to St. Louis. This shit had him crashing bad though. He figured he might as well get up and find a way to stay woke because shooting baskets like he was Kobe wasn't giving him any kind of motivation to finish this project right now and his new boss would chew him up and spit him out for not completing it. How was he supposed to pull a rabbit out of his ass in the middle of the night was beyond him, but it had to happen!

A lot of people would think being a computer-aided design drafter is an easy desk job but it's only easy on the days when the structure isn't a total shitstorm unlike Jackson, Mississippi's pipeline. The winter months are the absolute fucking worse because the pipes are constantly freezing over and bursting causing multiple homes to have low water pressure or no water at all.

There's always a boil water alert and everybody thinks it's simple to just replace a broken pipe not realizing the work that's actually required to replace the pipes of an entire city. Looking at blueprints on a computer day in and day out, mapping placements and making sure all calculations are correct is an extremely tedious job and ain't nothing easy about that!

Lester pushes through becoming the head of his department but recently there was a takeover with his company, and I stepped in as his new boss but regardless his plan was to knock me right out of this chair in the top office however tonight his only plan is to finish this last little bit of paperwork and yet his mind kept drifting off to this little cutie he's been flirting with on Facebook. She's been blowing his phone up because he promised her, he'd hit her up after work, but a lie doesn't care who tells it. After working at Cronix for eight years, he knew today was going to be hell.

He made his way to the break room and grabbed a redbull from the fridge, the security guard came in saying, "Damn, man you still here?"

He sighed and replied, "Yeah, man. I ain't got much left though ad then I'm out. Heading to St. Louis. Spending the holidays with my parents."

The security guard nodded as he said, "I hear ya man. Be careful on the road." He walked out but then quickly turned around and said, "Oh, yeah the big boss is heading this way."

He tapped the door frame and walked away while Lester shook his head in response. This was not the night he wanted to meet me but there was truly nothing else he could do to stop it. Just what he needed to make his night perfect. Everybody in the office talked about how I was a real ball buster! How I didn't play games and is always about business. He didn't mind as long as the heat wasn't on him.

I'm the new CEO of a billion dollar company so quite naturally Lester expected me to be what others would call a bitch, how-ever, if it was him, he'd be considered a big deal and handling business the way it's supposed to be handled. He crushed his can and threw it away just as I walked into the break room saying, "Mr. Walls, why are you still here? Marcus left hours ago."

Not trying to get his coworker and biker brother in trouble, he replied, "Just handling some last minute paperwork that I didn't get to earlier in the week."

I nodded and said, "I see. Mr. Walls you are such a hard worker. I wish we had ten more just like you."

Nothing he hadn't heard from the higher ups before. He replied with a smile, "Thank you. I appreciate the recognition. I'm really looking forward to moving up even further in this company. It's the reason I work so hard."

With an understanding nod, I replied, "I believe you'll get there in no time." I walked in and grabbed a bottle of water from the fridge as I continued, "Listen, I need you to come to my office. I want to show you something."

We took the elevator up to the top floor and as we walked into the office, Lester pictured his name on the desk. You should never work at a company for years with no goals in moving up and regardless of how much he respected me as a hardworking and strong black woman, he thought that I had no idea about his ambitions for the top position that I had just acquired.

I've been watching Lester for a while. He's absolutely an amazing worker but he could've been the worse in the building and I still would've given him the promotion to being supervisor of his department. With the rumor mill saying how much of a bitch I was, I needed something to butter him up before making my move. It had been some years since I saw him at Magoo's krumping and grinding on the dance floor with his bike club. I was fully committed to Dustin, so I wasn't interested in trying to hook up with anybody. Destiny had told me all about Lester and his new man stealing girlfriend so when she pointed him out in the club, I knew that I was going to stay clear of all the drama that surrounded their love triangle. God had other plans be-cause the guy she had pointed out was now my ambitious employee.

The world was small, but Jackson was smaller. Now some years later, here I was as his new boss, and he seemed to be none the wiser as to who I was. The only thing Lester wanted was my position in the company and was determined to get it by any means necessary. He stood alert, always staying professional. As a black man, he couldn't afford to let any higher up see him slipping into the guy he is when he's not at work. He spoke clearly, "What did you need to show me?"

I shrugged and said, "Oh, no reason to be prim and proper." He nodded but never changed his position. I walked closer to him and grabbed his tie while saying, "Mr. Walls, I'm going to fuck you and you're going to like it."

He chuckled letting his guard down a bit as he said, "Is that right?" I wasted no time in pulling him closer to me for a kiss. He had no problem with giving in to my needs. It felt so natural to be back in his arms with his lips pressed against mine. The way his hands caressed my body told me that he knew something about me felt familiar and I'm sure he'd figure it out eventually. If anybody would've asked him if he'd ever smash, he certainly wouldn't have denied the fact that he'd take my ass to pound town without a second thought about it.

Being about five foot two with full luscious lips looking like the next Angela Bassett in this piece, I already knew that I could easily walk in and own any room full of corporate men of all ethnicities. Any man says that they wouldn't get down and dirty with me was a straight up fool. I slid my hands down his abs and gently clasped his erection as I looked at him and smiled, "That's why you're my favorite in the building. You always come in ready to work."

As I stepped back, my fingers started to unbutton my suit while Lester followed my direction and unbutton his as well. I slid the zipper down on the back of the skirt and it dropped revealing my curvy frame and pudgy stomach wearing all black lace lingerie. I had been planning this moment from the second he caught my eye as I watched him hop off of his shiny purple Hayabusa, parking in front of the building and walking in like he was king of the world.

He admired my belly ring chain that went up my torso and around my neck along with my tattoo of dreamcatchers, clocks, and butterflies strung together like a garden etched beautifully onto my thick thigh. Lester watched as I slid unto the desk that he was planning on taking from me, not caring about what fell off as he made his way to me.

We kissed as if this wasn't our first time having sex in the office. As if we'd been waiting on this moment all day. He placed sweet kisses on my neck with light nibbles while diving his fingers inside of me. I was overflowing with excitement as my moans sounded off sweetly in his ear. He eased his fingers out to place them in his mouth so that he could taste my juices when I grabbed his hand and began sucking myself off of his middle and index fingers. That shit was the sexiest thing that Lester had ever seen causing him to dive his fingers back inside of me and finger fuck me until I was squirming all over the desk. Finally, he was able to get his taste of the sweetest nectar that he never knew existed. Pretty obvious that I was a woman that loved eating her fruits and veggies.

He began to make his way downtown giving me what he knew I'd love, and I didn't stop him as he started getting lost within my juices. While my hand rested on the back of his head pushing him in further as my hips rotated in a circle. When I felt his thick long tongue dart inside of my walls, I started knocking more shit off the desk looking for something to grab while arching my back higher in pure ecstasy. Lester should've known that I would've been a freak like this if only he remembered who I was.

I'm sure that he's heard all about how the ones as poised as me, are always the biggest freaks and I was proving that to be true as I pushed him off of me and hopped off the desk. He watched me drop to my knees, meeting his fully erect rod with kisses and licks while innocently looking up at him. The urge to look around for the PornHub cameras came over him for a quick second as he glanced around in disbelief at his new boss becoming his personal pornstar. I lifted up his rod, placing his sack into my mouth. I got real nasty with it, tapping his rod on my tongue, and he soon learned how much I loved gagging on his dick.

Only turned me on even more as he ran his fingers through my freshly silk pressed hair and gripped it lightly. The little nympho within me moaned so he gripped my hair harder while I started to go crazy on his dick. I enjoyed the feeling of Lester fucking my mouth. It's quite possible that I enjoyed it more than him. His knees were beginning to buckle, about to give out but he kept standing tall trying to take it like the grown ass man that he was. I knew he was reaching his moment, but I refused to stop.

Never switched up. Staying consistent. Staying the course. Lester wanted to say something because he didn't want any issues, but he blasted off in my mouth before he knew it and I happily swallowed him up in an instant causing him to moan louder than I was. I continued in a soft and gentle way, but that shit was too fucking intense, and he needed a moment.

It wasn't obvious to me, so he tapped me on the shoulder, and I stood up smiling as I spoke softly, "Why are you stopping me?"

I didn't need a reply. He had lifted me up while kissing me passionately like I didn't just have his dick down my throat. I wrapped my legs around him and he entered me standing in the middle of my office. He jumped around the office pounding me like he was Melvin in *'Baby Boy'* and I loved every second of ` my fantasy coming true. I've always wanted to get picked up and tossed around but Dustin was either too weak or didn't care enough to fulfil these sexual fantasies of mine. This red bull had him showing out like he was in Super Saiyan mode. He let me down and asked, "You don't need a break do you?"

My face turned up at him as I replied, "Boy please! We just getting started!"

I had my hand splayed across his chest pushing him back to the desk, forcing him to lay on it while I climbed my extra short ass on top of him. I started riding slowly and he watched as my body swayed with enjoyment. The moonlight shined through the big office windows cascading on my body, revealing my perfectly erect gumdrop nipples. I started caressing my thighs and hips as I rode as long and as fast as I wanted to. It's as if I was dancing on the dick the way my body rolled with my hands rubbing up into my hair.

I leaned down and started to kiss Lester on his neck, but the ride never stopped. His hands were all over me until they made their way to my supple ass. After a few smacks with my moans in his ear, I started to nibble on his earlobe as he gripped my ass and sped up the bounces. My kisses and nibbles stopped and all that could be heard was, "Oooh shit!" and "Fuckkk!"

Lester could hear his alarm going off on his phone and he already knew it was six in the morning. *'Damn'* he thought to himself as he still had a seven hour drive to make and here he was fucking the shit out of his boss. He lifted me up off of him and got off the desk. I was mad and about to go off on him because he had just interrupted my first true climax, but I was soon going to feel that and so much more. He spun me around and bent me over the desk as he entered me from behind. Whatever was left on the desk was on the floor by this time.

I reached my hand between my legs and started to massage my clit while Lester reached for my neck, lightly choking me. The moment that I accepted defeat and allowed Lester to have full control is when he placed both hands on my hips and beat the pussy up for this last round. I screamed out and he knew I was creaming all over his dick. His was right behind mine and just in time as his alarm was going off again. I looked exhausted and out of breath as I said, "I don't want to have to find you after the holidays. You better be here bright and early ready to work and don't worry about the paperwork you were doing for Marcus."

Stunned, he wasn't sure what to say but he replied, "Listen, I agreed to it. It's not his fault at all."

I shook my head with a smile and said, "Chill out. Nobody's in trouble. I never expected anybody to actually finish all of this work during the holidays, but you just love exceeding expectations. Happy Holidays Mr. Walls. Safe travels."

With a smile, he nodded and replied, "Happy Holidays Mrs. Love." As he walked away, he looked back at me one last time and that's when he had an epiphany.

Forbidden Romance

"There's nothing I want more in this world. Than somebody who loves me naked. Someone who never asks for love. But knows how to take it." - Naked by Ella Mai

Imani

The computer screen illuminated a plethora of tabs for flights to book going to Hawaii. Marcus reassured me that nothing was going to stop him from missing my birthday this year and no matter what I had planned that we would do it. I've always wanted to go on a cute little trip with my man. Things had been going great between the two of us but lately work has once again gotten in the way of everything.

Either he's way too busy or I'm too busy and slipping into depression wanting to be alone for weeks at a time. We rarely have time for each other now and it's making me wonder a bunch of things. The need to confide in my man about the weird events taking place in my life, wasn't something that I wanted to do. I wanted to keep all of my deep dark secrets to myself and pretend as if some things never happened while others never existed. After all of this time it was safe to say that we still didn't know a damn thing about each other. He comes over to my place. I went to his. Sex was the only thing that we seemed to have in common, but I held out hope that it could become more.

Just as I was about to text Marcus, my phone vibrated, and I rolled my eyes at the name that popped up. Destiny has been ducking and dodging me for the past two months as if I did something to her. I refuse to play along with the bullshit, so I ignored her call just to get a text that read *'You dirty nasty bitch'*

I simply stared at my phone completely confused. While trying to ignore the message, another one came in saying, *'Bald-headed hoe ass dick breath bitch'*

Trying once more to ignore the bullshit on my phone, I got up deciding to take a shower.

Working from home was the best thing that I could've done in life and today I was clocking out early to take a mental break. I stepped into the tub and turned the showerhead to pulsate, letting the water beat on my back, neck, and shoulders. The feeling was the next best thing to a massage at a spa somewhere.

My phone vibrated until it fell off of the bathroom sink. Although I had hoped that it was Marcus, I was sadly mistaken as I finished my shower, dried off and checked my phone, I had five new messages and not one from Marcus. The messages were from the same number that texted me earlier. They all had the same tone as well.

'Bitch you a slut!'
'Get your own fucking man'
'Loose pussy ass bitch'
'Probably got gonorrhea in the back of ya throat. Nasty hoe!'
'You a nothing ass bitch'

Within about thirty minutes, I found myself sitting in the driveway of Ace's house in Byram with a manila folder that had come in the mail earlier that day sitting on the passenger seat. He was the perfect somebody that I needed to talk to. After he noticed my car outside, he walked out and tapped on the window. I rolled it down and with a smile he asked, "What's wrong?"

I grimaced as I said, "But what's with the smile?"

He shrugged and replied, "You don't even like driving to Byram so it's kind of funny seeing you out here."

I nodded and went on to ask, "You right. You got some smoke?"

He leaned back with a surprised look as he answered, "You trying to smoke?"

He went back in the house for a minute and came back out. As soon as he got in the car, he fired the gas up. Watching me like a hawk as I pulled on the blunt and choked made him laugh and I said, "Man shut up! I just got a lot on my mind."

With a sigh, he replied, "What's up? Ole boy done fucked up already huh?"

I glared and said, "No! Everything is great with Marcus. I got this in the mail today though."

Ace started to cough so bad that he was tearing up. I chuckled because I knew what I had said was indeed shocking. He replied, "What the fuck is it?"

I shook my head with a shrug and replied, "I didn't want to open it alone. I know how I can be and I didn't want to get sucked back into depression especially with these text messages I've gotten today."

With a sincere voice, he asked, "What text messages?"

I pulled out my phone and begin to show him the messages while saying, "I think it's Terica. She's still pressed about our friendship."

As calm as day he replied, "Oh this again. You think Terica is doing this to you? I thought we went over this, Imani. Come on now. You're better than this. Why are you so caught up on her like this?"

I was applauded as I replied, "Caught up on her? She's harassing me! Who else would be telling me to get my own man and just snapping out like this? Who?"

He shrugged and said, "I don't know Imani. I just know it's not Terica. You never know who you done pissed off now that you're dating that biker guy."

I sighed and replied, "Wow! So you're just dismissing the thought of it being Terica?
Are you that in love with this girl that you can't see the person that she really is?"
Ace shook his head and said, "I don't have a girl and you're blowing my high. Why don't you come in? I cooked some red beans with rice, fried chicken, and cornbread if you want some."
Slightly hurt by how he had dismissed my intuition of Terica being a crazed psycho lover of his, I refused to turn down a meal. Just as those munchies started to kick in, I wondered to myself, *'When did he learn how to cook and why has he never cooked for me?'* His house was smelling great with the chicken fried to golden crispy perfection. I said to him while stuffing my face, "Ace, there's no way you cooked this!"
He laughed and replied, "Why would you say that?"
I washed down a mouthful of food with some red kool-aid as I said, "First of all you can't cook because if you could cook then you owe me a lot of meals from a lot of years where you done ate up all my food and had me cooking all of this time. This is crazy. I refuse to believe you cooked this."
With a smile, he shrugged and said, "Well looks like I owe you because I promise I really did cook this."
He went and brought the package back to the dining table. I let him open it and he pulled out a bunch of previously folded letters while a few pictures slid out and hit the table. He started to read one of the letters aloud,

To my love,
Every minute that goes by, I miss you more. I search for reasons just to be next to you. Each thought of you makes me crave you more. You are my fantasy come true. You are my dreams made real. The memory of your sweet soft lips placing kisses in every curve of my body sends chills down my spine. My body heats up and burns with desire

with the smallest touch of your hand. as it searches for juices to slip into and explore. I miss the way our bodies glide as the soft sounds of Sade play into the moans created by our love. Only you can take me to a place created with pure ecstasy. I become lost in you as you dig into the deepest parts of my soul.
I am yours. Forever yours.
I love you,
Imani

Ace just stared at me, clearly lost for words as I sat looking puzzled remembering the day, that I wrote the letter. I broke the silence as I said, "I wrote that like eight years ago. Why is that in the folder?"

He didn't say anything as he continued to go through love letters and the pictures that had fallen out as he said, "Damn, this motherfucker watching your every move!"

I snatched the picture from his hand and there I was sitting in Red Lobster across from Marcus. I frantically searched the rest of the pictures just to discover that they were all from the last few months. There were pictures of me at the gym, in the tub, and even sleeping. I searched some more and what seemed like a million pictures later, I came across some old polaroids that I wished never existed.

That moment when life becomes so surreal that you become speechless as if silence would erase what's actually happening. That moment where whispered words are too loud, and it feels like the entire world can hear your thoughts when in reality it's just you freaking completely out.

Ace was still looking at the pictures as he said, "Damn, I think I've seen too much." He handed me the picture and sure enough it was female in the bed wearing a black teddy with heels. She was on her knees smiling while being kissed on the neck by me. Silence filled the air while my throat just about closed up from being completely dry. I was frozen in space and time as Ace stood beside me and showed me another picture as he pointed asking, "Is this real?"

I looked at the picture to see the other female licking my stomach as I smiled into the camera. Fear kept my face down in a desperate attempt to avoid eye contact, cringing what he may be thinking. He took everything out of my hands and placed it back into the manila folder. I watched him take the package to the living room and start up the fireplace. I never moved as Ace placed the package in the fireplace. The smell of my past overflowed while the crackling sounds produced a musical symphony to my soul. Ace came back and walked me to the couch where together we sat down as he held me, and I cried into his arms.

They sat in front of the fire in silence until the package was completely gone and I found the words to say, "Thank you. I don't know what's happening or why but thank you for that."

He wrapped his arms around me, "I got you, Imani." I wanted to explain but that's a closet full of skeletons that I didn't think anybody was equipped to handle. I that knew opening that damn package was going to be bad but now the only thing on my mind was how to move on with a real life stalker on the loose. Ace went on to say, "I know you're not ready to talk about this now. I get it. I understand how private you are, but you have to understand, somebody else knows about y'all and they're torturing you because of it." He looked into my eyes as he continued, "Imani, I don't think you're safe. This person is watching your every move. You've been hacked on Facebook, receiving blocked calls and horrible text messages, and didn't you say you got some dead rats in the mail? Somebody is out to get you and I'm guessing it's because of you and her but I got you, okay. I got you!"

I began to cry again, and he held me tighter. I understood everything that he had said. He was right, somebody knew, and they were angry with me. I spent the night and decided to stay the next few nights in his guest room. He catered to me and never left my side but when Monday came we both had a job to be at and there's no telling what could happen next.

Bastard Out of Mississippi

"Never felt so ugly. Pretending that he loves me. Sometimes it's just that money. Never had to afford me." - Lose to Win by Fantasia

Jackson, Mississippi
2013 AD
-Broken Little Woman-

Chanice

She sat across from me in the booth of the Waffle House on High St smiling at me as we enjoyed our first mother and daughter date. The way the sun kissed her face had her beautiful brown eyes looking like a two round pools of honey while her light blue shirt complemented her bronze skin tone perfectly causing me to pull out my Nokia phone to snap a quick picture of her to remember the occasion forever while she says, "I'm so proud of you Niecy. You're doing a great job and making some good money too."
I shrugged not really thinking anything of her words as I had just turned sixteen only five months before. A sweet sixteen that I could never forget as Aunt Flo came to visit and I was laid in bed snuggled up under my mom like the big ass baby that I was. Nobody understood our relationship with me being adopted to Meme, but my mom was my everything. She was my sister. My best friend. My ride or die.
There was never a moment where she judged me for being me and she was the realest woman I had ever met. Didn't matter how bad

the truth was, she didn't mind telling it with full confidence. I knew that she was enjoying the moment from how she was cheesing so hard, but this wasn't an actual date because I was at work and didn't have any customers since the second shift was always so slow.

I had started my first job and would leave Jim Hill at one o'clock in order to start the two o'clock shift. Whenever I'd get off, I'd tell my mom all about the different customers that came in and the crazy conversations they would have with each other or the cook. I always invited her to come hang out with me during one of my shifts and finally one day she agreed. My mom was so ecstatic to spend that time with me as we never did anything together aside from riding around at night listening to music or talking shit about celebrities and life.

She used to be a major party girl, always keeping her hair done up in French rolls and curls with long blue almond shaped nails but as of lately she had thrown herself away for reasons that she kept to herself. I never once cared about her appearance and loved every moment that we spent together. The one good thing that Uncle Keith's death did was bring us closer together causing me to move in with my mom. She was the fresh start I was desperately seeking from Meme's house, and it helped a ton knowing that my mom stayed within walking distance of Jim Hill. It wasn't the fanciest environment. In fact, it was pure ghetto, but I didn't mind it. I was happy with my mom and JohnJohn. It was different but in the best way.

The cook walked over with a chicken sandwich made special for my mom before heading out to smoke a cigarette as I replied, "Mama, I don't do nothing here. It doesn't pick up until right before I'm about to leave. That's when I make the most tips."

While shaking her head with a smile, my mom bit into the sandwich that I had purchased when one of the second shift regulars came in grinning only wanting a cup of coffee and gossip.

I quickly got up and served him a hot cup of Joe and introduced him to my mom. She seemed so shy as she politely smiled back and chatted the nice gentleman up. I just smiled and watched the conversation because my mom was anything but shy.

She was outgoing and charismatic. People gravitated towards her without even knowing why. I couldn't understand how she did it, but I watched her every move trying to learn how to be as amazing as her. After my shift ended, I handed her the tips that I made so that she could have gas and cigarette money while we traveled back down the road heading to the studio apartment that we all shared together in Battlefield.

Suddenly, our beautiful mother daughter day turned into a scene out of *'What's Love Got To Do With It'* as JohnJohn's father was screaming at my mom for being gone all day.

With a stream of sweat trickling down his face, he slammed a stack of cd's across the back of her neck as he yelled, "Get the fuck out and take that little bitch with you!"

She spoke softly, "I don't have nowhere to go."

He yelled even louder while throwing the little that she had in a trash bag, "Well you should've thought about that before trying to meet other niggas!"

Tears rushed out as she pleaded, "Baby please! I wasn't meeting any man. I was sitting with Niecy at her job. I swear I was!" The truth wasn't something he cared to hear as he was convinced that my mom was only using me as an excuse to meet other men behind his back. She looked over at my brother and I with guilt ridden eyes as she said, "Y'all pack your stuff so we can find somewhere to go."

Within a second of her words leaving her mouth, he screamed out, "You ain't taking my son no gotdamn where! Get that bitch and leave! Go back to ya mammy's house for all I care!"

Believing that Meme wouldn't take her in after another fight with this lowlife, that idea was quickly dismissed. We got back in her white '86 Crown Vic with soft maroon plush seats heading to Downing St with the hope that we'd be welcomed in with open arms and we were until they weren't. Although they hadn't seen each other in a while, she knew that her best friend always had her back no matter what. Imani and her mom lived on HUD and although she had multiple people staying with her throughout the year as if she was a boarding house, when it came time for the inspection, everybody had to leave with the quickness.

A month later and my mom was stressing from trying to figure out where to go because she believed her and JohnJohn's father were officially done until he came crawling back like a fire ant. They sat in the kitchen as she folded clothes arguing about why she hadn't brought her black ass back home yet and she stood her ground accepting the breakup as she was tired of being beat on by a man that clearly didn't love her.

He gathered his keys and stormed out while staring at me like he wanted to kill me.

When I went to go check on my mom, she had a new fresh cut under her eye and I knew he had punched her in the face, but my mom denied it while saying, "Niecy go get your things so we can go back."

This was all so new to me, and I didn't understand what had transpired to make my mom change her mind when she had said so many times how happy she was to be away from that man. Still, we went back and the next day I had them all in a panic because I had went missing. I was hiding out with Imani unbeknownst to Imani's mom, hoping to never go back to witness the abuse that my mom was enduring.

I could've gone back home to Meme's house where my room was untouched waiting on me but then I would have to face the demons from my past. This was my fresh start and I felt like I couldn't possibly go back to Meme pretending like I wasn't getting harassed every day from the boys wanting to have sex or the girls wanting to fight because their boyfriends wanted to have sex. I could've been honest about the rape, but I was too busy accepting it as my fault and running from it hoping to forget it ever happened. JohnJohn's father got his act together when Meme had threatened to kill him dead if he didn't find her gotdamn grandbaby. She played no games when it came to me and JohnJohn's father knew she meant every word that flew out of her mouth. Luckily for him, my mom knew exactly where I was and called Imani who couldn't deny that I was staring her in the face shaking my head no. I went back in a squad car against my will as JohnJohn's father expressed how sorry he was for how he acted. Swearing he'd never act like that again and yet neither of us believed him, but we were both stuck with nowhere to go.

The following months helped me to understand that he was nothing but a crackhead as Meme had stated so many many times before. He'd smoke up all of his money and then beat my mom's ass for her money, just to beat her ass again for not having money when the landlord threatened to put him out or the lights were turned off. Whenever he was off dumpster diving for anything that he could take to the CanMan, my mom would confide all of her darkest secrets to me, probably hoping that I'd understand why she couldn't leave that man alone.

She had encouraged me to learn how to do hair and allowed me to practice in her hair. My mom would pick a random braid pattern in a magazine and request that style. While I attempted to recreate an Alicia Keys style, my mom rolled up a blunt and said, "When I was four years old, your Meme's first husband molested me until I was seven years old, and nobody believed me when I told them. It wasn't until Aunt Ethel caught him for herself that they believed what he was doing to me, but grandma believed me the moment I told her. I think she knew the whole time though. She always knew things like that about everybody."

She placed the damp blunt across the top opening of the lamp shade to dry and sparked up a cigarette as she waited and continued, "I loved me some Myrtis. She was a firecracker, and she didn't play about her children and her grandbabies. That's one thing I always could say about Myrtis."

I tried my best to act unbothered by the smoke circling in my face as my mom finished the cigarette and lit up her blunt while saying, "When I told your daddy he believed me. He was the first man to hold me when I broke down crying in his arms. They say that the first man's arms that you break down and cry in is the man that you're in love with and meant to be with."

She exhaled a smoke ball of marijuana that traveled straight up my nostrils as she continued, "I didn't know he was a crack head when I met him. He told me that he had a gambling problem. You were only six months old at the time. I had been drinking a little. Smoking a little. I was wild and baby your Meme wasn't having it. She likes to say she took you from me but really, I gave you up. I knew she wanted a baby after having lost her twin boys with Jim right before I got pregnant with you. The night before court, your daddy laced the blunt and I didn't think it was so bad until six years later when we had JohnJohn, and he had eye problems like your Meme."

She sighed as if her heart was breaking from the memories that she never shared with even her best friend while she said, "I probably should've let my cousin have him.

He was hers first. He was with my best friend too. I'm just the lucky one that ended up with him."

As soon as I finished braiding her hair, I said, "Mama this shit is ugly."

My mom grabbed the mirror and ran her fingers down the row of braids as she exclaimed, "Girl this look good! I like it." She opened up the magazine and pointed to a picture of feed in braids as she said, "I want that next."

I shook my head and said, "But that's her real hair. That's not weave."

With a smile my mom said, "Nah they done fed the hair in somehow where you can't tell. I'm telling you Niecy that's weave!"

Just as I was about to reply, the devil walked through the door with JohnJohn humming his happy tune and turning on Aretha Franklin's *'Chain of Fools'* as he started to clean up and cook. By now his predictable behavior was obvious to me. I knew when he was high as a kite, and I knew when he was needing a fix.

While JohnJohn played his video games, completely content with how life with his parents were, my mom and I continued to have girl talk but on a different topic as we laughed on the memories of Uncle Keith and Myrtis. We steered clear of speaking on Meme as to not awaken the devil inside of the man that was my brother's father.

About a year later and my mom's heart was filled with the feeling of failure and guilt as she looked at the white paper bag that I sat on her bed and before I could utter a word, she looked at me and said, "You're pregnant."

I simply nodded my head while my mom tried to reason with me before the news could reach Meme as she said, "You need to get an abortion. I don't want this baby hating you the way that you hate me."

The only words that I heard was *'You need to get an abortion'* and tears filled my eyes because I wasn't killing my baby that I already loved so deeply. Just as Dustin had run off, so did JohnJohn's father but not before smoking up every red cent of the rent leaving us broke and homeless causing me to drop out of school and figure out my life fast when Meme called with excitement in her voice of the news of her first great grand. Eventually, JohnJohn's father reached out with lies about him being in Slidell but was actually laid up with my mom's best friend until she put him out for not choosing her over my mom.

My mom stroked his ego over the phone telling him all about how she needed him and to hurry home while I just wasn't with the shits anymore. Although I hadn't given birth yet, I was a mother now and my first concern was my baby. The environment wasn't suitable for me, and I knew it was worse for a baby, but I had a room that was still untouched and still waiting for me about twenty minutes away. After trying my hand at those feed ins on myself, I texted my friend guy Nate to come and pick me up and take me to Meme's house. There were no ill words as I got up and cleaned the front of the studio apartment. As soon as I finished washing dishes, Nate had pulled up outside and I looked at my mom and said, "Okay mama, I'm gone."

A look of pain and desperation stared back at me as she said, "I knew you were leaving when you got up and started cleaning because you were too calm but okay."

There was nothing else that I needed to say because I certainly wasn't staying. The devil had been back for a month and his predictable behavior was still predictable. Despite my mom pretending as if he had changed, she knew he hadn't and instead of leaving like me, she stayed. When I gave birth, everybody was thrilled. Maybe because after so much death it was something to actually celebrate for once.

Another year rolled by, and I was out on my own doing the best I could as a nineteen year old mother in college. My mom adored being a grandmother as it was a chance to make up for so much that she had missed out on with me but thanks to the devil, a few harsh words caused me and my mom to fall out in the parking lot of a church.

When Brinae's mother asked me to be one of her bridesmaids, I wasn't happy about it! I already had way too much on my plate and didn't have the space for more obligations in my life, but this was my best friend's mother who had been a mother figure to me and an adopted grandmother to my girls, so I sucked it up and made sure to be in attendance for whatever Brinae's mom needed. My mom begged me to let her pick up the girls from daycare and I agreed while informing her about the wedding rehearsal that I would be in later on that day. Everything was going just fine until the devil was ready to drop the babies off and I wasn't at home. When my mom called, she was angry because he was angry, and I knew this when he pulled up driving like a bat out of hell. It was obvious to me that he was in need of a fix and was lashing out because of it.

He jumped out of the jeep and slammed the door as JohnJohn got one of the babies out of the backseat. As the devil was getting the other baby, I popped open the trunk to get the double stroller out while trying my best not to say anything about the obvious. The devil walked up to me shoving my baby into my arms with so much force that it made me stumble backwards from the truck as he started to get the stroller out with hate in his eyes. As soon as I snatched the handle from his hands, the words of my Meme flew out of my mouth, "You ain't nothing but a crackhead!"

He socketed me dead in my face causing my glasses to fly off and hit the ground.

I nodded and power walked with JohnJohn back to the church, swinging the doors open to a group of Imani's family looking crazy and confused as I slung the stroller into the church and gently sat my baby down at the door with JohnJohn following suit and running back to the jeep. I stormed back out as I watched the devil jump back into the jeep while my mom jumped out screaming, "Oh you want to fight?! Come on!"

The look on her face told me everything I needed to know. She was afraid and she didn't know what the fuck was going on, but she had better prove her love to that worthless piece of shit. Seeing the fear on my mom's face sent me into a rage that I never knew I could possess as I threw my hand in the air pointing in my mom's direction while screaming out to the devil hiding in the jeep, "I been waiting to beat yo ass!"

Every word ranged true but before I could even reach the jeep, Brinae, Brinae's mom, Vanjettia, and one of the groomsmen were struggling to hold me back believing that I wanted to fight my own mother. Not understanding the event that had just transpired between the devil and me. All I could hear was Vanjettia and Brinae's mom pleading, "Niecy stop! That's your mother!" Their words meant absolutely nothing to me since it wasn't my mom that I was about to kill. They all held on for dear life when eventually my mom retreated back inside the jeep and the devil sped off down the street.

Years went by and it was never discussed. We swept it under the rug and acted as if it never happened until one day, I had a full panic attack because he was beating on her, and I couldn't come to her rescue as Keith had done for Beverly. The fear of my mom being beat to death overwhelmed me and I wasn't okay until I was back in town laying eyes on my black queen. Of course, she acted as if nothing happened, and I realized I had to let her go just as Meme had. I couldn't save her if she didn't want to be saved. We continued our girl talks and expressed love for each other in the way that we knew how. There was never a day where my mom wasn't proud of me for being a wonderful mother and her daughter but when John-John called me only two weeks before Christ-mas.

A birthday that I shared with my mom; I couldn't process nothing he was saying.

Ironically, I was doing my hair and my phone rung with *'Mommy Dearest'* going across the screen. Since we had just talked two days before for at least three hours as we always did, I figured I'd call her back when I was done doing my hair. Not a second later and my phone was ringing again with *'Meme'* going across the screen. I felt something wasn't right because there was never a time where these two names popped up on my phone back to back like that. When I answered, it was JohnJohn's voice saying, "Niecy mama gone! Mama gone!"

In complete shock, I replied, "Who mama?"

With confusion and hurt, he says, "OUR MAMA!"

As he passed the phone to Meme, she spoke softly with hurt in her voice, "It's true Niecy. Katrina is dead."

I hung up and sobbed to myself while feeling a sense of relief because at least my mom wasn't living in hell with the devil anymore.

All Night Flight

"I've never really seen your type. But I must admit that I kinda like. So maybe if you have the time we can talk about. You being mine baby." - Sweet Lady by Tyrese

Destiny

Andre exclaimed, "How lucky are we to be in Miami right now?" Carlos never looked up from his phone when he chuckled and answered, "It's a business trip AntRob. It's not a vacation."
While shaking his head in disbelief and motioning around him, Andre replied, "Look at the bigger picture man. The business part is done. Have some fun. Let loose. Look at all of these beautiful women around us. Oh shit!" He took a shot of the patron that he had sitting on the table as he straighten his shirt, watching the woman of his dreams approach him with elegance and grace. I was wearing a cute light blue floral two-piece maxi dress and had a cute Farrah Fawcett curled wig glued down.
I smiled and spoke softly, "Fancy seeing you here."
Andre wasted no time in replying, "Must be fate."
He went to grab my hand as he licked his lips eyeing me like the juiciest steak he had ever seen when I stepped back and said, "Carlos are you going to put your phone down and give me a hug or what?"
Andre sucked his teeth and went back to drinking his patron, as Carlos looked up and smiled. There stood his crush from a few years ago, still looking as fine as I did when his brother's best friend, Chaos, introduced us at Kemistry. He stood up and wrapped his arms around me taking in my sweet scent. Ken cleared his throat in frustration interrupting the reunion that Carlos was enjoying

causing him to step back and say, "My bad man. Destiny this is my coworker, Andre. Andre this is Destiny." He paused and smiled as he continued, "An old friend."

I nodded and said, "An old friend huh?"

Carlos shrugged with a smile while Andre got up saying, "It's nice to meet you but looks like I'm no longer wanted at this table. I'll see you later man."

He walked off vibing to the music that blasted through his air pods, making his way up to a couple of women he'd been eyeing all night.

I giggled and said, "Interesting character."

Carlos nodded his head in agreement and asked, "What are you doing in South Beach?"

I shrugged and said, "Just here on business. I leave out tomorrow."

Carlos thought to himself, *'Maybe it was fate'* as he replied, "Damn me too. What do you say we get out of here and see what we can get into?"

I wrapped my arms around him, placed a kiss on his neck, and whispered, "Though you'd never ask."

For the next few hours or so we enjoyed the beautiful scenery that South Beach had to offer while catching up on what we had both accomplished as well as lost over the last few years. The outing only reignited old feelings that were locked away when I decided to choose his brother over him until he went and got married leaving me alone and heartbroken while Carlos went to Birmingham pushing papers in the mailroom and working his way up to executive status.

As we made our way back to the lobby of the Mondrian Hotel on West Ave, it was obvious that neither of us wanted the night to end so soon. I was no longer the young and naïve girl pinning for his brother that I once was. I had now grown to become a bold and daring woman going after everything I wanted without hesitation. I interrupted what would've been an awkward moment of silence and eye gazing when I placed my hand on the back of his head, pulling him in for a kiss.

His arms found their way around my waist perfectly and it was agreed in that moment to finish this night with a happy ending. Carlos eagerly escorted me to the elevator ready to make up for the lost time. The ride up to the eighth floor only heighten the moment that was filled with passionate kissing and fondling causing the other guest to become instantly turned on as they entered the elevator.

When the elevator dinged and the doors opened to the eighth floor, the female of an older couple cleared her throat as she entered the euphoric atmosphere. Carlos and I stumbled out into the hallway, giggling as if we were high schoolers, making our way to his suite. He pulled me close just as the door closed behind us, caressing my face while saying, "You're so beautiful."

He leaned down and kissed me while I pulled his shirt over his head. My eyes scanned his body admiring how beautiful his brown skin looked. I walked backwards towards the couch, stepping out of my heels, and unfastening my top with a seductive smile that Carlos loved. His slacks and briefs hit the floor in the same instance that my skirt slid down revealing my natural full figure shape. I used to imagine this moment a million different ways and here it was finally a reality. Another second couldn't be wasted as he met me at the couch placing kisses on my neck that continued down to my beautiful full breasts.

My head tilted back when I felt him nibbling causing me to moan and wrap one of my legs around him. He eased me down onto the sectional couch with his hand on the back of my neck, slowly entering my anxiously waiting pussy. Chills went down his spine when he heard me softly gasp in ecstasy as I realized he was much bigger than I imagined him to be. His stroke was slow and steady until he sat up and began to drive into me harder. The speed of his strokes continued from slow to fast with his hands on my hips, keeping me exactly where he wanted me.

When he moaned, I began to smile while pulling him down to me for a kiss. I wrapped my legs around him which prevented him from getting back up. As gyrated my hips beneath him, Carlos became weak all over his entire body, but I didn't stop. He took back a bit of control when he pinned my hands above my head as his strokes became deeper and rougher. My moans grew louder with each stroke. I was now the weak one as my legs slowly slid down from around his waist.

Carlos stopped and stepped back, stroking his rock hard trophy as he motioned with his head to the balcony window. Happily, I obliged, getting up and strutting to the balcony window. I placed both hands on the window and Carlos laughed as he unlocked the door and slid the balcony window back. My eyebrows raised in excitement realizing what he really wanted. I stepped out feeling the cool breeze that came off the bay across my breast causing my nipples to harden and my pussy to drip even more.

Carlos walked up behind me, moving my hair to the side and kissing the back of my neck while making sure I felt his throbbing trophy on my ass. His fingers lightly pinching my nipples at the same time I swirled my fingers around my clit. He bent me over and dived deep inside of my walls without a care as to who could possibly see them.

I held on to the small table that sat on the balcony and enjoyed every second of Carlos being in control. He could feel me becoming more relaxed every time he thrusted deeper inside of me. Loving every minute of this adventure, Carlos smacked my ass so hard, it was sure to leave a print but all I did was moan out, "Oh baby!"

Minutes ran by and it was obvious that I had tapped out from Carlos driving into me so hard. He stopped only to place my back against the window, lifting me up to finish making his dreams come true. I knew the end was nearing when I heard him moaning as he gripped my ass harder. He lowered my legs and looked at me once more to say, "You're so beautiful."

I smiled back and replied, "Maybe we can get together another time."

He nodded and escorted me back inside his suite, knowing that he'd probably never see me again. Instead of crushing my hopes and dreams, he made sure to save my number and offered to pay for my room if I stayed the night with him, but I insisted on heading back to my own suite. We kissed and parted ways.

The next day Carlos woke up to Andre banging on his door. He reluctantly got up and let the man in. Andre held true to his nosey nature as he asked, "So man what happened with you and ole girl last night?"

Carlos shook his head while yawning and getting ready for the flight that they both had to catch in the next few hours. Andre continued to make assumptions as he stated,

"I just knew you would've hit that. The way she was all up on you. Ain't no way! I would've most def given her what she was looking for."

Carlos continued to keep his stance on nothing happened while changing the sub-ject, "Did you get the email about the meeting on Monday?"

Andre sucked his teeth and went on into the conversation about work. Carlos was open to discussing any and everything, but he wasn't about to discuss his personal life with Andre. He talked too much. The entire company would know, and the meeting on Monday would be about the activities Carlos participated in versus whatever it was really about.

Time was winding down and leaving Miami left Andre the saddest. Carlos boarded the plane with memories of a night he'd never forget. He decided to make some notes in preparation for Monday's meeting while Andre felt it was best to sleep. He hated flying and sleeping helped him get through the two hour flight. The pilot was heard over the intercom after takeoff saying, "Folks, we have reached our cruising altitude now, so I am going to switch the seat belt sign off. Feel free to move about as you wish, but please stay inside the plane until we land... it's a bit cold outside, and if you walk on the wings, it affects the flight pattern."

A few passengers were heard giggling at the corniness of the pilot's joke and then a sweet voice asked Carlos, "Can I get you anything, sir?"

Carlos answered no before having to take a doubletake, seeing me once again with a big smile, he asked, "What are you doing here?"

I shrugged and replied, "Must be fate." Carlos smiled and decided to take a risk since Andre was fast asleep and the other coworkers didn't know anything about us. He asked, "Why don't you meet me in the bathroom?"

I replied as if I hadn't already planned it myself, "Say less."

As soon as Carlos pushed the sign from vacant to occupied, I had already hiked up my skirt while leaning against the sink with one leg on the toilet. He moved quickly unzipping his pants and snatching my waist to his as he darted his tongue in my mouth. I tried my best to contain the volume of my moans, but his deep pounding strokes were sending me into overdrive making it damn near impossible to do, moving me to bite him to keep from screaming out. The pain he felt from me had him growling lowly in pleasure. He whispered in my ear, "Cum on this dick."

Although I didn't want the moment to end, I gave in and creamed at the same time he blasted inside of me. Just as he leaned back pulling his pants up, we heard tapping on the door. The voice on the other side whispered, "Destiny hurry up girl."

Carlos looked at me with a raised eyebrow and I shrugged as I said, "I had to have a lookout duh!"

He chuckled and we both walked out as if nothing had happened. When he made it back to his seat, Andre was still knocked out with only about an hour left on the flight. The previous thoughts of never seeing me again had vanished and he begin to make plans to take me out the moment he was free to do so.

Last Rites

"I don't like your perfect crime. How you laugh when you lie. You said the gun was mine. Isn't cool, no, I don't like you" - Look What You Made Me Do by Taylor Swift

Destiny

Time was of the essence. Quickly, I rang the doorbell and dashed behind the building before the door swung open to the condo. My attire of black leggings, a black long sleeve turtleneck, black gloves, and a black mask that only showed my eyes which was hidden behind black Ray-Bans blended into the darkness of the night. Finally, the front door opened where a brown paper bag sat on the porch blazing in flames. As she screamed out with disgust, "What the fuck?"

I knew her heart raced in fear and anguish when she stomped out the fire and smelled hot shit on the bottom of those ugly ass pink Uggs of hers. With a smile hidden behind my mask, I spun from around the building striking her in the mouth causing lava hot waves of excruciating pain cascading down her spine from the metal end of my dad's baseball bat.

Cora held her mouth desperately trying to stop the blood and her teeth from falling out as she stumbled back into her condo, tracking shit stains on her freshly shampooed beige carpet. Slowly I followed behind her, spinning the baseball bat around in one hand with a black duffle bag straddled diagonally across my body while delivering another hard blow like a pro in an MLB championship game.

I've never played any sports but somehow, I was perfect as swinging this bat on this simple minded hoe that felt the need to have my name in her mouth. The man she married she couldn't keep home, and this made her lash out at the wrong bitch. When my bat met her abdomen, I heard the sweet sound of her ribs cracking which made her fall over in even more agony and hitting her head on the side of her living room end table.

I rolled my eyes as she cried out, "Take whatever you want but please don't kill me."

From busting the TVs to shattering the vases and Sammy Sosaing any and every glass object in sight, I wasn't wasting any time destroying her perfect little condo so that it would look like a robbery gone wrong. I went upstairs to the bedroom that she shared with my ex, Nate, and started bashing in the mirrors and ripping curtains down while pulling out the dresser draws and slamming them down.

It was as if the Tasmanian devil himself had paid her condo a visit. After I stuffed the laptop, phone, some jewelry, and her wallet in the black duffle bag, I made my way back downstairs while swinging at the walls breaking the cute little pictures that provided a false image of holy matrimony. Unable to move with tears rolling down her face, Cora's annoying voice pleaded, "Please. I won't say anything."

After walking up to her, I smiled as I bent down with a pillow in my hands and spoke coyly in her ears, "Oh I know you won't."

Before she could say another word, I had straddled her and was smothering her until she stopped moving. After checking her pulse to ensure that my mission was accomplished, I walked out into the cool night's breeze, skipping to Niecy's black Honda Civic that was parked on the next street while imagining what the neighbors would say to see sweet old Cora banged up like this. There was no time to truly reminisce and take in the glory of what I had done as I made sure to ditch the duffle bag in the woods during the drive back home, the same way Lorena Bobbitt slung her husband's penis of out the car window.

After crossing the state lines into Alabama, I cleaned myself up at some rinky dink motel off the highway where I tossed the blood stained clothes in the dumpster and quickly got back on the road. The drive was exhilarating as I blasted my music and realized that Market Place Lane had never experienced such a tragedy as this one. *'This is totally going to make headlines!'* I thought to myself with excitement and a grin across my face. The news would probably label this as the Woodstock Massacre while Georgia State Troopers and local police put out a statewide search for the killer not knowing that I was now six hours away in Clinton, Mississippi soaking in a bubble bath and listening to the soothing sounds of music.

With the candle flames dancing across the walls, a smile eased across my face as the gory flashbacks of my first kill invaded my thoughts. To reminisce on my actions seemed even more orgasmic than the crime itself. Interrupted by my phone lighting up with a text message from Nate that read, *'Wyd babe'*

My laughter filled the air, more sinister than I've ever heard before. That troll that he called a wife would die all over again at the message thread between her husband and I as he tells me all of the freakiest things, that he's ready for me to do to him after he finishes his drill weekend in Hattiesburg. A light tapping noise interrupted my victorious moment as Carlos spoke softly, "Hey Destiny you good?"

While rolling my eyes, I sweetly lied, "Yes, sweetie I'm fine. Just watching these TikTok videos." Without any hesitation, he opened the door and before I even realized what was happening, I screamed at him, "What are you doing?"

I knew that he was hoping to have a little fun with me from the way that I just popped up on him in the middle of the night and instead of taking Niecy's car back to her. I lied and told her I had picked up a few overnight shifts at Amazon's warehouse, but the truth was I never got the job and I've just been coasting by on the generous donations of the men in my life. A quick forty dollars here and another twenty dollars there really does add up when you have absolutely nothing.

He glared at me, unfazed by my words and with full disdain he asked, "What did you come over here for? I thought you were done with me."

With a sigh, I placed my phone on the black shag bathmat and stood up allowing him to see every curve of my body as the bubbles gradually slid back down into the water. Slowly I began to fondle myself with my right hand. I didn't need to actually do anything because I already had in a trance the moment I stood up. His mouth hung open wide with a slight smirk when he seen my left hand rubbing over my breasts and squeezing my hardened nipples. Seduction in my smile from seeing his thick dick protruding through his grey sweats. With a grin on his face, he shook his head at how wild he knew I was about to get. It was just something about a fire sign that these men in my life couldn't resist.

Enjoying the scene more and more, he bit his bottom lip watching me step out of the tub and walk up towards him. As I placed my hands on his waistband, I slid down to my knees along with his grey sweats and commenced to kissing his fat head that bounced happily in my face. After hearing him moan from the tender strokes on his shaft, I wasted no time with placing his rod down my throat, showing off how amazing it feels to have no gag reflexes while humming to the sounds of Shirley Murdock's *'As We Lay'*

Technically, I was done with him because it was his brother that I wanted. The one man that kept denying me knowing all he wanted was me but of course he had a loyalty to his brother. Maybe his friends as well. It wouldn't be much longer before I wore him down and gave him this cocaine pussy. I'd make him mine soon enough but until then I needed an alibi and Carlos was the perfect sucker for the job.

Just as he was beginning to really lose himself in the moment, my phone started ringing sending vibrations across the bathroom floor from the black shag bathmat. Abruptly I stopped, jerking his throbbing rod out of my warm mouth, rushing to answer the phone hoping it to be Nate. He groaned and sucked his teeth with an attitude as I said, "Just give me a minute sweetie."

While pulling up his grey sweats, he realized his freak show was over and walked away heading towards his man cave to relieve himself as he rolled his eyes and hissed, "Whatever."

I shrugged without a care and went on to answer my phone, "Heyyyyy baby. I miss you."

A female's voice replied, "Uh, what?!"

I glanced down at my phone to see that the caller ID did not say Nate. With a laugh and replied, "My bad girl, I thought you were Nate. What's up though?"

She seemed annoyed as she said, "Damn, so you don't know huh?"

I replied, "Know what girl?!"

Niecy sounded kind of out of breath as she said, "Lauren is dead."

With confusion, I screamed into the phone, "What the fuck are you talking about?!" I cared nothing about Lauren's simple minded ass because we were never cool like that but this was my godsister's best friend and I know how hurt she's about to be to hear. I asked, "So who gone tell Imani?"

Niecy quickly replied, "Shit you! I ain't telling her this! You know that girl has been through a lot these last couple of months. Why do you think I'm calling you?!"

She wasn't wrong. Imani had been going through hell lately and this was just another blow that could possibly have her going overboard and sending her straight to the crazy house. Immediately, I hung up the phone and began calling my godsister. No answer.

After wrapping a towel around me and walking out into the bedroom, I started pacing frantically as I continued to call repeatedly and still no answer. I left a voicemail. I sent text messages, Facebook messages, and even Instagram messages. The news was circulating all over social media and they all read the same thing. Lauren was dead and Imani needed to answer the fucking phone!

Imani

I couldn't bear the last thought and image of my best friend, Lauren being dead in a casket, so instead of attending the funeral, I paid her family some respect earlier in the week before the funeral. As soon as I made my way through the crowd of grieving family members and friends, there to comfort Lauren's mother, I overheard the bickering of Lauren's little sister and Greg in the kitchen as Shannon stated, "Why are you even here? Nobody wants you here." With a low sadden voice, I heard Greg reply, "She was my wife, Shannon. I loved her. Please don't do this."

A low bang came from the kitchen as I watched Shannon's balled up fists hit against the kitchen table as she hissed, "Loved her? You killed her!" Tears fell from Greg's eyes while Shannon continued digging even harder at him, "You're a piece of shit. My sister should've never married you. All you gave her was heartache and miscarriages. Get the fuck out! And yo ass better not show up at the funeral or my cousins gone beat yo ass!"

Although I should've kept walking, I continued to listen as the back door opened and slammed shut along with Shannon letting out a loud grunt of frustration. I shook my head at the crumbling effect that one loss could have to an entire family as I finally made my way to Ms Lisa sitting in the den. She sat on the old floral couch with her sister rubbing her back and swollen eyelids from the uncontrollable crying spells she had been having.

I walked up to her and held her hand as I sat down beside her. Ms Lisa looked at me and tried to smile recognizing her daughter's only friend in this world. She tried to speak, and another crying spell consumed her words signaling to her sister to grab the box of Kleenex that sat on the back of the couch. Silently, I rubbed her hand as tears flowed down both of our cheeks.

Despite the intense grieving moment we shared, the definition of an unfit mother was indeed Lisa. Over the years, all she ever did was praise Shannon for having a pretty redbone complexion like her father that was killed in Hurricane Katrina while she completely neglected the beautiful coffee bean brown skin beauty known as my best friend. She was the spitting image of Ms Lisa and for whatever reason both Ms Lisa and Shannon hated Lauren.

Aside from the woe is me act that Ms Lisa was putting on for the attention, the pain was real as her prized cow was now dead. Up until the moment that Lauren became an international model, she wasn't even worthy to be the shit on the bottom of their shoes but of course all of that changed when they could brag on how she was doing so many amazing things off in New York and Pairs, making all of this money, and giving them so many expensive gifts. Their bragging rights had died and apparently Lauren's husband, Greg was to blame.

I didn't waste too much time crying with people that truly didn't give a damn about my best friend. The plan was to make a few groceries after the visit which is why I ended up at Walmart but somehow my reality ended with me walking out with only snacks and a bottle of white wine. I was ready to go home and down the entire bottle and take my ass to sleep until suddenly, Destiny runs up to my car, hopping in the passenger side with a bottle of Patron in her hand. She was ditching one of her many men when she seen me walking out of Walmart. I wasn't even in the car good before seeing my back tire completely flat. I thought to herself, *'What is happening to me?'* I slammed my car door which startled Destiny as she said, "Damn girl. What the fuck is wrong with you?"

I pointed to the tire and replied, "Do you see this shit?! I can't catch a fucking break!"

She sighed, "Oh girl that's nothing. At least it ain't ya engine or ya transmission. Hold on, let me call my friend. He's a mechanic and he stay right around the corner in those apartments."

Destiny was right. It was just a tire, but I honestly didn't have the money for a spare tire, so I sent Ace a text telling him my problem and where I was. Destiny suggested that we walk to the apartments where the mechanic lived and just as we started our nature walk of South Jackson, I heard a guy say, "Hey baby you need some help."

From the way that Destiny was smiling all extra hard told me that whoever he was had to be fine and that I certainly did need his help. When I turned around, it was Xavier. Instantly, I was pissed and hissed, "What the fuck are you doing here Xavier?!"

He exhaled and replied, "Had to pick up something from Walmart. Why else would I be here? Better yet why are you here? You could've gone to the Walmart in Ridgeland. It's closer to you anyway. If you were hoping to see me then here I am."

I groaned, "You're the last person I want to see."

He smiled as he said, "You're cute when you're angry."

With sarcasm dripping from my words, I smiled back and said, "I'm sure your wife is cuter."

As he rolled his eyes, he nodded and said, "Baby, let me help you. You know damn well you mean more to me than some piece of paper."

Imani raised an eyebrow with her head tilted to the side, "But a divorce is just a piece of paper too. Besides, I have help coming. I don't need nor want anything from you anymore so please go."

He scoffed, "Your ungrateful ass is going to regret that."

Without any hesitation, Destiny asked, "Now bitch why you tripping when that fine ass man was just trying to help you!"

I rolled her eyes as she sighed and said, "Girl fuck him!"

Destiny smiled and replied, "I sure fucking will! That man is fine as fuck!"

With another eye roll, I sighed and turned around to see Ace pulling into the parking lot. After he changed the tire, he followed us back to my place since he was worried about me considering how I clearly had a stalker on the loose. We all went inside, and I grabbed three glasses from the top shelf and mixed us all some drinks while Ace fired the gas up and Destiny started her rant saying, "Girl why in the fuck is Chris back fucking with Chelsea. His bitch ass think I don't know though. I been knowing since day one. He stay lying and shit talking about she stalking him and won't leave him alone!"

Rotation was on me, but I was tearing up from damn near coughing up a lung. I had hit the blunt entirely too damn hard as I managed to say, "I don't know. I guess he love her but if she is stalking him why hasn't he called gotten a restraining order or something?"

Without even knocking on the door, Niecy walked in. Here was the real pro. Niecy and Ace could smoke each other under the table. She got that shit from her mom though. She was the true blunt monkey. Always rolling up extendos and calling them baseball bats.

Katrina always thought her sweet daughter would never in a million years touch a blunt. If only she could see her now. Smoking like she invented this shit. I was still trying not to die while they were both puffing with ease as Destiny eventually replied, "Girl, he don't love that bitch. He just ain't got nowhere to go since his back injury. Now he's a fucking freeloader with no job and too many baby mamas. That bitch is desperate and so is he!"

Niecy chuckled from the effects of the kush as she chimed in, "Well why you won't just take the man in and show him the love he's trying to find in her. I mean how does the saying go? Something about holding him down or something?"

Destiny just shook her head no. You could tell she was in the zone too when she started to lean back and talk low as she said, "Girl no! Just no! You know my place ain't in my name and even if it was that his ass can't stay with me. Not now, not ever. I done played the hold a man down fool once too many times. He don't even like to keep a job and all he do is fuck off with other bitches. He stay having me in drama so now the only thing he can do for me is eat this sexy fat ass when I call for it."

I just stared in disbelief while feeling the awesome effects of the gas. Ace was in his zone playing games on his phone or probably texting his multiple women. It was clear he was only there for the weed at that point. According to him, Niecy stayed with gas that puts him on his ass. Like mother like daughter. I replied with a delayed understanding of the conversation happening between us, "Wait, he eats ass?! I can't imagine fucking Chris. He's just not cute to me and now you tell me he eats ass."

While Niecy looked on with disgust on her face, Destiny laughed and continued, "You one of the few because all the bitches trying to get some of him. I taught him everything they love too. I turned that little baby into a grown ass man."

We continued our girl talk while Niecy lit up two more blunts. We had killed the Alize and Patron while working on the bottle of Nuvo. It was litmas at this point. Niecy turned her playlist on, and we all just started dancing around the living room. The drinking and smoking didn't stop. For a moment everything was good. We were all laughing, and I could feel Lauren there with us. This was something that I truly needed. I danced away the reality of my tatted-up brownie boo with that loudmouth and heart of gold being too beautiful to not have died in her sleep at the old age of 101.

When I went to the hall closet and grabbed a blanket to place over Destiny who had passed out on the couch, Niecy said, "Damn Ace, why you ain't got on that yet?"

As he shook his head, Ace sighed and replied, "I got bougie dick. Can't be out here fucking anything and everybody."

With widened eyes, Niecy just dropped her head with a smile, and I added, "Y'all chill. She's a pretty girl."

Niecy replied, "Now girl stop playing like you don't know yo girl likes to have a 'fun' time."

As Ace laughed, my face filled with shock as if I had been accused of being the *'fun time'* girl as I said, "How you gone talk about my godsister like she ain't your best friend?"

With her lips turned up, Niecy darted her eyes back and forth before saying, "Nah shawty don't pin her on me unless she making me money."

Ace chuckled and said, "Damn, Niecy you ruthless ain't it."

I chimed in, "I think she used to be a pimp."

Niecy smiled and replied, "The word is madam and nah baby I'm just about my business."

Ace was intrigued on what business Niecy had going on as he was trying to make some business moves with a big boss like her while I sat back remembering how Lauren couldn't stand Destiny in high school because she was this big ass hoe, and everybody knew it. She had slept with all of the football team, sucked up the entire drumline, not to mention she was giving blowjobs on the spiral staircase and bending over behind the cafeteria.

She deserved to be in the Hall of Fame for whoredom at Jim Hill and to top it all off, she got the chemistry teacher, Mr. Galveston fired. It was ultimately his fault for getting caught with his pants down during detention, but she's since bragged heavily on how she seduced him a few times before that.

After a few trips down memory lane with Niecy, she left and headed home to her husband while I climbed into my queen size bed where Ace had gotten in the bed and passed out hours ago. It wasn't a problem because it was more than enough room. I stared at the picture on my nightstand of Lauren and I cheesing like two kids at Disneyworld on her birthday from three years ago. Wondering to myself, *'Why did it have to be you?'* while still pretending as if I was okay. I cried myself to sleep trying to let it all go.

Bad Business Moves

"Make me your Aphrodite. Make me your one and only. But don't make me your enemy. Your enemy, your enemy." - Dark Horse by Katy Perry & Juicy J

Destiny

After not hearing from Chaos for a good eight weeks, my phone chimes with a message from Jeremy saying, *'Can't wait to see you tonight'*

I had no desire to reply until hours later when he showed up at my hotel room with flowers and a gift basket filled with all of my favorite goodies and dressed to impress.

He had on a navy blue turtleneck and black slacks. Although he was a bigger sized guy, he was looking fresher than Jidenna during an ATL photoshoot. My kitty purred slightly from his scent alone causing me to go googly eyed as he walked inside. It was as if I was inside a cartoon with the way that I turned my head following his scent. His first words to me after entering inside were, "Thought we were going to dinner."

Still filled with resentment from Chaos' rejection, I asked, "And why would I do that? Because you came up here with a basket full of treats?"

He smiled and said, "Yes, that's exactly why. Now get dressed and come on."

I sighed as I went into the bathroom taking a quick hoe bath at the sink and spraying my crotch down with Victoria's Secret body spray. I came back out wearing some booty clapping white and gold pants, a low-cut crop top, and skintight cardigan to match while rolling my eyes. Jeremy was such a sweet guy and truly adored me, but he was too nice. There was no challenge. No excitement. I needed bold and daring and with Jeremy it was giving goody two shoe vibes and *'Little House on the Prairie,'* but I certainly wasn't turning down gifts and free food, so I put on a somewhat sweet face and went on to make the most of it.

As they walked outside, he was much more of a gentleman than I've ever been out with. He opened doors for me and simply treated me like the queen that only he seen in me. Jeremy was really an amazing guy to do all of this especially since we had known each other since middle school. Whether it was our first date or not, he didn't have to go all out like this.

I would've been fine just hanging out at his house and having a few drinks because I really didn't want to be seen in public with the man, but I was pleasantly surprised when we pulled up at Olive Garden. The ball was in his court for the next few minutes before the food arrived. Jeremy chuckled, "I guess you're still mad at me." I shook my head no as I buttered my roll. He sighed, "Well that's good to know. I have some pretty good news to share with you and I wouldn't want anger to get in the way of that." While munching on my roll, I nodded in agreement and he continued, "I proposed to my old lady for real this time and we're getting married next month!"

I spit the roll out while choking on the rest. The man straight up started laughing in my face as I said, "Are you serious?"

He could barely speak amongst the laughter when he finally managed to say, "Hell yeah!"

I threw my napkin at him as I finally caught myself, "Well congratulations. I guess it's about time."

I gulped down the water that I had and asked the server for a refill while Jeremy continued to laugh so hard that tears rolled down his face. When he calmed down a bit, he says, "I didn't think you'd choke to death when I said it. I just wanted to take you out and properly thank you for introducing us. There hasn't been a woman that I've dated that could ever truly make me as happy as she does."
With a sigh, I regretted the day I introduced Jeremy to his fiancée. We were outside of my mama's house, and he stopped Niecy in her tracks saying, "Don't I know you?"
I couldn't believe what the fuck I was hearing. To think that these two people knew each other was completely mind blowing and sure enough, she replies, "You do look familiar."
He smiled showing that gap in between his two front teeth as he held his arms out standing up from his Impala as he says, "Damn, Niecy! How you been?"
They chatted it up while I watched in complete disbelief as she went on to have her bragging moment to me, saying, "Oh snap! This ain't your Jeremy. This MY Jeremy. I knew him first."
She had stopped by with that ugly ass girl Fatima. Everybody wanted Fatima. If not Fatima, then Niecy and if not Niecy then me. I wasn't about to allow Niecy to snatch another man away from me. She already had snatched Dustin and Nate. What more did she want from me? She couldn't have Jeremy too and hearing her nickname him 'Papa Bear' absolutely disgusted me even more. So, I put Fatima on Jeremy and his cousin. I knew she'd do everything that Niecy wouldn't do. She'd be a quick lay in the hay. Fucked and forgotten while I continued to keep his attention.
My plan literally backfired in my face as I sighed and asked, "Are you telling me my man-whore of a best friend would never marry me?"
While knowing I was full of shit but enjoying the idea that I could actually take him straight back from Fatima if I wanted was all I

needed. He replies, "You know that I've always wanted you since middle school."

His words made me heavily consider giving him a real chance at a relationship. He was the only guy that has ever wanted me for me and never judged me for being promiscuous. I had already fucked his cousin and best friend, but he still so badly wanted to be with me. Jeremy was always just a phone call away whenever I needed a ride or food or just a friend to hold me at night. A true upstanding fool! I'd call on him in need and then go off and fuck and suck every other guy in town while crawling back to him with those puppy dog eyes in need of his friendship.

Love can make you do some crazy things, but this was beyond crazy. He defended me as he believed every lie that I ever told while seeing the truth for himself. Being the only guy in Mississippi to say that he's seen or laid beside me while I was butt ass naked and nothing happened is not something that should be said out loud. It's actually considered a BIG problem when Thee Head Hunter herself refuses to go any further with you.

I smiled as I loved the feeling of being wanted no matter who it was as I lied, "We've known each forever. I would've love to been yours but I think you and Fatima are perfect for each other. Besides I'm still not over the miscarriage. I almost died. I want to see you happy though. Fatima perfect right?"

As he shrugged and sighed, he replied, "I just prefer to see a person in all of the sea-sons. A lot of people like to compare relationships to test driving a car, but I could settle down with a car faster than I could a woman. I like to see how she is in the summer and the winter. She's probably evil in the spring and sweet as pie in the fall. I can't see my wife in her during only one season but kudos to those that can, just saying it's not for me. Fatima's great though. Just had to take the time to get to know is all that I'm saying."

Before I could reply, I looked up and noticed the finest man that I've ever seen walking out the front door. I excused myself with a lie as I said, "Oooo I have to pee. Be right back."

After walking towards the bathroom, I doubled around to the front doors without Jeremy seeing me and slipped outside. I scanned the parking lot until I seen his fine ass leaning against a '17 red corvette while chatting it up with a few other guys. I stood nearby as if I was waiting on a ride while eyeing him up and down. He stood at about six foot four with the lightest complexion ever and green eyes. I twirled my hair and bit my bottom lip the moment that I caught his eye and he dismissed his homies to jog over to me. Another poor soul had taken the bait as he said, "Hey. You waiting on somebody?"

With the quickness I lied, "Oh yeah, I'm meeting my best friend Niecy here for her birthday. She said she was coming down the street."

He smiled at the fact that he a had a few minutes to at least get my number as he said, "Why not wait inside of my car instead of out here?"

The invitation I was hoping for as I nodded, and he took my hand to walk me to his brother's car that he was lying about. Instead of getting inside of the car, I leaned against the back of it hoping to entice him to just a little devilment as I spoke boldly, "I want to suck your dick."

An unbelievable moment had just transpired for him as he had never had a woman come at him so directly, but it definitely turned him on to know that they weren't kids playing games. To know that I was grown and knew exactly what I wanted gave him an instant rock hard dick but he still wasn't sure how serious I was until he was grinning with his pants around his ankles leaning back on his brother's brand new whip. I sucked him up as good as I could in the parking lot of Olive Garden while he enjoyed every second of a fantasy that he never knew he had coming true.

With my warm mouth wrapped around his balls, I stroked his shaft, and his knees went weak as I licked up his creamy goodness with a smile. Without any other words said, I walked away heading back into the restaurant to finish my little date but not before batting these fake ass lashes and giving him these poor ass puppy dog eyes for a few of his coins.

*Ba*ecation Vibez

"I get so lonely. I can't let just anybody hold me. You are the one that lives in me, my dear. Want no one but you." - I Get Lonely by Janet Jackson

Imani

I screamed into the phone, "Are you fucking kidding me right now?!"

After three years all I could do was shake my head while the tears rolled down my face by the bullshit that Marcus' bum ass was telling me on this phone. He was breaking up with me only hours before our trip to Hawaii for my birthday. He had been doing this shit every year and I was more understanding than I ever should've been for those first two years.

The first time he came up with the most unbelievable shit ever about how he wanted to get closer to God and be celibate. I refused to hear anything that Ace had to say about it because he seemed not to like anybody I ever tried to date, because clearly, I got a thing for picking the worse dudes to fall in love with. Marcus ghosted me for a week and then played victim as to why I was no longer hitting his line. Apparently, he only needed space and celibacy for that week of my birthday.

My words were clear when I said, "Don't say it."

So, Ace didn't say it. Like the one in algebra, it was understood that Marcus had played my ass to the left and most likely had another woman or a few on the side. Everything was perfect until my birthday rolled around the next year and randomly, I was single again. His excuse at that time was simply that he had to choose between me and his job after his supervisor saw him walking into a

house where well-known drug dealers were dealing. Of course, Ace had to ask, "How did they see him?"
I repeated the lie that Marcus told me and said, "There was a camera on the light pole outside of my house."
Ace walked outside while drinking a beer and stared at the nonexistent camera that caught the activities of the imaginary drug dealers dealing out of my house. I swore up and down that I wasn't going back because I should've been more important that the job. Ace gave me the best advice that he could. He was honest when he said, "You don't deserve this dude. He's a lying ass bum and this ain't got shit to do with his job!"
I didn't want to believe that it was another woman by the amount of time and attention he gave me. It was clear to Ace that Marcus was living a double life, but the shit had done hit the fan today. From the way I was screaming and crying, it's safe to say that I finally accepted the truth for what it is. In an instant, the phone in my hand went flying across the room, hitting the wall and landing on the floor. I stormed off to the bedroom only seeing red not hearing my front door open and close. The energy that I was giving was like a scene from *'Waiting to Exhale'* but when the smell of bleach circulated strongly throughout the house, my unwanted guest was hoping that I hadn't gone the Left-Eye route.
They followed the scent and sure enough, I was in the bathroom bleaching up all of Marcus' clothes, the Xbox, his brand new cowboy boots and anything else he had left but luckily for me, that's where my tantrum ended. A sigh of relief escaped from my unwanted guest causing me to look their way as I said, "What are you doing here Xavier?"
He shrugged as he replied, "Just wanted to see you. The door was unlocked, and it sounded like you were fighting."
Without a second thought, I replied, "Come to Hawaii with me. I'm not letting him ruin this trip for me."

What would Xavier look like turning down an all expense paid trip to Hawaii? A motherfucking fool is what he'd look like and Xavier for damn sure wasn't no fool. His only problem would be his wife crying and missing him, but it was nothing to tell her that he was away on a business trip instead of with me. A woman he'd been seeing for years that was half his age. He replied, "You don't think you can reschedule it?"

I rolled my eyes regretting the offer as I stood up and said, "For what? You got something better to do?"

Slightly appalled, Xavier said, "Damn I might!" I raised my eyebrows and with my arms crossed, I sucked my teeth in disbelief as he continued, "When we leaving man?"

A smile swept across my face, and I laughed while walking out of the bathroom and saying, "Like I thought. Flight leaves in the morning at nine o'clock so go home, get packed and be here tonight."

With a confused look, he asked, "Why tonight?"

He was walking up behind me when I turned around and said, "Because you're not going to wake up on time. You never do."

He knew I was right. Xavier hated waking up early to do anything unless it about money. It's the reason he pushed to become so successful in his line of work as an engineer to where he was finally able to secure his dream job at Cronix making a hundred fifty thousand dollars a year.

Letting down his favorite mistress during a time like this wasn't something he could do, and he wasn't going to deal with his wife's bad attitude about the trip. If he had went home talking about being up early for a flight the next day, then she would've done everything in her power to make sure he missed that flight, so it was best that he did exactly as I told him and just stayed the night in order to catch our flight.

It didn't take long to pack a few clothes and make his way back to my house just to see me and my godsister, Destiny, drinking and dancing the hurt away to the musical lyrics of Boosie's *'Adios'* on some fuck the bullshit vibes. One thing that has always stood out the most about me was how hood I really was. I loved shaking my fat ass in the middle of a crowd of people and just like my godsister, I loved the attention. Nobody ever thought that a big girl like me could move this ass the way that I do and the looks on their faces when I dropped it low was unforgettable. The liquor had me feeling friskier than ever as well as Destiny.

Together we danced around Xavier giving him a show of a lifetime. It wasn't long before she had whipped his dick out and started bobbing for apples while I kissed him with his fingers massaging my clit. It was crystal clear that I was back on my bullshit as this nasty little club scene went on all night until everybody crashed around four or five in the morning.

The alarm was going off and somehow, I was up and already shading the fuck out of Xavier's old ass for needing the alarm in the first place. All that mattered was that his ass was up. Any other night, he would've been sleeping until the next night after those strong ass drinks that Destiny made. Luckily for him, this was a fifteen hour flight and I knew that he was going to be knocked out most of the flight. After boarding the plane, he let me have the window seat while he got comfortable enough to doze back off when I said, "Thank you so much for coming with me."

Xavier shrugged and replied, "You know I got you."

We checked into the Presidential Suite at the Grand Hyatt Kauai Resort & Spa late that night after landing. Our room was filled with pink and silver balloons in the living room that said *'Happy Birthday Imani'* with a few more balloons spread across the suite. There were small liquor bottles tied to the bottom of the balloons followed up with pink rose and white petals on the floor. On the bed, the towels were folded into two swans kissing and a bouquet of roses laid in front of them. With an embarrassed look on my face, I said, "I told them to make it as romantic as possible but damn!"

Xavier chuckled and said, "Nah, they understood the assignment."

No need in allowing any of this to go to waste. Xavier grabbed one of the mini liquor bottles while I followed suit and we both went to downing a few of them then we went down to the pool and partied with the other guests. The next morning, I was up and at it again waking Xavier up to go hiking the Kalalau Trail with me. The first time he started to regret this entire trip as he soon found out that I had a fucking itinerary that I was trying to stick by.

He should've asked more questions but it's Hawaii and at least there were other people there hiking as well. It was actually fun despite the few moments where he only hoped that if he fell, they would at least find his body before he washed out to sea to never be seen again. All I did was laugh and make it seem like it was nothing to be afraid of, but as soon as the trail became narrow as hell and we were holding onto to the wall, my laughter stopped, and I wasn't playing any games anymore. When it was over, Xavier said to me, "It better not be any more death dares in ya plans miss lady."

I laughed until I started to turn red in the face as I forced myself to say, "I hope you can swim!"

I walked away before he could even answer while he thought to himself, *'Hell nah I can't swim. She act like I ain't black!'* That comment had Xavier completely stressed the entire night thinking that we were about to swim out in the ocean and get eaten by sharks. He knew he could float but he wasn't Michael Phelps or anything. The next day we slept in a bit which made him think that I was just being an asshole about swimming until I stepped out with my bathing suit on. He hoped like hell that I just wanted to go to the pool downstairs and before he knew it, we were jumping off a small cliff beside Wailua Falls. Shit was pretty fucking amazing! He didn't complain at all instead, he snuck up behind me and dunked me a few times. Later that night after we had showered and changed clothes, we had a private dinner on the beach.

The chef gave wonderful insight on the amazing Hawaiian dishes that we were eating and how fresh the lobster was since he had it flown in just for us. I had been planning this birthday trip for a while now and Xavier was happy that Marcus missed out because he was having the time of his life with me. The chef cleaned up and left while they walked along the beach enjoying the beautiful view that was before them.

The sun had gone down creating an alluring essence that Xavier had been trying his best to get entangled in the entire trip. To him, I was the most beautiful woman that he'd ever laid his eyes on. He has always loved me more than his wife but the circumstances surrounding our relationship made it impossible to truly be together, so he was caught off guard when I stopped and wrapped my arms around his neck, kissing him passionately. His lips were soft and luscious. I looked at him with a smile and he couldn't help but go in for another kiss. If this had been any other night, I would've stopped what was about to happen but here we stood on one of the most romantic beaches in the world, both sober, and in full control of our actions.

Using a mind of their own, his hands begin to pull the zipper down of the snug pink and white dress that covered my beautiful full bosomed frame. There were no objections from me as Xavier began to place kisses all over my body while caressing my sexy breasts. I stood in front of him eyeing him seductively as he pulled my lace panties off with nothing but his teeth and continued placing tender kisses on my ample thighs. He lifted my smooth leg onto his shoulders and went in to take a sip of my ocean. My hands massaging his bald scalp along with my moans indicating this is what I truly needed and wanted the entire trip.

Xavier placed two fingers inside of me and motioned them as scissors while suckling on my pretty pearl. My legs starting to buck and tremble as my moans grew louder causing Xavier to stop and lay me down on his shirt. I had enough energy to wrap my legs around his waist and right there in the sands of Hawaii, his dreams were coming true. From how loud my moans were becoming, it was clear that I no longer cared about getting caught by anybody. Xavier was trying to knock my bottom out, so he let my legs down and then pushed my thighs down into damn near a middle split and he continued giving me every inch of his pipe. Caught up in my warm juices, Xavier moaned in my ear, "I love you baby."

Immediately, my fingertips were scratching his back up. He gripped both of my shoulders securing me in place and he dived deeper into my ocean. I smiled and bit the corner of my bottom lip looking him dead in his eyes. The shit was making him weak and as soon as he let go of my shoulders and gripping my hips, I pulled him down, hands splayed across his bald head and kissed him. His hands gripped harder, locking me in place from sliding away from while my words staggered as I said, "I'm cumming."

It was sweeter hearing those words in person versus in his memories. He started going harder causing me to scream out with delight. Xavier knew eventually somebody was going to check out what was going on, so he pushed through reaching his climax. Despite the cool breeze coming off of the ocean, we were still drenched in sweat. He had plans to fuck me all over the suite when we got back to it but as soon as we got up and started getting dressed, everything about me had changed. The crazy fun girl that he came there with had shut down and was acting as if I hated him. When we got back to the suite, Xavier spoke softly, "I'm sorry. I thought that's what you wanted."

I shrugged and replied, "It is what I wanted."

Confused and not understanding the change in our chemistry, he tried to comfort me, and I moved away causing him to ask, "Well what's wrong?"

All I did was look him up and down and continue to shake my head leaving him even more confused than before and he remembered how he slipped just as I said, "I can't keep pretending like I'm nothing to you. I don't want to hate you, but I can't be with you. I'm tired of sneaking around. You need to leave her and come home to me."

In this moment, he knew I wasn't wrong. Xavier reassured me, "I hate this too baby and if it was easy to just walk away from her, I would but you know it's not that simple."

Seeing his smile was a turn on. Feeling his hug was a turn on. The peck he gave on my cheek was a turn on. Being around him was a turn on. There was no going back and there was no moving forward in our relationship. Forever a mistress, never a wife. A lesson learned.

_A F_ool In Love

"It took me by surprise I must say… when I found out yesterday. Don't you know that I heard it through the grapevine. Not much longer would you be mine." - Heard It Through The Grapevine by Marvin Gaye

Chanice

Despite what the outside world seen through the rose colored images that I posted on social media for family and friends, my marriage had only gotten worse.

After taking a walk on the crazy side, I randomly picked up my phone and signed into Dustin's Facebook account. He was in the middle of meeting some floozy at the Mustang Motel. I watched as the messages came in where he'd reply only to delete them as soon as he replied. I had been fooling herself to actually believe that things would get better.

We had started back going to church and it seemed to be all for nothing. Only making matters worse as he moaned and groaned about being too tired or too bored. He complained constantly about Pastor Jones being a con artist like Beverly. He hated everything about the church until they started stroking his ego. It was only then that they were okay in his book.

When Dustin walked back in the house, I sat on my computer in the living room multitasking with designing flyers for a special Capricorn winter wonderland show at the club, preparing for my first podcast episode, making sure that the grand opening for my hair salon, Beluv's Beauty Bar, went off without a hitch, as well as editing videos of dance routines.

Going viral while becoming the CEO of a billion dollar company along with a successful cabernet didn't mean that I could instantly sit on my ass and do nothing. It felt like the weight of the world was on my shoulders as I prayed for a team to help take some of the load off. The stress of it all caused the petty bitch within me to speak before I even realized what I was saying, "Damn baby you ain't gone give me a kiss?"

A guilty smile crossed his face as he walked over to me and bent down with his lips puckered as I turned away and spewed, "Don't put your fucking lips on me and you been fucking that nasty bitch in room 104!"

He leaned back with a face full of shock and confusion as he tried to formulate the words to plead his case as I continued, "I've already seen the messages, Dustin so no need to lie about it."

The bullshit spilled out of his pores as he exclaimed, "Baby I just went to go and smoke with her."

I rolled my eyes and went off, "Why the fuck is she sending you pussy pictures and yall meeting up at the hotel if you just want to smoke? Oh, you can't call Chris to smoke now? Can't call up nobody but you can hit up this random ass bitch to smoke. Nah keep them lies for ya mammy!"

He huffed as he tried a different approach as he said, "It just an impulse. I don't know why I did it. I didn't even want to. I really just wanted to smoke and the next thing I knew we were having sex, but I promise I didn't want to do it."

All I heard was, *'I slipped and my dick fell into her pussy'* as I laughed and replied, "Yeah okay Dustin. I slipped too and my mouth started sucking dick at work."

There wasn't nothing he hated more than being laughed at as he stormed off ready to cry to his mother on the phone. The next day we got up in full attack mode preparing for church. While Dustin walked around with an attitude that I decided to ignore, I snapped up a few pictures in the bathroom with my kids until he was finally ready to go. I no longer cared about the cheating, but I was indeed hurt by the reality of what my marriage had become.

In my opinion, he should've been more grateful at the fact that I didn't care and instead he walked around pouting like a little bitch. My only hope was to let God handle it and go on to church as a family. Everything was beautiful from what others could see until after service was over and Dustin claimed that he wanted to talk to Pastor Jones about his own infidelity problems as to why he couldn't stop sexting other women. I waited with the kids as I faked a smile with Mother Jones and her daughter, the First Lady of Jackson when Pastor Jones invited me into his office for an impromptu marriage counseling session.

Mother Jones agreed to watch the kids while I followed Pastor Jones into his office. From the moment I walked in I knew that I had walked into a set up as I seen the pitiful face of Dustin and the concerned face of Deacon Ellis. I looked around as I sat down next to my husband with the full understanding that I shouldn't have been the only female in the office as Pastor Jones started in, "Now Niecy, I have Deacon Ellis here because he needs the practice but Dustin came to me about his own issues and we won't get into that but what troubled me was that he said that you two have been fighting and that in your anger you've been throwing dishes and being completely out of control. I remember I had to teach my own wife how to be a wife as well. I know you know that you have to forgive this man for what he's done and that you shouldn't be so angry like that Niecy. He said that he was wrong for meeting the woman but that he didn't do anything, and I believe him. This is a hard working man and a good father from what I can see and that he's trying to be the best husband that he can be. Do you think that you can be a better wife and let the past go?"

I despised the idea of talking about my marital problems with anybody other than God because everybody had to pick sides instead of saying what was right. I smiled with sorrow and shame from the intense urge to clock my pastor right in the motherfucking mouth. I knew that I was a damn good wife to this lying ass bitch of a husband of mine and yet there he sat oozing with enjoyment of him, the pastor, and the gotdamn deacon ganging up on me. I had the right mind to flip the fucking desk and beat their asses with the chair but that's certainly not the Christian thing to do especially in the house of the Lord. With my now permanent fake smile plastered across my face, I replied, "You're right. I forgive him and I will certainly work on being a better wife for my husband."

The men smiled accepting the act that I put on as a mission accomplished. Another simple minded pretty girl that they all just got over on but as Myrtis' first great granddaughter, I only had one thought circling in my mind, *'Just wait until we get home!'* As much as I despised speaking on my marital problems, I'd never embarrass myself or my husband by fighting in public. I only liked handcuffs and police uniforms in the bedroom but aside from that I didn't want the drama and bullshit that law enforcement had to offer. The car ride back home was rather silent while Dustin believed he'd truly walked away with a clean slate. The lies he told himself.

Within minutes of walking through the front door, everything took a turn for the worse and we were both arguing and screaming in front of the kids. Tia cried out, "Please stop fighting you guys!" causing Dustin to put on an even bigger show and I made sure to match his energy as I said, "How the fuck you run to Pastor Jones, and you don't even like him? Thought you said you only trusted your cousin Clyde when it came to talking to pastors."

He hissed, "I'm trying Niecy! I could've said all about how you cheated on me right before your fucking birthday, but I didn't. I didn't know he was going to pull you in too and if I had known then I wouldn't have gone to him."

I rolled my eyes and boldly stated, "You didn't say shit because you know the reason why I cheated. We never have sex, and I told your ass before we said *'I do'* that I didn't want a sexless marriage. We fuck maybe once a fucking year while you're fucking every bitch you see on the gotdamn internet! And why the fuck you got to do this shit in front of the kids?"

After screaming in my face and small spit balls touching my skin, he scurried into the bedroom and locked the door with a fifth of whiskey in his hands. I wasn't about to just let him get away with traumatizing my babies and then go hide in the bedroom when all of this shit could've gone down in the bedroom in the first place. It was him who felt the need to ask, *'What's wrong?'* as soon as we pulled into the driveway and then again at the front door. Basically, switching roles with the hope of starting a fight. He had gotten his wish as I had him terrified from my short ass kicking the bedroom door in only to find him hiding in the closet cowering in the corner like the little bitch that his mammy raised him to be.

My anger only slightly subsided as I spoke calmly walking around the bedroom with the closet door open and the bedroom door frame hanging off as he asked, "Why do you have to be like this? Look at what you've done? Do you even care about my feelings?"

I heard his words loud and clear as I replied with a chuckle, "Your feelings? Oh now you it's about your feelings?"

He sipped his bottle of whiskey and continued to whine, "See that's the shit I'm talking about. You only care about yourself. Just because I'm a man don't mean I don't have feelings Niecy!"

While shaking my head in disbelief from not knowing how to even answer the bull-shit, I got up and walked into the closet and snatched the whiskey bottle away as I said, "You don't need this."

That bottle of whiskey must have been his everything because he got up pushing me until I fell down, snatching the bottle back out of my hands. Nothing about him surprised me anymore as I jumped up and started shoving his ass right back. We wrestled for control. His goal was to ram my head onto the floor while choking me into submission, but I managed to pull the lamp off of the nightstand and smash it over his head causing him to stumble backwards.

I was up again and heading for the kitchen with him hot on my heels. The moment he realized that I had opened the draw looking for a knife is when he ran out of the front door. I no longer cared who seen the fuckery that we called our marriage as I silently walked out of the front door as if I was Michael Myers. He'd certainly grow tired before I would, and I wasn't going too far with my kids in the house alone.

We both ran track in high school and despite the heavy amounts of weed that we had since smoked, he had lit the pavement up hauling ass. I walked only a few houses down before saying fuck it and fuck him. When I got back in the house, I locked the house down and let him figure the rest out for himself. It wasn't long before my mother in law was blowing my phone up. When I answered, Catrinea pleaded, "Please Niecy let him back in the house. He says it's cold and it's raining. Don't leave my son out in the cold like that."

The only thing I wanted to say was, 'Fuck you and your son' but you reap what you sow.

I looked at my kids and sighed as I replied, "He better keep his gotdamn hands off of me or he's a dead man walking."

Just like everybody else, Catrinea had taken the side of Dustin but played the role of the sweet mother in church praying for everybody's well being when in reality Catrinea was the biggest conman of them all and failed terribly in raising all three of her kids. If you wanted to know anything about any-body, then all you had to do was sit beside Catrinea and she'd give you an ear full of what the rumor mill had going on.

Everybody knew not to trust Catrinea, and all Dustin ever did was run to his mammy to be his yes man in all of his wrongdoings. The very type of mother that I vowed to never be.

He walked back in feeling victorious thanks to his bitch ass mama. I let him think what he wanted because I didn't make idle threats and the next time, he laid hands on me would certainly be his last.

After cleaning everything up, I sat in the living room crying and pleading with God to fix the shitshow that was my marriage. I wanted to provide my children with something that I didn't have growing up and that was a mother and a father. All I ever had was my Meme, Grandma Myrtis, and Uncle Keith while my brother JohnJohn was raised by our mother and his father.

Everybody around me at least had their mother but it was becoming quite clear that if my marriage didn't get any better that my kids would grow up to become toxic adults like so many others that I saw around me, not knowing how to love or be loved all because of what they had seen with their mother and father. I prayed for my husband to get saved and maybe that would change things for the better.

Drunken Confessions

"Like an appetite that's hungry. You can have some freaky fun with me." - Freak It by Lathun

Imani

Every woman needs at least one freak'um dress for ladies' night, but Destiny's entire warerobe consisted of freak'um dresses, freak'um shirts, freak'um shorts, and freak'um shoes. I watched her try on about a thousand different outfits while dancing in the mirror in her own zone repeating the lyrics, *'Just keepin' it honest. You wouldn't want a young nigga, if I wasn't whippin' this foreign'* to Tory Lanez's *'Say It'* and from what the streets were whispering, Thee Head Hunter was spitting nothing but facts...in this moment of course. I was rocking a sleek long black ponytail with a bang swooped to the right side looking like my own thick version of Kandi Burruss when ten outfit changes later, Destiny finally says, "Okay girl we got to hurry up if we still want to get in free."

I tilted my head to the side in disbelief feeling as though Destiny was trying to make it seem like I was the one holding us up from getting her ass rubbed on. She had already wasted about five hours getting ready just to wear the first outfit that she picked out. I was annoyed and more than ready to feel up on a cute guy or two myself.

Luckily for the both of us, Destiny had about seven different guys cashapp her twenty dollars so that we could get some drinks since it was free before midnight, but she wasn't done getting ready until just before eleven o'clock and we had about a twenty-five minute drive with the way either of us drove.

I stood up with keys in hand, heading to the car while Destiny hated everything about hitting the scene too early while I didn't mind being the grandma since I stayed sitting down and just rocking to the beat. I'd only get up to enjoy a few blues' songs and do a quick two step. A few times I might grind up on a guy or two but I wasn't getting down and dirty especially in my black skintight dress. It was no surprise that the music was blaring from down the street as we pulled up to this huge mansion deep in Madison. I would've settled for a simple girls' night out at One Block East or

Freelons but it was a must that I supported my girl, Niecy, with this FreakNik themed house party.

There was no dress code and as always Destiny had lied as there wasn't an entry fee either. All of Jackson and the surrounding areas had been talking about this event from the moment that Niecy joked about it during a live session on TikTok. I had no idea that she'd take it to the extreme like this but one this about Niecy, it was always *'Go hard or go home'* with everything that she did. As soon as we walked in, the security checked our IDs, as this was only for twenty-five and up. A grown and sexy event. Once we got past security, we were greeted by some baddies with a bag of car keys, a bucket of ice filled with mini liquor bottles and a tray of pre-rolled herb. There were only a few rules to abide by.

1. **Tip the waitresses!**
2. **No drunk driving!**
3. **No fighting!**

If this had been the club, we would've dropped an easy dub a piece just to get in so why not hand it straight to the waitresses and get tore the fuck up. Had me mad that I didn't sign on to be a waitress like Niecy had asked me to do. The vibe was chill at first as everybody simply stood around swaying to the beat that DJ Twigga had bumping. I seen way too many familiar faces and then Destiny spotted Chris off in the corner talking to some hoe that looked a lot like Chelsea. She kept her eyes glued to that man and wasn't worried about the man until the girl turned around and it was confirmed to be Chelsea.

Destiny rocked to the music beside me until she seen Chelsea walking to the back of the house to play a game of spades while I sent Niecy a text to see where the fuck she was. We all knew that Niecy was a party girl that didn't do the clubs but certainly the girl wasn't about to skip out on her own fucking party. As soon

as Chelsea walked out the away, Destiny was walking up to Chris smiling as she took his mini bottle of Hennessy out of his hand and gulped it down with ease. He nodded and said, "You want another one?"
Ready to do some damage in the worse way, she replied, "Yup. Two more."
While Destiny got wasted in the corner with Chris, I had started a grind session on some guy that looked like he was fucking the shit out of me to the beat of *'Dance'* by Big Sean. We continued to party until Destiny threw the entire vibe off, ruining everybody's night from being too fucking drunk. Since the mansion was hella packed and no one was the wiser, Destiny massaged Chris' dick until it bulged out of his pants so hard that he had to adjust himself a few times. She licked on his neck turning him on even more until he offered, "We can go upstairs if you want."
She shook her head no as she darted her tongue into his mouth with her hands releasing his dick from its cage. Instantly, she was head down bobbing for a cream shot while he looked around nervously hoping not to get caught but enjoying the feeling entirely too much to be a married man with six kids.
Everything was going just fine until having no gag reflects caused her to expel all of the contents in her stomach onto his lap. He slapped her off of him before he knew it with a disgusted look on his face. As his homie was off to the side snickering to himself after having witnessed the entire event, I walked over to Destiny and Chris with my new boo snuggled up behind me as I said, "Now why you get her drunk like this?"
Chris ignored everything from everybody in that moment. The embarrassment was too much to bear, as he took his Givenchy shirt off and tried his best to clean himself up. When he was done, he walked away knowing he'd never in his life fuck off with Destiny ever again. As she stumbled into the bathroom, I got my new boo's

number for a quick meet up another time and then took Destiny's drunk ass back to my place so that she could sleep it off. She woke up the next day angry with herself and lashing out at anybody in her path. It wasn't long before her first true love caught wind of the event and met up with her at their favorite hour motel to console her and remind her that she's still the baddest bitch in the land.

Chanice

If everything was preventing me from doing something then I knew it was one of two reasons, either it wasn't for me to do, and God was telling me to sit my ass down or it was exactly what God had for me and I simply had to jump a few hurdles to get to the finish line. After going viral and becoming a verified account on TikTok, it was a must that Femme Fatale IV actually showed out at least once for the people and for whatever reason we decided to host a FreakNik themed house party while looking like the freakiest nastiest schoolgirls to ever carry a book. Everything was going great until the day actually came and of course my wonderful and loving husband had the most to say as he asked, "Why would you throw a party and not make them pay to get in?"

I rolled my eyes while gathering my stuff and placing it all in my Femme Fatale IV duffle bag as I replied, "Because it's not about the money Dustin. It's about the exposure. It's just business. You wouldn't understand."

He scoffed as he continued, "You make money in business. You just want these motherfuckers to kiss your ass. I wouldn't dare throw a party and not charge a motherfucker. I didn't even let my brother get a tattoo from me unless he paid me. Hell naw! I'd make my own mama pay me! I ain't doing shit for free!"

Just as I was placing my array of the Crayon Case cosmetics in the bag, I said, "If this was your tattoo party then by all means make them pay but this is basically my coming out party. I can't explain to you how marketing works if all you care about is money." I spun around to see him still laying in bed in nothing but his boxers when I asked, "So you're not coming?"

With his phone in his hand and a beer in the other hand, he huffed as he replied, "For what? To watch you make a fool of yourself. Wearing makeup looking like a clown and shit. You know I don't like that shit."

While shaking my head, I spoke softly, "Well I like it. Are you sure you don't want to come?"

He sucked his teeth, and I knew a fight was brewing. I could either hash it out with him now and possibly miss my own fucking party or I could deal with it later when I least expected it. When he had the advantage causing me to lose complete control ready to burn the fucking world down. I chose later because I wasn't missing this party. I put too much of my time and energy into planning this event and I was more than ready to shake a little ass with my girls as if we were back in high school. He claimed to love dancing, but I never once seen him actually dance.

He never truly did anything outside of a humpty hump dance as a joke. None of us were the dancing machines like we were when we were younger but when you truly love dance then age ain't nothing but a number which is why everything inside of me screamed, 'FUCK HIM' as he spoke with an attitude, "Nah me and the kids will be good without you. I'll order some pizza or something."

His words stung just a bit. Not an ounce of failure rushed over my body as a mother but regret in being a wife certainly did. I grabbed my keys and headed out to pick up my dance crew. I rented a beautiful two story million dollar mansion deep in Madison with a beautiful lake in the backyard. We cleared the furniture out that was downstairs in order to have as much room as possible to dance. As adults, sex wasn't something that we shied away from, so we made sure to leave the bedrooms untouched in case anybody felt frisky. There was also one table left downstairs just past the kitchen in case anybody wanted to get a spades game going. I understood that dancing wasn't for everybody, and I didn't mind catering to all which is why I couldn't understand why Dustin made such a big deal about having an entry fee when he could've just come and supported me at the very least.

I had an old classmate and Brinae's ex from Jim Hill, set up the DJ booth on the balcony upstairs. Completely out of the way of the dance floor. My baby brother was finally released from prison, and it was a great thing for me because he finally learned how to fight and also bulked up from constantly working out. He was now perfect for security and checking IDs. Nobody wants to square up with an oversized giant especially if he was just released from prison. Any staff member from the cabernet simply became a waitress for the party which they were more than eager to do as their plan was to rack in as many tips as possible.

As soon as the ass shakers and big head hundreds started pouring in, me and my dance crew went upstairs to get ready in our schoolgirl outfits. Vanjettia and Brinae wore short black and gold plaid skirts, white low cut polo shirts, golden knee high socks and thick black school shoes. Shannon went with golden jeggings, a white tank top, with a black, white, and gold letterman jacket specially made for Femme Fatale IV and some all black hi top chucks. I was a rocking some black high waisted bell bottoms with golden suspenders over a white long sleeve turtleneck onesie and low heel ankle boots.

While I waited for my sorority sisters to come into town, me and Femme Fatale IV did our final fit checks when Imani sent me a text asking me where I was. Apparently, the party was going off without a hitch while I was upstairs with my dance crew making sure we were ready to make magic on this camera. This was our first house party as a dance group since Fatima's birthday party when I met Dustin. Before we stepped out, we all took a hit on the hookah that was filled with purp while taking a couple shots of Patron and we made our way downstairs.

I shook my head seeing Destiny's drunk ass stumbling to the bathroom with Imani trying her best to hold her up. It wasn't my problem as long as they weren't causing problems at my event. Brinae had her eyes locked on DJ Twigga as if we were back at Jim Hill and the moment his set was done, she had plans to take him upstairs and show him exactly why her stage name was Ri La Belle. It was my play brother that made the vibe electric as DJ FreekNastee held true to the theme of the party playing only the best ass shaking hits to make Femme Fatale IV cut the dance floor up. Just as I heard the Ying Yang Twins say, *'Why you wanna waste a nigga song, then? Sittin' yo ass down doin nothin'* my Delta Sigma Theta sorority sisters had finally entered the building ready to shake it like a dog on the dance floor. Once Femme Fatale IV had proven to be the baddest dance team that TikTok had ever seen, I turned around to see my childhood sweetheart hovering backwards like Ciara did on her 'Goodies' video. I felt slightly challenged as he started krumping with another guy as the crowd went wild from the battle. Childhood sweetheart or not, I certainly couldn't allow anybody to show me up in my own party. I signaled to Brinae to grab DJ Twigga as I snatched a random guy from the crowd.

The guys already knew what to expect as we eased them into our nasty world with simple twerking and ass shaking. Fatima and Shannon pulled up two chairs for the guys to sit in while me and Brinae, straddled them backwards and leaned forward placing our hands on the floor and securing our feet on the back of chair as we popped our plump soft asses vigorously while the guys grinned in ecstasy. DJ Twigga had two hands full of Brinae's ass when I leaned back up and seen the guy that was battling my childhood sweetheart sitting on the floor. I walked up to with my feet planted on both sides of him as I dropped into a spilt right on his lap causing the crowd to go completely crazy. Brinae followed suit and we both continued to pop our asses as we crawled away when Shannon noticed Chris in the crowd and made him sit in the chair for her own special lap dance as she crawled to him and used her entire body to massage his print.

It's a good thing he changed clothes or else he would've missed out on this epic lap dance he was receiving. Although Dustin and Chris were cousins that did everything together, they couldn't have been more different if they tried. The moment Shannon straddled Chris, he wrapped his arms around her thighs and lifted her up out of the chair slamming her body into his. The liquor and kush had definitely gotten him in the zone. As I stood next to my childhood sweetheart, we both cheered on anybody that touched the dance floor giving it their all while DJ FreekNastee went on to play a master mix of 2 Live Crew causing us all to gyrate and grind harder than before.

Just as my childhood sweetheart was about to dip behind me for a quick nasty grind session, DJ FreekNastee slowed the beat down and Femme Fatale IV started our party walk. My sorority sisters, Nina Renesie and Bianca Mion caught on quick and joined in as well. Unbeknownst to us, a few other Divine 9 members started their party walks as well as we all glided through the crowd to the beat of *'You'* by Piles ft. Tank.

It wasn't long before we were back shaking our asses and battling on the dance floor.

When I looked around my childhood sweetheart had left the party before even saying goodbye. I would've loved at least one dance, but that one dance would've turned into one kiss and that one kiss would've certainly turned into my legs in the air or me down on my knees. Either way it was probably for the best since I'm still a married woman.

ACT THREE

BARGAINING

"They made a deal and they liked the deal, until they had to pay the price."
-Brent Weeks, The Black Prism-

ACTS OF SERVICE

"I give good love
I'll buy your clothes
I'll cook your dinner too
Soon as I get home from work"
-Babyface-

Her Hearts Desire

"I put a spell on you. Because you're mine"
- I Put A Spell On You by Annie Lennox

Imani

"Baby, I want you to come over for my Christmas dinner party. It's going to be a bunch of my co-workers and a few friends from the church, so I need you not to look like you've been thrown away!" my mama exclaimed over the phone.

I sighed as I said, "I just seen you like two weeks ago and ma, I've just been really busy with work is all."

In a sing song voice, she replied, "I'm making your favorite!" Cheesecake was not my favorite. In fact, I had grown tired of it as a child but for some reason my mother thought that I really loved this simple ass dessert. She would make two and expect me to eat them both just to fuss at me all of the next year for being overweight. The irony. My mama continued, "I made an extra cheesecake so you could take home too."

In a desperate attempt to get out of going I lied, "I have to see if my car will make it. It's been acting funny lately."

My mama pursued without pause as she said, "Oh, baby I wasn't expecting you to drive. Willie is already on the way to pick you up so be ready. Now listen I got to go and check on my greens. See you soon."

I sighed as soon as the phone had hung up as I went and showered to prepare for this fake ass Huxtable style Christmas dinner. All I truly wanted for Christmas was to relax at home sipping on some mixed drinks as I sorted through the wreckage that I called my life. After eating this special brownie that Niecy had made while sipping on a perfectly mixed *'Fuck Me Up'* I was more than ready for these holiday shenanigans as I seen my stepdad pull into my driveway. I didn't let him make it out of the car good before I was locking my front door and making my way to him.

I couldn't deny that the night was indeed a beautiful distraction. My mama had decorated the inside to look like every single hallmark Christmas movie ever invented with Boys II Men's *'Silent Night'* playing in the background. A bunch of people that I never knew existed tried to remind me who they were and how they met. I stayed civil and played the role assigned. Some would say fake it until you make it, but I was doing anything to not face my own reality so why not share some laughs and sip some eggnog.

It's better than being alone on Christmas and for once nobody was arguing. After sending Ace a long apologetic *'Merry Christmas'* text, I continued to fumble with my phone all night hoping for a reply. He was still not speaking to me, and it was hurting me more than ever. I had messed up, but could anybody truly blame me when I was trying my best not to go completely insane.

Three hours later, and my mama was kicking everybody out. I had my cheesecakes and was trying my best to bum a ride so that I wouldn't have to be cramped up in my stepdad's two seat Porsche however nobody was heading my way. Everybody had other places to go make plates at so back in the little black Porsche I went.

The ride from Flowood, MS to Ridgewood Rd was more awkward than cramped and uncomfortable. I stared out of the window in silence and was more than thankful when we pulled into my driveway thirty minutes later. He was out of the car by the time I closed the car door and followed me into the house saying, "Hey, can I use your bathroom?"

I sighed and replied, "Sure."

As I poured myself a glass of Pink Moscato, he walked into the living room and said, "Imani, can we talk?"

With an annoyed tone, I replied, "About what?"

He stared at me for a bit and went on to say, "I know that no matter what I say, you won't believe me but baby you know that I love you. I know seeing me with her tonight hurt you and baby I just want to show you just how sorry I am and how much I love you."

I chuckled and shook my head as I spoke candidly, "By fucking your wife's daughter on Christmas night?"

My stepdad rolled his eyes and said, "Baby what the fuck is the problem? We've been fucking for years, and you never cared before so why do you care so much now?"

I hissed as I said, "Xavier when did I not care? I've asked you to divorce her several times and what was your reply? Huh?!"

He threw his hands in the air while saying, "Here we go again with this shit!"

Anger and hurt filling my words as I spoke, "Yeah, here we go again! Answer me though, if I had kept the baby, then what? Would our baby had been enough to make you divorce her or would I have to send my child to its granny's house so she could play the wicked stepmother? I mean really how would that have worked?!"

His words were calculated and cold as he said, "You killed our chance of being together when you killed our baby. Now you throw it in my face because I didn't leave my wife!" He scoffed and murmured, "Trifling."

My head spun with shock as I replied, "Oh wow I'm trifling now?! Exactly what the fuck are you, Xavier?"

He replied with a chuckle, "I'm a gotdamn God send. I'm the only man that was willing to love you. I wasn't perfect and you knew that, but I gave you all of my heart. You played me."

While shaking my head, I replied, "Xavier, I'm twenty-four years old. I'm not that eleven year old little girl that you met thirteen years ago. You couldn't possibly think that I would still be as naïve as I was back then."

He smirked as he looked at me with lust in his eyes saying, "Baby I know! I see the woman you've grown into. Hell, I helped you grow into her. I'm just trying to say I'm sorry for any hurt I caused you tonight."

I stared at him and asked, "What are you sorry for?"

Xavier was on his hands and knees begging, "Baby everything. I'm sorry for everything."

I knew every word that he uttered was a lie. I knew everything about him was a lie. Trying my best not to get wrapped up in his charm seemed to be so hard for me to do. He crawled closer until he was centered at my feet. He started to ease his hands up my legs as I spoke softly, "Please Xavier just go home." While ignoring my request, he started to kiss my outer thighs. A desperate plea for sex is all it was. I pushed him off, got off of the couch and walked over to my mantle as I asked, "Why did you marry my mom?"

He groaned in dismay and answered, "I told you why already. I've apologized a million times for that. I didn't know she was your mom, Imani. I really didn't" Another guilt free lie from the mouth of a conman.

With a sigh I said, "Dude you don't see anything wrong in what we've been doing? I mean most of it if not everything has been in the same house. Under the same roof. How are you okay with this?"

Xavier sucked his teeth while rolling his eyes and replied, "Imani do you hear yourself?! Do you really think I enjoyed doing things this way? I'm not trying to hurt you or your mother. I didn't plan any of this."

I looked away, disgusted with his arrogance while saying, "I didn't really see you saying no either."

He got up and walked up to me. As he placed his arms around my waist, he spoke softly in my ear, "I could never say no to you because I loved you." His breath on the back of my neck brought back each and every memory that I had worked so hard to rid myself of. He started to plant kisses of seduction along my shoulders as he continued to whisper, "I still love you baby."

It was years too late to do the right thing and push him off of me. A yearning desire to feel him inside of me once again was starting to take over. He's always been a gentle lover, taking his time to show his affection to every part of me making me feel a love that I never understood. He spun me around and started kissing me passionately driving me further into ecstasy while fondling both breasts, pulling them out to suck them one at a time like he was a junkie, and they were his addiction.

His excitement bulged out against my legs, exercising its desire for this one last high. After fully undressing me, he escorted me back to the couch where my mind, body, and soul started to enter into another dimension as he sat me down and lowered himself to his knees preparing himself for his favorite meal. He didn't miss a beat as he consumed my juices, treating me like I was the object of his obsession.

I thought to herself, *'Imani what are you doing?'* I was starting to scoot back, denying him the chance to express his feelings and thoughts with the vibrations of his tongue on my pearl as he fingered me slowly. He tightly held onto my hips, pulling me right back to him as he uttered, "Put them legs up. I want to see those pretty toes in the air."

I did as my lover requested just for those pretty toes to go numb and my legs to shake as he continued his mission of blowing my mind. It wasn't long before he stood up, leaving my pussy throbbing and eagerly awaiting his next move. Being an older man, gave him the perfect advantage because I never had to tell him what my body was craving for.

As he glided his shaft inside of me, his strokes were nice and slow like the beat of the song he was humming. Still pulsating inside of my walls, he lifted me up off of the couch, slowly pushing in and out every inch of him while he carried me over to the wall. Feeling as if my entire body would just go limp in his arms, I was reassured the moment he used a death grip on my ass cheeks to secure me in the air. Before I knew it, I was on top of him in the chair next to the radio. I wanted to show him the true woman that I had grown to become.

I wanted him to always remember me and what we had after tonight. Using my favorite position to control the moment and turn him into a bull in my own rodeo show until I exploded on top of him. His moans were so loud, that they gave me chills knowing how good I was making him feel. Thanks to this one man, I knew how to please any man as I eased down on my lover.

While stroking his shaft, I placed sweet kisses and little circles around the tip while his words echoed in the back of her head from the first time that I ever gave him head, *'All men love a warm mouth'* Hearing him moan as I worked out my gag reflects was giving me the much needed ego boost that I needed and wanted. His pressure was building up, but he had other plans in mind when he commanded, "Get up."

With the biggest smile on my face, these thick almond brown thighs stood up. My chubby stomach didn't stop no show as I positioned myself over the armrest of the couch while maintaining the arch of a demon. In his finishing move, each stroke was slow and sinful causing me to moan until I was screaming out in pleasure. As his speed increased, sweat was beginning to trickle down from his forehead and chest onto my back.

Seconds after I reached my last climax, he was out of breath slumping on top of me. No time was wasted, as he quickly grabbed his clothes off the floor talking about how much he'd missed me. I watched him get dressed while fighting the desire to say I loved him. He made it clear that he didn't want to stop seeing me, but I couldn't force him to be with me. It was time to move on now. He had a wife to love and cherish. A wife that was my mother.

*The Invi*tation

"You say that I've been actin' different, yeah. Funny how I finally flipped the script on you. When you the one who's double-dippin', yeah. You so sloppy, how I caught you slippin' up-Pick Up Your Feelings by Jazmine Sullivan

Chanice

Imani exclaimed, "Oooh this is going to be fun! I can't wait but Ace might not come, and I don't want to be a fifth wheel y'all."
She called Ace but he didn't answer so she sent him a text with the details, and he re-plied, "I'm sorry. I'll be out of town for that weekend."
Imani rolled her eyes as she searched her little black book of an iPhone for a replacement. Her hope was to make amends with Ace since he had become so distance after her birthday trip to Hawaii. She was doing everything to understand what the issue was between her, and her best friend has they had never been in such unfamiliar waters such as these. Regardless, she was a smart girl that knew how to give a man his space, so she did just that and didn't push the issue too much.
After a few more giggles amongst us, Dustin emerged from the bedroom saying, "Ugh go home ugly."
Destiny scrunched up her nose as she replied, "Boy shut up! I ain't going nowhere." While shaking my head, I continued to go over the itinerary that I had planned for this couples' retreat in Gatlinburg, TN when I asked Destiny, "Did you have somebody in mind that you wanted to bring?"
She shrugged her shoulders and replied, "Chaos might come if I ask him." I stared at her waiting for her to pick up her phone

when Destiny said, "Oh you want me to ask him now?" I nodded while trying to control my facial expression of being annoyed at the dumb blond that Destiny loved to play while Chaos answered the FaceTime call and she said, "Baby are you busy next weekend?"
He replied, "No, why? What's up?"
She turned the phone around to me as she said, "This is my best friend and she's rented this cabin for a couples' retreat in Gatlinburg."
Before she could continue, I replied, "Girl stop telling people that shit. We are not friends."
She giggled and changed her statement as she said, "You're right. We're sisters."
With a sigh, I placed my head in the palms of my hand while she went on to use her pouty lip and puppy dog eyes, turning the camera back to her and said, "I don't want to be alone. Baby will you please come with me?"
As Dustin headed back into the bedroom to play Call of Duty on his new Xbox, he yelled, "Ewww don't make that face. I almost ran up out of here."
Destiny rolled her eyes and continued talking to Chaos as she said, "Nevermind that dog that you hear barking in the background. That's my cousin." With a giggle, she added, "He's not actually my cousin but he's my cousin."
Annoyed with how many times that Destiny felt the need to tell the world that Dustin and her were basically kissing cousins, I chimed in, "You might as well just move to Alabama."
Imani snorted and spat her soda out as she said, "Niecy shut the fuck up! Girl you is stupid!"
The story of Dustin and Destiny was one that didn't make any sense and yet made all of the sense in the world. They had dated until they found out they were cousins or at least that's Destiny's side of the story. Dustin's is much different as he claims he never once liked

her because he doesn't like girls with big lips, and he makes it his mission to point that out whenever he sees her.

Chaos smiled weirdly on the phone from the exchange between us as Destiny replied, "Okay let me explain. My mom dated his uncle, and his aunt married my cousin while my dad is his great grandmother's nephew but we're more like play cousins."

Imani called it before I could as she said, "Baby y'all cousins!"

I shook my head with a fake smile recalling the recent events of my marriage as I said, "Welp let me book the flight!"

Destiny laughed and said, "Oh no send him to his mama!"

Chaos interrupts our little moment by saying, "Just text me the details."

They hung up and Destiny went on to brag about how she met Chaos and how big his dick was. She continued to speak on how amazing his sex game was until Imani says, "Girl don't you know you can't talk about what your man do or the next woman gone want to test him out for herself."

I nodded while Destiny scoffed and said, "Okay but Niecy's is married and you're my godsister."

Imani smirked and said, "Bitch I'm still single!"

Highly offended, Destiny decided to dismiss herself and head home but not before saying, "Baby I ain't worried. Do you see me? These niggas love me. They gone always call on Destiny. This mouth they can NEVER forget."

Imani and I laughed as Destiny strutted out the door thinking that she said something worth anything when all we heard was the words of a proud throat goat. I had a nigga mentality and simply understood why guys kept her around, but Imani was a different breed. She didn't mind testing waters and lakes that she wasn't used to.

After a few more giggles, Imani left and I started to make dinner for my family when Dustin walked into the kitchen to fix himself a glass of red kool-aid in complete bitch mode. I sighed from the mere fact that a fight was brewing, and I just didn't feel like fighting my husband anymore. When he spoke about his feelings, I tried my best to be more mindful of them and although we seemed to have been doing okay, I knew the shit was about to hit the fan.

With desperation in my voice, I said, "Dustin I think we should talk. I can clearly see that something is wrong, and I don't want us to fight about it later when we could just talk it out now."

I tried to place my arms around him with love and he stepped back saying, "Nothing's wrong."

As he walked away, I nodded and realized in a few days that he'd catch me off guard about something so small and start a screaming match that led to a wrestling match that led to me wanting to kill him and I didn't know how many more times I could walk away from committing murder. I was fed up and in an instant my humanity flipped off again and I was ready for war. When I walked into the living, he was relaxing in the recliner with his feet up watching cartoons.

I looked at my kids sitting on the couch and back at my husband as I politely picked up his glass of kool-aid and dashed the red liquid in his face. In complete shock he pushed the foot rest down and sat up as I said in a composed manner, "What's the fucking problem now?" He stood up and walked away as I started to taunt him enticing a fight, "Oh nah don't walk away. We don't walk away anymore remember?"

He headed into the bedroom as I followed behind him continuing to press his every button as he starts to pack his things and says, "I don't have to put up with this shit. I'm leaving."

I started tugging on his clothes and we started to wrestle once again with him trying to leave and me pulling him back as I screamed, "You ain't going no motherfucking where! Can't you fucking see I love you and I'm doing everything I can to fight for you! For us! What the fuck am I doing so wrong that makes you want to leave?" He threw his stuff down and yells, "You don't fucking love me. You don't fucking support me. You don't care about my feelings. You're fucking selfish and only think about yourself. Everything I do is for you and it isn't enough and I'm still here! I'm fucking leaving."

There it was. His fucked up version of his truth. While staring him dead in his eyes and pointing my index finger in his face, I spoke firmly, "You're a gotdamn lie! All I do is support you and love you. Leave! There's the door."

To the outside world listening at the wall, he sounded like the victim when in reality all I had ever done was support him in any and everything he ever wanted to do, and he fucked over it. He was a lazy son of a bitch that wanted to sit on his ass and collect a check for doing absolutely nothing.

Everything we had was because I pushed for us to have it. If it was left up to him, we would've been high off our asses and sleeping in our car. He was a piece of trash that I cleaned up and he stood before me yelling a bunch of bullshit in my face when it was him that didn't love or want me.

For years, I walked around feeling like chopped liver and not understanding why I wasn't good enough for him. There were times I walked around completely naked hoping he'd be turned on and he never was. *'Marriage is honorable'* is what Meme always said and divorcing a man over lack of sex seemed so wrong when he appeared to be a good man in other areas. No, he wasn't a good father but being a parent was a learning experience. No, he wasn't the cleanest, but I was prepared for that as I've always heard men can be rather dirty and disgusting. No, he couldn't manage a dime, but it was a lack of education as the public school system had failed him.

No, he's not at all consistent but his inconsistency came from his undiagnosed ADHD. Of course the frequent cheating he's done since I met him was because of impulses that were taught to him by his brother and his cousins as all they ever did was cheat on their women. Despite being the pastor's grandson, he hated church because the members were hypocrites which meant we couldn't even study the bible at home as husband and wife.

He was disrespectful to me in public only because he didn't know how to be a respectful behind closed doors. No, he never took me out because he didn't know how to be romantic. No, he couldn't cook but I taught him a few things as every adult should at least know how to cook one decent meal. He was hardly ever honest, but honesty was about the rarest thing to come by in these times. The only time he ever asked me what was wrong was when he knew I was pissed off and didn't want to talk about it until I had calmed down first. The only time we had sex was after we argued about it and even then, I had to masturbate beforehand because he refused to partake in foreplay or even simple flirting. Whenever problems would arise, it was me constantly trying to find solutions to make us better. I've now grown tired of trying to mend something that I never broke.

I knew that I was a boring little nerd to him only wanting to chase after success rather than fucking off doing nothing. My marriage was worse than the story of *'The Little Red Hen'* as he could never contribute to any business idea that I had. No, instead he'd come up with his own and want me to put all of my time and money in it while pussyfooting around in putting in the actual work for it to succeed. I'm sure he wanted me to put the work in as well.

I stood there counting the many times, that I should've left his ungrateful ass but stayed because of the fucking kids. At this point I just wanted to last long enough to make sure the kids were grown but who the fuck would want me now after having kids and his bitch ass to deal with as my ex. I wanted out and if he wanted to leave then he was certainly free to go.

I walked away heading back towards the kitchen to finish making dinner for my kids as I cried silently to God begging for forgiveness for how I threw a drink in that man's face. Although deep down I was happy to see him go, I felt like I was too much for any man to deal with. My anger stayed getting the best of me and despite how much I prayed, shit was only getting worse. I spoke freely as I said to God, "He's yours now. I don't want to deal with him anymore. I'm tired of fighting. I shouldn't have to fight a man that I call my husband. I'm tired of being angry. I don't want to be with somebody that makes me this angry all of the time. My kids will be just fine without him."

Dustin walked up behind me, and I refused to turn around as he said, "Baby I'm sorry. You know I'm not ever leaving you."

I turned around to face him as I sighed and replied, "You said some things that can't be taken back Dustin."

He nodded and held me and replied, "I know but I didn't mean them. It was just in the heat of the moment baby. That's all. I love you."

The damage was done as far as I was concerned. There was no apology to take back the moment that had just transpired. I wasn't sorry for throwing the kool-aid in his face. I apologized to God because regardless I disrespected my husband, but I wasn't at all sorry for it. His words stung and left a mark that was never going away. For a moment, 1 believed that she was free and yet here I was in his arms saying the words, *'I love you too Dustin'* while not feeling an ounce of love.

As I was telling my kids not to mimic the behavior of their mother when they're older and in a relationship or marriage, my phone lit up with a text from Imani asking, "Is it cool if Beau and a couple of his friends come along?"

I carelessly replied, "Yeah it's no problem."

Cooking had become me and my kids favorite bonding moment, so I allowed them to help with cooking the beef tips and rice while trying to salvage the rest of our day. We all sat down together and ate dinner while I decided to put my focus on myself and my kids from that moment on. God would handle the husband however he saw fit because I refused to fight for this bullshit anymore. The words of my mom echoed in the back of my mind, *'Girl Janay went dick crazy because they wouldn't let her get no damn dick'* and I realized that I too had gone dick crazy from not getting no damn dick.

Twisted Troubles

*"Pop-poppin' shit, you would think I went to school for chiropractin'. Lookin' good as hell today, just sent my nigga five attachments. Why did you confront me
'bout a nigga? Man, you bitches backwards"*
- Tomorrow 2 by GloRilla & Cardi

Imani

The last thing I wanted was to travel by myself, but I boarded a Greyhound bus and made it to Memphis within six hours. I would've loved to driven here and saved some time, but I preferred to sit back and ride when it came to trips instead of driving. I loved to take in the scenery. Nature is one of the most beautiful scenes that is often duplicated but nothing can be as beautiful as the real thing.

While trying to make amends with Ace and invite him to Gatlinburg for this couples' retreat, he'd declined my offer despite him talking about road trips and this being on my dime. He'd sent a text here and there but as far as talking on the phone or coming over, that was null and void. Instead, Destiny insisted that I give Beau a chance. She only wanted him occupied so that she could have her fun with Chaos.

With a stalker on my ass, I was having major *'trust issues'* and preferred to meet Beau at the cabin instead of riding with him. This didn't stop me from trying to talk to my best friend as I left him a voicemail telling him how I was leaving a week earlier so that I could stop in Memphis first to visit Greg. It wasn't much that I could do for Greg except be there for him but that's the least that I could do for him.

I've been calling Lauren's phone and it was still going straight to voicemail. It seemed foolish to show up to a place and nobody knew I was there, not even the person that I was coming to see. I've always been rather adamant about others calling or texting before popping up at their house and yet there I was in my hotel room getting ready to head out to a charity event that I wasn't even invited to.

I've heard nothing about Memphis except that it has great food and swap meets. While staying at a hotel near Beale Street just so I could experience Memphis and all it has to offer, I decided to get some sightseeing in and came across some pretty good places that I couldn't wait to really check out when I went shopping the next day after seeing Greg.

Being away from my own drama was beauty within itself making this an overdue treat to myself. The only thing that was missing was a friend to share it with and to my surprise there was Greg walking out of the Beale Sweets Sugar Shack. It took a lot to maneuver my way to him.

There were a bunch of people trying to get his autograph, a picture or chat it up with him. By the time that I made it to the front of what seemed to be a line for his attention, his bodyguard says, "Sorry, Mr. Hinton isn't seeing anybody else." I rolled my eyes and attempted to be nice, "I have some personal business with Greg." The bodyguard wasn't going for it. I sighed realizing that I was probably one in a million girls that's used this line with a celebrity before. As this Rikishi wannabe tried to turn me around, Greg noticed me and placed his hand on his bodyguard saying, "Yo, chill. I know her. What's up Imani? What are you doing here?"

I straightened my denim jacket and went on to say, "Crazy but I came to see you. I guess I found you."

He looked startled as he hugged me and said, "Listen, I'm heading to get a bite to eat in a minute. Why not catch up over dinner if you want?"

I replied, "No problem."

As I waited, I realized that his definition and mine of the term *'in a minute'* was quite different. I figured he'd finish up in about twenty more minutes; this man was there for another hour and a half. I waited, nonetheless. Finally, we left and made our way to Wet Willie's. I had traveled over two hundred miles to eat at a place called Wet Willie's but there were no complaints from me. His bodyguard stayed close by but not too close, he gave us space to talk freely. It was a must that we caught up with each other first. It's been almost a year since Lauren's death and about four years since we'd seen each other because anytime Lauren came to visit, she always came by herself or with Greg.

The charity event that's tomorrow had me reminiscing about the first time that I ever met Greg. I thought I noticed him before he ever met Lauren. There were many groupies swarming over him at the masquerade ball. At the time I was in love, and I just knew that I was going to be Mrs. William Xavier Smith one day soon. Lauren was the only person at the party that I knew having just come back from a runway show.

About a week after meeting at the party, the three of us hung out as if we were friends from the sandbox. It was no surprise when Lauren called me the next year saying that they had eloped. Greg seemed like the man of her dreams, and I couldn't have picked a better guy for her. He catered to Lauren's every want and need. She was living like a princess in that fairy tale come true type of love.

With hope that one day my own fairy tale would come true too, I cheered for my best friend from the sidelines. I never hung out with Greg without Lauren but in this moment, he reminded me so much of Ace. Just being able to chill with a friend was refreshing and what made it better was that he wasn't Ace.

Sure, I had entertained the idea of a relationship with him but in this moment his smile was enough to make me test out some murky waters with him. I was human after all with eyes that could see and Greg was still a very handsome man until he mentioned he had a new lady on his arm, but he wasn't sure how serious it was. It was still pretty new.

I was sadden at first until I realized how great it was to hear that he was actually moving on with his life. I didn't expect him to be single forever, however, he should probably move out of that mansion that he shared with Lauren. No new lady wants to share the same bed that a man shared with his dead wife. I thought to myself, *'It's just common courtesy.'* Greg's newfound relationship was the very thing that made me ask, "Greg, where did you meet this new lady? I hope not at a masquerade ball."

He smiled as the memories flooded in and he replied with a chuckle, "Met her through a non profit organization that I work with. The League. We do a bunch of different things from community events to politics."

I nodded with a smile as I said, "So listen, I'm here because I received some interesting phone calls from Lauren phone. I thought it was from you but when I tried calling back, I only got the voicemail."

He shook his head in disbelief. He seemed completely rattled by what I was saying as he replied, "Nah Imani, it wasn't me. I honestly thought that you hated me the same way that Lauren's family does." My heart dropped. It seemed as if I'd come all this way only to stir up drama and tur-moil. Knowing that I could've avoided Memphis altogether, I mumbled, "Wow. I definitely don't hate you and I feel so bad that you would think that."

He placed his hand on mine and replied, "Don't be. It's good to see you again and honestly, I wanted to reach out to you, but I didn't know what to say. We should've been sat down like this. It's something she would've wanted us to do."

He wasn't wrong. After almost a year, better late than never is what Lauren would've said. Since I had the chance, I asked, "I know this is a lot to ask, but do you know what happened? I know about as much as the rest of the world and it's still seems so surreal."

He sighed, "I just know we were arguing. It wasn't nothing major. We'd been dealing with trying to have a baby and at the time we'd had just experienced another miscarriage. It was the second one and she just wanted to be around you. I wanted her to stay home and rest, but she wasn't having it, so I offered to drive her. She didn't want me to drive, and I didn't want her to make that drive by herself, so I let her drive with her stupid ass model friend. I didn't understand it at the time that it was just grief and that she didn't want to be around me. In her eyes, I was the cause of her pain and she wanted to be as far away from me as possible. We argued over the phone during the drive, and she ended up blacking out when the car swerved."

His eyes started to water and together we fought through the tears. I hated myself for asking. I could've lived with a simple car accident but to know all of that broke my heart as I replied, "I shouldn't have asked. I'm sorry."

He sniffed, "It's okay. You deserved to know. She was like a sister to you."

I got up and hugged him as I said, "Thank you for telling me."

We shared a few tears and sniffles, but eventually pulled ourselves together and the rest of the night we shared laughs and memories of Lauren. It was a great turn around and at least in those moments I no longer felt like my trip was wasted. We exchanged numbers so that the next time we were in a city together, I wouldn't get detained by his bodyguard. Luckily, Wet Willie's was just down the street from my hotel, so I declined the ride that he had offered and decided to walk back. It was only about a twenty minute walk and that's including the multiple stops, that I needed to make as I took in the beauty of the city.

I felt free here in Memphis. There's no stalker here. There aren't any packages waiting for me at my room. There isn't any baby daddy drama here. I could be myself here or at least discover who I truly was without the chains of my past hindering me from achieving my goals. Nobody knew me here which meant starting over would be a breeze. I was starting to consider the move heavily as I remembered how I've always wanted more, and this was a beautiful city. Besides at the end of the day it wasn't Jackson, Mississippi.

I was almost at my hotel when I felt a spell of dizziness come upon me followed up with ringing in my ears. I was convinced that maybe I had a few too many drinks, but I didn't think that I'd feel the effects so soon. Everything around me started to spin topsy turvy and sitting down felt like the best idea, but before I could decide on what to do, someone had grabbed me from behind. I struggled for a moment as I tried to get away, but my attempts had gotten me nowhere. My attacker tightened their grip while placing me in the backseat of a black car. I knew exactly what was happening, but I never thought that this would be happening to me. Time moved so quickly and after minutes had passed; I finally blacked out.

Epiphany of a Lost Love

"Listen to your heart tonight. Come on, come on, come on. Make it alright, yeah. Come on, come out tonight." - The Secret Garden by Quincy Jones, Al B. Sure, James Ingram, El Debarge, & Barry White

Chanice

Lester opened his eyes as the bedroom door was slowly closing behind his head-ache. It was three in the morning and there stood Destiny in nothing but her lace nightie and a black silk robe that draped off of her shoulders. He had become the object of her obsession the moment he walked into IHOP and sat down in her section one night after clubbing with his bike club.

Chaos introduced them and she just knew she'd make him another notch in her belt, but she wasn't his type and Lester was never one to fuck behind his bros like that. This only made Destiny obsess over him even harder as she made her way down the ClickTight Rydaz lineup, hopping from dick to dick. It didn't matter if they were married or not as long as she had made it known that they had fucked Showout's girl.

The more Lester denied her, the harder she came as she slithered through his inner circle of cousins and uncles finally landing on his blood brother Carlos. She created such a commotion that even Lester's precious little wife thought that he was cheating on her with Destiny. It wasn't hard to believe with Destiny prancing around sharing the story of how in love her and Lester were. She had convinced herself of this fabricated story as she told anybody that would listen, and everybody believed her. Lester was living in a hell that he didn't ask for and all he wanted was an escape with nowhere to go.

Despite being a faithful and loving husband, his wife went on to have her own affair which wasn't at all a secret as everybody knew because of how careless she was with it. He tried to forgive her, and they even sought counseling but what good did that do when she had gotten pregnant by his brother and passing the baby off as his. It was then that he packed his bags and left refusing to endure another ounce of embarrassment by this foul woman.

Now here he was in a cabin in the woods of Gatlinburg, trapped in a room with the one woman he's contemplated several times on murdering. A prison jumpsuit didn't look so bad and then again running his bike off the side of the Reservoir didn't sound so bad either. Anything to rid himself of this crazy ass broad.

Any plans he had of a peaceful retreat was thrown out the window the moment his best friend Chaos, texted him saying, "I'm going to tell you now that Carlos is bringing Destiny since him and that girl broke up. I got to handle some business in Biloxi." Instantly, Lester's head begin to throb from the thought of him and Destiny being in the same room for too long.

It didn't take long for him to learn that Destiny was just a pretty face in need of a straight jacket. It made no sense to him why his brother would bring this crazy ass girl on this trip knowing the bullshit he's endured since meeting her. The moment he seen Destiny; his entire mood changed. He felt betrayed by Carlos. After already getting his wife pregnant, there he was parading around the one person he knew Lester couldn't stand.

Annoyed at even having come, he asks, "Destiny, what are you doing?"

She licked her lips and twirled her hair as she giggled and spoke coyly, "Oh no this isn't my room. I must've gotten all turned around."

He sighed as he pinched the top of his nose while saying, "Well, could you let yourself out? I'm trying to sleep."

Instead of walking out of the door, she walked closer to the bed, allowing her robe to slowly fall off of her body as she said, "Baby stop playing. You know you want me. Let me make you happy."

Lester jumped up out of the bed without even putting a shirt on as he shook his head and walked straight out of his bedroom leaving the door wide open. He was creeping down the stairs through the cabin hoping not to disturb anyone else's sleep. The more he walked in silence and darkness, the sooner he realized he'd leave at the break of dawn heading back to Jackson, MS. He needed to take in the mountaintop view out back, reflect, and figure out his next move when it came to the disrespect his brother was constantly putting him through. Lester went outside to the deck to plot his next move when I startled him as I spoke softly, "Couldn't sleep huh?"

Lester looked around and seen a breath of fresh air as I held out my glass of Snoop Cali Rose as a peace offering. I was wearing a purple fuzzy robe with house shoes to match. There was a light green blanket covering my legs as I sat in the patio chair on my iPad watching an old comedy special by Sommore. He took a sip from the glass and sat down in the patio chair beside me. He stared in amazement at the opportunity that had presented itself before him. Lester had been plotting for months for a chance to tell me who he really was.

There sat my childhood sweetheart, a boy I knew from back in the day before AOL and Yahoo was a thing. It was me and him saying Candyman or Bloody Mary in the mirror while he chickened out on the fifth time, and I never let him live it down. I was my own version of Chyna and Laila Ali, wrestling and boxing one day and then playing with my pink Barbie vanity set in those poofy ass church dresses that Meme loved for me to wear the next day. We were best friends at eight and eleven years old but for me, I was a young girl in love, and nobody was telling me otherwise.

There were plenty of times Lester has tried to speak up, but it never seemed like the right time. It was now or never. He tried to spark a conversation by asking, "Why are you out here?"

My reply sounded dry and slightly annoyed, "I guess I couldn't sleep."

Only a simp would keep trying. Call him what you want but I was never a sweet girl. I've always been mean and all that's ever done is turn Lester on. He knew exactly what I needed to make me smile like a kid going to Disneyland for the first time. He just had to tread lightly on these icy waters and remember what we had so long ago. Time was on his side since Destiny was too busy making her move on her next victim. I'm pretty sure her mission was to fuck every guy there or at least suck his dick. Lester was on a mission as well as he asked, "Why don't you remember me?"

With a puzzled look on my face, I chuckled and said, "I do remember you Mr. Walls."

He shook his head and replied, "Yeah but we met years before that moment in your office."

I was studying his face as I replied, "How did we meet?"

An evil smirk appeared on his face as he said, "At Magoo's. You walked up to me asking about my girlfriend. That was so weird."

I sighed at the memory. It wasn't what I wanted to hear but it is what had happened. He didn't seem to remember our childhood romance which was rather heartbreaking to say the least. The way he rubbed the back of his neck made it obvious that he'd mustered up a lot of courage just to stumble down memory lane to bring up this random moment. He took another sip of my wine as he carefully chose his next words with precision and accuracy, making this a sensual game of chess rather than a trip down memory lane.

I raised my left eyebrow, so he knew it was do or die. My reply seemed like I was even more bothered than before as I said, "Nothing was weird about it."

Silly games were for kids, and I was on vacation. Seeing Lester wasn't on my agenda but there he was, and I just needed him to be chill. Dustin was only a few steps away and just like him, I was trying to figure out my next move in the bullshit that I was calling a marriage however Lester is an extremely attractive man to me. He's chocolate covered pleasure that I didn't mind enjoying a few more times.

His smile was alluring enough to make me choose the wrong thing every time he asked. He wasn't a flashy guy but still managed to outshine everybody in the room. All I wanted in this moment was to enjoy the presence of a fine ass man, but Lester was tweaking and throwing off the vibe. Just as I had the thought to go back inside, Lester sighed and said, "You're always so bold. It's really attractive and also really intimidating for a lot of men but not for me."

This definitely got my attention. I sat up and replied, "Intimidating?" before allowing Lester to say another word, I laughed and said, "Wait. Shut up! Seriously?!"

With his hands raised, he exclaimed, "Oh shit you know how to laugh?!"

I went on a pinching frenzy while saying, "I can be rather abusive as well."

Lester laughed and replied, "Ya pinches feel like tickles!"

A few punches in the arm later and I asked, "Is that better?"

While looking me up and down, he licked his lips and spoke seductively, "You said you giving massages?"

When Tyrese said that Capricorn and Pisces were connected, he must've heard about me and Lester. He's the only guy to ever match my energy as we stayed wrestling because of hormones that we didn't understand at a young age. He understands it fully at thirty-one. Denying the excitement that rushes over his body whenever I walk in the room would be the worst thing, he could ever do to himself. All of his cares about any other woman fly out the window when he sees me, looking good as always.

I took a few glances at him and contemplated giving him that massage and a few thousand more. It only made it easier to give in to him knowing he's the first boy I ever loved. I was free to be unapologetically me with him. When I walked in as the last couple because Dustin could never afford to do anything early or on time, I almost ran for the hills to see the extra couple that Imani told me about was Lester and some random chick.

It was simple for me. This was a vacation before I walked through the door and it's still a vacation. I desperately needed a break from my reality while giving Dustin, the divorce lawyers, the pastor, and everybody else the illusion that I was giving this marriage my all while plotting my escape every single day. I was happily unbothered and figured why not get a slight upgrade on this vacation.

As I stood up, I pulled his arm, while saying, "I may have said that. Give me a hug and let me feel you up."

He happily obliged to the embrace and hoped it was enough to let down all of my barriers because he knew that there was more to me that just another mean girl, but those barriers had disappeared the moment he licked his lips. He couldn't resist another second as he leaned forward for a kiss. Excitement soared through his body when I didn't lean back, he continued until our lips had connected. His affection poured out producing an exquisite musical of moans between the two of us.

Curiosity had gotten the best of him in our intense make out session leading his hands to discover that I had nothing on underneath the robe. A natural body that I loved and embraced. To him, I was perfect and any other man that noticed me would agree. A beauty that surpassed physical features. Men desired me and wanted to have a woman like me, but men will be men. Boys will be boys. The conversations would suggest that lust wasn't off the list, it just wasn't first. I've always been a woman worth fighting for. He paused our session to say, "Come with me."

Without any hesitation, I followed my childhood sweetheart through the cabin and tiptoed upstairs behind him with the biggest smile on my face. We entered his guest room at the end of the hall. In the middle of the room, he watched me drop my robe while backing up to the king size bed seductively. At the edge of the bed is where he lifted me around his waist, climbing onto the bed while sweetly kissing me. I could feel the excitement ready to bust through those black gym shorts. There was no denying the monster that was ready and waiting to enter me once again. His kisses migrated from my collarbone, onto my breasts until he was suckling and caressing them both. This was a man that I had secretly fallen in love with all over again and didn't mind going to war about him.

It's safe to say that I fell in love the moment I seen him again at Magoo's and then again in my office and perhaps once more in this moment. This was a man I couldn't stop falling in love with. When he reached my honey pot, he looked up at me and smiled as he said, "I've missed you so much." Before I could reply, he dove straight in with his hands holding my thick caramel thighs keeping me steady. He didn't need instructions when he knew exactly what to do.

I've never hit a climax so fast in my life. It was like I was a virgin all over again with him after pushing out a set of twins. I wasn't about to say stop when the man had just started but he recognized every movement and moan I had so he adjusted to meet my needs and wants. The biggest challenge was not to wake everybody up while I drew a bit of blood biting down on my bottom lip, trying not to scream.

My fingertips begin to ache from gripping the sheets so hard after feeling his long wide tongue dart inside of my walls. He had my hips swirling in circles that made him think that was one good way to ride his face. The plan was him teaching me some more ways. My legs shook uncontrollably as he snatched my soul. With a glazed smile of victory plastered on his face, he stood up ready to give me even more while he pulled me to him. He teased me as he rubbed his head against my throbbing wet lips. Slowly, he entered inside which made me grip his forearms. Those punches may have felt like tickles, but these nails were digging into his arms giving him an ego boost. His strokes were only slow in the beginning. He just wanted to open my honey pot up a little. I was taking all nine thick inches like a champ!

As he flipped me over, I gave him the arch from hell. He stepped back for a second just admiring the perfection that was tooted up before him. The thought to go beat Dustin's ass for playing over this good ass pussy crossed his mind instantly. It was clear he wasn't getting his wife back. My childhood sweetheart held my hips tightly and wasn't going to take it easy with full intentions of shooting the club up. Giving me a few sweet long strokes before wreaking havoc, I had already started throwing it back before he could do anything, and it threw him off a little. The mission was to have me running all over this bed but instead I was fucking the shit out him from the back.

The minute I slowed it down, he took control trying to blow my back out and I loved every inch that he rammed inside of me. As he grabbed a hand full of my hair, he smacked my ass so hard that he had to hold my ass cheek knowing his handprint was going to be there later for him soothe when nobody was looking. He flipped me again and this time I wasn't his born again virgin. I pushed him down on the bed and straddled him like I was mounting a beautiful black stallion. The sheets peeled off the corners of the king sized bed as his toes curled and the moans of ecstasy tried to escape. I bounced this soft ample ass with ease and then bent down never losing rhythm nibbling on the bottom of his earlobe. His arms wrapped around my waist, and we sat up causing me to wrap my legs around him once more. This wasn't the finishing move he had in mind but it's the one that took him out.

Neither of us wanted this to end. The morning light was starting to fill the sky and soon the entire cabin would be awake. Silence filled the air, but it was more plotting than awkward. I had no idea how I was going to keep getting away with having fun with my childhood sweetheart, but I was going to figure it out. This wasn't enough for me, and Lester felt the exact same way. Everything was understood in the silence, I smiled at him, and he smiled back. As I walked out of the door shaking my head, he grabbed my arm pulling me back to him to give me the sweetest kiss goodbye.

Trapped In The Past

"I don't wanna be just a memory. And I don't wanna feel your wings break free. Because without you I'm lost in the breeze." - If You Let Me by Sinead & GRADES

Destiny

I was no different from any other woman walking the earth in search of a man to take care of me. After falling for one too many lies, I learned how to master the art of lying for myself. This only helped me get so far in life as there was always a better liar than me waiting to challenge my skills. I didn't know this when I met Nate. I believed everything he told me and his lies became an easy thing to fall in love with. When a man has insecurities within himself and comes across a woman that he believes to be out of his league then lies will become his best friend as he'll do and say anything to impress that woman however when the woman is easily impressible, well then that's a different story.

The moment Nate found out that the woman he'd been bragging about to everybody was actually fucking his roommate and his coworker, he plotted his revenge. It didn't matter who it was. He simply wanted me to hurt the way that he was hurting and if anybody close to me was willing then he'd make sure to have his fun right there in my face. He searched my Facebook friends list and was met with insecurities of not being good enough to approach any of them.

He stalked my page, searching the comments and hoped one homely girl of his stature would pop out for him to use and it never happened. I went on to brag my heart away about the amazing things each one of my many men did in and outside of the bedroom. As for Nate, he too was an amazing head hunter. We were a match made in hell since I never found him attractive. His dick rating was about half a star, and he was only ever good for being my do boy.

It's only when I shared this information with Niecy that the shit hit the fan because she seen a rather handsome guy that didn't deserve the bullshit that I was putting him through. She was young and naive when she sent Nate the friend request and conveniently, he just had to be around me when he checked out her profile after accepting the request just for me to scream out, "You can't talk to her. That's my best friend."

He waited until he was away to send his introductory paragraph as if he was applying for a scholarship at Cambridge. What he seen was a pretty and plain girl that he didn't want to use and had high hopes that maybe I did brag a little. Nate was more than prepared to prove himself and his rating no matter what the rating was because it was obvious to him that Niecy was only sending a friend request for one reason and that reason was sex.

Revenge had become a thing of the past as he placed it on the backburner the moment, he met Niecy. For him it was probably love at first sight. He was amazed at how perfect she was, and he was completely wrong in thinking that she wanted anything more than to be his friend. This was during a time when Niecy had way too much going on and couldn't process another obligation such as a relationship with any man when she was trying to figure out herself and get her life together.

I tried to warn him, but he was too busy caught up in his own head to listen. He just had to prove a fucking point. So they remained friends while Nate continued to pursue a relationship with Niecy despite it all. He wanted to be her prince in shining amour, rescuing her from all her troubles but he was constantly met with rejection. He decided to go back to his original plan of revenge except this time he wanted revenge for being rejected and he knew the perfect person to run to and execute his plan. As if coming back to me would be so easy. Killing two birds with one stone as they say. He told me how much he wanted her while telling Niecy that I was crazy and a liar. Although I was indeed a liar and a bit crazy over some dick, Niecy never cared because that shit didn't have anything to do with her and her bills.

This was the moment in which I fell in love with Niecy. She accepted all of me and never judged me for being a lying ass hoe. She listened to me and was honest with me even when I was fucking up. Couldn't no man walk up to her and tell her anything about me without her coming back to me telling me to watch they ass more. The truest and realest friend I have, and she refuses to become my lesbian wife. I'm a grown ass woman free to do whatever I pleased to do. Nate wanted to make Niecy jealous and crazy which was impossible to do when Niecy never wanted that man in any romantic way. His hope was to destroy our bond and yet all he did was make a complete fool of him-self. Nate was a man with a plan. I listened silently as Niecy talked to Nate with him on speaker...

Nate sighed and asked, "Why are you cockblocking me?"

With a chuckle, Niecy replied, "Sir, how am I cockblocking you?"

Unamused and slightly bothered, he says, "You told Destiny about my girlfriend."

In a surprised voice, she replies, "Oh damn. So you are trying to take her out on a date? Why didn't you tell me? I wouldn't have said anything."

He exclaimed, "I didn't think I had to worry about you. You're married!"
With a hearty laugh, she says, "Okay but you know the girl is a compulsive liar. How was I supposed to know that she was telling the truth this time?"
Nate groans at the truth in Niecy's words while saying, "Man I'm just trying to get my dick sucked in the back of the movie theatre."
Niecy shook her head at the craziness that she heard over the phone not knowing that I had every intention of sucking his dick, but she'd been pissed if she knew. I just wanted to witness her reaction and to see if she actually had romantic feelings for him the way that he claimed she did. It was obvious that everything she had been telling me was the truth. She didn't give a fuck about Nate, and I never cared about the truth of their relationship as only being friends. From the way Nate was acting and bragging on this girl meant that the bitch was simply a better liar than me. A complete fucking actress in need of a Golden Globe, an Academy, an Oscar, a Tony, and a gotdamn Emmy.
If Niecy loved him the way that he believed she did then I was impressed, and it only caused me to fall deeper in love with the girl. In the end, Nate simply didn't want me as anything more than a quick lay in the hay whereas he was ready to give his all to Niecy and I know it wasn't because of conversation. Sure, he'd confided so many things in her and that included his relationship problems, that Niecy always encouraged him to do right with. That was just Niecy being Niecy. It's the reason I hadn't pursued a relationship with her.
I knew she was just this nice girl that you really couldn't help but fall in love with. The more Nate pushed the issue, the more I hated their friendship while Niecy wasn't thinking about either of us as she was happily married to Dustin as a traveling hairstylist. When I wised up and seen Nate's true colors I cried to Niecy telling her,

"I knew it wasn't you because you wouldn't do me like that. I know he went after you first because I watched him on the computer at my house when he sent you the friend request. I told him that you were my best friend!"

Niecy shook her head and replied, "But Destiny, I sent him the friend request and weren't you fucking the roommate and his coworker?"

Without an ounce of regret, I replied, "But he didn't know that!"

As always, the point in my words flew right over her little naive head. Niecy knew men could talk more than women sometimes. It wasn't anything happening that close to home, and they didn't know about it. As time went on, I loved to tell everybody how we've shared multiple men together when we weren't even attracted to the same skin tone on a man. I just wanted her to see that it could've all been so simple to just be together and have as many men as we want together. Since she couldn't see the beauty in what we could have, I'd simply have to show her that it wasn't a man on the planet that would love her unconditionally, but I could. If she let me.

To others it might look like a competition. My girl just needed to see that ain't none of these men worth more than a quick nut. They all lie. They all cheat. They all talk. She wanted love. She should've wanted money. It's the only honest thing she was going to get from these trifling ass men. Amongst the lies, I proved my point as I went on to make my rounds to everybody in his circle as I had done with a bunch of other guys before and after him.

I started when I fucked his friend one night on the bed of the truck while Nate and Niecy sat inside the truck talking causing the moment to become rather awkward since Niecy had no intentions of fucking Nate. That was what I call killing two birds with one stone. To prove to her that he wasn't shit right along with his friends while proving to him that she didn't want anything more than friendship from him filled my heart with satisfaction, but the show must go on. I went on to the next friend and fucked him inside of Nate's truck outside of my mama's apartment. When Niecy had stopped by to visit, she called him to say, "Why are you sitting in the truck? Just come inside."

He replied, "What are you talking about? I'm at work."

While in a confused state from staring at his truck, she asked, "Are you in your car because I'm looking at your truck right now?"

At this point, everybody believed that I just loved DICK. All kinds of dick. Horse dick if I could get it. I was just trying to wake my girl up to the reality that these men ain't shit. Eventually Nate finally accepted what it was between him and Niecy and put his childish ways to the side. Whatever relationship problems Nate had going on was between him and the women he was with but after so long, a man will be a man.

If Nate wanted to get sucked up in the back of the movie theater, then by all means he was more than welcome to because I do love dick. Nate went on to accomplish his mission and picked me up later that night for a date to go see *'Harley Quinn: Birds of Prey'* and within no time, I was slobbing on his nob like corn on the cob in the back of the movie theatre.

A Mother's Love

"I got too mad and I said too much. Went too far and I almost cussed. No my mama didn't raise me that way. Lord I need a little help today." - A Little More Jesus by Erica Campbell

Quitman, Mississippi
2009 AD
- The Eve Gene -

Chanice

Whenever somebody would ask me how I felt about my great grandmother Myrtis, I'd always joked around saying, *'She was mean, but I loved her'* and they always took that to heart believing that I really hated the woman but in my defense, this was an inside joke between me and my mom that nobody else ever related to. In all honesty, words couldn't describe the love that I had for that beautiful, amazing woman. Over time I grew up to be just as mean as Myrtis according to the mommy friends I had met, and they loved warning each one of their children not to act up around me because I was mean and would whoop them when they got out of line. I held true to the nature of being Myrtis Lee Rogers great granddaughter and I made sure each and every mommy friend that I had knew and understood how much I didn't like no bad ass kids. Just like Myrtis, I didn't like no fast ass little girls that liked to sit and ride their heels and flirt with grown ass men. I didn't like the mannish ass little boys wanting to touch on everybody and their mama that never listened to anybody and I for damn sure didn't like the nasty ones that always wanted to play in somebody's ass.

My friends believed that I was abusing my poor kids and that was the only reason that they listened to me and made good grades in school. On the contrary, I never spank my kids because they aren't spoiled rotten. They respect me and I respect them. It's a mutual understanding that when they fuck up, I'm not sparing the discipline. Whether they fucked up at home or in school, they know that the possibility of a punishment was significantly high.

While I resorted to alternate forms of discipline with being a military drill sergeant issuing out burpees and planks, Dustin was constantly instilling fear in my children behind my back causing them to fear a whooping when they didn't have to. It's what he received as a child and yet it didn't do a damn thing for him because over the years the respect for his mother Catrinea diminished more and more. She was more afraid of him than she was our heavenly father and that only pissed me off. As the old saying goes.....I wish a ni... MY SON would!

Keeping an open door policy of honesty was perfect as I always sat my kids down having bible lessons from the Old Testaments and not sugarcoating it with coloring books and cute nursery rhymes. I left that for random playtime and instead of walking around screaming *'Respect your elders and your days shall be longer on the land'* or *'Honor thy father and thy mother'* as I witnessed my Meme and others do, I made sure my kids understood that no matter what they did in life they didn't want Jesus to say to them, *'Away from me for I never knew you'* and with love they listened.

Together we watched how others weren't teaching their kids the bible and how they acted bad as hell. Whenever my mommy friends would plead with me on how to get their kids to listen or respect them or do better in school, I'd tell them to send them to me, but they always refused because they believed that I was going to allow the German and white side of me to take over and beat them like I was the original slave master of Mississippi. The ones that did desperately want a break from their bad ass kids, didn't care what I did to them as long as they were gone away from them until they went back home singing praises of the amazing time they had at my house.

They couldn't understand why their kids loved me so much knowing how mean I could be while never understanding the love that I gave to each child as if they were my own. Whenever it was time to punish a child, they looked to me for approval on the only thing they knew and that was a beating, but I'd always choose a different route because many times, it was the parents that were spoiled and not the children but when you know better you do better. Myrtis was an extraordinary woman that showed love to each one of her kids in the only way that she knew but it was her love for my Meme that set me on the path of being the mean mama bear that I am.

During a parent teacher conference in fifth grade, Meme proudly walked the halls of Quitman Upper Elementary with me, her adopted granddaughter, by her side after listening to nothing but praise and high honor for my nerdy four eyed skinny self but the next day when I made it to class my teacher stopped me in the middle of the classroom just as the students were starting to pour in and asked, "Is your grandmother white or albino?"

I looked dumbfounded as I had never heard the word albino before. Meme had explained to me several times that she was a black woman but that she just looked like that. She told me that her father was Jamaican and German, but we weren't supposed to talk about it because the Germans were still trying to eradicate the product of a secret love affair now known as the black Brunners.

A look of terror filled her face as she told me how her brother Melvin was mysteriously killed after digging too deep into the Brunner side. It didn't take much convincing, but she still made me promise to never look because they were watching, and I'd be killed if I got too close to the truth. I heeded her warnings as she went on to give me a full account of the history of Myrtis and the Thompson side of our family as she was Cherokee and White from Tylertown, MS but Meme never once said anything about being albino.

To a child living in a black rainbow of colors from the lightest to the darkest, I just shrugged my shoulders and accepted that truth. I never questioned why my Meme looked completely white with wooly blonde hair that she'd use a relaxer on to straighten out the kinky curls only to use rollers and do a pushover style in the end. I never even wondered why her grey eyes shook and sometimes flickered golden embers nor what made her legally blind or even diabetic. The fact that she appeared to the world as a white woman but was absolutely black seemed to go completely over my head until I heard the word *'albino'* from this nosey ass teacher. Once again, I just shrugged and replied with the only answer that I knew to be true, "That's just the way she looks."

This white teacher ironically named Miss White patted me on my shoulder with a smirk and walked off without even explaining to me what the word albino meant. This puzzled me all day long and the second I stepped off the school bus I only had one question for my Meme that sat at the dining room table chatting it up with Myrtis like any other regular day. I walked in and with the sweetest voice Meme asked, "Hey baby. How was school?"

Standing in front of them both, I ignore her question and stand proud as if I'm Kevin Hart getting ready to cuss his teacher out because my question was in dire need of an answer and I didn't want to forget it, so I asked, "Meme, what's an albino?"

Curiosity had killed the cat and anger had consumed Myrtis as she replied, "And who in the hell wants to know?!"

Not Niecy! I didn't want to know a damn thing. As far as I was concerned, I had overstepped and just cussed the Reverend completely out and it was judgement day. Meme looked at her mother in a distressed manner as she asked, "Who told you that word?"

I darted my eyes at Myrtis who was inches away from getting up on her good leg and beating somebody's ass as I softly repeated the words of my teacher, "Miss White asked me if you were white or albino and I know you said you're not white so I just told her what you told me. That's just the way you look."

Meme pursued her lips and nodded her head as she said, "Baby go do your homework in the room."

As I walked away, Myrtis was going the fuck off. I'm pretty sure all of Clarke County and possibly Meridian could hear Myrtis screaming, "Who this bitch think she is asking about my gotdamn baby? It don't motherfucking matter what the fuck you are or how the fuck you look. Bitch better sit her motherfucking ass down and do her motherfucking job before I have to go up there and beat her ass with the butt of my gotdamn gun!"

Once Myrtis had calmed down, I had official become a true ride or die for my crippled old grandma. It was exciting to witness the *'crazy'* emerge from within. As we sat outside underneath the carport, I looked at Myrtis and said, "Grandma, if you were robbing a bank, I'd drive the getaway car."

Myrtis looked a little stunned because we never watched any black gangster movies such as *'Boyz N Da Hood'* or *'Belly.'* Movies like *'Jason's Lyric'* was something my mom tried so hard to get me to watch but I was a sucker for *'Sweet Home Alabama'* with Reese Witherspoon or *'Miss Congeniality'* with Sandra Bullock. So, to hear her great-granddaughter proclaim such a feat was a little troubling I'm sure but at least she knew that I didn't mind going along with her on a crazy ride.

The mutual understanding of *'Don't fuck with Linda Jean'* created an unbreakable bond between us causing Myrtis to teach me how to make homemade banana pudding and allowing her more sassy side to show while still instilling the morals and values of praising God and getting saved with the evidence of speaking in tongues. We had our own thing and I cherished it. I adored Grandma Myrtis but after Uncle Keith's death, I found myself in an unfamiliar place and at seventeen years old, I had gotten pregnant by Dustin and was a high school drop-out.

Around Valentine's Day, Meme wanted to visit Myrtis since her health was declining more. I walked around like I had been chopping onions all day with a face full of regret and a belly bigger than the sun. I knew Uncle Keith would've been so disappointed to see me like that and I could feel the disappointment seeping from Myrtis. I kept my head down and helped out as much as I could while trying to avoid the obvious. One thing about getting pregnant is that now everybody knows for a fact that you've had sex. I was embarrassed and disappointed in myself and being in that house only made me feel worse. As I sat in Myrtis' room, an unexpected visitor came bursting through the carport door screaming, "I'm sick of your ass Wewe!"

Nobody knew that Wewe was even in town while his girlfriend stormed through the house with him hot on her heels as Myrtis laid calmly in the bed and said to me, "Baby hand me my purse."

I knew exactly what was in the purse, so I made sure to handle with extreme care. Just as the girlfriend made her way to Myrtis' bedside, Myrtis had already reached into her purse and politely placed her gun onto her lap with her finger resting on the trigger while staring at the girlfriend and waiting on her to finish her rant. Instantly, the girlfriend settled down and whatever was troubling her so intensely before seemed to suddenly disappear as she spoke with ease, "I'm just so tired Ms Myrtis."

Myrtis nodded her head while Meme crept in and instructed me to come out of the room but like Cecily in *'The Color Purple'*, I really wanted to stay and watch what transpired next. It was rare that people pushed Myrtis to this point of no return. Quite frankly it was a death sentence that everybody understood except for Wewe's girlfriend.

I never knew what Wewe had done to that girl, but she must've been just plain stupid to barge in on Myrtis the way that she did, regardless she never came around again. Meme and I stayed with Myrtis for a month before heading back to Jackson, Mississippi. This I was thankful for as I didn't have to be a walking disappointment in the house she once shared with Myrtis and Uncle Keith any longer.

Just as I was walking out of Myrtis' bedroom from cleaning the bathroom, Myrtis sat up slightly and with a firm voice she said to me, "Niecy you're not the first and you won't be the last. Hold your head up and walk like you know God got you."

I didn't understand her words at the time, but it was comforting to know that Myrtis wasn't completely disappointed in me as I had believed she would be. Two months later and I had taken my GED test and even attended the graduation ceremony while preparing to attend Jackson State University for the fall semester. Dustin had broken up with me the moment I got back to Jackson and was engaged to some new girl while playing father to her little girl. All I could do was shed one lonely tear as if I was Johnny Depp in 'CryBaby' and didn't worry about a boy too afraid of being a father to children that he had laid down and made.

Just as things was starting to look up for me, Myrtis' health took a sudden turn for the worse and the family was gathering for yet another funeral. Although I didn't understand my situation, Meme did, and she made sure that I sat this funeral out because during Uncle Keith's funeral I didn't realize that I experienced my first panic attack in the midst of my grief. She had to make sure to protect her first two great granddaughters from their young mother having a second one at seven months pregnant. I was heartbroken and months after becoming a mother, I looked at my girls wishing Myrtis could've held out just a bit longer to meet her first two great great granddaughters. They look and act so much like her sassy self.

I had accepted death as a part of life and all that mattered to me was making sure that I got to meet that amazing woman again one sweet day. In order for that to happen I had to make sure that I got saved and that meant being Holy Ghost filled with the evidence of speaking in tongues. My prayer closet didn't have the fancy ottoman and silk *'I Love Jesus'* scarves or the pretty pillow to rest my knees on but I made sure to run to God with every problem that I faced in every situation no matter how big or small. I could see how God was working in my life, pulling me through hardships that couldn't be explained and when I finally got it......I GOT IT!

I didn't have Myrtis to call so I called Meme to thank her for her love and her guidance.

If it wasn't for those two ladies, I would've never felt God's love coursing through my body one beautiful afternoon in August after my mother's death. It was as if I was on fire and yet I wasn't sweating or tired. I couldn't control myself and the only words that I could utter that made any sense was *'I Love You Jesus!'* My children stood by watching me praise in a way that they had never seen before. So used to the normal claps and jigs that we all did to a little gospel music, but this wasn't claps and jigs and wasn't any music playing as they watched me fall unto my hands and knees uncontrollably worshipping our Heavenly Father that they had only heard about in the bible lessons. It wasn't long before a new language had broken through, and I knew I was speaking in tongues.

By the time, the Holy Spirit had released me, I was able to finally explain to my children what had happened. Now my girls are more than ready to be filled with God's love. It wasn't until now that I realized what Myrtis meant when she said, *'You're not the first and you won't be the last. Hold your head up and walk like you know God got you'* because she was right. So many others had gotten pregnant even younger than I had. At the very least I was already working and had turned eighteen before giving birth. I had gotten my GED and was going off to college. Sure, it wasn't ideal, but it could've been so much worse. I had no reason to hold my head down in shame because God definitely did have me.

Sinister Sisters

"I've never been in love like this. A love like ours. I pray for it on my knees. Every night for some hours" - Hrs & Hrs by Muni Long

Destiny

Here we were face to face not making a move. I thought to herself, 'Why is he here with that homely looking slut dangling from his arm? Always looking like a one night stand gone wrong.' It was obvious to me that Showout's new arm candy meant him no good and yet he paraded her around as though she was God's gift to the world while I stood here barely able to continue faking this smile as Niecy hammered on and on about her plans in this new business move for her umbrella company TriBrid Productions. I was more concerned with how my first love was burning a hole into me.

I wore a sexy emerald green, strapless, hugging all the right curves, can't help but notice me dress. You could say I wore it just for him. Everything was sitting just right as it showed off my smooth legs, and hugged my curves, giving every man there a reason to look in my direction. I didn't think that green color would be so enticing but I couldn't find a bomb ass red dress for Niecy's grand opening. We couldn't stop locking eyes with each other. The man had it going on with his ducktail tux. Nothing was better than a man that could do both. I wanted to melt into his arms from the way he stood looking like a chiseled god, getting me all hot and bothered without even knowing it. I had to cut Niecy off as I said, "I'm sorry boo but I'm needed elsewhere."

I made my way to the guest bedroom in the back of the house. Looking at his fine ass had me overflowing and needing a relief. I knew I wouldn't have made it through the night without bringing my silver bullet. After I locked the door to get comfortable on the chaise by the window, I slid my black panties to the side and started making circles with my bullet on my clit. All I could think of was his hands all over me until I heard light tapping at the door. Thinking to myself, *'Who in the hell could that be?!'* I didn't want to stop because I had just started but I didn't want to cause a scene, so I rushed and put my silver bullet up, fixed my hair and opened the door. Of course, it was the man that I wanted the most in the world. He asked, "Are you okay? Why are you hiding in here?"

Dustin walked right in and closed the door. We've known each other for too long for him not to care. Although we met at the beginning of our ninth grade year, the attraction was undeniable. We immediately started dating and love was an easy and simple thing in ninth grade. For two years it was beautiful and then our mothers met during a church convention in Jacksonville, Florida. The reality of us being first cousins was too much for either of us to bear and so we simply stopped talking. We stayed away from each other as much as we could, but it seemed as though fate itself just kept bringing us back together. Now his wife was someone I considered my best friend. A sister even and despite us being cousins, I still couldn't resist this man. I needed him every single day.

Sometimes I despised the little family that he had created with Niecy, but I understood the image that he needed to maintain. As the grandson of a pastor, he couldn't go off and marry his first cousin which left me alone unable to truly settle down with anybody else. My heart was with him, and no other man was going to be able to take his place. was coming along to change that.

I understood that he was concerned because of how I just ran off but I'm on a different mission right now and it was the wrong time to show concern. All I wanted to do was jump some bones and rock somebody's world, but I was giving it my all to be a good girl. He looked at me in a weird seductive way that I always fell for as he continued, "Were you leaving?"

I forced a smile and said, "No, that's not my plan. I was just trying to go to the bathroom dang Shad."

He had this funny smirk on his face, while locking the door. Somehow, my body instantly knew all of the impure thoughts racing through his head as I watched him walk up to me with a smile saying, "You are looking mighty fine in this dress young lady." He started softly running his fingers up my arms and around my neck lifting my chin up for a kiss as if I wasn't horny enough. I wanted desperately to respect my best friend's marriage but too much of me just didn't care in that moment. It wasn't the first time that we had betrayed Niecy and the way it was looking it wouldn't be the last. Dustin and I stopped caring about being cousins well before he met Niecy as we had already done everything under the sun. It didn't matter if we did it some more. He always seemed to know exactly when I needed him the most and like always here, he was ready to cater to my needs in any way that I desired.

While my heart and mind took the time to figure out the best way to say no, my body had taken control causing me to grab the back of his head, bringing him to me. I wanted him right then and there and I wanted him to know it. He grabbed my ample ass as we kissed, squeezing it like he missed me as much as I had missed him. It had only been a couple of weeks since we had been in each other's arms, but we were already sharing moans as if it had been years. He pushed me on the bed and with ease slid that skintight dress up and ripped my panties off. I just laid back and prepared myself for the magic that I knew Dustin was about to create with my body.

I watched him lower down to his knees and I knew exactly what he wanted, so I spread my legs with my knees bent as a trail of his kisses started at my thighs and ended at my moisten outer lips. Dustin pressed my thighs open even more and went to suckling on my clit. Instead of running like I normally did, I slid deeper into his mouth, like I wanted him to eat my soul out. My head tilted back with delight as it had been too long since I last felt this man's mouth on my body. I could barely control myself the moment I felt him slide his finger inside of my sweet spot. It never took long for me to climax when I was with Dustin. Almost twelve years later and he had only just begun to truly explore every inch of my body.

I started to shiver and in went another finger; my hands pushed him right on in. My breathing became staggered but that didn't stop my hips from swaying on his face. I wanted to scream as that hallelujah moment quickly approached sending my body into another world. Dustin continued stroking his fingers in and out as he lightly suckled on my clit and that's when I began to run. The pleasure had become too much for me to take. Dustin stood up with a smile knowing he had given my body more than what it needed. I felt the need to show him up because he was feeling a little too sure of himself.

I pulled him by his waist and started to unbuckle his sexy white slacks as I pulled them down with boxers intact. My old friend was already rock hard and standing at attention. I licked and stroked him with only my tongue taking all the time in the world, slowly sucking the tip and stroking his shaft. As soon as he started moaning, I was dripping once again. I knew that I was the only one that could make him feel like he was a man. I pulled out my silver bullet and gently rubbed it against my throbbing clit while deep throating him. The goal was to make him remember me whenever he fucked his perfect trophy wife despite that being my best friend.

The man was unable to fully be mine but at least we had our secret love affair. He tried to hold in his groans as much as he could. I never stopped sucking him as the bullet swirled on my clit. I was a pro in his mind and no other could compare making him lose his mind each and every time. My ego grew too big for my head because I knew I had him. As my climax slowly approached, I sped up the motions on his rod while both of his hands were now gripping my secured lace front with his mouth wide open trying not to scream out. He was ready to blast off as I moaned out from the climax that I was experiencing. I gripped his shaft a little tighter and sucked a little harder. I was going to make sure he knew that I was Thee Head Hunter of the Sip!

His legs were shaking so I eased off still stroking as my old friend shot all over my face. I smiled at the victory lap that I'd made. Just as I stood up ready to keep this freak show going, another damn knock came on the door. We both had completely forgotten about the fact that they were at Niecy's grand opening after party. It felt like it was just us this entire time. Dustin pulled his pants up and motioned for me to get dressed No matter how he felt in the moment, one thing for sure and two things for certain Thee Head Hunter of the Sip could never compare to that Million Dollar Pussy that he was married to. He wasn't about to get caught up with me at any time regardless of the history and love that we shared.

I pulled on his arm before he could leave out and said, "We need to talk Shad." He looked me up and down and replied, "What's wrong?"

I laid my heart out on the line as I answered, "I'm in love with you. I've been in love with you since we were fourteen. You can't tell me that you're not in love with me.... not after what we just did. It's clear that you don't love Niecy."

With a grimaced look, he replied, "Of course I love Niecy. I wouldn't have married her if I didn't but you're right I love you too. It's not what I planned on. It just is what it is, ya know?"

I pulled him in closer and tried to kiss him, but he turned his head while I said, "Baby just get a divorce. We could move where nobody knows us. We don't have to be here in Mississippi to be happy. We can make a home somewhere else."

Dustin pushed me off of him and said, "I'm not divorcing my wife. Why is this all of a sudden, a problem for you?"

I sighed as I said, "Because I'm pregnant Shad."

He shrugged and said, "Okay. What that got to do with me?"

With pain in my voice, I replied, "You're the father."

While shaking his head, he chuckled and said, "Nah, find somebody else."

Taken back by his arrogance, I said, "What the fuck you mean find somebody else? I've only been fucking you!"

Dustin grabbed my arms and slammed my back against the wall while whispering firmly in my ear, "Shut the fuck up! Bitch you ain't pregnant by me." He looked me in the eyes with coldness in his heart as he said, "We ain't never did shit because we're fucking cousins."

As soon as he released me, he walked out the door leaving me in tears remembering the lie that we've been telling Niecy for all of these years. He didn't want Niecy to know anything about our past because Dustin was the biggest hoe in Jackson, Mississippi and one more ex-girlfriend that Niecy considered a friend would've been the nail in the coffin for her especially his cousin. I never cared before but now I was carrying his seed and I wanted to keep it.

I wanted him as well and hoped like hell that love would've been enough to make him come home to me. Everybody knows a baby won't keep a man, but I had to try considering Niecy got pregnant at seventeen and it seemed like that's all Dustin needed to change his whoreish ways and become this perfect husband. After only days of them being married, he was still sneaking out to meet me in my bedroom and yet I didn't have his heart. Neither did Niecy. This I knew all too well.

The man only married her because she was the sole beneficiary of her grandmother's life insurance that was worth over four hundred thousand dollars, but Niecy was also the hustler that I never cared be and because of that, lady luck was on her side causing those thousands to quickly turn into millions.

Niecy had his pockets and that's something that I could never afford, and a baby was only going to make things worse. I gathered myself together and headed out, strutting right past Showout hoping to make him turn his head as he was always going to be next in my lineup of men but instead his eyes were fixated on Niecy. The woman of the hour.

Fraudulent Behavior

"Ain't nothin' but a gangsta party, ahh shit, you done fucked up now, you done put two of America's Most wanted in the same mother-fucken place at the same" - 2 Of Amerikaz Most Wanted by Tupac & Snoop Dogg

Imani

The way this day ended was no surprise. I could feel the vibe change as soon as Greg entered the room this morning. It had been maybe a couple of weeks since I was supposed to be in Gatlinburg and already I had been beaten and raped by a demented sociopath. He was unusually frustrated as he spoke, "You know Xavier, I've been wanting to meet you for some time now. Do you remember your ex Nicole McNeal?"

Greg had replaced my constraints with a shock collar and dared me to escape. I stayed put like a trained dog and every time he came back; he would sit in the center of the room and stroke his Glock as if he was jacking off while directing Lauren and I to perform the perfect love scene. Xavier was tied naked to a chair and forced to watch us have sex but any time that he became aroused, Greg would use a taser gun, inflicting pain and control over what Xavier was allowed to enjoy and what he wasn't. The days when I used to enjoy Lauren and Xavier, adoring and craving every moment with them was long gone. Nothing about this was pleasurable or desirable, however, we had to fake it until we made it. If we refused, complained, or acted as though we weren't enjoying ourselves, Greg would press a button on a remote causing the collars around our necks to shock us.

Xavier was in a daze could barely able to comprehend the events surrounding him. I had hoped he'd eventually master how to control his erections but that certainly was not the case. In mere seconds of us kissing, he would get aroused. Before we finished, he would have passed out from being tasered so many times. Lauren mentioned days before that she could see Greg growing tired of him and today seemed to be the day. While we just sat in the bed waiting for directions, Greg continued, "Come on Xavier! I know you remember."

Xavier mumbled, "Yeah, I remember."

Greg clapped his hands with a big creepy ass smile and said, "I knew you did. I bet you remember her daughter too. What was her name?"

Xavier looked confused as he replied, "What?"

Greg punched him in the face like the man owed him money and said, "Don't play coy with me Xavier. What was the daughter's name? It's a simple question."

He groaned, "I don't remember."

Greg smirked, "You don't remember huh?" He pulled out his Glock along with a picture out of his back pocket and held both up to Xavier and yelled, "What's the little girl's name?" Without hesitation, Xavier replied, "It's Amaia. I remember now. Her name is Amaia."

Greg chuckled and said, "I bet you do remember."

Xavier didn't say anything. He just sat there trembling and watching Greg as he took out another picture and said, "This is Amaia too." Greg seemed normal for just a moment as he looked over the picture with sadness in his voice as he continued, "This was the last picture I took of her. Her eighteenth birthday. This was the happiest day of her life and it was also the last day. I threw her this huge party, but my biggest mistake was inviting Nicole's sister.

It didn't take long for them to start arguing. Messed up a perfectly good party with some old ass drama. That simpleminded bitch said that Amaia was the reason that she had to leave you. Amaia started crying and ran away. Found her the next day lying dead in a ditch on Hooker St from an overdose. I guess being the reason for her mother's misery was too much for her to bear. Do you know how Amaia could be the reason that you and Nicole had to break up? What you didn't want kids or something?"

Xavier stuttered, "I I I I have no idea what that's all about."

Greg stroked his Glock as he asked, "Didn't she leave you?"

Fear had surfaced on his face as Xavier replied, "Yeah man she did but I never knew the reason why?"

With a chuckle, Greg nodded and said, "Fucking a ten year old ain't a reason?"

While shaking his head, Xavier said, "Nah, man that wasn't me."

Greg stood up as he replied, "It wasn't you?! Do you know how messy it was to learn about you? It wasn't until I tied her ass to a bed and soaked her ass with gasoline that she finally told the truth. It was a secret she'd take to her grave, so I had to put her ass in the grave to get it. My mother was sick and should've been locked away in prison for allowing that shit to happen to my sis-ter. I didn't fault Amaia or my aunt. She was nothing but a child but to know you took ad-vantage of my sweet baby sister. It really did something to me."

Greg began to pace as he waved his gun around and continued, "Maybe it was learning that my mother hated my baby sister for being more beautiful than her and fully gave her up to a grown ass man?" Greg stepped up to Xavier placing the gun to the side of his head as he said, "Nah she created you but to go along with some shit like that is what fucked me up." He tapped the gun on the side of Xavier's temple and said, "Nah, it was definitely learning about you taking my wife's innocence. That was the nail in the coffin for you."

Xavier tried to explain while Greg continued pointing his gun in his direction, "What you want me to say man?! I don't know why I like little girls. I don't know why I did it! If I could take it back, I would. I really would. I'd never touch her or another little girl. I won't even look their way. I'm sorry man. Please man!"

Lauren chimed in, "Baby it wasn't all him, I wasn't a baby and I didn't do anything I didn't want to do. Let's just leave. Just me and you. I'm sorry about all of this. We can go anywhere! Baby please put your gun down. We don't need any more blood on our hands."

POW!

Within seconds Greg had shot Xavier in the head as he said, "He's a grown ass man. He knew what the fuck he was doing. Why do you think he kept getting hard when y'all fucked? He still like that shit and if he could, he would've fucked you right now. He's not remorseful. He wanted me to spare his life and for what? He was only going to fuck up another kid's life. You were a child Lauren. What's his excuse?!"

Xavier sat there lifeless with a bullet hole in his head as the blood oozed from the hole and down his face. The walls painted with blood splatters while I just stared at Xavier and his beautiful brown glassed eyes staring right back at me.

Lauren was already sobbing as Greg started to untie Xavier and haul his body away whereas I couldn't speak. I couldn't move. I couldn't seem to form the tears that Lauren had flowing. I sat emotionless as the one man that I've loved for thirteen years was put down worse than a dirty dog. Those last few moments played over and over again in my head in slow motion. His voice I couldn't erase.

Finally, Lauren dried her tears and broke the silence between us, "You do know he's dead because of you."
With a face full of shock, I replied, "How the fuck is this my fault when you're the one that's supposed to be dead?!"
Lauren scoffed, "Insurance fraud is the easiest crime to get away with. Murder isn't! I wouldn't have ever known about Xavier if it wasn't for you!"
As I shook my head in disbelief, I sighed and said, "I wasn't the one that told Greg though."
Lauren hissed, "He's my husband Imani! I confided in him about Xavier because he took advantage of me. Of you! Of our age! He was a grown ass man and we were barely teenagers. Then he goes and marries that bitch of a mother of yours and thinks he can have his cake and eat it too. Yes I told him but if I had known that I was adding fuel to a forest fire I certainly would've shut the fuck up! Xavier was my first love. The last thing I wanted was to see him dead."
With a chuckle, I replied, "So you're mad because your first love was my first love was my mom's husband?! Yeah fuck that and you're actually shedding tears over this shit? What is wrong with you?"
If looks could kill, I would've burst into flames from the way that Lauren had started to look me up and down with pure disgust as I said, "It's you. It's always YOU! No guy ever chooses me especially after they meet you. Doesn't matter how good I look or how good I fuck them, they always choose you, but Xavier chose me, and Greg married me and look where I'm at now? A dead bitch with MY first love's brains splattered across the fucking walls and being a sex slave with the one bitch MY HUSBAND truly wants, and you have the nerve to ask me what's wrong with me? Bitch you're what's wrong with me. I wish I never met your fat busted ass."

I nodded as the pain from my ex best friend's words hit harder than any punch she could've thrown as I said with tears filling up in my eyes, "Wow okay."

Lauren was completely right about Xavier. It was completely my fault for Lauren's first time with Xavier and all the multiple sessions thereafter. I never understood why Lauren started hating Xavier so much because I was too self-absorbed in my own issues to care about anybody else's. I never seen him as this pedophile predator because everything I did was by choice. Or so I was led to believe.

There were no threats from him to kill my family or to keep it a secret. We didn't think things through. Xavier was sweet and careful in his gestures. For the most part I sought him out and he went along with everything. He didn't deny me anything. He gave me everything that I wanted and more. It was the thought of having his baby that I couldn't accept. That's when I started to really see how wrong everything that we'd been doing was.

I glanced over at my ex best friend and spoke softly, "Lauren, you're right about Xavier and I should've realized it a long time ago. Can we just work together to try and find a way out of this?"

Without hesitation she replied, "There's no way out of this Imani. Whatever Greg is going to do next, he's going to do it, whether we want him to or not."

I sighed as I replied, "We can't just give up."

Lauren yelled, "We're wearing shock collars locked in the basement in the fucking middle of nowhere. What about that don't you understand?!"

I groaned, "I understand it just fine Lauren but we have to make an escape plan before he kills both of us next."

She leaned in with a smile and whispered, "I already have a plan."

Before I could say another word, Greg had barged back in the room saying, "What plan Lauren?" She didn't speak. She looked at me and I looked back at her. Greg turned his focus to me and said, "What fucking plan huh?"

I didn't say a word. I didn't know how to reply because saying I didn't know would've only angered him more. I had mentally prepared myself for what was to come next. He came closer to me and began to snatch off my collar. A million thoughts were racing through my mind, *'Was there another line up at the door waiting to sodomize me or maybe he's about to take his anger out on me because I didn't answer him!'* He began to choke me as I felt him force himself inside of me.

This was something new. His violence wasn't as intimate as it was in this moment. He's been very particular in feeding me with a long handle spoon while allowing others to abuse me. His love for his wife denied him of being with me the way he truly desired unless it was with Lauren as well. There was nothing that I could do other than cry and gasp for air. Eventually, I gave up, closed my eyes, and accepted my fate.

***Divorce Par*ty**

"I don't care if we on the run. Baby as long as I'm next to you. And if loving you is a crime. Tell me why do I bring out the best in you" - Part II On The Run by Beyonce & Jay Z

Chanice

After tossing and turning all night, I finally got up with the intense urge to go through this man's phone. If the feeling was this strong then I already knew that whatever I found was going to bad. Sure enough, him and Alaysia had fallen in love with each with plans to move in together. It probably would've been hurtful if it wasn't comical as he had shared the same message to about ten other bitches that he'd fallen in love with and planning to move in with. These were some hellified impulses. I put his phone back on the nightstand and attempted to go back to sleep. I laid in bed beside him as he slept peacefully when I looked over at him and thought to myself, *'You just a dirty fucking dog.'* Just as the thought occurred, he barked in his sleep, and I was flabbergasted.

That intense urge to search his wallet came in stronger by the second so I got back up to satisfy this overwhelming feeling. When I opened the folds of his wallet, two mini yellow Ziploc bags dropped out. One was filled with a white powder and the other contained two blue pills. Inside the billfold sat three lifestyle condoms and a small red straw.

I've always been green when it came to drugs, but I wasn't stupid as I knew I was holding cocaine and jiggas in my hand. Everything started to make sense as to why he would have the sudden outbursts of anger or why random charges equaling over five thousand dollars

was coming out of joint bank account. The only thing I could think to say about the condoms was, *'At least he's using a condom!'*
Either way I was officially done. I wasn't angry. I was finally satisfied with a legit reason to let this man go without wondering what I could've done to be a better wife. I laid back down with a sense of peace and slept like a baby well into the afternoon before waking back up. When I did get up, he was up on his phone trying to hide what he was doing. I sat up and said, "I'm not angry when I say this, but we shouldn't be together. You know after all of these years, we'll always be friends but we're not in love with each other."
That same sad pitiful look appeared across his face that he had in Pastor Jones office as he said, "Don't do this. I don't want to get a divorce. I want to be with you. I love you. We've been doing this thing for too long. Sure we fight but that's normal. It's what people in love do. Are you saying I'm not worth fighting for?"
With the kids spending the weekend with their godmother, I got up and started getting dressed as if I was going to handle business with the club as I sighed and replied, "I'm saying that Destiny is on the way to pick you up and take you to your mom's house."
He stood up and said, "Niecy, what the fuck? We were just talking about opening my restaurant last night and now you want to break up? You know how ready I am for this. I see you with all this success and I ain't gone lie, I'm a little jealous. I want to be like you."
He continued without knowing that his words fell on deaf ears, "I mean I thought I wanted to do music but I'm just not feeling it but this restaurant baby. This restaurant is for me. I know it is. I've never wanted to do something so bad as this. It's my passion. I just didn't know it until now."
Emptiness is what I felt. I no longer cared what his dream was, and I wasn't investing into shit with him. Meme had once said to me, *'Niecy you need to find a man with a dream and God will bless that man.'* At the time I was only nine years old sitting in the small

bedroom that I shared with Meme in Quitman, Mississippi so I didn't understand why or how God would bless that man, but my mission was simple......find a man with a dream.

Meme didn't say shit about the many men that had dreams and no ambitions or about the ones with dreams and no potential. Dustin was a lesson learned for me. I needed a man that knew exactly what he wanted and how to get it without becoming America's Most Wanted. I smiled as I got the keys to my 20' Lincoln Navigator and said, "There's no rush on getting out but Destiny will be here soon so don't have her waiting and be nice to her please."

While I headed for the front door, he started following behind me with tears in his eyes as he said, "Baby please! Why are you doing this? It's like you don't want us together!"

After I hopped in my truck, I slid my shades on and before driving off with a straight face I replied, "Remember be nice."

He fell to his knees watching his dreams of success drive off heading to Hampton House Apartments. With Big K.R.I.T's *'King of the South'* blasting through my speakers, I danced freely as a single woman in my driver seat. As far as I was concerned, the rest was just paperwork, and I didn't give a damn about the law of the land. Between me and the good Lord, I was single and was going to act accordingly.

I parked my truck and eyed the apartment building with a knot forming in my stomach. This was my first time ever popping up on a man and my nerves had my hands slightly shaking as I thought to myself, *'Please don't call the police on me'* I guzzled down the bottle of water that sat in my cup holder as if it was Hennessy giving me liquor courage as I hopped out and went to the downstairs apartment door.

After a few knocks, Lester finally answered the door with a confused look on his face eyeing me up and down as she said, "You seen me calling you."

He replied with a smirk, "I was doing a live on TikTok."
As I rolled my eyes, I replied, "Oh are you going to let me join in?" His smile grew bigger as he nodded and stepped back allowing me to come in when he asks, "What if I had a girl over here?" I shrugged while surveying the apartment looking for any sign of a female and say, "I didn't come to fight. I came to hang out."
With a chuckle he replies, "You something else. How you been though? How are the kids?"
Instead of sugarcoating the truth like I normally would, I said, "Everything's a shitshow right now but I'm pushing through. Got anything to drink?"
A pained look surfaced on his face as his said, "Want some water?" I shrugged hoping for something much stronger as I turned on my playlist and vented to the one person that I thought would possibly understand me. He listened and gave the best sound advice that he had to give while cracking a few jokes as he said, "I can't picture you kicking a door in. That's like watching Elmo on some gangsta shit." While he had himself a good ole laugh, I glared at him as I said, "Elmo be with the shits when it comes to Rocco though."
He nodded and said, "Yeah but Elmo ain't kicking doors in on Sesame Street." With a shrug, I spun around in his office chair and replied, "Probably because he ain't got no fucking feet."
Our conversation continued as we switched topic after topic until we were up making TikToks for his page. He had a nice following, but he hadn't gone viral yet. Between trending dances and skits, we ended up roasting each other on his live which brought his numbers up significantly. When we finished, he put me on to navigating the world of social media more than just entertaining family and friends. He had my full attention as I wanted to learn as much I could about social media marketing. It wasn't hard for me to fall for a fine ass man like him that could teach me something actually worth knowing.

It wasn't long before my stomach started rumbling as I clapped my hands together and said, "Okay get ya black ass up so we can go get something to eat. I'm hungry." Reluctantly he followed suit and grabbed his motorcycle keys and helmet while handing me the spare helmet. I shook my head trying to shake my nerves away from riding a motorcycle for the first time as he chuckled and helped me put the helmet on, he says, "Don't worry. I got you."

There was no doubt in my mind that he did but that didn't stop the butterflies fluttering into huge knots in my stomach while my mouth dried up worse than the Sahara Desert. My only hope was to make it to the bike without going completely weak in the legs and dropping right where I stood. He hopped on his purple Haybusa with ease and held out his gloved hand for me to join him. I figured a walk on the wide side couldn't be too bad as I grabbed his hand and slid on behind him. While he zipped down the road, I held on for dear life trying not to crush his ribs. The ride was comforting and peaceful as I remembered how it felt to ride on the back of my pawpaw's F150 in the country or whenever I zoomed through the yard on the go kart.

Those butterflies disappeared within an instant as I realized I was scared for nothing. I could ride holding on to Lester any and every time he offered. When we arrived at our destination, hunger suddenly reappeared with a vengeance. After getting off the bike, I finally noticed that we'd arrived at Southern Delights which was a brand new upscale restaurant in Madison. It was the second most talked about hot spot in Jackson as my cabernet was still reigning in the number one spot. When we entered, Lester made himself right at home, bypassing the hostess stand and going to a corner booth in the back of the restaurant.

The vibe was low key as the lights were dimly lit with black cushioned booths and a huge bar in the center. From the way that Lester walked in, it was obvious that he was probably a regular as

a pretty snow bunny made her way to us with a smile and said, "Ooooo Showout who's this?"
I didn't think it was possible for a dark skin man to actually blush but there he was turning completely red in the cheeks as he said, "This is my old lady Niecy."
With a chuckle, I say, "Really old lady?"
That infectious smile appeared as he continued, "We've known each other a long time Niecy."
I squinted my eyes at him wondering if he had finally remembered our childhood romance or if he was simply referring to how we met at Magoo's. Before I could get my answer, the pretty snow bunny says, "I'll let Beau know you're here. What can I get y'all to drink?"
He ordered a Bourbon & Honey while I kept things cute and ordered a Passion Fruit Margarita. We sat next to each other with his arm stretched out behind me as I leaned into him snapping up a few pictures simply because I had started to dip my toes into the art of photography and being in this restaurant had me feeling myself when a tall handsome vanilla king approach our table sporting a nice brown beard that made me picture him as a lumberjack in the woods of Shubuta as he smiled and said, "What's up Showout?!"
Him and Lester shook hands while Lester said, "Hey man! I had to bring my old lady out to your restaurant."
The grizzly bear of a mountain man nodded his head as he looked my way and said, "Damn Showout, you better keep this one in the house." He took a quick look around his restaurant and looked back at me and said, "You are way too pretty to be with this man. If you need help escaping, just let me know."
I couldn't contain my laughter as Lester replied, "Hey man! What? I'm not holding her hostage." He looked at me and asked, "Baby, am I holding you hostage?"
I shook my head and replied, "Nah baby it's just Stockholm Syndrome."

His friend's laughter was contagious as we all laughed until the tears started to well in our eyes. He went on to ask, "What a pretty lady like you trying to eat tonight?"

I replied, "I like steak but what's the chef's special tonight?"

He nodded and replied, "Sayless. You'll be biting into heaven when I'm done." Just as Lester was about to say his order, his friend interrupted him by saying, "I already know what you want man."

With Lester's hands raised in the air and his face scrunched up, his friend walked away as I say, "So he's the reason that you can just walk in like you own the place." He rested his hand on my shoulder and it sent vibrations throughout my body as he replied, "Oh yeah Beau is my biker bro. He just opened this restaurant, but he's been cooking for forever. Pretty fucking amazing at it too."

I looked around surveying the atmosphere as my money making wheels started spinning in my head when I asked, "Hey, what's your dream?"

It was a question he had never been asked as he pondered for a moment before replying, "When I was younger, I thought about opening up a dance studio. Maybe even a dance team and enter into some dance competitions but I'm too old for that now. But you know I'll still bust a move though."

He appealed to my better nature in many ways and although he was still legally married, I adored the man that sat beside me and wanted to see him happy. Some would say take your time and quite frankly time was of the essence. I was ready to seize the moment with this beautiful dark chocolate God of a man. With a sweet smile, I said, "I have a building that's perfect for a dance studio. All my kids do is dance, and I can't teach them the style of dance that you do but I'd love for you to teach them."

As he nodded, he said, "Yeah but I don't have the time to get the studio up and running or to get together a dance team. I'm working about five different jobs right now just to stay out of trouble."

I giggled and shrugged while saying, "You should probably quit then."

Lester contemplated my offer of having his dream studio while hoping that accepting this opportunity didn't mess up what was developing between us. With a look of admiration in his eyes, he smiled and caressed my thick thighs as he leaned in closer and whispered into my ear, "Well I guess this is my two weeks' notice."

I could feel Lester's soft warm lips planting a kiss on my neck. While closing my eyes, I tried my best to keep my composure as I spoke low and seductively, "Sir, don't get raped in this booth."

His hand gently caressed my cheek gliding down to my chin as he lifted it and kissed me as if we had the entire restaurant to ourselves. I embraced the moment and we continued into an intense make out session in the back of Southern Delights and he was definitely a southern delight for me.

By the time we released each other, it was obvious what our next plan was as my hunger had suddenly subsided with a different hunger now in place. My mouth watered craving to taste him while my pretty pink panties were officially soaked.

The pretty snow bunny from before came back out and gave us our plates. In front of me sat a plate of Herb Crusted Filet of Salmon while Lester held out his hand for me to take as he started to pray over our food while a plate of Carne Asada Steak sat in front of him. We ate over light conversation while trying each other's meal when he asked, "How's your brother?"

I replied without processing the question as I said, "Well he was in prison for a felony hit and run but he's out now. I gave him a job working security at my cabernet." After the words escaped my mouth, I exclaimed, "Wait! So, you know my brother?"

He scoffed and rolled his eyes as he said, "You know damn well I know your brother." With a smile, I nodded and replied, "Took you long enough."

As he gripped my thigh, he looked at me and said, "I've known since Magoo's."

My body was overheating from his touch making this entire interaction damn near impossible to withstand as I said, "Well Tutu, why are you just now saying something?"

He shrugged as he said, "I was waiting on you to say something."

I looked up into his eyes as I spoke coyly and said, "I'm gone beat yo ass when we get home."

In the sexiest way, he licked his lips and leaned over to whisper in my ear, "And I'm gone wear yo beautiful ass out."

There was no reason for me to reply. It was time for the check. It was time to go. Just like clockwork, Beau had reappeared with a smile on his face as he inquired about the meal, "So pretty lady what did you think?"

I smiled and closed my eyes as I gave him a chef's kiss while saying, "Magnifique!"

Sometime later and Lester and I were tonguing each other down and ripping our clothes off in his bedroom. My shitshow had fully turned around as I was reeling in the feels of a blissful dreamland fantasy with my childhood sweetheart.

The Masquerade Ball

"Even though I'm only in your town for one night. I got enough time to rush through the drill. Girl, tell me how you feel deep down inside."
- Feels So Right by Lloyd

Imani

Dozens of people poured out to endure a night of anonymity and laughs while I walked around surveying the room watching others as they gravitated towards somebody they knew or wanted to get to know. I felt like I had stepped inside of *'These Are The Times'* music video wearing a full-length royal blue ballgown snugging my full figure frame. You'd think I would've gotten the matching mask with the stick instead of the silver one that stays on but messing up my hair was the least of my problems. I'd been living in OKC for a year and had yet to make any new friends. I could blame it on being busy with work and yet I was the part owner of a massage parlor in Uptown with my best friend who was constantly away doing runway shows in Paris and Milan.

Even with working for myself and making my own hours, I had yet to find the time to explore the city. I thought joining a Facebook group would help and at first, I was excited for this meet and greet. The members in the group seemed outgoing and just as destitute of friendship as I was. For the most part, I was just a lurker. I'd like a post here and there and then move on to another app altogether, but I forced myself to get out and meet somebody tonight. Male or female, it didn't matter!

The decorated black and gold accents made the room alluring in every sense of the word. At one table a few females had started to make small talk. I figured I would start there until I felt the staggered breathing of a raspy voice say, "Good evening beautiful."
I didn't have to turn around as he walked from behind me. I looked him up and down admiring his approach as well as his attire. He really took the dressing up to heart. The other men had on ordinary suits, but this guy had went all out wearing a black and gold cavalier vest over his shirt. Normally seeing a guy with a cane like his would give me pimp vibes but the cane was a great accessory with his gold mask. If England had a black king, he was definitely him. I couldn't help the impure thoughts that begin to invade my mind as he introduced himself, "I'm Greg. Thank you for coming out tonight."
I blushed when he took my hand and kissed it as I replied, "My pleasure. I'm Nini. Do all of the guys here greet a woman like this?" He shrugged, "I can't speak for the others, but my mom insisted on raising a gentleman."
His smile was infectious and his smell intoxicating. I could've jumped him right then and there especially with this ball taking place in the ballroom of the Embassy Hotel. It's been so long since I'd been with somebody, and he was perfect in every way. We sipped some champagne as we talked, and I learned that he was an NBA player for the OKC Thunder as well as the host of the group and party. I explained to him how I wanted to meet a friend and he thought he would introduce me to his new friend girl. There stood my best friend, Lauren, looking stunning. She wore a black strapless gown with a train. Her hair all pinned to one side with barrel curls flowing down.
Lauren had known Greg for a while and never once mentioned anything to me about knowing him. It was clear to me that they were more than friends. It could've been the sips since she was

drinking something much stronger than champagne. She couldn't keep her hands to herself and the same for him. I wasn't at all upset about it because I too wanted to be more than his friend. When the ball came to an end, Greg walked away to tend to business while Lauren asked, "Hey my honeybee, you wanna hit the club up after this?" I figured why not since I had nothing better to do. Lauren informed me, "I brought back some pieces from Milan that you might like. They're upstairs in Greg's suite. That's cool?"

I shrugged and we made our way upstairs to Greg's suite. Lauren made sure that I knew that this was her first and last night staying with Greg. His lifestyle was too much for her taste. I laughed while Lauren put some music on and handed me a bottle of green apple Ciroc to occupy my time while she dug through her Hermes bags of designer clothes. An hour later and we had tried on what felt like a million different articles of clothing while completely downing the bottle of Ciroc and working on a second one. We were both winding and singing in only our underwear when a throwback came on. I was all in the zone singing, *'And you ain't gotta call me ya boo, just as bad as you wanna fuck, I wanna fuck too!'*

Lauren was in front of me singing with our legs linked together as we grinded on each other to the beat. I wondered if my best friend was just in party girl mode or if she was about that life because I was feeling rather frisky. Lauren has always been beautiful to me, and sure curiosity had gotten the best of us in the past but since we been adults, she's decided to do things a lot differently. She's always been like a sister to me, so I always respected her wishes but seeing her in nothing, but these white lace thongs and matching bra was everything to me. Lauren placed her hands on my neck and pulled me closer while she darted her tongue in my mouth. As I cupped Lauren's supple ass, we grinded harder to the beat of *'The Nasty Song'* by Lil Ru. Moans started escaping from both of us, mixing with the sounds of Lauren's freaky ass playlist.

I could feel kisses on my ass cheeks making their way up my back and to my neck. I opened my eyes to see Lauren easing down to my aching pussy. That didn't explain the nibbling that I felt on my neck. Lauren spread my chubby legs open and slid my black lace boy shorts to the side. I tilted my head back as I heard that same raspy voice from before say, "I'm sorry. I couldn't help myself."
I replied with a whisper, "Don't stop."
Not sure who I was actually talking to, but I didn't want Lauren nor Greg to stop. I was enjoying them both. In that same second, Lauren slid two fingers inside of me and I shuddered from the satisfying wave of pleasure that came over my body. With Greg cupping both of my breasts, Lauren began to circle the tip of her tongue around my clit while Greg continued to plant kisses on my body. The music seemed to enhance every single thing they did. It was perfect. They were in harmony to each other and the beat. I screamed out in bliss from Lauren slurping up juices like an ice cream cone melting on a hot summer's day. She stood up and smiled saying, "My turn."
Greg nodded his head, and she went and sat back on the bed with one leg propped up. I climbed into the bed on all fours and pulled her lace thongs off, slinging them to the floor. In no time, I was two fingers deep tickling Lauren's insides while rubbing her pearl with my thumb causing Lauren's hips to sway to Tha Joker's *'Blow Your Back Out'*. Greg walked up to my perfectly positioned ass and smacked it. I just knew he was about to enter me from behind, but I was sadly mistaken when I noticed him get on the side of the bed and Lauren starting to gobble him up. My mouth watered, craving my own taste of his kingkong sized chocolate bar. The mixture of ecstasy filled the air as Lauren couldn't continue to control herself. She started to squirt all over the bed causing me to chuckle and say, "Oh baby, I wasn't done with you."

I went in to devour my best friend in the way I knew she truly wanted. Lauren screamed out, "Fuckkk!"

I hummed, "Mmm hmm." Knowing the vibrations would be electrifying to her already sensitive pearl. I lightly suckled her while Lauren managed to swallow Greg's load, not leaving a single drop behind. He got off of the bed and made his way back to me. His sweet friend tapping my pretty almond brown ass a few times and my hums grew into groans of anticipation for his next move. He teased me with his sweet friend by slowly rubbing the head against my pussy. I wanted to feel him inside of me so damn bad. Lauren was pulsating inside of my mouth while moaning, "Shiiiittttttt!!!"

When I finally finished, Lauren was laughing, while Greg was waiting ready at attention. I turned around to meet his sweet friend face to face and motioned for Greg to come closer as I sat on the edge of the bed. I took his sweet friend inside of my mouth with ease and commenced to sucking his soul out. As I sucked, Lauren sat beside me and began to rub my wet pussy while kissing on my neck and shoulder blade. This only made me want to taste his cream even more. He ran his hands through my sew in as he moaned out, "Damn."

Suddenly, I could feel the warmth of his cream hitting the back of my throat causing me to slow down just a bit. When I was done, I closed my eyes and laid back on the bed, allowing Lauren to continue strumming the strings of my pretty guitar. Lauren moved her hands and before I could open my eyes, Greg had replaced her fingers with his warm thick tongue. I though Lauren was wonderful, but Greg was perfect. He made me melt inside of his mouth while Lauren suckled on my breasts and my fingers now strumming the strings of Lauren's pretty guitar. Greg caused me to become all off beat making Lauren giggle.

She knew the effect that Greg was having on her best friend as he darted his thick long tongue in and out which only made me buck each and every time. He was truly turning me out in the worse way, if that was even possible to do. I considered myself to be somewhat of a pro in the game of satisfaction, but Greg was proving that I was nothing but a beginner just learning how to shoot my shot. When my moans grew louder and turned into screams of pleasure, he pulled me in closer and started shaking his head making me lose my ever loving mind and the little bit of composure that I had left was gone.

He took both of our hands and pulled us off of the bed while he laid on his back. Lauren grinned as she looked at me and said, "You ready to ride?"

I laughed and got on top with the quickness to show her just how ready I was. He caressed my thighs and gripped my ass as I rode him slowly. He bit his bottom lip and looked at me with admiration rather than lust. That moment was exactly what I had pictured when I first met him downstairs, so I sped up. He threw his head back and gripped me harder. Lauren climbed on the bed and placed herself on his face. Together, we rode him in unison like the best friends that we were, kissing each other until he couldn't take either of us a second longer. Lauren hopped off of his face saying, "Damn, I thought you would've had this on lock."

Greg smirked and replied, "I got something for yo ass. Come here!" He made me get up and had Lauren laying down as he pulled her to the edge of the bed and started jackhammering her while instructing me to ride Lauren's face. Although I was a little hesitant, wondering if Lauren could handle herself, I went ahead with it and sure enough Lauren was handling herself just fine. He made us stop midway and had us scoot back on the bed, I spun around and leaned down into the sixty-nine position with Lauren.

Greg smiled as he stroked himself to the scene of us pleasing each other. He rubbed my ass and smacked it, once again making me yearn for my own rough nasty session with him. It wasn't long before I was moaning like crazy as Greg had entered his fingers inside of me while Lauren continued to have her way on my clit until I tapped out. I rolled over to the side of Lauren while hearing both Lauren and Greg laugh at me.

I mustered up just enough energy to get back inside of Lauren with my ass tooted in the air enticing Greg to do whatever he wanted. He happily walked up to me and gave me exactly what I had been desiring the entire night as he entered me slowly and started to pump in and out. When his speed increased, so did mine and Lauren went moaning crazy.

Greg started to sway his hips as he danced inside my walls, so I did the same with my fingers inside of Lauren making her squirt once again. Seconds later and I was throwing it back while feeling my last climax quickly approaching. Within no time, Greg was groaning and trying to catch his breath as he started to slow down his pumps. The night had ended while we showered together....

SPLASH!

As I jerked from the freezing cold-water that Greg had just doused on my face, he knocked on the wall behind me as he said, "Wake up sleepy head! We've been waiting for you to join us." My eyes becoming more focused as I looked around with regret wishing so badly that I could turn back the hands of time.

ACT FOUR

DEPRESSION

"There are wounds that never show on the body that are deeper and more hurtful than anything that bleeds."
-Laurell K. Hamilton, Mistral's Kiss-

RECEIVING GIFTS

"If I gave you diamonds and pearls
Would you be a happy boy or a girl
If I could I would give you the world
But all I can do is just offer you my love"
-Prince-

No White Angels

"It's another day's journey and I'm glad... I'm glad about it, I'm so glad to be here." = Another Day's Journey by LaShun Pace

Jackson, Mississippi
2014 AD
-Women's Intuition-

Chanice

The sun shined brightly into the room where I was asleep in my bed with Meme in this little apartment that looked as if it had been abandoned. Everything seemed so run down on the inside, but the sun shined in so brightly as if someone had come and snatched the curtains off during the hottest day in Mississippi. There were torn clothes and sheets everywhere. The bathroom looked as if the toilet had overflowed. The tub and shower hadn't been cleaned in what looked like forever. I woke up having to go to the bathroom, but I kept seeing my mom walking around.

I became upset believing that Meme lied about cremating my mom. I looked to the side of me which was a doorway that leads out to another room where my mom is laying in her bed. I tried to wake Meme up to tell her that I kept seeing my mom. Meme doesn't even open her eyes and says with a groggy voice, "It's not really Katrina. It's remnants of her is all. It's just memories of what her and JohnJohn used to do. Use my bathroom instead."

I decided to lay back down instead of going to the bathroom until I realized that she said my brother's name as well and I reply, "Wait did you just tell me that JohnJohn is dead?"

She finally opens her grey shaky eyes and looks at me as she sighs, "Yes."

I ask, "When?"

She replies, "Sunday."

I begin to freak out thinking that Sunday was the day before and I start to cry and lay back down to hold Meme's hand as I ask, "Are you okay?"

Meme replies, "I have to go." and then she rushes out of the bed and walks out of the apartment.

I scream out, "Wait for me!"

But she doesn't. Instead, she continues walking out of the apartment until she disappears into the clouds as if the apartment is floating in the sky. Tia and Tamara were still just toddlers trying to follow behind her as I dashed to the bathroom while calling their names but somehow, I ended up in my mom's bathroom which was worse than Meme's bathroom which made me sprint back to her Meme's bathroom.

When I flushed the water splashed back out like a fire hydrant and I woke up lost and confused as to why I would have a dream like that. So many times, I've dismissed these dreams as just me having eaten something too spicy, but I've since learned to pay more attention to my dreams and pray harder after each one. It was just something about this dream that I can't seem to shake. I sensed something was wrong but instead of thinking too much about it, I dismissed it as just a weird dream.

I didn't allow the what ifs and worries to plague my thoughts instead I sat up in my bed and finished making the preparations for Tia and Tamara's fifth birthday bash. My phone vibrated showing an unknown MS number and I ignored it while continuing to work on the menu for the party. The theme was *'The Princess and The Frog'* and I had gone all out with planning this since this was my first time throwing a birthday party.

I wanted it to be extra special for my girls so I handmade everything myself, from the colorful tutus and birthday shirts to the amazing King Cake and beignets. There was a life sized balloon of Tiana and a happy birthday banner that I had strung together on birthday streamers. I only cared to use the colors Gold, Purple, and Green and insisted there be a seafood boil for a bunch of five years old because it was mandatory to be as authentic to New Orleans as possible. Thanks to living deep in the country, I decided to set up an obstacle course for the kids like the ones I used to have during field day in elementary school. One thing me and my classmates loved was trying to race through the course while hopping in a sack or walking like a crab so I knew that these kids would go completely nuts over this one huge game until it was time to eat and open presents. The party wasn't for another two weeks but I had already filled my closet with over twenty gift bags filled with chips, juice, candy, and mini toys as a thank you for each kid that came. The vibrations of the second phone call made me stop and answer the phone, when an older female's voice spoke, "Good morning. Is this Chanice Brunner?"

I replied, "Good morning. Yes, this is her."

The caller continued, "This is the morning supervisor of the nursing home where you're listed as next of kin for Ms Linda Brunner Liggins. Is this correct?"

Flashbacks of her dream flooded in as she replied, "Yes, that's correct."

The caller said, "I regret to inform you that she passed away in her sleep last night."

The feeling was that of a hollow tree. Dark and empty. An undeniable pain formed into tears and the inability to breathe which consumes you and causes you to lose track of time and space took over me. It's a feeling that I've dreaded since the day my Uncle Keith died. After having already lost so much, I knew one day I'd lose my Meme as well. So, when her health started to take a turn for the worse, I placed her in a nursing home so that she would have the proper care she needed.

I visited her as much as I could but working and being a single mother made that hard to do and now Dustin was trying to step up and be a father five years after the birth of our daughters. It was all proving to be a lot, but I was certainly giving it all that I had and staying prayed up about it. I dreaded having to plan a funeral and I didn't know how to tell my girls that their great grandmother was gone right before their birthday. After hanging up, I called Dustin even though he was at work at McDonalds as the daytime shift leader. He answered on the second ring, "Hey what's up?"

Trying to accept the words without breaking down on the phone, I say, "Meme died last night in her sleep."

He was calm as he said, "Damn. I'm leaving work right now."

We hung up and I allowed the tears to flow freely down my cheeks. It seemed like it only took seconds to replay all of our beautiful memories together. Time seemed much longer in the moment than it did reliving them. If only I could turn back the hands of time and be a better granddaughter. I cried harder over the mistakes that I'd made. The harsh words I recalled saying as a rebellious teen. The days when I didn't call when I knew that I probably should have. It all hit so hard as I wished I'd said I loved her more.

I would've paid more attention to the recipes. I would've listened more to the history lessons of our family. I would've catered to her more and made sure that my love was known. Although I wished I could've done more, I knew that Meme was very proud of me. There was never an ounce of doubt in her mind that her grandbaby would become successful just as she told me that I would be.

It had only been a week since the last time that we'd sat down and talked about everything under the sun and everybody. Meme looked at me with hope in her eyes as she said, "Baby, I see you sitting in an office behind a big desk one day."

I raised my eyebrows while shaking my head as I replied, "Nah, I can't do no desk job.

I have to be hands on."

Meme chuckled and continued, "Because being a pimp is so rewarding huh?"

I darted my eyes at Meme, silently invoking my right to plead the fifth while Meme continued, "Oh you thought I didn't know huh? I tell you this, I'd rather my grandbaby be the pimp than the hoe."

I chuckled and looked away still slightly embarrassed at what all Meme may actually know. She was a lot like Myrtis when it came to just knowing some stuff. God gave her dreams and visions constantly. I couldn't do any wrong without her telling me about a dream she had. She'd tell me how she was a true prophet of the Lord and I'd just listen.

All I ever seemed to do was listen until things started happening in my life and I wanted to talk and had nobody to talk as all of my heavy hitters, my mentors, the people I turned to for guidance in this messed up world was out of the game. Meme went on to say, "It's more to life than what you see if you just believe. Don't settle for no trash baby. God got something big with your name on it and all trash gone do is make sure to fuck it up. Leave the past in the past. Don't double back."

I knew all too well that Meme was referring to me and Dustin getting back together as I replied, "Meme, he's the kids father. He says he's wants us to try and be a family."

Meme turned her nose up while shaking her head as she laughed and said, "He ran off with Destiny but that wasn't his destiny." She looked at me as her eyes flickered specs of golden embers as she smiled and said, "That man gives me hives. He act like he don't mind playing booty games too. Gotta watch his ass Niecy. Something ain't right about that man."

While not trying to upset Meme, I say sarcastically, "Don't worry. I'll watch as well as pray like I always do."

Unconvinced and feeling weary, she re-plies, "I'm proud of you baby. My baby! You are a good mom and I know you'll be a good wife too. One thing I want you to remember is this...... it's not how you start the race but how you finish it."

As always it didn't take long before Meme was dozing off in mid conversation from taking her medicine. I tucked her in and went back to my apartment in Ridgeland Ranch. Now days later, I was sitting in my dining room in the salon chair of my makeshift salon when Dustin walked through the door as I was wiping my tears away. Without saying a word, I felt his warm embrace from behind causing me to find the last bit of strength I had to push through for her girls.

I didn't want anybody's input on how this funeral was going to go as Meme and I had already planned it out months before her de-cline. If anybody got up trying to sing *'His Eye Is On The Sparrow'* I was going to pop their ass right in the mouth in front of everybody. I went to my computer to design the obituary in remembrance of Uncle Keith with Meme's sweet smiling face floating in the clouds as doves circled around her head.

The millions of pictures on the inside with a tint of pink is what I wanted for Meme as well, but I didn't want a bunch of tears and sad sob stories because Linda Jean was a hellcat much like her mother Myrtis and this was a celebration of a homegoing that only true saints understood. If they weren't shouting for God, then it was best that they stayed their asses at home. My mom said to me once, *'You're supposed to cry when a baby is born because of the cruelness of this world, and you're supposed to rejoice when a person dies because they're going home to be with the Lord'* and if I could've had a brass band marching through the streets then I would've but I settled for some good old fashion southern style church instead.

Dustin made sure to have blunts and liquor on deck and at times it's what I needed but never what I wanted. It seemed as if he truly was just as heartbroken to know how much the mother of his children had lost and caused us to come back together in what everybody believed to be true love. It's quite possible that I never loved Dustin as anything more than a friend.

I understood that in life you'll experience a number of loves but only one would be the realest and the truest of them all. I didn't put my faith in men to be that love for me. Instead, I only ever looked to my Heavenly Father to provide that true love for me. I loved Dustin for who he was and never what I wanted him to be or had hoped he could be. We met at my first house party. My first taste of freedom. I remember Fatima being so mad at me for not wearing what she said to wear to her birthday party. Something simple, a white spaghetti strap shirt and blue jeans.

"Girl where is your white shirt?" Fatima asked while rolling her eyes and turning to look at the rest of the girls wearing the suggested attire correctly.

I lifted the black shirt and replied, "I have it on underneath. I wasn't sure if it was cool since it's beige."

Fatima scoffed and Brinae said, "It's cool Niecy, at least you made it. Let's go over the routine before people start showing up. Just take your black shirt off before the party starts."

I nodded and got in position. The lineup consisted of four girls, from shorted to tallest. Brinae was first. I really loved me some Brinae. She was cinnamon brown like me but a couple inches shorter than me. I'm 5'2 and at the time I was skinny like a stick whereas Brinae was thicker than a snicker. I was the only one in the lineup with no butt or any kind of frame to be exact. A little boobage is the only thing that I had.

At Jim Hill, Brinae was already so pretty and outgoing. Making friends wasn't hard for her but I felt connected to her after the grapevine shared with everybody how she was having problems at home with her mom which resulted in her leaving to stay with a relative at the beginning of the school year. We had just auditioned for our high school's version of Delta Sigma Theta for a week and then some days later she just stopped coming to school. I related to her pain. Home was simply a four-letter word learned in school and not the warm comforting place we all seen on The Cosby Show or Family Matters.

Brinae introduced me to her play cousin, Fatima, who was cool with me before I walked into her birthday party wearing this black on black outfit. It wasn't my intention to stand on somebody else's special day. All of my blue jeans were dirty because being in that very moment required sacrifices. My fresh start came with a change of lifestyle, and I didn't mind having dirty clothes for a month or two because I had freedom and a clean slate from the rumor mill that surrounded Meme's house. I desperately accepted that change, but I didn't need them knowing that. What happens at home, stays at home. *'We don't tell our family business'* is what Meme always says. I had become used to the struggle, but I had hoped that one day I would get away and travel the world. I wouldn't dare say no to the right opportunity.

Brinae's play cousin was the tallest of us all, so she was placed at the end of our line, Fatima was a powerhouse in my eyes. She's completely beautiful, a talented dancer and singer, and of course smart. She reminded me of my cousin, Sheena. Tall and light as a sugar biscuit. Compared to me, these girls were extremely popular but that could've been because everybody at our high school were friends from middle school or the neighborhood whereas I was the new girl in the neighborhood and at school. I was in unfamiliar territory and in desperate need of friends when I spotted a familiar face with Imani being my mom's best friend's daughter and supposedly my cousin. Imani introduced me to Brinae during choir and we bonded over everything. We loved singing and dancing but then our love for reading caused us to see boys in a totally different light. We combated our hormones by starting a dance team similar to the Dancing Dolls and this was our first party to show off our moves and impress the boys that came.

Between me and Fatima stood Shannon who I had seen before in class and at the auditions. She was another dazzling sugar biscuit that was just as goofy as me. I wasn't sure of Shannon's home life because the grapevine only cared to speak about her under her clothes than her family life. It was really hard to believe that she was doing so much. I couldn't understand where she found the time for boys and class but word in the hallways was that lil mama was coming through like a wrecking ball as soon as the report card said, *'Promoted to 9th Grade?'* Didn't make any sense to me considering she was by far the prettiest of us all. All Shannon had to do was walk in the room and the guys would swoon to her. It's beauty like hers that made me question my own sexuality. She was talented, outgoing, and outshined all of us. She was the only one of us that actually made the school's majorette team, the step team, excelled in choir, and had style. It was as if she was really just doing us a favor by joining our little team.

Shannon and Brinae were the true dancers, so they made up the routine. I didn't consider myself a dancer because Uncle Keith didn't allow me to watch BET or listen to rap and hip hop. During the summers, I'd visit my mom and she'd try her best to cram years' worth of Uncle Luke and Dru Hill that she swore the kids around her enjoyed. Un-fortunately, I preferred singing my heart out to *'I Hope You Dance'* by Lee Ann Womack and the only cd that I had with black artists was a MoTown complication I got for free in one of those get five cds for $1 ads that came in the mail.

My favorite song on the album was *'I Can't Help Myself'* by The Four Tops. My mom al-ways encouraged me to get up and dance when I was with her at her best friend's house as Imani and the other kids would put on a show twerking, dipping, shaking, dropping, rolling, popping, and whatever else they were dared to do. My mom celebrated dancing and music. She's the only reason I ever wanted to join a dance team.

When the guest started to pour in, Brinae and Fatima got excited and directed the lineup to the bedroom. Fatima was smiling hard as ever as she said, "Girl he came!"

Brinae replied, "I told you he would and girl he brought Chris too! That's my man so hands off. He's the light skinned one with the green eyes."

I etched a mental note of the description of the guy that Brinae was claiming. I didn't know much about *'girl code'* but I knew not to mess with their man. Luckily for me they hadn't noticed that my black shirt never came off. My beige spaghetti strap shirt had my little boobs looking like I was Dolly Parton and that had me so uncomfortable. I knew nobody at this party, and I spotted a grown man off in the kitchen during the practice, so I simply folded the bottom of my shirt up and followed the girls out the door.

The boys were standing at the end of the hall where it splits off to the living room and the den like some sharks waiting on chum, propped up on the wall trying to be cool. I peeped Chris within seconds since he was the only light skinned boy in the group. I've never been attracted to light skinned boys. I never liked Bow Wow or Lil' Romeo but I was loving everything about Sammie, Mario, Tyrese, and Usher.

The entire group of boys were a bunch of darkies. Temptation at its finest! They were covering the entry to the den where the party was and as soon as I turned away from them heading to the living room, one of them grabbed my arm and pulled me to him. My first instinct was to punch him dead in the face but instead I jerked my arm back while giving him a death stare. He leaned back with his hands held up like *'Don't shoot.'*

The entire time I tried to ignore him, but he was the cutest of them all. I had already pegged him as a cocky little asshole from how he grabbed my arm. After we finished our dance this guy and his group starts to dance their little dance. Their steps looked a thousand times better than ours. I was only slightly impressed though. The back of his black windbreaker said, *'Blue Satisfaction'* and that's when I knew he was going to be one of those extra freak nasty fellas like Pretty Ricky but he wasn't at all like them.

Once they finished their dance, he never danced again. I had dismissed the thought of him as nothing else stood out about him. He talked to every girl that was there and he kept eyeing me like he wanted to talk but was too afraid. Probably because I was in my mean girl mode from him pulling my arm like a heathen.

As the party died down, I tried calling my mom but no answer. She had fallen asleep as always. If I called enough, I knew she'd eventually feel the vibrations and answer the phone, but my phone died by the time she finally answered. I asked Brinae, "Hey girl do you think I could use your phone to call my mom?"

She took her phone out of her back pocket and her face frowned up as she said, "Oooo damn girl mine just died. Let me ask around and see who got a phone you can use."

Brinae walked off while I stood in the doorway of the living room, slightly hidden from sight. I wasn't a party girl or the popular girl. I didn't like attention. My desire was not to be seen in the spotlight. I preferred being at home and talking on the phone. I guess I had been sheltered for too long to actually appreciate the freedom I had finally been given.

I was learning how to be social but, in that moment, my social meter was overflow-ing, and I was ready to go home. I looked up and seen Brinae coming back. She says while holding that heathen's arm as if she forced him to come over, "Hey this is my play cousin, Dustin. He said that you can use his phone."

I looked back and forth between the two of them feeling like this was a set up but even more surprised that he would let a mean girl like me use his phone, so I asked, "Are you sure?" He shrugged his shoulders and replied, "Yeah, it's cool."

After my mom answered, I decided to flirt with the boy a bit. I was thankful and I had been a little rude earlier. We exchanged numbers and became friends. Everybody knew about us, but it was about a year before we ever actually had sex and within only a few months I was pregnant. Right before Myrtis died, he broke up with me claiming that he needed space and a month later he was engaged to some new girl.

Now five years later, he was back in my face wanting to try as a family. Everybody around us was in awe at how magical our love was causing me to open up my heart and accept being in love. Regardless of my side hustles, Uncle Keith, Grandma Myrtis, and Meme raised a lady while my mom Katrina raised a fighter. Three months after Meme's funeral, Dustin had proposed during a lunch date at Chili's. Two weeks later and we were at the Justice of Peace saying, *'I do.'*

The lesson that I learned with Dustin was that *'The counterfeit always comes before the real'*

*His Favori*te White Girl

"Don't need permission. Made my decision to test my limits. Cause it's my business. God as my witness." - Dangerous Woman by Ariana Grande

Chanice

My phone vibrated on the nightstand, and I answered without even looking, still half sleep and groggy as I heard Destiny crying hysterically into the phone saying, "Oh my God! I thought you were dead."

Barely above a whisper, I mumbled, "What are you talking about?"

She screams, "Didn't your house burn down last night? It's all over the news Niecy! Your house, the strip club, and the salon. Someone was trying to kill you! Where are you?"

Believing this to be just a horrible dream, I chuckled and said, "Laid up in Showout's arms."

She scoffed and hung up the phone while I rolled over and placed my phone back on the nightstand as I felt Lester's arms wrap around my pudgy waist as his warm words brushed across the back of my neck into my ears as he spoke softly, "What about my arms?"

My eyes bulged like they were about to pop completely out as I jerked forward rolling over onto him reaching for the remote controller that sat on his nightstand and frantically flipped the TV on turning to different news channels that all said the same thing. An image of my cabernet burned to the ground.

My salon still in flames as the fire department had been working overtime to put the fire out. The images of my house showed only the concrete slab and blackened remains as if it never truly existed. My heart shattered into smithereens as I broke down crying in

Lester's arms. All of my hard work was up in flames, and I knew exactly who to blame.

I was ready for war as I called Dustin's number maybe over a million times as it went straight to voicemail like he had blocked me. That wasn't going to stop me from raining hellfire on him as I jumped up getting dressed when his sister called me back crying into the phone saying, "Niecy, please leave us alone. We just want to be left alone."

I screamed, "Girl what the fuck are you talking about?"

She sobbed harder, "I know you know that he's dead Niecy. He's fucking dead because of you! So why are you calling his phone? We can't even deal with his death because our mama had a heart attack and died after identifying his burned body. Please just leave us alone."

The call ended and I stood frozen trying to understand everything that was happening around me. I had fallen into zombie mode just as I had when I lost my sweet angel baby, Jordan Danielle. Barely hearing. Barely replying. Just looking. Lester drove me to the salon where the fire department had finally put it out and started to examine the cause as the fire chief took me to the side and said, "I know how devastating this is right now, but you need to know that an accelerant was used in your house and at the salon meaning that these two fires were intentional however your night club was due to faulty wiring. It was electrical and completely accidental."

I heard him loud and clear but truly registered nothing he said as I replied, "But nobody was hurt right?"

A sadden look fell upon his face as he spoke with sorrow in his voice, "I don't know how to say this but there were two lives lost in these fires. A security guard at your night club. He was pinned by under a piece of the ceiling as he was trying to save a young woman. She's already given her statement to the police but..." He cleared his throat before continuing, "We found your husband in the master

bathroom at your house which is also where the fire started. We're not sure what exactly transpired but we do know that an accelerant was used making it intentional. I'm truly so sorry for your loss."
Without any emotion I nodded while picturing Dustin fucking up the wires in my club after welcoming my brother home from prison. His evil smile plastered across his face as he doused my salon with gasoline and pranced around the house in victory snorting his favorite white girl. As if a scene out of *'Final Destination',* I saw him standing in the bathroom with his hand over his heart gripping his shirt in an attempt to rip it off while trying to catch his breathe. He collapsed as one lonely tear fell out of his eye while he flicked the lighter in his hand. Just as he took his final breath, the lighter dropped, and flames ignited around him Whatever made him think he could so easily get away with this is the very reason why he didn't.
Unlike that horror movie, I didn't gasp from the revelation of what could've happened. When in zombie mode, the pain is numbed to barely a fraction of a pinch. The emotions suppressed into a chained up ball hidden deep within my soul. Sure, I'll eventually reflect on everything one day and most likely bawl my eyes out until I have a headache and drift off to sleep but until that day came, this is what the world seen. Someone with not an ounce of emotion. I walked away feeling weak and defeated as Lester leaned against his lifted Silverado with his arms held out. I walked straight into his embrace allowing a few tears to fall silently into his black and white hoodie.
We rode around the city for a while which was soothing, especially when we entered the countryside of Terry, MS. Seeing the beauty of what God created was always something that I enjoyed doing. Watching the way the leaves on the trees swayed when the warm spring breeze came through or how the honeybees buzzed off in the distance surrounding the pretty blooming flowers. There isn't

a painting that could truly capture the feeling that nature gave to me. When we pulled up to a beautiful golden yellow house sitting on about two acres of land, Lester looked at me with a huge smile as I realized that I was probably about to meet his parents, Bishop Walls and his First Lady.

As soon as I was about to hop out of the truck, he says, "Wait here." He jumps out and jogs into the house while I admire the spacious green yard imagining how my kids are going to love coming here to run and play outside when he comes back opening my door and holding out both of his hands for me to jump into. The only way I can ever get inside or out of this monster lifted beast of a truck is with his help, but I loved it because I loved how it felt to be in his arms. We walked up the stairs of the red bricked porch and through the double doors.

The inside looked as if it was a staged house that I had seen only in California when Sheena and I visited her aunt on her dad's side. I've never seen a staged house anywhere else aside from the pictures on Zillow, but I could only assume that maybe the First Lady was a decorator in a past life. We didn't walk far as I turned around and he'd gotten on one knee with a small, opened blue velvet box containing a ring in the shape of a snowflake in his hands as he said, "I've been waiting on this moment my entire life. Niecy will you please marry me?"

Without a second thought, I smiled and said, "Yes. Absolutely yes!" He jumped up hugging me and placing the ring on my left hand as he said, "I bought this house after the couple's retreat. I know the timing isn't perfect, but I couldn't wait any longer. I want you and the kids to move in. I've prayed on it, and everything feels right with you. I've known that you were my wife since we were kids. Especially when I threw up on you and you didn't go crazy on my ass."

The horror of the memory forever burned into my brain caused me to laugh while I said, "You're the only guy to ever throw up on me and I'm really hoping it doesn't happen again."

He tapped his stomach with a huge grin on his face and said, "Stomach of iron now baby!"

With my lip tooted up to the side, I went on to say, "Mmmmm so far so good but do my kisses still taste like chicken?"

His eyes bulked as he started to laugh uncontrollably while holding his stomach of iron. Tears begin to well in his eyes as he tried his hardest to get control of himself when he finally managed to say, "Baby no! I was lying. You have the sweetest kisses. I can't stop kissing you. I need to kiss you right now. You got my sweet tooth aching."

As he walked up to me, wrapping his arms around my waist, I shoved him off with a smile saying, "Seriously! I thought I had halitosis after that. Constantly brushing my teeth and praying that my breath didn't stank!"

He lifted me up as he said, "Baby you've been perfect since the first day we met. You're the sweetest girl I've ever met. You're the reason that I want to give you everything."

Within seconds we were christening every room in our home with the kids' rooms staying untouched. My prayers were being answered in ways that I couldn't imagine. Definitely more than what I bargained for but certainly everything I could've ever wanted.

Later that night, Nina dropped the kids off after having another fairy godmother filled week of tiaras and tutus while I had gotten up bright and early the next morning fixing pancakes, eggs, and bacon with fresh fruit on the side for me, Lester, and the kids. The kids love how I allow them to be as creative as they wanted to be as they got the food coloring and made rainbow pancakes while dashing a little cinnamon and vanilla in the batch. They even taking it a step further and slicing up a banana for a couple pancakes while dropping a few blueberries in some others. We laughed with pancake batter everywhere while dancing around to the soulful sounds of *'Good Love'* by Johnnie Taylor before switching it up to singing Paramore's *'Still Into You'* before sitting down to eat breakfast.

Lester sat with a plate of food fit for a king as he said, "All of three of you are just some oreos. You look black on the outside but you're really just as white as you wanna be on the inside."

Nothing we hadn't heard before as the three of us shrugged and commenced to throwing fruit at him when he opened his mouth and caught a grape with a grin of victory. We had promised them a trip to SkyZone and maybe even some robucks as long as they cleaned their room where they had draped all of the sheets and comforters over their beds and dressers because it was a must that they built themselves a fort and traveled to the land of Narnia to meet Aslan. Lester indulged in their extraness as he had nailed the sheets to the walls to give them an even better adventure and when I said, "Dude you're putting holes in the sheets."

All he did was shrug and say, "We'll just buy some more."

While shaking my head, I replied, "Is that right?"

He walked up to me and wrapped his arms around me as mine naturally held unto his waist. He kissed me with a sly grin and said, "Yeah didn't you know I was a millionaire."

I shoved him off of me, I laughed and said, "Boy when did you become a millionaire?!"

He walked off heading to gather more sheets while saying, "When I won a million dollars playing the Powerball. Duh!"

As if my life couldn't possibly surprise me more than it already had, I still had to pause and process the possibly of his words being factual. The first night living with Lester as a family and it was already more than I had prepared for. It was the complete opposite of what I was used to and yet it was everything that I had prayed for. Lester didn't have to prove anything to me and yet it had walked up to me with his proof that he was indeed a Powerball winner of a million dollars. He'd won years ago and didn't squander it doing a bunch of nothing. Instead, he waited. He prayed and when the moment was right for him he made his first purchase with his winnings which was my ring and our house.

Although I was grateful. In love. Completely happy with this man. I still had business to attend to and deaths of loved ones to deal with. While the kids and Lester enjoyed a day at SkyZone, I went on to meet up with Destiny at her mom's house. It's where she'd been staying for awhile and she was hating every second of it but that was her problem. Not mine. I pulled up and walked straight in since they never locked their doors. Such an odd thing to me considering how my grandma Myrtis would sit in the house with all the doors and windows open but the screen doors remained locked unless I was outside playing with rollie pollies and making mud pies. She wanted to embrace God's light rather than turning on a bunch of lights and running up her light bill. Pretty sure it's just a country thing but it's something that I do as well. Once the sun goes completely down, then and only then do we turn the lights on and close the windows and doors. And don't even get me started on thunderstorms! We allow God to do his work while staying far away from the windows.

There Destiny was laid in her bed that was in the den that she shared with her kids. Her mother and the kids were at church while Destiny was too weak to get out of bed from the constant crying spells she had endured. I placed my hand on her back and said, "What's wrong girlie?"

She sniffed and wiped away her tears as she replied, "I just hate to see you lose everything like this. You're such a good person. You don't deserve this."

My eyebrows frowned a bit at how she was more hurt than I was but maybe it's the fact that in my misery I still had so much to be thankful for. I lost everything that I had worked for but I hadn't lost everything. I still had my kids. I still had God and despite it all God was already giving me what I truly deserved. I patted her back and replied, "Oh honey you know God got me."

With a nod, she says, "But I know you're heartbroken over Dustin. He was the love of your life."

Zombie mode still in effect as I simply nodded wondering to myself, *'Am I heartbroken? Was he the LOVE OF MY LIFE?'* while saying, "Honestly, I'm just empty. I know it was all an accident but let's not talk about it right now. I wanted to see if you had heard anything new about Imani. Ace wanted to get a GoFundMe started which I think is an amazing idea. We can't let her story die out in the media."

As she shook her head, Destiny says, "I really don't believe she's missing. That girl laid up with some nigga getting dicked the fuck down. You know Imani a hoe."

I frowned and replied, "Imani is not a hoe. She just started getting some dick. Her mama had her as a prisoner all her life."

Destiny nodded and said, "All the more reason that she's probably just somewhere getting dicked down now that she can finally get some dick."

I rolled my eyes and sighed as I said, "So the girl just up and dipped for some dick? Left her place, her good ass job, and everybody behind for some dick?"

Destiny shrugged and replied, "You got a better reason? I mean who the fuck here would want her and she look like that?"

Instantly, I regretted making the trip. Destiny wasn't the prettiest girl and yet her ego had her feeling like she lived on top of the world. She constantly judged and belittled everybody's appearance around her when she could've stood to look in the mirror a few times at her own flaws. Imani had Destiny beat and that in itself is the reason why Destiny was trash talking Imani in this moment. Suddenly, she tapped my ring with her stiletto shaped nails as she exclaimed, "Oooo that's cute! I love the snowflake. It's perfect since you're born on Christmas. Dustin really loved you Niecy."

I pursued my lips and replied, "This isn't from Dustin, but we'll talk about it later. Since you clearly don't give a shit about your own godsister, I'm going to go see Ace so that we can figure out something about Imani."

She scoffed and rolled over pulling the covers over her head burying herself deeper into depression as I let myself out.

Heaux Talez

"Cause I got you sprung off in the spring time. Fuck all your free time. You don't need no me time." - P*$$Y Fairy(OTW) by Jhene Aiko

Destiny

My phone lit up with Niecy's name when I declined the call again as I rolled my eyes. It had been only a few days since I last since her and we argued about the whereabouts of Imani as well as the accidental fire that wasn't as accidental as Niecy believed it was. Dustin had already confided in me that he was in serious debt with a druglord and needed about a hundred thousand dollars.

His plan was to burn down her businesses and the house down and use the insurance money to pay off his debt while using the rest to start over in a different state with me by his side. It was the perfect plan until he fucked up and got caught up in the flames from being a dumbass. I didn't feel like continuing an argument that didn't produce any solutions to any of my problems while believing that Imani was safe wherever she was, I went on to do just as my baby daddy instructed me to do and that was find somebody else to claim our seed that grew inside of me.

I stood in Hideaway sipping on whatever Chaos had ordered for me. Looking just as clueless as ever as I was rocking my red stilettos, tight blue leather pants, and see through white crop top. It was a cowboy themed birthday party and although Chaos had invited me, I seemed to have missed the memo as different groups of trail riders gathered on the dance floor swaying their hips to the country sounds of *'Keep On Rollin''* by King George. This just wasn't my scene, but I was going to do what was needed in order to impress the guy on my arm. I leaned forward and said in his ear, "What's going on? I'm so lost right now."

Chaos replied, "They're just line dancing. Come on I can teach you. It's pretty easy."

I pulled my arm back while politely declining, "Oh no I can't dance. I got two left feet."

He walked back up to me and placed his hands on my hips as he said, "You ain't got all of this for nothing."

Some of his biker bros walked up to him, eyeing me like I was the best cut prime rib in a butcher's shop, while saying to Chaos, "Oh damn son, this you?"

With a smile from Mississippi to Cali, Chaos replied, "Yoooo what's up Ken?"

I smiled as I sipped on my drink seductively trying to be the sex symbol that I knew I was when Ken smacked my ass and said, "Damn Chaos! You sure you handling all of this?"

Without a second thought, Chaos replied, "Oh it's getting handled tonight!"

Maybe others would've found offense to the conversation and lack of respect taking place but I for one found it to be invigorating. I adored the attention that all of the guys gave me but what I loved the most was when they all fell to these knees to worship the sex demon within me. A succubus true to my name. I started rubbing on Chaos' crotch hoping to entice my new prey. Ken was a pretty smooth brown with locs damn near touching his knees. He looked rather innocent which he was definitely easy.

It wouldn't take much to get him to blow a quick rack and I knew if Chaos owned a successful trucking company, then his boys had to have some pretty deep pockets as well. Nothing felt wrong about fucking all three of them and then letting the deepest pocket know that he was going to be a daddy in about seven more months. Unfortunately for me, a couple of the ladies walked up to his buddies and pulled one of them onto the dance floor the moment *'Flex'* by Cupid came on. I was just going to have to make it work out with only Chaos and Ken.

It was only an hour later when the birthday boy was getting kicked out for being too wasted and trying to fight one of the guys from a different trail ride group. Chaos grabbed my hand and left ready to finish the night up at his place and as soon as I got inside his royal blue Camaro, his right hand was deep inside of my pants, swirling around in my wetness. In a matter of seconds, I was tooting my bare ass up with my head down in his lap and a mouth full of dick.

When we reached the stop light on Lake Harbour, an older gentleman looked to his left and did a double take at the prettiest moon he's ever seen in his life. Chaos sped off as soon as the light turned green, swerving in and out of the lanes on Spillway hoping not to draw attention from the police because he had no intentions of stopping me from doing what I felt was necessary. What should've only taken twenty minutes, turned into thirty minutes real quick but finally the drive was over and we pulled into the driveway of Chaos' 4 bedroom house that sat on the Reservoir.

Within a flash, we were inside and stripping out of every piece of clothing that we still had on, making our way to his bedroom where I laid across the bed with my head dangling off the side of the bed. Just as Chaos was about to wreck perfect havoc in me, I motioned for him to come around the bed bringing me face to face with his delicious looking award winning dick.

As I held the base, he fed me his trophy dick as I laid there with my head upside down. I relaxed my throat in order to take in every inch while he increased his speed giving me a reason to feel like I was that bitch. Feeling the love taps of his sack against my forehead as he massaged my hardened nipples, caused me to crave a more forbidden treat just as his body started to tremble.

Suddenly I could feel another set of hands glided up my thighs along with warm kisses on my love handles. I had completely forgotten about Ken. He had been trailing us this entire time and when we came in, he simply sipped his whiskey and watched our little show while stroking himself. Once I was done with Chaos, I was going to bend it over for Ken but luckily for me, his whiskey had him being frisky. He massaged my clit just as Chaos' creamy delight exploded in the back of my throat.

While savoring every single drop, the boys switched positions and it was now Ken's beautifully crafted dick in my face awaiting his turn as Chaos tapped his trophy dick on my throbbing pussy lips. I lifted his rod and opened my mouth wide, allowing him to drop his sack into my mouth. I licked, kissed, and lightly suckled his balls until I purposefully slipped my tongue further behind his sack.

Ken jumped back as he squealed, "Shit!"

I giggled as he came back for me while Chaos begin to hammer my walls down. Ken was more forceful in my mouth than Chaos as his balls slammed against my forehead from him fucking my mouth like I was a blow up doll. Chaos gripped my hips hoping to secure me in place as he continued to ram me for dear life while Ken kept pulling out denying me a taste of him.

He was too busy enjoying the feeling of my tongue deep between his ass cheeks. Although enjoying it felt wrong, the feeling was too satisfying to deny as moans escaped from this unknown pleasure that he never knew existed. His rod was the hardest it had ever been causing him to stroke as I ate creating an overwhelming urge to grip my secured wig and stop me as I heard him say, "Damn you a nasty little bitch!"

With ease Chaos flipped me over and they had switched again with Chaos sitting on the bed as I took him in my mouth once again while Ken massaged my ass cheeks. Ken returned the favor as he started to devour me from the back and moving further down to the front. Going back and forth as I swayed my hips from side to side spreading my juices across his face.

Ten minutes later and Ken was still eating with no intentions of stopping while I had sucked Chaos dry. He had gotten up and left only to return to Ken finally stopping only after his hunger was completely sated. I had experienced at least four orgasms back to back before Chaos was back inside of me, slamming his balls against my swollen clit. They had created a sexual game of hopscotch, as one jumped in the other jumped out. Just as Chaos had blasted off once more, he hopped out and there stood Ken with his rod in his hands as he contemplated his next move.

With my ass still tooted up on the bed, Ken rammed his dick deep inside of my anal canal and begin to mercilessly blow my back out. I had gone numb for the first few minutes until I was able to become more relaxed which made me grind my hips trying to fuck him back. Feeling his sack slamming up against my throbbing wetness was mesmerizing to me. It wasn't long before he was exploding again. Slightly sore and tender from the tightness of my asshole, Ken removed his rod and rubbed it against my wet lips, entering with ease. He gripped both sides of my hips and commenced to pounding away in an attempt to rip a hole straight through me.

A slap of fire landed across my ass cheeks causing my eyes to water. I was speechless but loving every minute of the pain that I felt. He wrapped his left hand tightly around my waist as his right hand gripped onto my shoulder blade as he said, "Whose pussy is it?"

Unable to speak from a mouth full of Chaos' dick, I hummed the words to his dismay causing him to jerk my head back and ask again and I whimpered, "Yours."

Satisfied with my answer he pushed my head back down onto Chaos' dick, increasing the speed beyond what I could handle causing me to choke harder than I ever had. Despite being able to barely breathe, I creamed on Ken's dick and he released his hold around my waist. When he noticed me trying to take a break, he pulled me back into my position as he said, "Nah don't run. You're my bitch now!"

Without a second thought he rammed harder, and tears started to slowly fall from my eyes. It was a pain that I hadn't experienced and yet I enjoyed it and hoped like hell it was worth it in the end. Eventually I felt him explode within my swollen and tired walls. I slumped over on the bed, unable to move as him and Chaos laughed as Ken slapped my ass with a kiss on my cheeks. Chaos walked into the master bathroom to get a bath towel and face towel and handed it to me to clean myself up while Ken went into the kitchen and got himself a Gatorade. I was without a doubt wore the fuck out but mission accomplished.

After maybe twenty minutes of contemplating my life and the many choices that I had made, I finally mustered up enough energy to go clean myself up. I wasn't at all ashamed of what I had to do to secure a father for my child. As soon as I turned the water off from washing up, Ken was kneeling down and parting my thighs for another hour long eating session. My phone was vibrating again with Niecy's name appearing across the screen. Chaos yelled out, "Yo why the fuck Niecy keep calling you?"

I moaned loudly with pleasure, "Ignore it!"

He nodded and tossed the phone on the living room table as Ken stood up, lifting me unto the bathroom counter and fucking me for dear life all over again. He whispered into my ear, "You gone have my baby?"

A sense of accomplishment soared over my body. I couldn't contain my excitement as I smiled eagerly and moaned, "Yessssss!"

Delusional Dreamer

"Insane in the membrane. Insane in the brain. Insane in the membrane. Crazy insane, got no brain." - Insane In The Brain by Cypress Hill

Imani

I silently watched Lauren drink an entire bottle of Remy in celebration of her latest attack on Greg. These random moments of her talking to me has been the only interaction that I had with anybody now that Greg has remarried. She's celebrating the idea of her putting in an anonymous tip of Greg committing insurance fraud and murder to the police. I urged her not to do it because of what's going to happen when he finds.

I thought that Lauren would've known better but this sudden need to get revenge consumed her. Greg marrying Nina has been the only thing that she can think about. Anytime she comes down here, it's to talk about Nina and how she's been sent from The League. A few of the things she's shared with me has given me a little hope.

Such as one little tidbit is that Greg has been gone a lot lately, parading around his new little wife. Lauren feels invisible and my name is never mentioned in any of these talks. Thanks to her misery needing company, I've been allowed to leave the room in the basement. With her focus centered on all things Greg and his focus on all things Nina, I figured I could at least use these distractions around me to try and escape. I knew exactly where the front door was and on the few times that we left; I believed that I could make it to the nearest store to get help. The only thing that I was afraid of was The League. They could've been anybody.

Lauren had once confirmed that those random guys in the beginning were all familiar faces to her. That's the only reason she went along with it. None of it was new for her. I didn't want to believe it at first, but it was making a lot of sense. These people knew that Lauren was still alive, and when she killed their girlfriend, it was enough to convince The League that she needed to be eliminated since the girlfriend was part of The League as well. The courage to run made the plan so simple, however the fear of getting caught hovered above my head pouring out every ounce of bad luck the universe had to offer. I should've made sure that Greg was gone before I tried anything because if he caught me then my time was up. He used to have these designated date nights with him and Lauren before he caught her with Xavier. Now he's given them to Nina and my only hope is that tonight is date night. This would be great for me since it takes Lauren a couple of days after her drunken cries for attention before she can function correctly again. I knew that she was well past wasted because she was crawling up the stairs. Even her farewell words were distorted and lagging at the same pace as her feet. I was surprised when she made it out the door without falling down the stairs.

A few minutes had gone by, and I hadn't heard the keys locking the door. Just as I had hoped, the girl was too drunk to lock the door as always. A smile of hope made its way across my face. Maybe it was the anticipation or anxiety, regardless it was uncontrollable. It felt like now or never. My heart was pounding about three hundred beats per minute while I crept up the stairs. I was on the verge of a heart attack by the time that I placed my hand on the doorknob.

I thought that I was ready and that I'd be in the hallway inching to the front door within no time but instead I stood there as if I was an ice sculpture frozen in time forever holding this doorknob. I could've made it out of the door, but I didn't even turn the knob. Every fiber in my body was frozen solid while fighting fear itself in an attempt to leave it all behind. Another battle that I would evidently lose. It's amazing how fear made me quickly retreat to my room.

Only seconds had went by and, the sound of keys locking the door let me know that my once in a lifetime chance at freedom was destroyed by fear. For over a week, I would listen at that door for their voices. If I heard none then I'd pick at the lock on the door with a couple of small pins that I had found in the corner of my room. It seemed to take forever but after only a few days I was able to unlock the door. I had to practice getting it opened faster while Lauren was still making random visits which didn't feel all that random once I started to keep up with my days. If any members of The League stopped by, then she'd would come down to the basement to drink and be loud.

This happened every Friday from what I had been able to gather. I'd sneak a few looks at Lauren's phone after she became sloppy drunk and every single time, she staggered out the door, she left it unlocked. This helped me to know that today should be the first of January, making it a year since I got here. The date was shocking to see at first. So many things I know that I've missed out on with my loved ones, but it was also the motivation that I needed to get away from here as soon as possible. If tonight I was successful in escaping, then it's only so many options that I had. It was a fact that I wasn't going to get any help from the nearby houses or stores because Greg trusted going to only a few places when I was allowed outside, and they were always close by. It was vital that I avoided those places without a doubt.

While I sat at the door listening to Greg and Nina giggle, I knew that I couldn't allow fear to win again tonight. This entire time I hadn't heard anything from Lauren, so it was safe to assume that she was sleeping some liquor off. So far, everything was lining up perfectly. As long as I wasn't in the room, it was easy to know when somebody left and came back because you could easily hear the garage door opening along with the chirps of a car alarm followed up with the sounds of scuffling feet making their way down the hall, getting closer to me but veering off in the opposite direction instead. I waited patiently for confirmation that they had left so that I could make my escape. My heartrate slowly increasing when the sounds of the garage door closing gave me the signal that I was waiting for.

With a deep breath, I started to pick the lock. My hands were sweating causing me to constantly stop and wipe them on my night-gown. What used to take days only took two hours this night. The first step was completed. Gently, I twisted the knob and softly pushed the door open. It was dark as all of the lights downstairs were turned off. I stayed against the wall hoping that with each step that I took that I didn't bump into anything. If something were to fall, it would certainly wake Lauren up because it was way too quiet. I even had to get a handle on my breathing as I managed to get from the basement to the front door. Another huge accomplishment for me that I'd have to wait to celebrate after getting away from here. I started to unarm the alarm when the headlights of a car rolled across the wall.

Quickly, I ducked down and peeked from behind the wall into the foyer and hoped it was just a car making the wrong turn and turning around. The lights around me turned on as I suddenly had to struggle to hide. Greg had come back earlier than I had expected, slamming doors, and screaming at the top of his lungs, "Bitch wake your drunk ass up!"

As he stormed up the stairs, I swiftly made it out of the front door. The night was still, dark, and cold. There were only a small number of houses in the vicinity, so I hid on the porch wondering if Nina was in the car or not. The only sounds that I could hear was Lauren screaming, "Fuck that bitch and fuck you too!"

With hope that their arguing would draw attention away from me and the dogs wouldn't notice me running was nothing but false hope. They started barking as soon as I sprinted off towards the road. As luck would have it, they were still chained up and I no longer had anything to worry about with them. Once I got past the houses, I was in the middle of nowhere and unsure of which way to go but it didn't stop me from running. Real freedom was within my grasp.

I couldn't wait to get to the police station and turn them both in and hopefully they find The League as well. I didn't want to look over my shoulders for the rest of my life in fear of them. Out of breath, with a burning throat, I had run from one street just to walk past three streets because I wasn't sure who was a part of their organization. Knocking on one of the member's houses late at night in an attempt to run away from my master would be the death of me and not at my master's hands.

I needed to get further away to the next town at least, and I couldn't waste time doing it. I darted across the street into an old KMART parking lot. There's a gas station in the far distance that I psyched myself to believe was just a few more steps ahead when in reality it's a mile up a hill and I'm already on the verge of freezing to death with only my adrenaline getting me this far. I cared nothing about the cold weather when I jolted from that porch wearing nothing but a nightgown and socks, but it was starting to catch up to me as I continued to walk towards the highway. There was no turning back.

Abruptly I was stopped in my tracks by Greg's white '16 Ford Fiesta slamming into the side of me. I laid on the ground in agony praying that he'd finish the job by putting me out of my misery right then and there. Instead, he jerked me up and slung me into the backseat. What I thought took me at least four hours, seemed to take Greg about ten minutes before he dragged me out of the car and back into the house, pushing me down the stairs.

I hit the floor lighter than I did the pavement when he hit me with the car, but the pain remained the same. I was once again moaning in agony clutching my stomach. The sadistic laughter of Lauren during my return caused me to glance at her where I noticed that she was sporting a fresh black eye with a nice busted lip to match. I also noticed the shock collar was back around her neck. It wasn't hard to understand the type of shit that we'd both stepped in.

Greg shut the door with a loud bang announcing that he had entered the basement. He violently escorted us both to the couch where we awaited our final judgement. He snapped, "You two evil bitches!" His focus towards Lauren as he said, "You think you did something huh?"

She hissed, "The same way you thought marrying that hoe was doing something?"

Greg shook his head as he groaned, "Lauren." He started to clap his hands, with an overwhelming sigh, "Congratulations, you done fucked up now! Do you know what happens when the League doesn't want you in their little club anymore? Well my dear wife, they make it seem like you've never existed."

Lauren's laughter interrupted his rant, "Well I'm dead so I already don't exist."

He scoffed, "Oh, this shit is funny to you huh? You know for a dead bitch, you laughing real loud." She laughed even harder, and he punched her in the mouth. She was spitting out blood when he asked, "Ain't shit funny no more huh?" He grabbed her face and whispered, "I ain't going down for this shit by myself." She spit in his face, and he returned the favor with the butt of his gun to her nose.

That's when he walked up to me and stroked my face with the gun. He began to slide the barrel from one side of my face to the other. He stopped at my lips after the third slide, slowly parting them and forcing the gun into my mouth while saying, "Suck it before I blow your brains out."

Family Portrait

"So you're having my baby. And it means so much to me. There's nothing more precious. Than to raise a family." - Forever My Lady by Jodeci

Destiny

A sharp pain shot through my groin in mid step causing me to bend over in pain unable to continue standing. I held my vagina feeling as if it was ripping apart from me while using my free hand to brace myself on the wall. I was unaware of what lightening crotch was, but I was learning rather quickly that it was normal symptoms of the third trimester in pregnancy when baby is the size of a watermelon and has settled into their position awaiting their big debut. I had finally made it back to bed after eating a cup of ice. While trying to catch my breath I attempted to get further into the bed and take a nap when Ken stumbled in drunk off his ass from a night out with his biker boys as he mumbled on, "Baby I love you! I love you! And they don't see what I see. Why don't they like you baby? I love you."

I sighed as I watched him stumble up to the bed reeking of nothing but liquor and cigarette smoke as my pregnancy nose was in full overdrive. If I gagged, I was sure to throw up. He certainly didn't care about getting in bed with me smelling like that while still rambling on about how his boys didn't like me. I didn't give a rat's ass about them. A couple of hours later, I was up going to the bathroom once again. This was the first night that I'd been unable to truly sleep in this pregnancy.

No matter how many times I readjusted my body pillow that Ken hated, I still couldn't get comfortable. Not to mention the many trips to the bathroom that I had to endure. Braxton Hick's were starting up as I was more than ready for the end of this pregnancy. Only six more weeks to go and I still hadn't had my baby shower. I laid back down only to be up again from being uncomfortable and having to pee. It was at three in the morning when I realized that I might have been in labor but quickly dismissed it because it was still too early to have the baby. I was only thirty-two weeks pregnant.

Baby had other plans as the pains grew stronger lasting longer. The next time I woke up I knew that I was in fact in labor. I nudged Ken to wake him as I refused to deal with the pain any longer. Unaware of what was happening Ken sat up still reeling off the effects of his boys' night and asked, "Is everything okay?"

Unable to reply until after the contraction had passed, I finally managed to say, "Baby it's time."

He obliged still unaware as to the fact that the baby was coming. I wobbled out the front door and into the car and Ken rushed us to the hospital while the contractions were hitting me back to back barely giving me even a second to breathe and lasting even longer. Six hours later and we were welcoming a beautiful baby girl named Aaliyah Kadence.

Slightly underweight but perfect in every way with a head full of hair. I stayed in the hospital for only a couple of days, and it wasn't long before depression set in triggering the crazy bitch within to come out and play. Multiple people stopped with every pink hair bow and onesie that they could find just to awe over this bundle of joy but the very next day a special visitor made me want to kill Ken's ass.

In walked his best friend of seven years. A pretty plump redbone wearing an open red and black plaid shirt over a white *'In Living Color'* t-shirt with denim shorts and red and white chucks. She was cute but plain and even on her worse day I knew I had that bitch beat however I was down for the count unable to do a thing for the man. His best friend had come into town just for him because if the bitch cared so much about meeting me then she surely would've made the trip a lot sooner, but I already knew what it was when he excitedly told me that she had actually come into town.

This was my worse day as I smiled and sat up in the hospital bed from nothing but resting after having pushed a whole human out of my vagina the day before. Ken had freshened up prior to his best friend's arrival as if he was going on a damn date. Putting on his very best with a button down shirt, fresh pair of jeans, crisp J's, and his favorite chain while spraying on some AXE body spray and sure enough, the bitch asks, "Is it okay if I steal him away for a few minutes?"

Ken stood by with a huge smile on his face awaiting the green light that he knew I would give as this was only his best friend of seven years and despite them trying to date once, it didn't work out so there was nothing to worry about. Everything in my gut told me to say no but I didn't have any other options to choose from. I needed this man happy in order to take care of me and my baby that he'd just signed the birth certificate to. I smiled and nodded and watched the man walk out of the hospital with another woman only a day after I had given birth to the daughter that he was happily claiming.

Several hours passed before Ken's return and he went straight into the bathroom to freshen up again. There was no doubt in my mind that he had been fucking that bitch, but I couldn't say a word about it. He came out of the bathroom taking the baby from my arms with a smile big as ever and a glow that was brighter than the sun while he danced around the hospital room singing to baby Aaliyah with a father's love in his eyes.

I sat and watched in agony at how I had to swallow each hateful word that tried to come up. The moment that he was sleep and the baby was back in the nursery, I eased my way out of the bed and went to the bathroom where his clothes were tossed to the side on the floor. I picked up his boxers and sniffed the crotch, confirming my suspicions. His unique scent of passion went up my nostrils turning into a loathing scent of resentment as I exhaled.

Days later and I was finally at home trying to settle into motherhood with this man when another unwanted guest left me feeling uneasy from their visit. My mama walked in with her nose turned up from the disarray that surrounded me as she said, "With Vincent you could've had a maid and a nanny."

I sighed as I dismissed my mama by saying, "Have you heard any news on Imani yet?"

As she shook her head, my mama's saddened voice replied, "No nothing since her friend filed a missing person's report. I just hope they don't find her dead in a well somewhere. Such a pretty girl despite that trifling ass mother of hers. Still a damn shame how she just let that man have his way with her and she's on the gotdamn news crying about him being found in the Mississippi River like he didn't deserve it. Good riddance if you ask me."

Nobody asked but my mama didn't mind continuing her rant about her ex best friend. As if she was any better but what happens at home stays at home. As long as the topic wasn't about me, then I enjoyed talking with my mama about any and everybody but the moment that my mama set her aim on me, there was no saving me from the double edged daggers that flew out of my mama's mouth.

I chimed in with a lie, "All this time and I never knew. She never said anything to me and as small as Jackson, Mississippi is I thought

I would've seen him at least once before. Especially when it seems like we just always know the same people."

My mama scoffed and replied, "No yall just fucked all of the same people like motherfuckers ain't gone talk." She shook her head and continued, "It breaks my heart to know I raised nothing but a lying ass hoe."

The truth never bothered me when it was somebody else that was saying it but when it was my mama, I always felt the need to defend myself as I exclaimed, "What have I lied about now?"

My mama hissed while holding baby Aaliyah, "You think I don't know that this is Dustin's baby?! Why not abort it like you did Vincent's? I'm not going to stop Niecy when she beats your ass because you could've left that girl's husband alone."

Without any hesitation, I denied the allegations as I said, "I never slept with Dustin, and I never had an abortion. I told you that was a miscarriage, and I didn't know I was pregnant." My mama was pissed at the utter disregard for her intelligence as she spoke through her clenched teeth, "Bitch lie again, and I'll beat your ass myself."

I snatched my baby out of my mama's arms in order to have some sort of shield as I replied, "Believe what you want."

Before my mama could say another word, Ken had entered the house holding a boutique of roses and sunflowers with a box of chocolates. He looked at my mama and said, "I'm so happy that you're here. Would you be able to watch the baby? I got something special planned for your daughter."

Unimpressed, my mama quickly replied as she started for the door, "I can't. I'm late for my hair appointment."

Ken shrugged as his plan B folded and he went back to plan A. He had surprised me with a spa day at Massage Envy. An undercover reward for allowing him to spend the day with his best friend of seven years. It was enough to create a hint of forgiveness but not enough to make me forget although I needed just about anything to get my mind off the bullshit that my mama had just pulled.

Once I was dressed and ready to go, he stood in front of the door with a smile as he said, "Thank you so much for making me a father." He kneeled down and opened a small box containing the cutest little promise ring and continued, "If you accept me, all of me then I promise to always take care of you."

Nothing about his approach impressed me but I smiled and jumped for joy with tears in my eyes as if it was my very first time accepting a ring from a man. It wasn't engagement ring or a wedding ring, but it was a start to a commitment of a lifestyle that I needed. He stood up and kissed me still awaiting his answer but believing my reaction to be the 'yes' he needed while I threw caution out of the window and unbuckled his slacks, pulling them down as I lowered myself with them.

There wasn't a thing that I wasn't willing to do to secure a stable future for myself, but I'd be damned if he stepped out on me again. As I pulled out his already rock hard dick, I licked the tip while stroking the shaft as I looked up saying, "Yes baby. I'm yours."

Blackjack

"Mount Everest ain't got shit on me. Mount Everest ain't got shit on me. 'Cause I'm on top of the world. I'm on top of the world, yeah." - Mount Everest by Labrinth

Chanice

With the money Ken acquired from hitting the jackpot on a slot machine at River-walk in Vicksburg, he went on to purchase a house in Brandon with the plan to open up an underground casino. It started out small as a game night amongst the men of ClickTight with only a poker table and a speaker until Destiny came in and renovated the entire house to give it a true casino vibe. She went crazy with that man's money buying a blackjack table, a roulette table, a craps table, a pool table, a Mississippi stud table, 2 slot machines, and a wooden liquor bar for the dining room. Each table game was placed in it's on room with the slot machines lined up in the living room.

In celebration of becoming a father, Ken invited the guys over to have a game night, but Ace was too depressed over Imani and declined while Carlos had jumped full force into a brand new relationship with my sorority sister, Mion and she wanted in on game night as well. Since all of the guys included their girls, Destiny huffed and puffed until Ken agreed to let her in on the festivities as well. Unbeknownst to Ken, this was perfect for Destiny considering she cared nothing about game night as her only hope was to get Lester off to the side and steal a kiss or two.

Maybe even give him a quick blowjob in the closet if he was down for it.

With a live stream going on Lester's TikTok page, Mion bragged on how she'd take every red cent the guys had in a quick game of Blackjack and all three guys had a hearty laugh until Mion dominated them at the Blackjack table. She claimed she didn't know how to count cards, but she was racking up like she knew. After losing over two thousand dollars, Ken exclaimed, "Girl, you lucky I ain't got security to throw yo cheating ass out! That was the baby's money damnit."

Carlos defended his lady by saying, "Aye chill out. You can't gamble ya baby's money man!"

Ken scoffed and replied, "I wasn't. Ya girl just swindled me out of it. Straight up hustla. She could sell fish to a fisherman!"

Mion flipped back her long knotless braids and replied, "I'll take that as a compliment." I chimed in, "Let's get something going with this pool table though."

Instantly we all left one room and went into another one that was upstairs as we gathered around the pool table where it was me and Mion versus Ken and Carlos. Lester decided to sit this one out, just to admire me from a distance. It was hard for him not to stare, and it was even harder not to bend me over that pool table in front of everybody on live and in this room so sitting this one out seemed to be the best idea, but Destiny kept walking into his view, licking her lips and bending over with her ass tooted up in a desperate attempt to get his attention.

He sighed and sipped his D'usse & Lemonade while hoping Ken would check his girl. He turned his attention to the comments and entertained the five thousand viewers that he had watching and asking questions. The female commenters were on Destiny head about the amount of thirst they witnessed her displaying for

ShowoutKing as side bets of a female mud wrestling match between Destiny and I started up.

He made sure to kill the excitement of a fight as he wanted no parts in that whatsoever! Everybody might see Elmo when they see me, but Lester knew a crazy ass Chucky doll could emerge at the drop of a dime if I was ever truly pissed off. Once he noticed that Destiny had left to see to the baby, he took a quick bathroom break as me, Mion, and Carlos entertained the viewers in his absence. Ken was too busy being a sore loser in his makeshift casino to care about anything or anybody else. Just as Lester thought he had escaped the shedevil, Destiny walked right up to him as he was exiting the bath-room and grabbed his crotch while boldly whispering, "I wanna suck your dick."

With discontentment, he tried to gently move her hands off of him before anybody seen them and just as he moved one hand, she placed the other one on his crotch, squeezing slightly harder than before. Lester was a man that didn't partake in drama and no matter what he did or didn't do with Destiny, it was forever going to be his word against hers. The last thing he needed was his childhood sweetheart catching him in a comprising position with this crazy broad.

He just didn't think that I would believe that my so called best friend was a compulsive lying ass hoe when in reality I knew all too well of her crazy antics but Destiny was only going to do what he allowed her to do. He sighed and replied, "You got to let me go." Destiny smiled at the challenge that walked away from her as she plotted how she would snatch his soul the next time she seen him.

The night grew closer to an end as we all played board games, card games, and even charades while enjoying mixed drinks and munching on different plates of food pre-pared for us by Beau's head chef of his restaurant, Southern Delights in Madison. Things were going well so far despite the tragic events that had recently happened in my life with the disappearance of my cousin, Imani, the death of my husband, Dustin along with losing everything that I had in a house fire but as soon as Destiny started to drink, everything took a turn for the worse.

Mion sat back and watched her like a lioness protecting her king as Destiny carelessly flirted with all three guys. Mion went on to claim her man as she started to rub on his crotch, licking and whispering in his ear while lightly kissing his neck. Her flirtatious behavior was at an all time high with him as he flirted back. Mion made it very well known that if Destiny wanted Carlos again, she'd have to go through her to get him. It's not a challenge that Destiny wanted to take on since the girl couldn't fight at all, so the liquor became her very best friend. Mion was a pretty ass firecracker when it came to her man and unlike the rest of the meek and humble women in his past, she didn't mind checking a bitch about hers.

Nobody else had seen the sudden change in Lester from the act that Destiny was putting on. Normally he was a complete goofball, always cracking jokes and talking mad shit but this night he was rather quiet, reserved, and to himself. I hated seeing the strained look on his face and it caused me to wonder if I had done something wrong.

Since my house burned down, he's been my knight in shining amour as he's accepted me and my kids into his life but transitioning from the single life to a ready made family, I'm sure wasn't something that he had planned. He's gone from enjoying quiet nights alone to being attacked by three oversized midgets. There's absolutely nothing quiet about us as we're constantly talking louder than men during the Superbowl about anything and everything. Movie nights are the worse because we interact by screaming at the characters the moment one does the most horrendous act against common sense.

My girls are true to my nature as we stay pranking the man at every turn he makes. Whether it's walking into the house, unable to turn the lights on because we've unscrewed the bulbs and started blasting him with nerf bullets or it's the simplicity of switching the sugar out for salt, he's certainly endured the worse and not once did I ever think maybe we were getting on his nerves until now. We've certainly tried to make up for our prankish nature by catering to him with different things that we know he'd love but when a person is tired of you, it's nothing else that needs to be said. I knew all too well that a man could and would put a woman out for anything and it was looking like my time was coming to an end from the way that he sat seeping with contempt.

Although he reassured me, I hatched a plan to sneak him away from the group for our own seductive game night. It started with us locking eyes during a game of charades and then there were the unseen touches as we moved around switching players while eating and drinking. His demeanor changed for the better as wicked promises of pleasure made it incredibly hard for either of us to ignore the intense emotions that developed from the way that we were staring each other down. It was only a matter of time before I went M.I.A for a quick game of hide and seek.

As Mion turned to Carlos, she asked, "What's the strangest place you've ever had sex?"

He smiled and replied, "The Purity Retreat."

Destiny chimed in, "With the church?!"

Carlos nodded while Ken laughed and said, "Wasn't nothing pure about that retreat."

Carlos shrugged with a smile and said, "I regret nothing."

When I pulled the card, I turned to Destiny and asked, "What would you not want to find in your partner's bedside drawer?"

She shook her head and said, "A double sided dildo."

I just burst out into laughter knowing exactly who Destiny was referring to while all the men sat silently in horror trying not to stare too hard at Ken as he tried to deflect by saying, "Why in the hell would I have a double sided dildo bay?"

Destiny replied with no emotion, "Hell if I know. I'm just answering the question."

A few raised eyebrows and some side eyes later and Mion had started feeling the liquor a bit too much as she had started to grind her nice little fatty in Carlos' lap to the beat of *'Buttons'* by The Pussycat Dolls while I claimed to be sick from the calamari and needed to lay down in the guest room for a bit. Lester caught the hint and moments later, entered the guest room only to find me nowhere near the room. Instead, there was a folded up note and small flashlight sitting on the end table, and it read, *'When you camp out at night, you're always prepared. It's nice to have this in case you get scared.'*

Lester wasted no time making his way outside to search the backyard for a camp-site. He spotted some string tied to a tree with another folded note. Eagerly he went to the tree to read the note, but it was blank. As he looked up, he noticed another tree with a string tied to it but no note, so he followed the assumed breadcrumbs that his Gretel was leaving him as he entered the wooded area behind the house.

Five minutes later and he walked up on me sitting on a red blanket wearing a cute wave rider blue lace butterfly crotchless panty set from Savage X Fenty. Surrounding me was a bucket of ice with wine and two glasses beside it. There was a covered bowl of fruit and a can of whipped cream in her hand.

It's never been a moment where Lester was left speechless, but this had him completely zoned out as he kneeled down not caring about the wine or the fruit and begin to kiss me. He paused to simply say, "You're such a good fucking girl!"

I smiled in response and placed my hands on his face pulling him closer to me. His smile, his touch, his presence was all electrifying to me. Our kisses instructed him to grip my thick thighs the second that our lips touched. Instantly, he begins to caress my sweet spot with his fingers. In and out. One finger. Two fingers. The more I moaned, the more he fingered. His thumb wrestling my pearl simultaneously with his kisses leaving passion marks around my neck. My nails digging deep into his forearms from the intensity of his fingers stroking in and out. His mission was to dominate me in ways that he'd only dreamed of.

He took his fingers out ready to taste my sweet nectar until I grabbed his hand and suckled both fingers with a smile only meant for trouble. It was a reminder that I was still the boss, but he was the only one that could control me. His rock hard mandingo pressed against my inner thigh causing me to wrap my legs around his waist ready for his next move. Lester danced his tongue around my nipples gently biting each one. He suckled and kissed all over my body before placing my legs on his shoulders and meeting my elevated honey haven. After placing an ice cube between his lips, he commenced to rubbing it across my throbbing pearl. I could feel him teasing me with his tongue at the same time. The mixture of coldness and warmth sent me into an enchanted frenzy in these woods.

Lester continued to work his magic when I uttered the words, "Yessssss daddy!"

I had an orgasmic explosion in his mouth leaving him glistening in the moonlight as if he'd just come up out of the ocean. He crept back to his original position with my legs back around his waist. As placed one hand around my neck and the other gripping my hair, he slowly entered me keeping his strokes slow and steady. I could barely feel the tugs he gave my hair or the grip that lightly tightened around my neck. He was giving me mind blowing climaxes that echoed off of each other.

He stroked like he was going half on a baby with me. Both of my legs made their way onto his shoulders once again, folding me up like a lawn chair. He sat up giving me a look that I knew was going to send me into a blissful insanity. His stroke sped up only slightly forcing me to whisper the words, "I love you."

Taking each inch with a smile, I felt the coldness of the melting ice on my pudgy belly. He was caressing my breasts and keeping my entire body entertained. What I wouldn't give to have this forever. Time had escaped us, and we could hear Destiny drunken voice invading our out-of-body fantasy as she screamed out into the woods, "NIEEEECCCCCCYYYYY!!! Girl you better not be out in these damn woods hunting deer and shit!"

We stared at each other smiling as Lester never stopped stroking. He sat up and instructed me to get on all fours. He wasn't letting my arch from hell get the best of him this time. Gripping both sides of my hips he pounded into me with the only intention of making me know who the fuck *'Daddy'* was. He bent over on top of me still pounding as his soft lips placed warm tender kisses along my spine. I was stuck in a trance not knowing what to do. The moment he blasted off into my walls, I knew I was never letting him go.

We took only a few seconds to gather our breath and get dressed to sneak back inside. Luckily for us it was only Mion and Carlos woke in the living room getting ready to head out. We tiptoed through the kitchen and went out through the garage to his lifted black Silverado. Next time, we planned on taking a trip to Vegas for a real casino night.

Breaker of Chains

"You've got a feeling, a soul, that I need in my life, babe. Oh, oh, oh-ooh-woah. And though we may grow, I don't know why we don't grow apart, babe - ICU by Coco Jones

Imani

During the moment of me tending to another busted lip on Lauren, she randomly asked, "What made you think you could get away?"
Remembering my escape attempt from months ago, I shrugged and replied, "I never thought I could."
Lauren nodded with understanding and stated, "A suicide mission in other words."
I agreed, "Whatever gets the job done."
She placed her hand on mine and spoke softly, "I wish I could be you."
Silence was my only reply. I didn't have the energy to entertain Lauren's many sad excuses as to why I had to be here for almost two years enduring any of this. I continued to nurse to her wounds, praying that my end was near. No matter how it looked. Greg had been out of control for the last three days since his arrest, becoming more of a monster than before without any remorse for his actions. Even in the midst of his rampage, Lauren says, *'He's just angry because I sent in that anonymous tip. He'll calm down eventually?'*
It caused Nina to leave him and the League to mark his file as dismissed. Now, he's on his own without any help to battle the

multiple criminal charges that's piling up against him. He wants to keep Lauren alive so that she can admit to her part in all of this while Lauren is saying, *'I'll do everything I can to help him because I love him, and I don't want to ever lose him!'*

The words of a complete fool. As Greg comes in waving this gun around with his feelings of authority still in question from the stunts that we've pulled, he snatches me away from Lauren with one swift move and he motions for me to go sit down on the couch while grabbing Lauren next. He then sits in a chair across from us and looks us up and down as he scratches his head in silence. The feeling of powerless and fragility consumes me as I watch him decide what he wants to do next.

With no need for either one of us, he's feeling desperate and dangerous. Despite beating us black and blue for committing the ultimate betrayal of tipping off the police and trying to run away, his beautiful Nina sold him out to the police. She told them all about how he was holding us hostage in the basement even though it was only me truly being held hostage.

Lauren didn't have a desire to leave him. She was the Tiffany to his Chucky, but the police now have a different story. After snorting another line of coke, he was still fuming as he said, "When the police showed up at the restaurant to arrest me, I wasn't worried because I knew they had nothing on me. Then they fucked me with sandpaper and no lube by turning my wife against only before they told me that my dead wife tipped them off to me committing insurance fraud and murder."

He paused for a moment as if he was recalling what happened then he chuckled and sighed, "These summabitches had the nerve to tell me they found a charred body in the Mississippi River along with my gotdamn wallet." That creepy ass smile seemed to appear out of nowhere as he continued, "The shit slipped out, but I still called my lawyer and got my ass out of there."

The lines of coke he's been snorting for the past couple of days is starting to get to him as his face glistened with sweat. The gun laid on his lap as he tried to wipe the sweat from his face with his white muscle shirt. The sounds of a can dropping outside of the basement door made Greg jerk his head up, alert and ready. He looked back and forth with the gun in his right hand and placed his left index finger on those big soup coolers, instructing us both to be quiet.

Lauren agreed with a nod, and I did the same but deep down everything in me wanted to scream out for help. I knew that Greg would shoot me dead if I made a sound. He inched up the stairs and slowly eased the door open. When he didn't see anything, he was convinced it was all in his head. On his way back down the stairs, somebody kicked him in his back, and he stumbled down the stairs, causing his gun to slide across the floor while this other person came charging down the stairs in full SWAT uniform.

I wondered, *'Where's the rest of the swat team?'* There wasn't anybody else and Greg didn't stay down for long. In mid step, Greg swung and knocked off the helmet while Lauren and I moved near the foosball table in order not to get hit as the fight ensured. Greg was weak and off balance in the beginning, but he didn't allow that to stop him. He still tried to fight but this other guy overpowered him.

The guy had Greg in a headlock from behind until Greg flipped him and he hit the floor. It didn't affect him has he popped back up like Muhummad Ali ready to box. When he turned around, I realized the other guy was Ace. He was handling his own just fine until Lauren slid Greg's gun closer to him without me seeing her. For a split second I thought to run to Ace when I seen Greg reaching for the gun but instead, I screamed out, "Gun!"

Luckily, it was enough to get Ace's attention for him to kick the gun away. Greg grabbed his ankle and Ace hit the floor sounding off like thunder in a storm. My hands trembled at the sight of Ace wrestling to get Greg off of him. The last thing that I wanted to see was Ace get killed. I wouldn't have been able to live with myself being the cause of his death.

Greg had the advantage and reached for the gun again, but Ace jabbed him in his side causing him to ball up giving Ace the upper hand as he struggled to get the gun from Greg. It was too much to watch. Every second lasting longer than an hour and yet if I blinked too hard, then I'd miss it all. Greg tried his best to punch Ace in the face without letting the gun go, but every punch that he threw, Ace blocked it and then the gun sent off a shot.

Instantly, I turned away and buried my sweat drenched face into my dirty night-gown. I allowed the tears to freely fall wherever they wanted to. A minute passed by, maybe more and I could hear crying and the words that came through, "Baby wake up! Wake up baby please! I'm sorry. Okay I'm sorry!"

A hand rubbed my back and I turned to face Ace in his attempt to help me up while pointing the gun at Greg. I stood up with my eyes glued on Greg. Lauren laid in his arms as he pleaded with her to breath and come back to him. She gasped her last breath as the blood poured out of her chest. She was gone, and we all knew it. He continued to hold her as he started to rock back and forth crying.

Ace thought we would be able to slip out the door while Greg grieved over Lauren until Greg stopped us in our tracks when he sobbed as he said to me, "Imani, wait." I stopped but Ace lightly tugged my hand, urging me to leave while we had the chance and yet I stood there waiting for something that I knew I didn't want. Greg sat on the floor soaking wet from sweat and covered in Lauren's blood.

He looked at her with his red tear filled eyes and shouted, "It should've been you! You should be dead! Nicole didn't deserve this! She was the love of my life, but you and that pedophile ruined her." He paused and looked down at Lauren as he gently stroked her hair and placed a kiss on her forehead while saying, "I only got married to make you mad baby." His eyes shifted from Lauren to me as if he were looking for confirmation that him marrying Nina was forgiven. Even though Ace continued to urge me to leave, I stood still. Greg spoke with a broken heart, "I know I could never be Xavier but baby nobody could ever be you."

I had hoped she would move, a cough or something. The only reason that I've been standing here this long was to see if she'd come back. I related to Greg's disbelief, but his intentions were never pure. This was somebody that I loved from the very first day that I met her. Granted we indulged in things that we should've never done but my love for her was real and seeing her dead was the one thing that I never wanted to see.

Maybe Greg was right. Maybe it should've been me after all I was still the one that encouraged Lauren and Xavier to have sex never knowing they were already talking. I was still the one encouraging the threesomes. It was me that enabled all of the behavior, but I never forced her to do anything. I loved her and only respected her when she declined.

Lauren was broken long before she ever met me, while Xavier was a pedophile on the day he approached me. I hated to even think it but maybe I wasn't the culprit. Maybe just maybe, I was actually the victim. Within the blink of an eye, Greg had drawn a second hidden gun from behind him and pulled the trigger with the gun aimed at me. There were two shots that sounded off before Ace shoved me up the stairs and out the door. We ran out of the house and at the same time SWAT and local police ran in to arrest Greg. Everything was in a blur as the paramedics tried to assess my wounds while Greg was escorted out in cuffs with that creepy ass smile on his face. The coroners rolled Lauren body out behind him and the moment he seen the black body bag on the stretcher, he became hysterical causing a few SWAT officers to taser him.

The squad car pulled off with Greg still going berserk in the back seat. The coke and the heartache of Lauren's death was stopping him from even feeling physical pain. The feeling of being free from Greg didn't set in until I was at the hospital. Ace rejected any notion of him leaving my side after detectives entered the room to get my side of the story.

I replied with what I knew and when I wasn't answering their questions, I wondered, *'How am I supposed to live a normal life after this?'* It wasn't a lot of information to give to them because I didn't know the names of any members in the League. To top it all off, I didn't even know where I was being held. The detectives decided that they would talk to me at a later time so that I could rest and heal.

When they walked out of the door, Ace stood up to hug a female waiting in the hall beside the door. I squinted my eyes trying to see if it could've been Terica, but she was too tall. It wasn't until she walked in that my body started to tense up with my hands using the last bit of strength that I had to grip the rails as Ace introduced Niecy's sorority sister, Nina.

She held both hands up as she stepped forward speaking as softly as she could, "Imani, I am so sorry for what has happened to you. I'm an undercover detective that was assigned to infiltrate the League. We've been trying to take them down for at least six years now. They've been operating a sex trafficking ring, drug smuggling, money laundering and a bunch of other outrageous criminal activities. Thanks to Ace we were able to take down everybody in connection to Greg." My eyes drifted to Ace as she continued, "If he hadn't asked us to look into who was terrorizing and stalking you, we would've never discovered that it was Greg. He was the thread we needed to pull to dismantle the entire organization."

As he placed my hand in his, he stated, "I wanted to tell you everything about what Nina was doing, but I couldn't or else it would hurt the sting operation. I'm sorry for pushing you away. I only did it to protect you." He didn't need to apologize for saving my life. If anybody needed to apologize, it was me for accusing Terica of being a jealous stalker and treating him like a suspect. I wouldn't be alive right now in this hospital bed, if it wasn't for him. I smiled and said, "It's okay. I'm sorry for being crazy and please tell Terica that I'm sorry as well." I turned to Nina and continued, "I'm really happy to know that you're an agent and not a part of the League as well."

She smiled as Ace replied, "What are you apologizing for? You had every reason to be crazy."

Nina chimed in before leaving, "You are an amazing woman. A true survivor and that's nothing to apologize for." She hugged Ace and went on her way. A feeling of gratitude came over me because of my best friend Ace. He stayed the night with me at the hospital despite me telling him that he should go home and get some rest. He refused to leave me alone, since he felt that I wasn't ready to be left alone yet. I stopped trying to get him to leave because he was right, I wasn't ready to be left alone.

*A Low Down Dir*ty Shame

"If I can't be with you. The world could not go on so every night I pray. If the Lord should come for me before I wake. I wouldn't want to go if I can't see your face."
- Heaven Can Wait By Michael Jackson

Chanice

Brinae was out breath as she ran to catch up to me while I was leaving my office as she said in between breaths, "Bitch....I just...hold on!" She placed one hand on her stomach and the other on her forehead as she took a deep breath as I patiently waited for her to get herself together when she finally managed to say, "Girl, the fucking Les Twins and Beyonce are in the audience!"

I nodded with a smile and replied, "Well it's Femme Fatale IV from the infamous Moulin Rouge of the South. They were bound to come eventually."

She looked at me as if I didn't understand what she had just said. We may have taken French in IB together, but this girl knew for a fact that she was speaking English. Brinae grabbed my shoulders and shook them as she tried her best to snap me back into reality as she said, "Bitch I said Beyonce! Is in the motherfucking audience!" With a hearty laugh, I shook my head with tears forming while saying, "Yo chill the fuck out! You better put on a damn good show."

It was as if Brinae had completely forgotten that she had literally left her dressing room in her undergarments to peek out of the curtains and then run to my office with the hot tea after one of the guys from Team Flye told her about the special guests in the building. Her eyes bucked and she realized that she still had to get dressed and possibly take a shot to settle her nerves because this wasn't something that she ever imagined happening to her. Brinae quickly replied, "Shit!" and ran back to her dressing room to finish getting ready for the show.

After purchasing land just outside of Clinton, Mississippi and a year of construction, I was finally able to open the doors of the new headquarters for TriBrid Productions. As much as I missed my cabernet and salon, I didn't backtrack or attempt to start over. I simply continued on with my ultimate dream of a successful umbrella company. Working as the CEO of Cronix, I learned a lot about making the best investment deals for me as well as all of the amazing tips on real estate.

I've been able to walk away as CEO while incorporating my new business skills in my own soon to be Fortune 500 company. With Lester's help, he brought in every chapter of ClickTight Rydaz to help host this fundraising show in order to help the community of Jackson, Mississippi after a deadly tornado swept through destroying most of the city leaving us all to figure out ways on how to rebuild one of the poorest cities in America. Femme Fatale IV and Team Flye came together to showcase several different dance routines that had the intense moves of krumping along with some sensual slow grinding by Lester and his guys that paired so well with the jazz struts and majorette moves of us ladies. Together we were the perfect cherry on top of a dance sundae.

I stood by the stage as I watched the influx of people swarm in from all over the state and surrounding areas. Femme Fatale IV and Team Flye had the internet buzzing before the big day even arrived, bringing in busloads of people to witness the show and we made sure that they got their money's worth.

Vanjettia walked up to me while rolling her eyes as she said, "I just seen that stupid ass hoe walk in."

I chuckled and replied, "As long as she paid the entry fee and doesn't cause any trouble then I ain't worried about a thing."

There was a time when Vanjettia and Destiny used to hang out as buddies but somewhere along the road, they started to hate each other. It could've been the obvious that Destiny had probably fucked her man after they met at Wingfield. I never cared because it was never my problem. The moment that Destiny spotted me, she waved while walking towards me when Vanjettia says, "Not today devil." and walked off.

As I shook my head, Destiny walks up and says, "Girl I got something to show you!" She pulls out her phone to show me how Beau had been liking up her posts on TikTok, leaving heart eye emojis in her comments, and messaging her on SnapChat. I sighed and said nothing wishing that I had a blunt to help me ignore the bullshit but looking around the fundraising event and the success that it brought in was enough to make me simply shrug my shoulders and ask, "You must be here for AntRob's birthday?"

She replied with a smile, "Yup and I'm leaving with Beau." She continued in a singsong voice, "I'm gone get some dick!"

With a smile I nodded and said, "Go ahead. Enjoy yourself."

Without any hesitation, she replied, "Oh I am!"

A few moments later and *'Night of Viegre'* a special two-hour Virgo themed show dedicated to AntRob for his birthday had started. The audience watched in awe and amazement while the mayor, Chokwe Lumumba and the First Lady of Jackson were sitting beside our special guests chatting it up with eager smiles.

After a few comical musical parodies, the show moved on to one of my favorite new-comers, Lapin Neige, which is French for snow bunny. She was giving her best rendition of *'Circus'* by Britney Spears with the birthday boy seated centerstage as she twirled and sashayed around the stage in her white majorette boots, shimmery stockings with a silver and white corset and top hat to match.

AntRob was grinning harder than a kid in Candyland. Just as the music switched out to
'Money' by Cardi B, and four dancers wearing shiny white and green majorette outfits, jazz strutted out and danced around the birthday boy as Lapin Neige made her way backstage for a costume change. As the audience drank champagne and cheered for the birthday boy, a rather flamboyant male walked directly up to me and said, "I see you're doing quite well for yourself despite being a widow."
I squinted my eyes and sighed as I replied, "I'm sorry but do I know you?"
He shook his head and said, "No but we certainly do need to talk."
The only thing that I wanted to do was enjoy the show like the rest of the audience. I had worked so hard on this with Lester and knowing that Queen Bey was in the audience had me wanting to make sure that the show didn't have any hiccups but of course tonight I'd have to deal with every damn body wanting to talk! I escorted him to my office and as soon as we sat down, I asked, "So what business do I have with you sir?"
He looked around at my office with his nose up in the air as he said, "Aside from all of my regulars leaving City Lights for Femme Fatale before it burned down, I wanted to meet you so that I could apologize to you face to face. I can see that you're an amazing businesswoman and..." He paused for a moment as his eyes begin to water up.
I handed him a box of Kleenex and he continued, "Thank you. I'm sorry I don't know why this is so hard. I never expected things to go this way and I've tried to move on but I needed closure in order to do that. The guilt has been eating me up causing me not to be able to sleep at night. I just needed to say that I'm sorry. I know you didn't know but Dustin and I were in love. We've been off and on since high school."

There was nothing about what the news that was shocking to me. I had my suspicions for a while, but I hoped like hell that I was wrong. He certainly would've never admitted to it as religious as his family is. With one look I knew exactly who he was causing me to sigh and ask, "Is your name Alaysia?"

His tears stopped flowing and he twisted his head as if he was flipping back his long Brazilian hair that he didn't have when he replied, "No, Alaysia Santee is my grandmother in my gay family, The Infamous House of Santee. How do you know her?"

The urge to burst out laughing at the fuckery was overwhelming and yet I simply shook my head with pursued lips and replied honestly, "Well that's who he was talking to before he died so I naturally assumed that it was you. You don't have to apologize for a thing that you and Dustin had going on. I guarantee you, I'm not hung up on it at all."

I may not have been hung up on it, but this man certainly was, and it was obvious that he was about to tell Alaysia exactly how he felt about her fucking with his man. He got up and before walking out of my office he said, "I tip my hat to you milady because you're one hell of a woman."

I nodded as he walked out while I giggled to myself and sighed as I looked over the papers on my desk. There were a bunch of IRS notices and past due bills in Dustin's name. He had taken out multiple loans to support his coke addiction as well as paying off his many side hoes. The insurance companies were being flaky with me on the account of the fire chief's final report of all three fires being arson and with no suspects to point the finger at, all of the blame rained down on me. I suppose it's my nonchalant demeanor that made him feel weary of my alibi, but life was better to deal with once I shut off my humanity.

If this was an episode of *'The Originals'* then it's obvious that everybody would be dead but instead of me going on a killing spree, I simply shut down and got deeper into my work. Anything to ignore the pain waiting to consume me the moment I allowed myself to feel anything. Once the show was over, Lester headed out to Jacksonville, Florida for ClickTight Rydaz annual weekend kickoff while I picked up the kids from Nina's and headed home.

After Sunday service at Word of Life at Highland's campus, Lester sent me a text and let me know that he'd see me sometime the next night. I was missing my man something fierce, but he needed to enjoy himself with his biker brothers and I needed to take the time to relax especially since I was already starting to freak out from being over two weeks late. We've never discussed, and I wasn't sure if he was up to having any with me. I've always been fine with whatever God gave me but, in these times, everybody was settling for one and two kids whereas I always dreamed of a big family of about eight kids only because of my grandma Myrtis.

She had eleven kids in which I thought was beautiful and my Meme only ever had my mom which I thought was rather sad and lonely, but I witnessed how mothers truly didn't want all of those kids like Myrtis. Easy to say that I'm simply a different breed but I've already gone down the rabbit hole of having a child with a man that didn't want any kids. Not a trip I wanted to make again. So, if Lester didn't want any with me then that meant the end of us because I wasn't aborting my baby if there was one.

After I soaked in the tub with a glass of wine and candles lit, I decided to hook up a charcuterie board and read a book. Something I hadn't done in forever but just as fate would have it, I was up answering the front door at eight o'clock at night to Lester holding a huge Popeyes bag filled with two or three boxes of chicken and a smile on his face as he said, "Surprise beautiful. Did you miss me?"

I shook my head with a smirk as I tried my best not to jump on him from the excitement of him finally coming back home.

Just as he entered into the dining room and sat the food on the table, the kids ran out jumping on him the way I originally wanted to, welcoming him home with love. We ate at the table as he told us all about his biker filled weekend when I got up getting a second glass of wine and heading into the bedroom. He walked in behind me with a serious look on his face as he pulled out two boxes of pregnancy tests as he said, "Shouldn't you make sure that you're good before you drink like that?"

With an eye roll, I sucked my teeth and asked, "How do you know that I even need a test?"

He shrugged while opening the boxes and said, "I just know you haven't said anything about bleeding this month."

My nerves caused me to chuckle as I said, "So you're tracking my cycle?"

As he placed the digital and dye Clearblue tests on the bed, he replied, "You make it sound weird. I'm just observative is all."

With my lips pursued together, I reluctantly picked up the digital test to face my worse fears. Whether the test was negative or positive, I wasn't at all ready to know the outcome. I had a ball of emotions ready to explode like molten lava that I had been burying further down each day. This moment was going to be the key that caused all of those emotions to spill out in the worse way and that's what I had been avoiding when I first realized that I was late. He followed me as I walked into the master bathroom. With my nerves in my throat I asked, "Could you not watch me pee?"

His face scrunched up from the audacity of my words as he said, "With everything that we've done?"

A moment I figured I could have alone in order to try to control my nerves that were literally unraveling before him as I said, "Yeah but we haven't had any golden showers."

He gave a half smile as he replied, "You never know what the future might hold."

Clearly standing his ground in watching, I still pleaded, "Baby please."

His hands raised in the air as he said, "How about I just turn around? I won't look."

With an aggravated sigh, the rest of his words seemed to fade out as I rolled my eyes and I hiked up my 'black girl magic' sundress and sat on the toilet. I was still in control. My nerves hadn't gotten the best of me or at least I thought as I said, "Okay okay just shut the fuck up." I sat there in silence for only four seconds before saying, "Okay don't just stand there. Say something."

He went on to talk about whatever he was saying at first, asking me questions as I finally peed on the stick. The worse was over but my hands were now trembling as I wiped, flushed, and went to wash my hands. It wasn't something I wanted him to see. When I turned around, he had picked the test up watching the timer run out for the results as I said, "You're supposed to let it sit."

My words meant nothing to him as he replied, "It's going to do the same thing regardless."

I sat on the bed with my hand holding my head as I prayed for it to be negative. I really needed it to be negative. A baby with Lester wasn't something that I was ready for. After he walked up to me and held the test out and it read, *'Not Pregnant,'* the biggest sigh of relief escaped my body. Still unsure of why I was a month late but regardless I wasn't pregnant.

Unbeknownst to me, I didn't take another breath after the huge sigh of relief. Instead, I sat frozen on the bed unable to process anything happening, but I could feel Lester's arms wrapping around me, pulling me off of the bed as he kissed me saying, "Breathe Niecy! Breathe!"

Suddenly, it's as if I was awaken from the deepest slumber, attempting to catch my breath while my body continued freefalling in a moment of weakness. Silly me to think that he was the one overreacting as I believed that I was actually in control and breathing just fine but my legs had gone weak while time seemed to speed by us as he continued to hold and kiss me saying, "Breathe Niecy! Breathe!"

It wasn't until he felt comfortable enough to let go that he did and that's when I realized that maybe I wasn't breathing correctly. I was in a daze as if I had literally just landed on my feet when the tears welled in my eyes at the realization that I had lost everything and that I had nowhere to go. I was completely alone and although Lester had been nothing but a Godsend to me, I never took the time to process my emotions. To ever properly grieve any loss that I had experienced starting with my Uncle Keith. I had been in zombie mode since the age of fifteen and whenever something major happened all I did was shut it out refusing to deal with the pain.

My biggest fear was going through hyperemesis gradvidarum again and giving birth to another stillborn child. Of all the losses that I had experienced, that was one that I couldn't take again. Even if the child didn't die, hyperemesis gradvidarum was a devil that I didn't want to tango with again. My dream of a huge family didn't need to happen, and I understood why so many true mothers stopped after one or two. I had become content in what I had, and I didn't need any more if it meant going through that again.

Once the atmosphere had calmed down a bit, he sat down beside me on the bed and asks, "What are you afraid of?"

I pressed my lips together and sighed as I replied, "Nothing."

He nodded as he says, "Well you just stressed yourself into a panic attack."

With a shrug, I said, "I don't know maybe my body just needed a reset."

He sighed heavily and spoke softly as he wrapped his arms around me once more pulling me into him, "I don't mind using condoms. I can even pull out with the condom on if you like."

One thing he's always been great at doing is making me laugh in any situation. With honesty and love, I laid my head on his chest hearing the beauty of his beating heart as I said, "I do want more kids. I'd love a wild little boy running around."

After a chuckle or two he got up locking his arms and twisting his body on his heels as he said, "You sure you want a boy by me? He's going to be dancing all over the house."

With a smile, I got up to join him as I slow winded my hips in a circle and said, "You know boys take after their mothers."

His mouth turned up in disbelief as he placed his hand around the nape of my neck pulling me into him for a kiss before saying, "I'd love to see you pregnant so I can rub and sing songs to your belly all day and give as many foot rubs as you want."

With my arms wrapping around his neck, I stared at him in amazement as I replied, "I'd love that too."

He lifted me off the floor as he said, "Practice makes perfect."

*Jungle F*ever

"I know you wanna love, but I just wanna fuck" - B.E.D by Jacquees

Imani

Before I could make it home, Beau was sending me a text asking if I could come through. After everything that I'd been through, everybody just assumed that I'd want to be alone but that was the furthest thing from the truth. Being around people kept me from drifting down memory lane, constantly replaying the horrid details of what I went through with Greg and Lauren.

When I got to his place in Fondren, I sat in his game chair in his bedroom, staring at the man that I should've given a chance to years ago when we met at Last Call when Destiny pointed out his ClickTight Rydaz motorcycle club as she told me all about some guy named Showout that was obsessed with her. Although I've never been one to like cream in my coffee, Beau was the exception to the rule.

He stood at about six feet tall looking like the perfect oversized pooh bear minus the belly. His full brown beard had me ready to moisturize it every time I looked his way. Beau has always been a complete gentleman any time that we hung out. He'd cook and we just chill and talk shit while having a drink. I didn't want him, but my body did. There he was talking about his ex who he thought was the love of his life breaking his heart.

It was safe to say that we both needed a release. I had issues of my own that I was still dealing with. Beau had become a huge deal since the last time I had seen him. His restaurant was the hottest thing in Mississippi thanks to servicing Niecy's cabernet with his amazing fine dining skills. Despite how busy he was with the restaurant; he was still the only one that hadn't changed around me treating me like some absent minded victim that needed to be handled with care.

Not once did he ask what happened or offer a moment to share what the word in the streets. He just needed somebody to talk to about his hurt feelings and how somebody had done him wrong. In the end, I just wanted an escape from my own harsh realities from the lemons that life threw my way. It wasn't until I was watching him walk around in nothing but his gym shorts with his white tube socks and Nike slides, folding his clothes while rambling that I started to want more than his company and simple conversation. For some odd reason, I was nervous about my approach with a man she had never been with, but in mid conversation I interrupted him by saying, "So Beau we fucking or what?"

With confusion on his face, Beau raised his eyebrow and smirked causing me to smile back from the utter shock and disbelief that I had placed on his face. I've always been a bold and daring woman and yet Beau still needed time to process what was happening. He should've known by now that nothing was ever what it seemed with me, but it was obvious that I had done a number on him because instead of answering my question, he simply grabbed the keys to his Dodge Ram and said while shaking his head, "Let's ride out so you can clear your mind."

Highly disappointed in his reply, I just shook my head and got up to ride with him. I didn't understand how anything about my approach came off as if it was joke. I thought to myself, *'Is he no longer sexually attracted to me?'* Guys claim to want a bold female, an outspoken female, a female that says what's on her mind but when she's bold enough to say she's horny, they just brush it off. Granted, the only reason I was there was to fuck off, but my plans had changed, and the feeling of rejection had now made it my mission to get some act right. When we got back to his house, I looked at him and said, "You playing."

The aggravation in my voice was loud and clear as he smiled while still looking crazy and confused says, "What did I do?"

I scoffed while thinking, *'How the hell he don't know what he did?'* While shaking my head, I sighed and answered, "You still got your clothes on."

He started clearing the bed, finally catching the hint and realizing that this was not some childish game that I was playing with him. I got undressed and he followed suit. Sadly, to say my mind frame had changed just that fast. Awkwardness had set in as this was my first attempt at sex since my horrendous captivity with Greg and Lauren. Although I could still talk a big game, actually executing my plan was something different. My kitty wasn't even purring anymore! I stared at this Irish king naked thinking, *'When all else fails, suck some dick'*

There was a time when I truly enjoyed pleasing a man. It was always a complete turn on to hear a man moan and I had started something that I needed to finish. As I placed both of my hands on his chest, stepping a few steps forward and pushing him up to the wall, I kissed him while gently massaging his dick and planting sweet kisses all over his neck and tattooed chest. Slowly, I dropped to my knees and began to ease him into my mouth, I stroked his shaft and continued to kiss his tip with a few licks here and there. All he could say was "Oh."

I couldn't help but chuckle while speeding up the pace with the only sounds being heard were moans, oh fucks, shits, and slurping. Beau grabbed my head and began to thrust himself deeper into my mouth. My wild side was finally starting to emerge as the awkwardness quickly disappeared. His legs started bucking from the way that my lips created the perfect suction along with my hands stroking him into weakness.

This was my signal that he was getting closer to his moment. I continued on my mission until I heard him moan, "Ooh shit Nini!" causing me to gush like a fucking waterfall. It was just like music to my ears. I went from fast to slow and back to fast again, but the goal wasn't to make him bust. This was simply me jumping back into the saddle.

As I slowed down to a complete stop, I got up walked over to the bed and laid back on it while grinning from ear to ear. Beau walks over and climbs on top of me as he begins kissing me on my belly. He places his hand on my kitty and feels her wet and ready purring for a release. With a devilish smile, Beau grabs his monster sized vanilla creamsicle thinking he's about to slide it in until I say, "Oh no sir." I placed my hand on his head and eased him on downtown to where he was truly needed. After the blowjob he just received, I wasn't letting him skate by on reciprocating the energy and pleasure.

He chuckled and smiled as he replied, "Yes, ma'am."

Beau had me running all over this damn bed in nothing but pleasure. White men can't jump but they sure can eat some pussy! He seemed right at home as he savored every single drop. His hands caressing every inch of my body from rubbing my thick thighs to gripping my ample soft ass to the gentle squeezes on my pretty size D breasts was sending multiple surges throughout my body. He was definitely owning up to his biker boy name as Treasurer from the way that he cherished my body as if it was a diamond dipped in gold.

I was squirming to the point that I almost pushed him off of me. I could barely take another second, but I couldn't afford to deny myself this much needed orgasm. I shuddered as if I was a volcano erupting in blissful orgasmic erosions. Beau held my hips tighter during this intense climax and the moment I was done, he stood up with a smile and a shiny ass beard feeling victorious.

I had no energy or need to push him back down. I would've given him some type of applause but was still too weak to even lift a finger. He knew he had done the damn thing as he said, "Damn, it's been a while for you huh?"

I rolled my eyes from the obvious as I said, "Shut up and fuck me already!"

With my kitty was completely swollen from this exquisite head work leaving me sensitive to the slightest touch and the moment Beau pulled me to the edge of the bed, entered me slowly, I couldn't help but moan loudly. While biting my bottom lip, I dug my nails into his sheets, ripping them clean off of the bed. I pushed him to the side and hopped on top when I started taking him for a ride into nirvana.

Rotating my hips in a circular motion like I was the hoola hoop champion of the south. My fast circles turned into circular bounces and back into slow sensual circles which only made him moan louder. By the time I started gripping his dick, he was sweating and saying my name louder each time. That's exactly what I wanted him to do. He uttered, "From the back."

Once we switched positions, I realized how I had fucked up by giving him control. The sound of his big bear hand slapping across my ass cheeks echoed as a tear fell down my cheek. I screamed out, "Ooooh shit! Harder!" Clueless to the mission of destroying my walls that he was on, I quickly learned when he squeezed my hips and commenced to slamming his entire soul into mine. Our energies had connected, and it seemed like this is where we both needed to be. Constantly switching positions and before I knew it, my legs were in the air. This was the position that got him though. For a moment, I thought this St. Paddy motherfucker was never going to nut. It was at least forty-five minutes later before I contemplated taking a break for a bottle of water or something. As soon as he exploded, he rolled over panting with a victorious smile. All I could say was, "Damn."

Completely out of breath, he replied, "Yeah I know."

There was no denying that this was a great decision on my part. I didn't need love. I just needed to jump back in the game with somebody that I didn't mind being my nastiest with. We laid in the bed together as the TV played *'Captain America: Civil War'* in the background until I received a phone call from Blue Pointe Apartments informing me that I was approved and could move in today for the 2 bed 1 bath apartment that I had applied for earlier in the week.

I quickly got dressed and rushed to get to Ace's house so that I could pack up the little stuff that I had accumulated since staying there. Ace had gone over and beyond for me considering that I lost everything from being held captive by Greg and Lauren. I came out alive, but I came back to nothing. No job. No place to stay. No car. No money. No clothes. NOTHING! I've been staying with Ace until I could get back up on my feet but that hasn't been easy. It took me a couple of weeks to adjust after leaving the hospital.

When I wasn't able to sleep through the night, Ace would be there with laughs and snacks. We'd binge watch different Netflix series before he'd eventually fall asleep from exhaustion while I stayed awake. He was able to work from home during that time so that he could help me if I had an episode. Once I was able to sleep through the night and the nightmares decreased, I knew it was time to try and get back to working. Of course, I had the option of getting a job with my previous employer but the job I had was no longer available.

Ace suggested that I apply at Cronix where he worked, but he never once mentioned how Niecy had the job waiting for me whenever I was ready. She's the reason that I got the job two months ago as their Creative Director in the marketing department. The interview with the head of the department was more of a formality than it was actually seeing if I was a good fit for the position. It's great being able to have somewhere safe to stay with a great paying job.

Things were starting to look up. I was almost back to the independent woman that I once was. I pulled up just as he was walking back inside the house. I quickly hopped out of the 2017 Nissan Sentra that Ace helped me get and excitedly screamed, "Guess what?!"

He nonchalantly replied, "You're really an alien."

With my eyes squinted, I said, "What? No, shut up. I get to move into my apartment today!"

Without a care, he said, "Oh, the ones around the corner?"

Blinded by the excitement of having my own place again, I darted for the door as I replied, "Yes sir!" He came into the guest bedroom that he had loaned out to me when I noticed that he wasn't actually helping me pack as he would get an article of clothing from my suitcase and place it back inside of the dresser while casually talking about eating some hibachi for dinner. I stopped him by saying, "Hey my guy what are you doing?"

He shrugged and replied, "Trying to see what you want to eat tonight. What are you doing?"

I motioned to the suitcase as I said, "Uh trying to pack. What you're not tired of me yet?"

As he shook his head, he replied, "I just don't understand what I did to make you want to leave. I mean are you sure you're ready for this? You do know you can stay here for as long as you like Nini."

With a confused look, I said, "Ace you haven't done a thing wrong. You've been more than a friend to me. You're like the big brother I never knew I had. I wouldn't be ready if not for you. Thank you but every grown woman needs her own place."

He sighed, "You don't have to thank me. What are friends for?"

He finally started to help me pack and even trailed behind me to the apartment so that he could inspect it. Some would say he was going overboard but I appreciated everything that he did no matter how overboard it might've seemed. When I was getting stalked, I took this overboard nature for granted. That's something I'll never do again. It felt damn good to know somebody was protective of me and cared for me without wanting anything from me but my friendship. After shopping for a few household supplies, we ate Chopsticks on the floor of my new but empty apartment.

Baby Blues

"I ain't got seventy days. Cause there's nothing. There's nothing you can teach me." - Rehab by Amy Winehouse

Destiny

Just like any mother with a newborn, I was having the hardest time sleeping at night. It was well known that becoming a mom wasn't a walk in the park and that it would take some time getting back to the woman that I once knew. Pregnancy in itself seemed beautiful but the emotions that I had to battle were starting to take its toll on me. Ken had been the perfect father as he cooked, cleaned, helped with the baby, loved on my new mommy curves and stripes, while planning romantic dates and trips for when I was ready.

All he ever wanted was to be a father, but his relationships never worked out as no woman ever understood him like me. I worked hard to prove that I deserved all of his love and that he had no reason not to give it to me. The only problem was that Ken still had to work and make sure that the bills were paid. He wasn't able to be around the entire time although he would've loved to give all of his time to our baby girl as well as me, love certainly didn't pay the bills.

After he left for work, I laid in the bed ignoring the cries of baby Aaliyah while tears rolled down my face onto my pillow not understanding what I was feeling. I was supposed to be happy as I had finally accomplished the one thing that I wanted which was to be taken care of by a good man. It's all any woman truly wants and yet I laid in bed feeling hopeless and forgotten with mounts of *'push'* gifts from Ken gathered around me.

Anger had sat in as I forced myself out of bed to tend to the now screaming baby that needed to be fed and loved. I quickly fixed her bottle, fed her, and changed her only for baby Aaliyah to continue screaming. I tried taking deep breaths to calm myself down as the screeching cries were becoming too much for me to bare. All I wanted was for baby Aaliyah to go to sleep so that I too could maybe get an hour of rest but that just wasn't happening. I slung baby Aaliyah onto the bed where she bounced from her back onto her stomach as I screamed, "Why won't you just stop fucking crying?!"

My screams of frustrations mixed into the cries of baby Aaliyah as I ran to the bathroom locking myself away from the baby that I now realized that I should've aborted like I had done so many times before but like a fool I believed having a baby this time would work in my favor to secure a better future for myself.

As the doorbell rang, I quickly gathered myself and placed baby Aaliyah in her swing as she continued to cry. I opened the door to Niecy standing there with a pan of Chicken Tetrazzini that she had made just for me as she said, "Figured you could use the company."

With a nod, I smiled and stepped back allowing Niecy to walk in. She went straight to the kitchen placing the pan down and then to the beautiful baby Aaliyah to soothe her from crying. I walked up to Niecy with a baby syringe trying to force it into baby Aaliyah's mouth as Niecy asked, "Is this her medicine or something?"

While shaking my head, I replied, "No, it's wine. It'll help her go to sleep."

Niecy slapped my hand away causing the syringe to fly in the air landing on the couch as she yelled, "Don't make me beat your ass!"

Knowing how crazy Niecy could get, I decided not to push the limit any further as I walked away into the kitchen to fix myself a plate of Chicken Tetrazzini. Niecy continued to rock baby Aaliyah and instantly she calmed down from exhaustion with her eyelids so heavy that they could barely stay open as I watched Niecy smiling as she unknowingly looked into the pretty brown eyes of her dead husband, Dustin.

She sighed and it was obvious that she had realized the truth but said nothing to me as I rambled on about how happy I was with Ken and how I wanted to have a hotel party now that Imani was no longer missing. It would've done no good to confront hash out the details my betrayal to her or what she would judge as disgusting. I was having a hard time adjusting into my role as a mother whereas it seemed as if it came so natural to Niecy. It was the middle of the day, and I was wearing a baggy shirt, with mismatched house shoes, no wig or bonnet, and dark circles under my eyes. A sight I would've never believed if I hadn't seen it for myself in the mirror.

After baby Aaliyah was fast asleep, Niecy laid her down in her crib and came out to me pouring shots as it was time to celebrate this moment of silence. The house was a mess with clothes everywhere and dishes piled up in the sink as I handed her a shot of vodka while saying, "When are you going to start dating again?"

Niecy took the shot and replied with a smile, "Well I didn't plan on it, but it's gotten pretty serious with Lester."

I laughed to keep from crying in a fit of rage as I said, "Girl no! Showout ain't nothing but a hoe and he's crazy as fuck! You know he fucked Cynthia and his cousin's wife before they got married? Don't you see all of those women in his comments on social media. I'm telling you he's fucking the one that keeps commenting under everything. That's why she's doing it. You need to leave him alone. I don't approve!"

While shaking her head, Niecy said, "I don't need pussy patrol ma'am! I'm not worried about none of those women on social media or who he was with in his past."

With a smile, I said, "But Niecy you're so pretty. You could do so much better than being with his hoe ass. He's still in my inbox too. Constantly trying to meet up and fuck and everything." As I tapped the kitchen table I say, "I tell you what. When Ken gets back, we can go to Old Tavern tonight for some drinks. Maybe meet somebody new with a brother or cousin for me, huh?"

Niecy sighed heavily before saying, "I've never had somebody as fine as Lester ever look my way though. Plus, I done licked on him so I gotta see it through. Besides Ken gone beat yo ass if he finds out."

I scoffed as I exclaimed, "Ewww girl no! Licked him where?! And girl fuck Ken. He touch me and I'll run his ass over in his own car!"

She smiled and replied, "Okay crazy and below the belt duh!"

My only wish was hoping that this girl would believe me but no matter what I said or did, she never believed me and all I ever wanted was the best for her. I sighed and replied, "Do you see how he's always on live and posting TikTok videos. The man just wants to go viral and he ain't cute enough for that. He has no fucking talent. He's boring. I can't watch you fall for another man that's just going to drive you crazy. I still want to beat Dustin's ass for what he did to you!"

Niecy sat silently shaking her head with her lips pressed together and humming *'mm-mmhmmm'* while I continued, "I just want to make sure you get some good dick in your life. I can call up a guy right now. He's definitely your type because he's black as oil and loves eating pussy. Used to eat me out all night."

While still shaking her head, Niecy chuckled and replied, "Nope. You've told me all about your many men and how they all like to tap dance around on a person's crazy button. I'm wayyyy too violent for that shit plus God told me not to fight anymore. He petty like that."

I rolled my eyes dismissing the entire statement about my many men while focusing on the craziness that Niecy had uttered about God as I say, "You can't say that. God ain't petty."

Niecy sighed as she surveyed the room observing the mayhem that I called my happy life while choosing to remain silent at the blatant display of pettiness by the hands of God that was laid out before us. She shrugged her shoulders and continued, "I'm just saying. Why put me down here with heathens and devils that constantly test my gangsta and tell me not to fight them?"

I giggled and replied, "Probably because you take shit too far and use a two by four to knock them out."

She sucked her teeth and replied, "That was a big bitch. I didn't feel like fighting no big bitch. Had to make a point and had to make it quick."

With a smirk, I said, "Okay but even the point was a bit much don't you think?"

She rolled her eyes and said, "Coming from the one throwing desks and getting expelled from school. Pot meets kettle bitch! Pot meets kettle!"

While throwing my hands up in the air, I exclaimed, "She threw a book at me first!"

Niecy shrugged and said, "Just throw the book back. Y'all both missed so that was definitely a bit much don't you think?"

I looked at Niecy with a bit of gratitude as we shared these laughs together because her love was pure. The guilt of sleeping with Dustin was becoming overwhelming but the reality of being HIV positive was even more gut wrenching. I was refusing to take my medicine and was not only fine with dying but fine with passing it along to any man that I could.

It was ultimately their choice to sleep with me without a condom. Niecy was the only person that I knew I could confide something as big as this to and yet when the question of *'Who gave you HIV?'*

were to come up, I would've been too afraid to face the music of my actions as I'm was sure that it was Dustin but there she sat HIV negative. No stds. No diseases. In complete bliss while I sat in complete misery.

It was believed by everybody that Niecy only ever wanted Dustin and although he stepped out with everybody around her, we all believed him when he said he really loved her. It's just the way that life was and everybody had accepted that monogamy was a thing only between fictional characters.

Other than that, there has never been a story where true love prevailed, and monogamy existed in the same time period. The men envied Dustin for having his cake and eating it too and the women cursed him a thousand times over for always leaving them with nothing but a bad back and a kid or two to remember their time together.

Although I didn't want to be the one to rain misery on my dear friend's parade of love, I certainly didn't mind dipping in the gossip pool with everybody else while adding my own two cents in. After a while, the snickers and whispers of Niecy not knowing what Dustin did behind her back was all Jackson, Mississippi could talk about until now.

She walked around a proud and wealthy widow having the luxury of not going through a divorce where Dustin would've walked away with half of all that money. He wouldn't have cared what Niecy would've done after the divorce was finalized, just as long as he was good. At the same time, everything that Dustin had been doing was coming to light in the midst of their break up and just like the rest of the city, I stayed quiet on what I knew to be true.

Baby Aaliyah started to stir making cooing sounds on the baby monitor as I sighed and said, "I don't know what to do. All she does is cry."

Niecy chuckled and replied, "Should've sucked more dick."

I glared at Niecy while holding back the urge to say who my baby's father really was as I rolled my eyes and said, "Girl whatever. When do your kids get home?"

With a smile, Niecy replied, "Oh they didn't have school today. We're heading to Hurricane Harbor in Houston in the morning for their twelfth birthday. It's not much but it's something."

Jealousy and disgust ran through my veins like hot lava as I got up and started to wash the dishes, once again ignoring baby Aaliyah causing Niecy to see to her once more. I was ready to clock Niecy right in the mouth for simply being happy when she should've been just as miserable as me. When she walked back in holding baby Aaliyah, I replied, "They'll love it but it should've been Disney World."

She nodded as she sat down at the kitchen table and replied, "Maybe next time." She looked around once more and slid a business card across the table as she said, "This is just in case you're ever feeling overwhelmed and need somebody to talk to."

I picked up the card and instantly felt offended as I hissed, "A therapist? I just had a baby Niecy! Shit ain't gone be peachy fucking perfect."

We were both single mothers of kids by the same dead man and Niecy understood the emotions of being a new mom without any help. I was lucky enough to have Ken whereas all Niecy had was her legally blind grandmother at eighteen years old and a set of twins. She of all people knew how real baby blues could be and I know that she simply wanted to offer me some professional help.

After baby Aaliyah was quiet and content, Niecy left while I held a small knife in my hand believing that this pain would be the only thing that gave me the much needed relief of the intense and overwhelming emotions that seemed beyond my control. Even if only for a moment, the sting of the blade sliding across my wrists made me gasp is pleasure casting all my troubles aside.

ACT FIVE

ACCEPTANCE

"The ache for home lives in all of us. The safe place where we can go as we are and not be questioned."
-Maya Angelou, All God's Children Need Traveling Shoes-

QUALITY TIME

"It's not all in vain
No, no Lord, no
Cause up the road is eternal gain"
-The Clark Sisters & Dr. Mattie Moss Clark-

Iyanla: Fix My Life

"*I remember syrup sandwiches and crime allowances. Finesse a nigga with some counterfeits, but now I'm countin' this.*" - HUMBLE by Kendrick Lamar

Imani

I stood at the door patting my foot hoping that my mama wouldn't answer and that I could have left knowing that I tried without the extra work that's required. The door opened after the third knock and there stood my mama in nothing but a bra and panties looking like she had just woken up. The early morning sunlight made her squint her eyes and cover her face and yet it didn't stop her from recognizing her daughter as she grunted, "Well aren't you a sight for sore eyes?"

Waiting patiently for her to move, I smiled, "Hey mama."

She wasn't at all as excited to see her only child even with the recent events that's happened. I was abducted and tortured for almost two years by my best friend and her husband and of course my mama didn't care. She stood to the side as if I was a salesperson and she needed the entertainment. I walked in remembering the last time that I was there was Christmas and that damn party that my mama insisted that I attend.

With a sadden look on my face, I looked around to see that the decorations were still up. Nothing was different from that night other the pale scent of Newport's and the eerily feeling that you get in every horror movie right before a terrible jump scare. It wasn't hard to figure out that Xavier must've been snatched up after leaving my house that night.

We sat down in the living room across from each other and before I could start talk-ing, my mama asks, "So what do you want because I don't have any money?"

I shook my head while saying, "I didn't come here for money. Am I bothering you by being here?"

My mama cleared her throat as she replied, "Of course, I'm bothered that my one and only daughter has been back for months and hasn't come to see her only mother."

Baffled by her words, I took a second before replying. Normally I'd be pissed at the utter display of bullshit that I was being shown but in these days, I was unable to hold true anger in my heart for even a second. My mama's goal with every word that came out of her mouth was to belittle you, manipulate you, and completely make you think that you're crazy.

It was the reason that I kept my distance for so long but even distance didn't stop me from feeling worthless because of my mama's words and actions. My deep breaths gave my mama the pleasure that she needed in knowing that her words had affected me negatively and yet I was more surprised at the care she didn't give versus the attitude that she always had. I didn't want to say the wrong thing and cause an argument, but I wanted to be honest with her as I replied, "Mama, I haven't done anything in the months that I've been back but try to heal and get back on my feet. I would've come to see you sooner, but this transition hasn't been easy. I'm here now though. Better late than never, right?"

I smiled but my words didn't transfer as appealing as my mama spoke with her natural condescending tone, "Had you been here, it would've been easier. Always in the fucking streets running up behind some damn body that don't want you."

I sighed. Silence filled the space between us. Only my mama could make a big deal out of trying to get back on your feet however I didn't come here to argue with her. I just wanted to talk to her and express my truths and feelings and it was as if my mama knew exactly why I was there with the way that she was trying to deflect this conversation as it's happened several times before. Whenever I tried to come clean as a teen, my mama did everything in her power to not only dis-miss my feelings but to validate her actions for treating me like shit beneath her shoe.

I only ever had my best friend to talk to and in the end, Lauren used everything against me. I could feel the moisture from my mouth disappear as I begin to speak softly, "Katrina used to question me about YOUR Willie and when she told you that you needed to watch him around me, you just stopped talking to her. Kept me away from my dad's side of the family all because Katrina warned you about your pedophile of a husband."

My mama sneered as she interrupted me, "That lying bitch! My Willie ain't did nobody wrong. All that bitch ever did was lie on everybody while fucking everybody's man. She had a lot to say but couldn't say how she stole JohnJohn's father from me. He should've been my son. My Willie was a great man, and you know it!"

And the award for Toxic Mother of the Year always went to my mama. This was the time for us to forgive each other and move forward from this but I finally realized that it wasn't going to happen unless both par-ties wanted it to happen only after accepting their part in the bullshit that we caused. My final attempt to share my truths was when I said, "No mama, he wasn't good to me, and he wasn't good to you either. He took advantage of my age, and he used you. Everybody could see it."

Memories started to flood my mind from the mean mug that sat on my mama's face. Suddenly I was feeling worthless as I remembered the days when I'd get cussed out for being too fat and eating up all of the food simply because I wanted a second piece of chicken from a twenty piece box of chicken that was being split between three people. Shame covered my face thinking back to the days when my mama pushed me onto Xavier multiple times when I was a teen.

The many car rides that I tried to get out of would make my mama cuss me out and force me to ride with the man knowing he only wanted to fondle me freely in the privacy of those car rides. Sometimes he'd go out of his to get an hour room and have his way with me. My mama always turned a blind eye to the many times that I wanted to talk to her when Xavier wasn't around. The fact that her husband was only with her for her daughter left her with a feeling of rejection that made her find any and every reason to beat on me or call the cops to take me away with the story that I was a troubled teen that was constantly attacking her in her own home.

Angrily my mama spoke with her hands balled into fists, ready to swing, "If you've got something to say, then bitch I suggest you say it."

Softly with a timid tremble, I uttered, "I'm sorry mama."

My mama hissed, "Sorry for what? Fucking my husband?!" My silence and body language was all that my mama needed to understand precisely what I was sorry for. She nodded as she sucked her teeth and said, "Another nothing ass hoe. I fed you and clothed you and made sure you had a roof over your trifling ass head and in return you go and fuck my husband? That nigga should've killed your nasty ass!"

Her anger was expected. Her words were not in the least bit surprising to hear. I gave an attempt at explaining my side and how it started as I said, "But mama I tried to tell you. You just never wanted to hear the truth. He wasn't a good man mama!"

The waterworks started going while the blame rained down on me as my mama said, "Your fat ass could've said no! You wanted him. Too fucking fat and lazy to go out and get your own man to slop around with. You ain't never tried to tell me shit because your nasty ass loved fucking him. And now you want to blame somebody for

the shit that you loved. You're not going to blame me for that shit. I didn't make you do anything that you didn't want to do."
A realization of truth appeared on my face as I spoke boldly, "You know what mama. You're right. At the end of the day, I never said you made me do anything. I'm saying it wasn't hard to do it when you treated me like a piece of shit. I was a child that didn't know ANYTHING! I fell in love with how he showed me love and affection after the bullshit that YOU would do. Oh yeah, I definitely loved fucking him and I did it because I wanted to. I don't deny that, but I tried to tell you. It was you that wouldn't listen."
My mama became irate and started going off and as I stood up to leave, she was ready for war over a dead man as she said, "Bitch I wish you would hit me!"
I shook my head while my mama got into a fighting stance ready to defend her reputation as a wonderful wife and mother. I walked right past her and out of the front door. For all of the times that I tried to reconcile with her after an argument, I promised myself that this time I would never look back. The only actions that I was responsible for were my own and I admitted that I was wrong.
When I needed a mother, mine wasn't there. I had to learn to be my own mother and patch up my wounds the best way that I could. When I needed love, it was Xavier who gave me his messed up version of it. When I needed protecting, it was my best friend that came through no matter how jealous she was deep down. My mama was too self-ab-sorbed to ever truly care about me but that's okay because I still loved her and wished her nothing but the best in life. After leaving my mama's house, I headed to Dr. Simone Julez office in Madison for another therapy session in helping me move on from these inner demons that I had to face. Dr. Julez was so well educated with all of her degrees and different awards plastered over

the walls. I was so impressed with how this well educated black woman was all extra proud of her African heritage.

She had a couple of Mother In Law Tongues in the corners, abstract paintings filling the walls, fertility statues beside the door, and this beautiful water fountain next to the bookcase. She was even dressed like one of those women from Ace's church that think they're from Wakanda or somewhere, so the first thought that ran through my mind was that she's probably going to tell her to pray about it, but Dr. Julez was nothing like what I had imagined a therapist to be like.

As soon as I came in and sat down, Dr. Julez didn't skip a beat, "You've made a lot of progress since our first session. Are you still having nightmares?"

I nodded with a sigh as she said, "Some nights I do. Everything replays over and over again. I still can't get Lauren's face out of my head. I've tried just about everything I could think of and still I jump out of my sleep. I can say it's slowed down a bit. The nightmares are here and there now. I suppose it could be adjusting to my new apartment."

Dr. Julez clasped her hands together and continued, "Imani, this is all very normal. It's only been seven months since you were found and rescued. There's no guarantee that the nightmares will ever stop." I took those words in with a grain of salt. It wasn't what I wanted to hear her say but everything that she said was right. Overall, I was still healing, and there was no sure-fire way to get rid of these nightmares. She continued, "Have you finally spoken with your mother yet? In our last session you mentioned your desire to mend the relationship."

I sighed and replied, "Yeah that's not something I really want to do anymore. I think it's best if I stayed out of her life for good."

Dr. Juelz nodded with understanding as she said, "You'd be surprised at the outcome. Communication is a start."

I started to fidget with my fingers as I glanced out of the window. I shrugged and replied, "I understand that but regardless I know she hates me plus I tried the communication thing. Nothing changed." Dr. Juelz leaned in and held both of my hands in hers as she sweetly explained, "The only thing that should be of importance to you is that you don't hate you. We as humans cannot control the emotions or actions of another person and we are not required to. If hating you is what she chooses to do, then acceptance is what you have to do for you." I smirked and said, "I accept it and then what? Endure her toxic evil ways until she just randomly decides to love me?" Calmly she spoke, "Accept not endure. You should never stay where you are not respected. Accept your life for what it is with her and not what you want it to be. We all want wonderful loving mothers; however, we do not get to pick our parents. Imani, you are grown, you do not have to endure anybody's toxicity or evilness. You must love yourself enough to leave a person that treats you like this no matter who that person is."

I nodded and said, "That's something I realized after talking to her. I love her and ultimately, I forgive her, but I have washed my hands with her with love in my heart. I still only want the best for her, but I am no longer worried about her the way I used to be. I am only concerned with getting my life back on track and seeing what the future holds for me."

The session ended on a positive note with Dr. Julez prescribing me marijuana to combat my anxiety from the traumas that I experienced, even though I was expecting Dr. Juelz to say that I needed to look over my mom's toxicity and continue to endure her ways since that was my one and only mother. It was refreshing to be able to walk away from somebody that would only cause me heartache.

The memories of my childhood flooded in as I thought to myself how the conversation should have gone if my mama loved herself correctly. It's impossible to love anybody when you have no love for yourself. Self love is a sense of freedom within yourself where you are no longer bound by stereotypes and the norms of society. It's when you can look into the mirror and see beauty and perfection in your flaws.

With a smile on my face, I drove down I-55 towards Byram, no longer feeling the guilt for not wanting to deal with the toxic traits of others even if that meant no longer dealing with my own mama.

Tennessee Whiskey

"She a shy girl, but she a freak deep down. Pussy royalty, needs to be crowned. We should leave town, sex is better overseas." -Nasty by Russ

Chanice

His voice was low and demanding as he whispered in my ear, "Come sit on my face."
I tried my best not to react where anybody else could see. I darted my eyes to the side and watched his fine black ass walk away. My entire body was on fire ready to follow him like the lovesick puppy that I was, but I kept my composure, and it was a good thing that I did. We were in the middle of filming our first episode of *'The Melanin Midas Empire'* which was a reality show on Bravo that focused on how I moved as a businesswoman while showcasing the multitude of talent that surrounded me.
Lester and I were taking the art of dance to another level as we had started a small fifteen city tour for Femme Fatale IV and Team Flye with guest appearances from the Les Twins and the Jabbawockeez while Chris Brown performed his songs from upbeat to slow for most of our routines where he'd sometimes commence to a quick dance battle with Lester.
The dance battles only made Lester live up to his name of being Showout King. Nobody cared who actually won as it was just nice to see a fine ass dark skinned man and a fine ass light skinned man dancing on stage. While we were we on break during the tour, we

dabbled in extracurricular activities for the show as well as for our own personal entertainment. We were currently in Arizona getting ready to tour the Grand Canyon on horses, when I turned around to see Destiny standing at the kitchen table that was behind me, holding a coffee mug with a clear attitude. I dismissed her body language until Destiny asked, "Did his crazy ass say something to you?"

For whatever reason, I loved playing dumb with Destiny just to see what she'd say and do. Asking for permission to spread my legs had never been my thing so I couldn't understand why she thought that I cared to confirm or deny what I had going on with Lester since it was so obvious to everybody around us. She should've been lucky to even be able to tag along but the hoe in her was never satisfied. I didn't miss a beat as I replied with a confused look, "Who?"

Destiny rolled her eyes and said, "Girl, Showout. He didn't say something to you just now?"

I shook my head and shrugged, "If he did, I didn't hear him."

Unfortunately for Destiny, I wasn't about to feed into her delusions of any kind. I've always known that she was worse than Janay when it came to skipping in the crazy land of wanting some dick and naturally acted possessive about any boy that even looked her way. There was never a real reason behind why she felt the need to claim every hydrant that she pissed on but that's exactly what Destiny loved to do. It could've been something as simple as a kiss and dinner and she was planning their wedding date, so I've always been dismissive about who Destiny claimed as hers. Always tuning her out since all the stories sounded the same in the end. They fucked and they didn't want her.

It's been years since I actually encouraged the girl that I once considered a friend to be better or even telling her everything like when we were in high school. All of her crazy schemes made that null and void. Destiny has always been a compulsive liar to any and everybody that she's ever met but I believed that with time Destiny would let that pain and hurt go. After so long a Capricorn's heart turns cold no matter who is it and then there's no turning back to what you once had with them.

Blinded by my big doe eyes and baby face, Destiny believed that I was too much of a good girl to ever really do her wrong and go after a man that she claimed to love. She knew that I accepted her hoe ways and fucked up stories and she loved me for it, but I was no longer with the shits. Sis was bad for business, and I had to be careful about who I allowed to attach themselves to my name. Katrina Chanice had become a brand whereas Destiny was still the same selfish and lying jealous hoe that she's always been.

Destiny continued in a whisper, "Cause I was gone go upside his head if he was. Bitch he been fucking the shit out of me every fucking night!"

I giggled as I sipped my tea and said, "Nah na not every night. That's crazy how he just jumps from my bed to yours."

Destiny threw her hands up and replied, "I know right! But how am I going to say no to that dick? Carlos is bigger though."

I continued to sip my tea as I chuckled at how my words always seemed to go over her head. Either she was an amazing actress, or she was really fucking stupid but it wasn't long before Ken walked in and smacked Destiny on the ass while saying, "Good morning bay."

Destiny softly scoffed and replied, "Morning."

Imani walked in and spoke with excitement, "Y'all gotta start a YouTube show like the Ellises. Man, y'all are sooo cute. It would go straight viral!"

Ken eagerly replied, "I'm with it. What you think bay?"

Destiny did her *'I'm about to lie'* giggle and said, "Y'all already know I'm with the shits!" Ken eyed me seductively as he openly flirted, "We'll need somebody to hold the camera."

Chaos replied with disgust, "Ain't nobody got time for that unless y'all don't want to go horseback riding? So what's up?"

Destiny was about to decline until I started a TikTok dance and begin to sing, *'When the sun goes down, on my side town!'*

Chaos and Carlos joined in, *'That lonesome feeling comes to my door and the whole world turns!'*

Destiny and Ken looked in horror at the scene taking place before them. Both of them extremely jealous of the show taking place before them. We danced and walked away with no care in the world, laughing and ready to do a quick TikTok video to Brooks and Dunn's *'Neon Moon'* as soon as we got around the horses. This was all the proof Destiny believed that she needed.

For her, it was so obvious to know that I was getting flipped ten ways from Sunday by Chaos and Carlos. She lived in her delusions, believing what she told herself instead of the truth that was presented to her. Still believing that she'd successfully blocked me from Lester, she was left to witness me carelessly flirting with Chaos and Carlos in her face. After marrying Dustin, I apparently, wasn't allowed to have another one of her men.

Ken mixed them some drinks for this nature adventure that Destiny hated as she was by far the biggest hater of nature. All wildlife creatures, the sun, the outside itself was a hell no for her. I on the other hand was a true country girl at heart and loved everything dealing with nature until the mosquitoes started tagging me but aside from that I loved being outside and I had been wanting to go horseback riding for a while.

Being with my childhood sweetheart only made it extra special for me. Imani tried only because of Ace but eventually the beautiful views of the Grand Canyon erased all of her fears and doubts.

While my sorority sister, Nina convinced Chaos to take her on a wagon ride instead, hoping to get her in a better mood since she was no longer feeling the trip and ready to go home. Ken was working hard to convince the masses that he was about that country life. He'd say anything really to get in a girl's pants or be the coolest guy in the room and at this point he was feeling forgotten causing him to compete with everybody for the spotlight.

Destiny was the true definition of a city girl and all of this *'True Life: Day in the Life of a Country Mofo'* was becoming a drag especially when the horse bucked and almost had Ken flying down the trail. When Destiny attempted to mount the horse, she started crying real tears because her leg wouldn't swing around to the other side like the guide had showed her four times. She panicked and screamed, "I'm having heart palpitations y'all! I can't do this shit!"

Lester and I were already down the pathway enjoying the ride and taking in the gorgeous view that surrounded us when we heard Destiny screaming. We laughed to ourselves and continued on while Destiny and Ken stayed behind at the stables, drinking and letting the misinformation that Destiny gave herself about me to be the reason for the inappropriate schemes that she silently plotted to herself.

Almost four hours later, we were all back at the AirBnB in Scottsdale. Too tired to do anything else for the night. Ace suggested a movie night in the theater room and yet nobody was really feeling anything aside from going to sleep except me. With a bowl of popcorn in one hand, I walked into the theater room with a smile ready to watch this *'Candyman'* remake and the amazing gory scenes it had to offer all by myself. Although Lester wouldn't admit it, I knew that he still wasn't a fan of horror movies, so I didn't bother asking him to watch it with me.

This was one of my many guilty pleasures and I didn't mind enjoying it alone. The movie had barely started when the door opened making me roll my eyes as the sweet idea of being alone flew out of the door however, I was relieved to have Lester sit down beside me. He leaned closer to me, and I thought he was going to whisper more naughty commands in my ear but instead he begins to nibble on the bottom of my earlobe. I laughed and said, "I know you see me watching this movie."

He teased as he said softly, "I'm not stopping you."

He continued planting kisses with light nibbles on my neck while his hands squeezed on my breasts. I placed the popcorn aside and started kissing him passionately needing him in every way. I stood up and seductively rolled my hips taking off my shorts. His gym shorts were pulled down to his ankles and his rod standing at attention when I straddled him in his seat. I rode him like I was back on the Grand Canyon trail. He moaned lowly in my ear turning me on more and making me speed up slightly.

I had one hand on the back of his neck nibbling on his ear when I whispered, "Say my name."

He let out a small chuckle and moaned, "Niecy."

I continued my ride for a few minutes longer before getting up and spinning around, mounting him once again. With my hands on the recliner in front of me, I popped this ass for pimp like I was back at Freelons creating a slaying sound that echoed through the horror music that played on the screen. A murder was taking place onscreen and, in the theater room, yet both killers were filled with pleasure and satisfaction from their actions.

Lester gripped my hips and caught the rhythm to the point where sweat drenched our bodies making the stings of his ass smacks linger longer than before. I damn near ripped a hole in the seat trying not to scream out in pleasure. Even though I leaned back up, Lester kept stroking as much as possible while rubbing my pearl. He wasn't about to sit back down so he turned to put his back on the wall which is exactly what I wanted.

I leaned back down with my hands on the floor allowing Lester to pound me out as much as he wanted. He slowed down in confusion when my leg lifted into a spilt as my foot rested on the wall. He raised an eye-brow at the clear observation of me wanting to be slutted out like his personal little pornstar in the worse way. Just as he was about to speed up is when my other leg raised up and I started pussy popping on his American bandstand. Every time he thought he had me in check, I showed out in a different way.

He dipped out and quickly picked my short ass up so he could taste my sweetness and I wasted no time returning the favor with his shaft in my mouth. Lester could bust a few times and still be ready to bust again with the hardest mandingo in the land. When 1 heard the doorknob shake is when Lester let me down and I sat in the recliner with his dick filling my mouth up again while hearing him whisper between the knocks on the door, "Don't worry Niecy, I locked it."

With my hair entwined in his fingers, he stroked my face making me moan with satisfaction. My hands massaged his body with excitement. He could feel the next load ready to shoot out but when he looked down to warn me, I locked eyes with him and softly hummed with approval to what I was eagerly desiring. My throat filled with his warm elixir while my suction eased up slightly as my strokes continued. Lester was still rock hard when his knees buckled just a bit making him grab the recliner behind him.

His breathing staggering as I sat back grinning, watching him regain his composure and knowing his competitive ass was about to blow my back out just like I wanted. With nothing but trouble swimming in his hazel brown eyes, he grabbed my legs and pulled me to the edge and with no warning he started plowing me with only one intention and that was to put my ass to sleep.

The sounds of him pounding me recklessly cascaded louder than the music coming from the movie. Lester no longer cared who heard us. It was probably time that we made things official and told everybody any-way. He leaned down and kissed me as he shot off in my walls for the final time.

Fatal Attraction

"Don't you see that I got baggage. My heart's way too hard to manage. I can't give a nigga my trust." - Bare With Me by Teyana Taylor

Destiny

My mama spoke freely, "What made you choose this poor imitation of a man?"
As I rocked my baby, I vigorously shook the six ounce baby bottle of powdered milk and replied, "A poor imitation of a man. Seriously?"
My mama stood at the window in the living room watching Ken carelessly flirt with the young beautiful neighbor next door as she said, "I certainly didn't stutter." She sighed and continued, "The house is nice. The car is cute. The baby isn't deformed and yet this was the best you could do?"
I shook my head and said, "What the fuck do you want from me? How is this not good enough for you?"
Taken aback, my mama replied, "For me? I don't live here. This was clearly all for you!" I scoffed as I said, "Oh so that's the problem? I don't have enough space for you. I didn't find a man with enough money or value to buy you a house as well. Is that what it is?"
While shaking her head, my mama sighs and says, "You didn't find a man at all. You found some low life little boy to shack up with. You could've done so much better, but you never listen."
I sat down and fed my baby as I said, "What exactly was I supposed to do? Just smile and look pretty?"

Without hesitation, my mama sarcastically replied, "That's about all you're good for." She sighed and continued, "Destiny men are simple, but it's more than just treating them nice and expecting them to treat you nice."

I rolled my eyes at the words that my mama was saying. The shit never worked for me. All I ever got was fucked and forgotten. A bunch of broken promises and fake ass engagements rings that turned my ring finger green. I concluded years ago that I wasn't the pretty girl that my mama claimed that I was. It obvious to me that I was nothing more than a cold pot of grits left on the back burner of an abandoned house.

The men my mama had hoped that I would snag, wasn't checking for me unless it was to bust a nut, leaving the money on the nightstand, and tiptoeing back home to their perfect little wives. After so many rejections, I've grown accustomed to my place in these men's lives, and I didn't dare to stray from the position in which I worked so hard for. With my head down, avoiding eye contact, I lied, "I'm happy with Ken. He treats me nice and what we have is wonderful."

My mama scoffed as she spun around saying, "What you have here is a joke. That boy don't love you and ain't gone give you shit without your name being on it. You're a gotdamn fool and I don't need you calling me when he kicks your stupid ass out."

With an aggravated tone, I replied, "Maybe you should leave?"

My mama nodded her head as she picked up her Michael Kors purse and walked to the front door before saying, "It's your life Destiny. Live it how you want to."

A simple *'See you later'* or *'Goodbye'* would've sufficed but my mama needed her words to sting with a reminder of her disapproval at how I chose to live my life. The type of attention that I craved from a man only came from being what my mama would call is *'his lap dog.'* I needed a master. Someone that dictated me beyond the bedroom. It wasn't disrespect. It was pleasure and it was a preference that only a certain few knew exactly how to master. I wanted to surrender to the power of a man however too many men fell for a beautiful face, becoming whimpering cowards in the heat of the moment.

Although my mama seen a poor imitation of a man, I seen a king. No man was perfect as they all had flaws and they were all natural flirts. I could care less about what this man did outside of the home, as long as he paid the fucking bills. I'm not here because of love and I understand that a man loves having his toys. I didn't mind being this man's puppet, doing any and everything he wanted and needed. This was the catering effect of compromise that I gave to all of my men.

To lay down and become their nastiest fantasy while getting up only when they said to and cleaning the house up like the good Stanford wife that I pretended to be, despite the missing wedding ring on my ring finger. This wasn't love. This was a business deal. Take care of me and I'll take care of you.

After putting baby Aaliyah down for her nap, I started on dinner while Ken sat on the sofa with his feet propped up on the living room table, drinking a bud light as he yelled at the basketball game on the TV. I tried the best that I could to ignore my mama's disapproval but the broken little girl within me felt the need to say something especially after seeing who the little neighbor bitch was, so I walked up to him and spoke boldly, "So you fucking this neighbor bitch?"

Completely dumbfounded by my approach, the only words that came out of his mouth were, "Am I fucking my friend's ex wife?"

Hearing that bitch's name come out of his mouth instantly pissed me off. He was playing dumb with me when he should've known better. I drew my hand back and slapped him. The sting had him feeling like he had gotten hit with a hot cast iron skillet. I was inches from his face yelling about disrespecting me with this bitch. He sat there with his eyes closed taking in deep breaths as I continued screaming while feeling my hot breath in a mist of sour cheap vodka induced blunts. Patiently, he waited until I was done screaming to reply, "Yeah, I'm fucking her. Been fucking her for years and I don't plan on stopping. Not for you or any other bitch ass motherfucker!"

I sighed and began to rub my forehead from the headache that I had caused myself until seconds later when the entire mood changed again as Ken had gotten up storming into the bedroom to pack up my shit. I pursued him while pleading and hoping to explain how I didn't care and that it didn't matter but he wasn't hearing anything that I was saying. I cried out some more hoping to appeal to his better nature as I said, "Baby I'm sorry. Please just hear me out."

He shoved me into the wall creating a huge dent as he screamed, "Bitch keep your hands off of me!"

I screamed louder waking baby Aaliyah up as I said, "What the fuck does she have that I don't?"

As he continued to pack my things, I started throwing punches on his back. His infatuation with me was only because I made everybody believe that I was Show-out's girl but being his ex-wife was better. He slung me onto the floor where I grabbed his foot to stop him from leaving out of the room with my things.

He kicked me off accidently causing pain in my left eye that would later become a black eye, but he wasn't apologetic about the shit because he wanted me to get the fuck out. I followed behind him out the front door and down the stairs still trying to snatch my things from him as he yelled, "Bitch gone! Get the fuck off my property!"

I charged him with a closed fist, and he blocked the punch. Anger had finally taken control as he lifted me up and body slammed me into the windshield of his black Ford Fusion. Unable to scream as the hit had knocked the wind out of me, I rolled off while holding my back and walked up to him, hacking up a wad of spit aiming it right for his face. He stepped back and paused for a moment realizing the utter disrespect as I charged him again, kicking him between the legs.

When he bent over in pain, I started landing punches in the back of his head and he body slammed me onto the ground, pinning me in the grass. He had me locked down with his entire body while he cuffed my hands with the handcuffs that he'd snatched off of the dresser. Before he stood up, I could feel the fire from his hand onto my left cheek making my left eye throb more in pain.

He dragged me back into the house with a need to release his frustrations without re-morse. When he's happy, he's just horny all of the time. It's not romantic. It's not pas-sionate. It's just a lot of sex. One day, he's into BDSM to the fullest and the next it's just a moment that just passes by. I never cared as long as he was satisfied but I also never fully experienced the torture that he could inflict when he was angry. Ken tried his best not to allow his dark side to be seen and it was the reason he didn't mind having me around. I knew how to soothe the villain within keeping him locked away forever but tonight I left a triggering impression.

Safe words didn't exist in this darkness while limits and boundaries were meant to be crossed. No woman has ever lasted more than a few months with Ken because his villainous nature always seemed to run them off. He was always too rough and completely selfish. He never catered to a female's body or cared to explore what set her body on fire. Instead, he preferred to be the fire in the worse way. Always looking for new ways to inflict the most unbearable pain to the point of death until their bodies gave up. Those angry days could last for weeks, and every little thing only made it worse. There was no escaping the anger. He didn't care to hear me moan or to pleasure me. This was strictly for him. If it made him happy then he was going to do it as much as he wanted to.

After dragging me back inside of the house, he slung me unto the bedroom causing my head to hit the bedpost as he closed the door and locked it. He went and calmed baby Aaliyah down until she dozed back off to sleep. Ken had an array of his special toys hidden in his guest bedroom in a chest in the closet.

Since I felt the need to talk a lot of shit, he took out his scold's bridle along with his thick leather belt and made his way back to the master bedroom. I was sitting up on the bed attempting to plead my case once again, "Baby I'm sorry. I didn't mean any of this. I love you and sometimes I just get a little jealous is all. I. I shouldn't have blown up on you like I did."

Ken nodded his head as he took the cuffs off of my hands. I rubbed my wrists with a smile as he commanded, "Take your clothes off."

Eagerly, I did as I was told not caring what he had in store for me. Once I was naked, he placed the scold's bridle over my head. An old fashion dog muzzle made just for men to humiliate women with. Delight filled his eyes as I stood before him completely naked looking like the fool that I was. He placed his hands on my shoulders and turned me around, instructing me to lay on my stomach on the bed. He tied both of my hands and feet to the bedposts and with an evil grin, he commenced to beating me with his thick leather belt until my skin broke causing mini streams of blood to ooze out.

My silent sobs were heard as low whimpering groans of agony and misery unable to speak because of the muzzle and barely able to breath because of the pain while the words of my past echoed in the back of my mind, *'Treat them nice and they'll treat you nice.'*

At Last

"I like what you're sayin. Boy, it sounds real good, real good. But are you ready for a real woman, To test your manhood." - This Lil Game We Play by Subway & 702

Imani

Awe filled silence was in the air as DJ 51/50 started to play a song while the lovely couple began to dance their first dance for the second time with the pictures from their first wedding flashing across the wall behind them. A lot had changed in their appearance, but time was still on their side. Five kids and thirty years later and she still looked amazing in her peach colored wedding gown. Her locs were longer now with beautiful salt and pepper streaks that were pinned up under her crown. His hightower fade had faded away as he was now bald. They swayed together in harmony until the music stopped An uproar of applause came as they walked hand in hand from the dance floor with smiles wider than ever.

The epitome of black love at its finest. I yearned for the day when I could look in the eyes of my forever love with a burning desire that lasted for decades. They walked around thanking family and friends for attending their vow renewal. When I noticed that they were coming my way, my first instinct was to run and hide because I didn't know those people from Adam, and I didn't want to explain how I was a last-minute invitation and not crashing their beautiful ceremony. They approached me at the table and the happy bride wasted no time in saying, "I'm so happy you could make it! I have been wanting to meet you. You are just so beautiful!"

Her husband chimed in, "Where is that knucklehead boy of mine? I can't believe he'd leave you over here by yourself. You're too beautiful to be left alone. It's some vultures in this family and he knows that."

Understanding the confusion, I replied, "Oh no I'm not who you think I am. I'm Ace's friend. I'm not his girlfriend, Terica."

She smiled, "It's Imani, right?"

I nodded with a smile. Her husband says to her, "Baby don't butt in."

Her side eye was hilarious. I giggled to myself as she said, "Honey will you hush. Now Imani I know who Terica is but I'm happy that you're not her and I'm hoping to see much more of you."

Just as I was about to reply, Ace walked up and said, "Mom, you're badgering her. Let her breath a little."

She glared at him as Bishop Walls replied for his First Lady, "Boy where you been? You're supposed to be with your date. You know how your cousins are when they see a new pretty face."

Ace stepped to the side to speak with his adopted dad while his mother continued to get to know me as she said, "I have heard so much about you. Ace talks about you all the time. I am thrilled to finally meet you. We have this annual church trip coming up soon. We'll be heading to The Potter's House. It's our first joint concert so of course Bishop TD Jakes and Pastor Joel Sims are expecting this to be the revival of the nations, and I hope you'll be able to attend."

With an intrigued look on my face, I replied, "Oh wow, I didn't know he was doing all that but umm, I hope so. This has been a wonderful ceremony. You two are just beautiful together. I mean the love just flows."

She nodded with a smile and spoke as she stared at the Bishop, "It still amazes me how we've made it work for so long. Not every day has been filled with roses and lingerie and despite having five kids we've managed to keep our eternal love flame burning for all of these years. Oh yeah there were days that I could've really bopped him upside that bald head of his in the name of Jesus but the days like this where you say the love just flows, those days happened with ease way more than any bad day we've had. I've prayed that all of my children find a love like ours if not better."

As nervous as I was to watch them walk over to me, sitting beside me at this table looking at Bishop Walls and Ace was not so bad after all. She loved her family, and it was something I had not ever seen before in my life. A mother's love. I wondered, *'Is it possible to possess this kind of love for a child when you never experienced it yourself?'* I looked on with hope in my heart that one day I too could look at my husband and children with the same prayers in my heart.

Being around a family filled with love and morals is something that I didn't know I was craving for until now and after today I knew that I was going to hound Ace about any and all family or church events from now on. It was possible that I might meet a cousin that's right up my alley! I agreed, "I'm sure they will. They all have these great role models as parents. I don't think you have anything to worry about."

She looked at me as she said, "I like you Imani. I hope my son sees what he has before it's too late."

I shook my head, "Oh no we're just friends."

Bishop Walls and Ace stepped back to the table as she stood up and said, "Yeah, I remember saying those words about thirty years ago. As a matter of fact, I didn't want to admit it at first, but I fell in love with him the day I met. Now, I don't know what life could be without him."

Bishop Walls smiled as he said, "Mi'Lady get your nose out of that and come on and cut this cake with me."

They walked off while Ace and I shook our heads in laughter. The older generation stayed with the hooks up especially during a wedding. They see two people in a crowd smile at each other and immediately they think those two people should get married and have babies. That is not how relationships and love work. Although I didn't mind my future in laws being Bishop Walls and his beautiful First Lady, I was confident that Ace was not my future husband.

Over by the DJ booth, I watched as Carlos was a second away from popping the question to Mion while Lester and Niecy glided across the dance floor in an enchanted trance as the Walls boys two younger sisters entertained the twins, Tia and Tamara. What I saw was two people that seemed to have gotten it right. The marriage, the kids, and the careers. No generational curses. All chains broken. I wanted to learn a lot from people like Bishop Walls and his First Lady.

Ace waved his hand in front of my face while saying, "Earth to Imani."

I shook my head and replied, "Sorry. Your parents are beautiful together. It's hard not to watch them."

With a nod and a smile, he says, "Yeah, I hear ya. They got their own vibe going on. I hope my mom didn't get on your nerves too bad though. She can sometimes be too much with her spidey senses that she thinks she has."

I laughed and inquired, "Really spidey senses? Sounds like Niecy's mom. That's cruel of you to say but no she didn't get on my nerves at all. I enjoyed talking to her. I would like to know what all has been said about me though. She said she's heard a lot about me." I nudged his side and continued, "So spill. What have you been saying sir?"

With a straight face he replied, "Huh? What you mean?"

I raised an eyebrow, "Dude, what have you been saying about me to your mom?"

He smirked, "Nothing. Just told her who you were since you were coming to the ceremony."

I mocked our favorite movie, *'You ain't gots to lie Craig!'* while rolling my neck and circling my finger in his face.

He gently grabbed my hand while looking me in the eyes. It was something about this moment that created a tingling sensation over my entire body. Ace has never made me feel faint like this before and I couldn't understand why I felt the way that I did as he asked, "Would you like to dance Miss Shelton?"

I stuttered, "S..s..sure."

As we hit the dance floor, DJ 51/50 had the building bumping with the best sounds from the 70s, 80s, and 90s. The crowd started a soul train line because why not? Both Ace and I had beads of sweat forming on our noses with shiny foreheads to match. Most of the men had pretty much gotten undressed from the formal attire they were wearing.

If their shirts weren't completely off, then they were wide open or had a few buttons undone. It looked as if somebody came along and poured gallons of water on all of them. The ladies that wore heels were now barefoot with the heels pushed to the side as they tried their best to drop it low in their gowns.

My favorite slow song blasted through the speakers at the request of Niecy. Those without dance partners left the floor as well as the ones too tired from twerking and jigging. I wouldn't dare sit my favorite song out and Niecy knew this. Ace placed his arms around my waist with my arms around his neck. This style of dancing wasn't something that was popular in Jackson, Mississippi.

Maybe it was too sensual for their taste. Some prudes refer to it as sex on the dance floor but to a true dancer it is simply the black Tango and Niecy and I loved to do it every chance that we got. A cameraman walked in circles around us causing the crowd to form a circle and watch as both couples grinded to the Haitian beat that played in the background.

Ace had never heard of the Kompa until I showed him after Niecy showed me. Aside from the grinding of our hips in close proximity, there's the in and out swaying of our bodies as we dance together in harmony to the beat of the music. It's as if we're a stream of water flowing with the music. Thankfully for Niecy, Lester had a bit too much of the hunch punch and had loosen up a bit. As the oldest of the five, he had an image to maintain in front of Bishop Walls and his First Lady. The image went out the door as he grinded his hips into Niecy as if he invented the Kompa himself.

At the end of the song, Ace dipped me and as I slowly came back up, he held me closer as if he wanted to kiss me until an uproar of applause and praise for our dancing broke the trance that we were in. We quickly left the dance floor and headed outside to cool off and get some fresh air. The sun had gone down showing the dark star filled sky while the wind blew slightly here and there. A storm was coming in the coming up days but tonight the weather was as perfect as it could be. Standing amongst parked cars and chatting it up, there was a vibe that I hadn't felt since before my trip to Hawaii. An undeniable chemistry between the two of us that I had been trying my best to deny.

Must be something about weddings and vow renewals that bring out something in you that you never knew existed before. It could've been just the scenery or maybe the energy from the dance, but I was seeing Ace in a totally different light. He has always been fine to me and there was a time that I wanted him to be mine, but we settled back into this friendship because of his playboy ways and me being caught up in all the wrong things. That has been so long ago though. We've graduated, gotten jobs, and have grown mentally. He's no longer the playboy he once was. He's actually become a true and faithful man.

Ace went from being my best friend to my only friend and nobody wanted a replay of how lustful hormones could mess up a friendship. The goal was to stay drama free and yet the energy between us had a lot of emotions floating around in the air. After that dance everybody was convinced that we were definitely more than friends. He stood in front of me saying, "I don't know if I said this, but I love this dress on you."

I looked down caressing the black strapless velvet felt gown that hugged all of my curves and draped around my ankles. The spilt came up to my thigh in which I had hoped wasn't showing too much, didn't have time to find anything different. An online purchase that I was forced to stick with. He continued, "You feeling all over yourself is only making my view better."

His comment made me blush and it was obvious that he was indeed feeling himself. Ace hadn't flirted with me since before Hawaii, so I asked, "Are you high?"

He chuckled, "I wish I was high. Just trying to shoot my shot and missing is all."

I nodded and replied, "It's not the first time you've missed."

He stepped closer to me until we were inches away. Our energies becoming more intense as he said, "Why don't you stop blocking my shot then?"

He paused and stared at me. This moment had me terrified. Dealing with involved men were lessons learned that I wasn't trying to learn again and yet I hadn't pushed this man back or tried to laugh it off like I knew that I should've. I was intrigued.

As he leaned in closer, my eyes closed in anticipation of his next move. I heard the words, "Where the fuck is Ace?! I want to see him right fucking now!"

He jerked away from me and turned around to see Terica wobbling through the parked cars trying to get to the building. I watched him walk up to her and try to get her to leave only to realize she was completely wasted and should not have been driving in the first place. Terica fought him while trying to lick his face. It looked like she was trying to take him down in front of everybody.

Whatever she was drinking I wanted no parts of it. She was going to feel horrible in the morning. Lester came out and seen the commotion and offered to help figure something out with her. She wasn't listening and constantly yelling not realizing where she was. This had a few more people come out and watch them try to tame her drunkenness. I slipped away and left. I was lucky enough to park on the side of the road away from everybody else. It probably would've been better to let Ace know that I was leaving or to even say goodbye to his parents, siblings and Niecy, but I was too ashamed to face him or them after that moment that we had before Terica came.

For a split second, I was envisioning doing some of the nastiest things to my best friend at his parents' vow renewal. The thought of Bishop Walls and his First Lady catching their son wilding like that made me shake my head at the heathen that she was. Luckily, Terica did come and set us back on the right track. I knew that if I stayed then nothing was going to stop me from picking right back up where we left off.

It was obvious that we were both just caught up in the moment of things and not actually wanting each other because it was clear to me that he's in love with Terica since he was still entertaining her. Seeing Terica was the sign that I needed to keep respecting his relationship and remain his friend. I needed a man that wasn't caught up on any other woman. A man that only seen me. I wanted a relationship like what Niecy has with Lester. I wanted true unconditional love.

Celebrity Deathmatch

"Y'all haters corny with that Illuminati mess. Paparazzi, catch my fly, and my cocky fresh."
- Formation by Beyonce

Chanice

Another couple filled trip spent in Los Angeles, the City of Angels where the excitement of attending our first ever award show had us all on edge. Chris Brown was not only nominated for Album of the Year, but he was set to perform for the first time after twelve years at the Grammys. He wanted to use both Femme Fatale IV and Team Flye with him and Lester doing a dance battle like they did on the mini tour we just had. So, it was safe to say that the pressure was on to be better than perfection. For us this was Breezy's version of Beyonce's Coachella, and anybody could get cut off with the quickness. The reality show producers were living for the stress that we were under hoping to get all of the best scenes of us fucking up or crashing.

Unfortunately for Marcus the trip came to an end as soon as he arrived. Lester spotted him carrying his luggage out the door to his Uber. Lester and Chaos decided to meet him outside and see why he was packing up the SUV. Marcus knew he'd have to explain his early departure to his boys, but he wasn't sure how his wife would feel if he did considering she was the reason they were leaving.

Lester was the first to ask, "What's up man? I know you're not going to miss out on ATV riding and the fight tonight."

Nina peeped out the door signaling for Chaos to come help her on the grill and he happily obliged. Marcus and Lester laughed as

Marcus answered, "Yeah man I know but wifey ain't really feeling the trip no more."

Anger was starting to appear on Lester's face as he asked, "Was it Destiny and her flirting with you?"

Marcus' face became distorted as he quickly replied, "Oh hell nah! We all know how Destiny is and that hoe knows better. You know wifey would kill her." Marcus sighed and continued, "Listen, don't say nothing to nobody but I had a thing with Imani back in the day. I ain't trying to get caught up. I'm only Tail Gunner on the bike other than that I'm just Marcus. A faithful ass husband and a damn good father."

Lester's expression was filled with understanding and relief. He knew the struggles that his biker brother had with chasing every floozy's tail that walked past him. He shook Marcus' shoulders and congratulated him with pats on his back while saying, "Yooooo man it's about fucking time!"

Marcus smiled and shushed Lester at the same time, "Chill chill. Wifey still can't know. I don't want any problems on the flight back home. We've already hashed everything out. That shit so far in the past." Lester nodded and said, "No worries. You know this is safe with me." He smirked and rubbed his bald head while asking, "Since bro code is activated, what's up with you and Niecy?"

Lester shook his head and replied, "What you mean?"

Marcus chuckled, "Last month, in Arizona? The guys say you locking doors to watch movies. We only locking doors for one reason my guy."

He grinned hard as he remembered the night vividly and replied, "Just don't be surprised when she becomes Mrs. Walls next year."

Marcus shook his head, "Boy you wild with that one. She got a whole best friend named Destiny that's still fucking crazy about you."

Lester shrugged and said, "Shit happens." Marcus' wife startled them both by singing, "Impossible things are happening every day!" Both of the guys sighed with relief, thankful that she only caught the end of the con-versation. They said their goodbyes and Lester watched them drive off heading to the airport. Inside the house, drama was stirring in the kitchen when Destiny noticed Ken laughing it up with Nina as she said, "What the fuck are you doing?!"

Ken squinted his eyes with a sigh and replied, "We're just talking."

Destiny didn't back down and got louder saying, "Okay but you came here with me and we're fucking engaged. So what the fuck?"

Ken rolled his eyes and Nina tried to explain by saying, "Girl I almost blew my face off fucking with this grill. Ain't shit going on."

Destiny was heated as she hissed, "Bitch mind your fucking business! Ain't you supposed to be sucking Chaos' dick?"

The loud commotion caused Ace and Lester to enter the kitchen as well when Nina replied, "Bitch you real pressed about some dick but understand I ain't one of those little scared ass hoes you can just talk to any kind of fucking way. I'll dog walk your ass from here to kingdom come!"

Destiny was ready to throw a stool at Nina when Ken grabbed her and pulled her back from the kitchen island as I stood beside Nina and yelled, "Have you lost your fucking mind?!"

The camera crew weren't at all prepared for the scene taking place, but it didn't take them long to catch the vibe. I was pissed because every black reality show had to have some fucking body fighting like some damn dogs for ratings and so far, everything had been copacetic. This was the worse time for me as I was stressed out of my damn mind, and I didn't need to see any of this shit on the TV during primetime on a fucking Thursday and spreading across the media becoming memes.

They were going to chill the fuck out or walk their asses back to Mississippi from the way that I was feeling. Ace went to calm Nina down when Destiny spewed at me, "Bitch fuck you! The only reason you got this fucking show is because you killed your baby and joined *'The Illuminati!'* You killed your whole fucking family for money and trying to act holier than thou in front of these fucking cameras!"

I sighed and walked away only to black out, turning around to jump over the kitchen island on Destiny ass. The moment I landed on her, I was connecting each and every punch to her eye sockets, nose, and big ass mouth. Within a second my hands were around her throat choking her out as I slammed the back of her head into the beautifully tiled kitchen floor. Everybody around me had disappeared. It was only me and this gnat that had been annoying the hell out of me for years. Lester and Ace struggled to pull me off, but they managed to save the poor girl from death.

Now Ken was snapping off from the fact that I flew across the room knocking him down as I landed on Destiny. He yelled out, "Bitch I'll kill your motherfucking ass!"

Which only pissed Carlos off as he yelled, "You gone kill who my guy?!"

Ken didn't stutter as he spoke loudly, "That crazy ass bitch that just put her fucking hands on me. Who the fuck you think? If you want it, you can get it too!"

While wiping blood off her busted lip, Destiny mumbled barely above a whisper, "Niggas done got killed for less."

Mion shook her head and said, "Yo for real y'all chill the fuck out. Girl you just got your ass beat. It's best you shut the fuck up. It's not even this serious!"

Carlos was heated at the fuckery as he says, "I wish I would see a pussy ass nigga put his hands on a female."

I whispered to Lester that he needed to get the NDAs from the producers because this shit couldn't air on the show and wasn't not one bitch gone utter a word of what the fuck just happened, but this only pissed Destiny off more as she spoke freely, "If you fucking him, then just say that. He wouldn't be the first nigga you stole from me!"

Here I was ready for round two as my head jerked around so fast that I almost gave myself whiplash and said, "What nigga I steal from you?"

Destiny spoke proudly, "Uh bitch Dustin, Nate, Chaos, Carlos, and now Showout!"

In an instant, Lester screamed out, "I was never your fucking man!" Destiny didn't hold back as she continued spewing hateful lies in the air, "You want to deny all of the shit we did! All the times you said you loved me and had to think of me just to fuck your wife! You literally just told me the other night how you were only using Niecy and didn't give a shit about her but now you want to act like we never existed?"

Imani knew too much shit had hit the fan in that moment and said, "Aye man maybe y'all should leave. Shit shouldn't get this deep."

Ken yelled, "I ain't going no motherfucking where!"

Unfortunately for Destiny she didn't calculate the amount of anger that had filled the room from her rant until Lester blasted off, "Where the fuck you getting this crazy ass shit from? I ain't never fucked with you on that fucking level and I ain't never said no shit like that about Niecy."

He spun me around and looked me in the eyes as he declared, "Baby I ain't never said no shit like that to her or anybody. Every fucking body know how I feel about you. I fucking love you!"

I pursued my lips and exhaled as I said, "I know baby. I love you too." With a quick kiss, I turned around and continued, "I need everybody to sign NDAs right now. That goes for the camera crew and producers too."

Ken was defiant as he said, "I ain't signing shit!"

Carlos smirked and replied, "Bruh, just fucking stop."

Destiny shook her head and said, "Y'all ain't fooling nobody. All of y'all done joined that devil shit! You ain't finna have me signing nothing."

My laughter caused an awkward silence as I attempted to walk closer to Destiny when Lester wrapped his arms around my waist, pulling me back into him, as I sighed once more knowing that I was about to test the limits of my restraints as I smiled as I said, "You either sign it or I slit your fucking throat. I ain't joined shit. Bitch, I am 'The Illuminati', so keep my fucking name out cha mouth."

Ken's eyes bucked with fear as if actual horns had sprouted from my forehead as he said, "This bitch is the fucking devil."

With the biggest smile, I replied, "Nah baby, the devil ain't got shit on me."

As the camera crew had already stopped filming, the producers handed everybody NDAs along with a pen when Ken rushed up on me causing Lester to slide me behind him as Ken yelled, "Bitch you think I'm about to join this shit?!"

Carlos calmly said, "Big homie you need to move the fuck back. You too close."

Ken looked Carlos up and down and said, "Nigga fuck you. I do whatever the fuck I want."

I scoffed and walked up as Lester placed his arm out signaling for me to stay behind him as I said, "It's okay Carlos. He can do whatever the fuck he wants but his ass ain't leaving until he sign these motherfucking papers!"

Nina had been ready to rock Destiny since the first day she met her. She never cared about how or why the bitch was around, but she was a hoe and Nina couldn't stand no nasty ass hoe so as soon as she seen Destiny take a step towards me, she had strung the bitch up in a headlock forcing her to sign the NDA.

As Destiny struggled to breath, Ken wanted to protect her but before he could turn around good to help break her free Carlos had already knocked Ken's ass flat out. Destiny stood in horror afraid of what was to come next. The only thing coming for her was an Uber to take her ass to the airport. She didn't need to worry about her luggage. I had no problem in sending it right behind her. The moment Ken came to, he was surrounded by everybody with a pen waiting on him to sign the NDA. As soon as he did, he was sent packing as well.

After a successful performance, we spent the last day of the trip sitting around reminiscing on the childhood romance that Lester and I shared. Telling Ace, Imani, Mion, Chaos, and Nina all about how I always had to fight the boys for touching on my butt but then turn around and kiss on Lester in the closet thinking we were hiding our little relationship from Carlos.

I hadn't changed much. Still had a hella smart mouth and still ready to lay hands when needed. Carlos and Mion said their goodbyes because as far as Carlos was concerned, everything was right in the world now that his brother was truly happy with the girl that he couldn't stop talking about for the past twenty years. He had betrayed his brother in the worse way and making sure his brother came to the first couples' retreat was his way of making up for his fuck ups. He was only there to distract Destiny as much as possible. After Ace and Imani dipped out, Chaos and Nina followed behind them. Eventually, it was just Lester and I in this oversized mansion of a beach house. I calmly suggested, "Let's hop in the hot tub."

The jets were beating on my back along with Lester massaging my feet giving me a relaxing sensation. His hands started traveling up my legs until he had pulled me to him. I sat in his lap with my legs wrapped around him as he darted his tongue in my mouth.

His mandingo growing harder by the second causing me to smile a devilish smile knowing nobody was there to interrupt us.

I looked at him with amazement at how he could finally be with me the way I always wanted. He was my dreams come true. There was only one question that remained as he said, "Why did you start calling me Tutu?"

With a chuckle, I blushed from the memory as I replied, "Because you're always just too too much. Always so extra."

Lester smiled and shook his head while understanding that my mom was something else and everything about her had definitely rubbed off on me as he said, "Yeah, let's not tell nobody that."

I giggled and said, "Okay, Showout."

He smiled and kissed me again. I stood up and got out of the hot tub. After wrapping myself with a towel, I motioned for him to follow me. We were back in the kitchen with me in the fridge looking for snacks. When I made it back to the kitchen island, he wasted no time spinning me around and getting on his knees while placing my leg on his shoulder.

I braced herself against the island top as he started in on my waterfall. My moans were like a symphony coming from heaven. The louder I got, the more he showed out eating this pussy. It wasn't long before both legs were on his shoulders.

I was slightly running when he grabbed my hips and forced me to stay put. He stood up with my legs still on his shoulders. I grabbed his face pulling him closer to me as I looked into his eyes and said, "I love you, baby."

He licked his lips then kissed me passionately while slowly dancing within my walls. He spoke softly in my ear, "I love you more."

My knees beginning to tremble as sweat dripped off of his forehead onto my breasts. I held his head, clenching his now overgrown locs as I moaned loudly from reaching my climax causing me to try and catch my breath. I leaned back while raising my butt slightly for him to grab allowing him to continue to hammer me with my weakened legs on his shoulders.

It wasn't long before I had leaned back up wrapping my arms around his neck as he lifted me off the island. While my legs dangled over his arms, my dreams were coming true as he repeatedly slammed my body onto his rod hitting the bottom of my ocean floor. I was just entering into my thirties and still experiencing firsts with a man but at least it was with a man that adored me in the right way. He entered into the living room ready to wear my ass out on the brown leather couch. With my face down and ass up, he bit his bottom lip as he rammed all nine thick inches into me with no remorse.

After he exploded, we sat on the couch for a few minutes giggling and laughing about how good it felt to be grown together and not little kids hiding in a closet kissing and discovering ourselves. I got up and grabbed his hand heading to the game room. I spoke seductively, "Let's play a game of pool."

Lester chuckled as he inquired, "Butt ass naked huh?"

I nodded as we entered the game room and said, "Yup! Butt ass naked now rack em up." While shaking his head, he replied, "This shit ain't gone last long."

As soon as I bent over to break them, Lester was behind me stroking in and out of my nice snug walls causing me to not even hit the cue ball. His fingers twirling around my clit made me moan out, "Oh God!"

He bent down planting tender sweet kisses on my back while saying, "It's okay baby. Let it out."

I creamed instantly on his rod making me turn around as he placed me on the pool table pushing all the strips and solids to the side with some rolling into the pockets. We made the sweetest love before heading to the shower. I had never had so much sex in one day, but I was loving every minute of it.

The water flowed down over our bodies as we washed each other until Lester was ready for another round. He quickly spun me around, pushing me against the wall while kissing my neck and massaged my breasts. I was going to take as much as he could give and hoped this wasn't a one time thing. With a smile I turned around, lowering slightly to my bestest friend in town.

I took him in my mouth, slowly maneuvering him as far down my throat as I could. I wasn't trying to be a head hunter but I did want to please my man as much as he had been pleasing me and Lester seemed to be very well pleased with everything that I had been doing. My hair now soaking wet as I continued bobbing and stroking his shaft. The feeling was sensational to him as I stroked and licked him as if he was a lollipop.

One ball. Two balls. Both were in my warm wet mouth. There he was once again ready to buck from the pleasure. I hummed happily at his reaction knowing the vibrations would help him along the journey. My alter ego had appeared as I locked eyes with him while my fingers swirled on my pearl as fast as I sucked. As I moaned from my climax approaching, he filled the back of my throat with his milky filling while I squirted for the first time.

After swallowing every drop, I laughed and said, "Finally!"

To my surprise, Lester was actually going soft. This man was a walking Viagra pill, always on hard but surely, he was tired after the shower. Probably just needed a quick nap so he could go again. We were butt ass naked in the bed knocked out with *'Candyman'* playing a second time. Eventually we'd finish the movie.

It's A Wrap!

"Know that you, you dug your own grave, now lie in it. You're so cruel, but revenge is a dish best served cold." - I See Red by Everybody Loves An Outlaw

Destiny

I stood in the kitchen seasoning and preparing this meat to go into the oven to be roasted. I massaged it with olive oil and stuffed rosemary and garlic cloves around the sides of the pan. There were cut up potatoes, carrots, onions, green bell peppers, and celery as well. While using the butter injector to ensure this meal would produce the most exquisite flavor that I've ever created, the cries of baby Aaliyah echoed throughout the house. I sighed as I ignored the cries for attention while continuing to prepare dinner for Ken. He was out with those damn biker guys as he always was. Loneliness was setting in as he was hardly ever home since the disaster filled weekend, we had a few months ago. Imani reached out only a few times, but Niecy was no longer answering my calls anymore.

At first, I was sad and fucking more seemed to lessen the sorrow until Ken stopped coming home at night and whenever he did, it was only to spend time with baby Aaliyah and then go to sleep. I was slowly losing everything around me and not even my own mother bothered to check in with me. Imani stayed in a world of her own never caring about anybody else unless it directly affected her. Although I've always been surrounded by people, loneliness was something that I was used to. The still quietness of an empty place on the other hand was not. I enjoyed the company of others as it was the background noise that I needed to ignore the demons that I needed to face.

The oven dinged to indicate that it was done preheating, and I slid the aluminum wrapped pan inside with a smile. I couldn't wait to serve my man this delicious meal that I created all by myself. Baby Aaliyah cried louder for a mother's love and finally I washed my hands and walked to the door of the nursery where my nine month old had stopped crying. While shaking my head realizing that phantom cries were a major pain in my ass, I went back into the kitchen to finish preparing dinner when Imani's name lit up on the screen of my phone as it vibrated on the kitchen table, I answered, "Hey Imani."

With a chipper voice, Imani says, "I just got some furniture in my apartment and I know you and Niecy aren't speaking right now but I'd love for us to all get together and have a girl's night. You know just let bygones be bygones."

As I rolled my eyes, I replied, "I'm good on that. I don't have a problem with her or any-body."

Imani sighed as she said, "But Destiny we've known each other for too long. We're basically family. You know we all got hotheads and will go off and say shit that we don't mean. It's been months. Let's just smoke a blunt and dance this shit out."

I chuckled and replied, "All your ass do is get high. You ain't got shit better to do other than get high all the fucking time?"

Appalled in my reply, Imani says, "Bitch you smoke more than me! Probably high right fucking now! Do you always have to be a miserable ass bitch?"

The baby's cries echoed again causing me to say, "Yup! Now let my high ass go tend to my baby. Something you wouldn't know anything about."

After I hung up in Imani's face, I stepped to the doorway of the nursery, once again baby Aaliyah was sound asleep. I sighed and leaned against the door frame as I took a long drag on my illy while dumping the ashes right on the floor as I reminisced on the days when I wasn't trapped in the house like a light skinned nigger, barefoot and pregnant, cooking for my master and his bitch.

Times had changed from when I was the one that made the guys drool over the simple fact that I knew how to have a good time behind closed doors and not tell the world about it. They didn't mind donating a few dollars because of it either. Now here I was playing house just as my mama called it. I didn't want any of this shit. Maybe with Dustin but that dream went up in smoke and now I was the one left holding the diaper bag with a screaming baby on my gotdamn hip. I shook my head as I tiptoed away hoping not to disturb my sleeping baby.

With the clock ticking, I drained the rice and turned the vegetable medley off. I wanted to impress Ken so badly with this meal. He'd become so distant from me and although I hated what my life had become, he wasn't about to leave me without cause like so many others had already done. After setting the table with candles and wine, he walked in with excitement on his face. I hurried to meet him at the door as I took his hand and said, "Baby I cooked something extra special just for you."

He smiled and said nothing as he followed me to the table where I pulled his chair out and poured him a glass of wine. Ken eyed the table while I started to fix his plate and he said, "Damn baby why you do all of this?"

I spun around and sat his plate down before him and replied, "Because you deserve it."

The meal looked amazing and without hesitation, Ken dug right in with his eyes closed savoring each and every bite. I sat across from him admiring how I had accomplished the goal of pleasing him with only a simple meal. The plate was almost cleared as he said, "Oh I'm gone need another plate baby. Damn this is good."

I sipped my glass of wine and replied, "Anything for you baby."

He looked around and asked, "Where's Aaliyah? Did she just go to sleep?" With a blank look on my face, I stared at Ken, and he became agitated as he asked again, "Destiny, where's Aaliyah?"

I blinked my eyes once and replied, "You just ate her."

With another bite heading towards his mouth, he paused and frowned his eyebrows as he said, "What the fuck did you just say?" Before I could utter a word, Ken yelled the question again, "Bitch don't fucking play with me! What the fuck did you just say?" I chuckled as I watched him process the words he'd heard while looking at the plate that once held the roasted remains of the baby, he seemed to love more than me.

Orgasmic delight filled my soul as I watched him fall out of the chair trying to scoot it back in an attempt to check on the dead baby that he'd just eaten. When he made it to the nursery there was nothing but her soft pink and purple polka dot blanket in the crib with her binkie. He ran back into the kitchen, slamming his hands against the table as he screamed, "Where the fuck is my daughter?!" Unbothered by his irate demeanor, I replied, "I told you. You just ate her."

He slapped fire from me which I didn't even feel. After the recent months of enduring a side of Ken that nobody should ever meet, I had become impure to his hits. He'd have to hit me with an eighteen wheeler in order for me to feel the pain at this point. I sat up straight and wiped the drop of blood from the corner of my mouth. Tears flowed as he pleaded with me, "Please Destiny stop bullshitting. Where's the fucking baby?"

I sighed not understanding what was so fucking hard for him to get as answered, "I cut the crying bitch up and served her to you. How does she taste? Like chicken maybe? Or is it pork? Steak even?"

Horror and disgust filled his face as he realized that I was dead ass serious in everything that I was saying. The days of him coming home and being a wonderful loving father were no more. I couldn't stand the massive amount of attention he gave to my daughter while fully neglecting me. It was obvious that he was only sticking around for the baby and the love that he claimed to have for me was never real.

I could feel my time was just about up. His stomach turned sour as he recalled how amazing each bite tasted going down. While his knees went out causing him to tumble down to the kitchen floor, disbelief sat in as he frantically tried to get to his phone and call the police. A knot formed in his stomach creating a pain that he had never felt before.

Suddenly I heard the cries of baby Aaliyah once again echoing loud as ever. As I stood up to go check on her once more, I looked over at Ken thinking to myself, 'Death would've been too kind' as he suffered and gagged, praying to throw it all up when the dispatch answered and he managed to say in a whimper, "She killed our fucking baby!"

It wasn't long before the police were at the door trying to understand the nature of the call as nothing this severe had ever happened on the Reservoir before. A few burglaries but never anything truly newsworthy. The occasional domestic violence calls from couples that were trying to prove a point but never wanting to leave. Cases of missing kids maybe but murder cases weren't common in the outskirts of Jackson, Mississippi. They walked into the kitchen where the food was still out and took pictures of the scene.

From first glance it didn't seem like anything was wrong or out of place but as the true nature of the story flew out of Ken's mouth, the police couldn't bear the sight of the 'meat' in the pan being baby Aaliyah. They continued to walk through the house in search of the baby where they found me in the nursery. Rocking back and forth in the rocking as I had finally calmed down baby Aaliyah. In my arms was her balled up pink and purple polka dotted baby blanket as I sung, *'I'll love you forever, I'll like you for always, as long as I'm living my baby you'll be!'*

The tragedy hit headlines like a blazing wild fire and everybody that knew me were stunned to say the least. Many in disbelief watching Ken crying on their screens about a baby that he soon learned wasn't even his. My mother felt shamed as the guilt rained down mostly on her for raising such a vile creature. My so called friends denied ever knowing me and the many men that I loved acted as if I never existed. I was now the Jeffery Dahmer of Mississippi and nobody wanted to be associated with my name.

Years would go by and my name would be an urban legend in the streets of Jackson and surrounding areas with the story constantly being twisted becoming even more horrific than the one before. I was a pretty face and a good time, only knowing desire and using sex as power. Misery was my only friend and despair is what I craved to spread. Love and happiness was only a Marvin Gaye song or rather vocabulary words that I learned in elementary school.

While awaiting my trial, I donned myself the true Harley Quinn as I kept drawing black diamonds on my red jumpsuit. I was hated inside the walls as much as I was outside the walls as nobody could understand how I went through with such a heinous crime. The entire world had picked up on the story as I sat in the courtroom with a smile every day for the next three weeks that I was being tried. Reporters from Dateline and other shows visited me as well as publishers seeking a book deal to tell my story. Hulu producers sought after a mini documentary while Netflix created an original movie based on the events of what happened. Songwriters were inspired just like Sam Cooke was in *'One Night in Miami.'*

Podcasters and social groups discussed the topic in great detail while sociology professors felt the need to have social experiments about child abuse. OB/GYNs and pediatricians worked with physiatrists and therapists to create a more thorough exam to discover postpartum depression or in my case postpartum psychosis. This little country town was stunned to say the least. The State of Mississippi was forever changed whereas the nation was mystified as the news continued to travel overseas. Arguments arose on CNN as to the cause and nature of my mental state while the Sunday sermons referred to such a tribulation as another sign of the end of times.

This international attention had me gleaming as I paraded around the prison feeling invincible. Prayers went up against me and for me but not one person came to my defense on judgement day and yet they all watched on their screens giving my trial the highest ratings of them all. The gory details along with the testimony from Ken was more than enough to throw my ass under the jail. I was found guilty and the world rejoiced as justice had been served.

***Puppy* Love**

"For the way you're something that I'd never choose. But at the same time, something I don't wanna lose. And never wanna be without ever again. You're the best thing I never knew I needed." - Never Knew I Needed by Neyo

Jackson, Mississippi
1999 AD
-The Shy Queen-

Chanice

"I can't stop the car!" He yelled out as he pumped the brakes with his hands raised dramatically. He looked over at my mom and gave her a wink and continued on in his overly dramatic prank that was meant to scare me and the boys my mom was babysitting. We all sat in the white station wagon frozen as the car slowly inched closer to the apartment building. I was stuck in the middle between Tutu and my brother JohnJohn when Tutu decided it was every man for himself and jumped out of the car. My heart was racing as I whipped my head around to see him rolling along the ground to what he considered was safety.

My brother's dad stopped the car instantly and placed it in park as he frantically got out to check on Tutu who was perfectly okay as he said, "I thought you couldn't stop the car man?"

Whenever fear or excitement took over my brother's dad, he'd stutter really bad and this was one moment where his heart was in his throat thinking that he'd hurt somebody else's child in the middle of his innocent prank as he yelled, "A. A. A. A joke man! It w ww was a joke!"

I'm pretty sure we all knew it was a joke, but it seemed like I was the only one that witnessed the behind the scenes moment that happened between him and my mom whereas Tutu was convinced that he wasn't dying on that day. For whatever reason, his attempt at survival completely pissed me off because how dare he scare me like that! When we made it into the apartment heading to my brother's room, he was grinning from ear to ear as all the boys hammered on and on about how cool it was that he jumped out of the car. I rolled my eyes as I said, "It wasn't cool. It was stupid. You could've really hurt yourself you know."

He looked at me still smiling as he started to pout his big soup coolers making kissing sounds while saying, "Awww you like me huh Niecy?"

I was only eight at the time and he was eleven and one thing was for certain, I definitely did not like Tutu! I frowned my face up as I replied, "Eww boy no!"

He continued to mock me as he went on and on about how much I liked him because I cared about him being hurt. My mom only ever babysat boys so that my brother would have friends since I only visited during the summer. This summer was no different than any other summer and Tutu seemed no different than any other boy that my mom babysat.

All of the boys liked me, and I was constantly making business bad for my mom by fighting and being rude to the boys. I never let up and there was never a boy I liked, not even Tutu. He was going to believe what he wanted but he was annoying and when him and the boys started to sing, *'Tutu and Niecy sitting in a tree. K I S S I N G......'* I gave him one chance as I said, "Shut up!"

He continued the song on his own with a huge smile plastered across his face. I was never good at throwing because I always missed my target but somehow in my anger, I was the perfect pitcher for any softball team as I threw the small purple kid's meal toy at his head. I just knew I was going to hit the wall and he'd taunt me some more but at least he'd stop singing that God awful song of us being in love, kissing, and having babies. He screamed, "Ouch!" I looked at him with horror from the toy hitting in him in the head and causing him to bleed. An apology would've been the right thing to do but unfortunately, I was too busy gleaming with accomplishment from actually hitting him, making him bleed, and shutting him up all at once. The younger boys ran to my mom from the little droplet of blood that didn't even need a Band-Aid to tell her how I was abusing Tutu. The boy wasn't crying or anything. He wasn't even hurt but leave it to my mom to force me to apologize. Her heart was still racing from him jumping out of the car only hours before and here I was only making matters worse. We stood face to face as he smirked from my mom saying, "Niecy look what you did! You owe him an apology. You could've hit him in the eye. Don't you see that he's bleeding?"

Oh, I seen it and I wished I could've popped him again, but I sucked it up and apologized through gritted teeth because my mother told me to. Tutu was never bothered by the moment. In fact, he enjoyed it and started being a little nicer to me. We became the best of friends to the point where I wasn't having a good day until Tutu and his brother showed up. I was so excited when Meme said we were staying in Jackson, and that I could start school with Tutu. She got an apartment upstairs from my mom in Virden Addition and whether upstairs or downstairs, we'd do the same thing, wrestle. Trying out every WWE Smackdown move on each other. If it wasn't wrestling, then it was pranks.

One prank gone wrong was when I watched him sleep on the floor with his mouth wide open as I let a harmless little spider crawl inside. Me, my mom, and all the boys just stared at him when he woke up because the spider never came back out like we all thought it would. I just wanted to laugh about how he slept with his mouth opened while the spider crawled in and out but that's not what happened, and nobody wanted to tell him, so I mustered up the courage to say, "A spider crawled in your mouth when you were sleeping."

He was pissed as he jumped up and stormed off to the bathroom saying, "Why didn't you wake me up? Why would you let a spider crawl in my mouth?"

It was a great question that I didn't have an answer for. Safe to say he didn't trust being asleep around me anymore. He also wasn't with the scary movie pranks like saying Candyman five times in the mirror but locking people in closets and bathrooms were right up his alley. Being the biggest asshole of the year was an award he won just by being alive. It didn't matter because I was matching his energy at every twist and turn that he made.

As soon as school started, Meme had a diabetic sugar crash causing her to pass out in the middle of the grocery store. I had no idea what to do aside from getting her a lemon and a peppermint like she always told me but this one was the worse of them all and it landed her in the hospital for days which turned into weeks. Eventually she ended up having gallbladder surgery before finally being released and coming home.

I stopped going downstairs to my mom's because I was busy taking care of Meme. Before school one morning, I was cooking her some breakfast. Something simple. Eggs, bacon, and cinnamon rolls. I had already run her some warm soapy water in the hospital pale to wash up with and drug it across the apartment since it was too heavy to carry. Just as I took the cinnamon rolls out of the oven, Tutu was calling out my name.

When I opened the front door, there he stood with my brother and his as he said, "Come on, Niecy before we're late for school."

Time was of the essence, and I wasn't anywhere close to being ready for school. I still had to brush my teeth and get my shoes on but only after fixing Meme a plate of food and emptying the hospital pale. I looked at him with a strained look on my face as I replied, "Go ahead without me."

His eyebrows lowered with confusion, and he said, "It's okay I'll wait."

I may have been only eight, but it was in that moment that I started to see Tutu differently. He wasn't just the fun boy that my mom babysat anymore. There stood a boy that cared about me because in all honesty the school was across the street. He really didn't have to wait. I would've been fine walking by myself, but he refused to let that happen and when I was finished seeing to Meme, I hurried out to Tutu who wasn't at all mad about how long it took me. He didn't mock me for being slow or anything. In fact, he smiled as if he was truly happy to see me.

We didn't wrestle as much after that. I pulled away. Being a CNA at eight was taking a toll on me and whenever I went downstairs to my mom's apartment it wasn't to wrestle and play pranks. It was to escape the reality of taking care of Meme who was just as bad as Myrtis when it came to who cared for her. Sure, my mom could've done it, but Meme didn't want my mom to do it. She despised my brother's dad, and he despised her as well.

She didn't want to make matters worse for my mom and always sugarcoated everything rather than actually seeking the help that she needed. It wasn't long before she decided to move back to Quitman. She left the apartment for my mom since she was getting evicted a third time and said I could stay as well. That lasted all of the first half of school because by the time December rolled around, I was heading back to Quitman in the back of Uncle Keith's white car.

After Meme left and my mom moved upstairs, Tutu and I had become official *'boyfriend and girlfriend'* as we weren't in the tree kissing but in closets, bathrooms, and anywhere we got a chance to, you'd find us kissing. If kissing would've gotten me pregnant, then I should've had about seventeen kids from all of the make out sessions that we had. The kissing came to an abrupt stop one night when he came back from his cousin's birthday party. I had waited all day for him to come over and it wasn't until late at night that he came but finally my boyfriend was home.

He walked in and there I was like a Shih Tzu ready to hop on him and kiss him all over, but he wasn't feeling good and declined my kisses. With a sad pouty face, I just looked at him wondering what I could do to make him feel better but for him he must've thought I was just so hurt that he didn't want to make out with me, and I wasn't. Instead, I hated seeing him feel so bad. His demeanor was the complete opposite of the boy that I had grown accustomed to, and I didn't know what to do. He said he'd eaten too much candy, cookies, and ice cream. Well now I wanted to beat his cousin's ass for providing my boyfriend with all of those sweets that was now causing him misery!

Tutu couldn't bear to see my sadden face and came over to me and we started kissing. If he wanted me to hold him and rub his head, I would've done it because kissing isn't something that was going to make him feel better until it did. Just as he stopped, his head tilted down and he threw up in my lap. I'm sure he felt embarrassed but at least his stomach wasn't hurting anymore.

The transition back to being sweethearts wasn't a good one. I pulled back even more than before. For me, him throwing up was a sign that we didn't need to make out like that anyway and if any of the adults had known, then I would've been hung out to dry. I just wanted to chill out and that's exactly what I did. Everything that made us like each other had ended. No more wrestling, pranks, or even mocking. We were in the weirdest space and talking it out never crossed our minds. Then one day we both took it too far and everything we had came crashing to an end.

It was the fight of the century. Much bigger than any fight Floyd Mayweather has ever had. My feet were on the wall as I rocked back and forth in Meme's recliner. In front of me on the floor was both of our brothers playing with dumbbells that constantly hit the wall causing my brother's dad to yell out, "Stop hitting the wall."

That was the first warning. I looked at them and they looked at me. It was already understood that it was only going to take one more warning before the devil appeared ready to whoop somebody's ass about hitting this wall. We said nothing to each other, and I continued to rock back and forth while they continued to play with the dumbbells hitting the wall. The second warning came as he yelled out again, "Don't make me come up there. Stop hitting the gotdamn wall!"

Another look passed between me and our brothers and once again we continued in what we were doing when my mom thought she could intervene by yelling, "Whoever is hitting the wall, please stop!"

Tutu opened his big ass mouth and yelled back, "That's Niecy kicking the wall."

I darted my eyes at him and dropped my feet with the quickness as I yelled back out,

"No it's not! That's Carlos!"

We both jumped up and rushed to the bedroom door where my mom and brother's dad were sitting on the bed shocked at us as we fought it out with words about who was hitting the wall. Neither of them said a word but one thing about me, I can't stand a fucking liar. I didn't like lying and I didn't like being lied on. Within a second I had hit him in the back with the remote controller that I was unknowingly holding.

He wasted no time scooping me up and pinning me on the hallway floor, locking me up where I was unable to move my arms. We rolled around on the floor causing the air vent to fall off. The asshole in him had emerged and all of this was simply a ploy to get me back in his embrace as I felt his warm lips kiss my neck. I was now angry and embarrassed from what was transpiring in front of my mom.

After he finally let me go, we sat down beside each other in the living room. Crisscross applesauce. The boys hammered on and on about how Tutu got the last lick and won the fight. He sat beside me grinning a false victorious smile and I looked him in the eye with a straight face and clocked him right in his cute ass smile. Tutu and his brother didn't come back after that. My mom was upset with me and said that I took it too far.

My brother's dad unleashed his wrath on me with a whooping that left a gash across my right thigh. It was as if Meme sensed the drama and when she called, I didn't have to say anything about what had happened. There was only one rule that my mom had to follow and that was that nobody especially not my brother's dad was to put his hands on me. Meme and Uncle Keith was at the door only two hours later telling me to pack my stuff and that I was going back to Quitman.

Over the years, I thought about Tutu here and there but never enough to go searching for him. It wasn't until I was out at Magoo's one night with Destiny that I saw him again. It was his cute ass smile that reeled me in all over again. He was wearing a red shirt with the sleeves cut off and bold black letters on the front saying CT for his bike club ClickTight Rydaz.

I looked him up and down as Destiny bragged about how he couldn't leave her alone. I noticed the way he moved to the music. His nice fit body fully in sync with every beat that vibrated along the dance floor. His faded blue jeans and cowboy boots were a very impressive look for a dark skinned chiseled god such as himself, as the memories of our childhood romance flashed in and out like a black and white movie or an episode of *'I Love Lucy'* while simultaneously fading out everything that Destiny was saying as I continued to admire my childhood sweetheart all grown up.

Those full soft lips calling out to me. His arms protruding with ripped muscles and his hair now flowing as medium sized locs with bleached ends. He'd grown some stubble across his chin along with a small moustache across his top lip. The finest man in the building and it was my Tutu just chilling in his zone.

After Destiny made her final attempt in securing the idea that her and Tutu were destined to be together, I asked, "So what's her name?"

She looked puzzled and said, "Who?"

I nodded in his direction as I replied, "His girlfriend. The one he chose over you because she was the better image for his parents that are pastors."

The look on her face was priceless as she thought I hadn't been listening to her bull-shit of a rant, but I heard what I wanted to hear. She shrugged her shoulders trying to dismiss the entire topic as she said, "I don't know. He won't tell anybody her name. He doesn't want anybody to know her name."

Without even turning my head, I looked at her out the corner of my eye because a lie doesn't care who tell it but that was the stupidest shit that I had ever heard. She had been talking about this man and his man stealing girlfriend for months, but this was my first time seeing him. I sighed and took my lemon drop to the head before walking off in Tutu's direction. I walked straight up to him and asked, "What's your girlfriend's name?"

It was obvious that he didn't recognize me and I'm happy for it because I didn't need to travel down memory lane with him although I wanted to so badly. I was supposed to marry Dustin the very next day. This was my last night out as a single woman and all I wanted was to be a good wife and mother, but I felt like I had to prove something to Destiny. It was annoying how she acted like the world revolved around her cocaine pussy and deep throat.

The moment he looked at me with those hazel brown eyes and smiled sent orgasmic waves throughout my body, and I could've ridden him like a Harley right there on the dance floor. We weren't kids anymore and I no longer cared about getting caught by any adults because all of my family was dead and gone. As a matter of fact, making out was only going to be the beginning if we ever tested those waters but instead, he answered my question without any hesitation as he said, "Dominique."

I walked off soaking with satisfaction from hearing his deep voice and I told Destiny the name of her archnemesis, but the atmosphere had changed. Dominique was no longer the problem and probably never was. The fact that I so boldly walked up to the finest man in the building and received the scared name of his precious little girlfriend, proved to Destiny that I was her archnemesis and because of that she started to move differently with me. Everything became a competition between us even though I was the married one and she was the single one.

Dreams Do Come True

"When your lips touch mine. It only confirms. I found true love in you."
- A.D.I.D.A.S by Ro James

Imani

This new intern has been arguing with me over this design for the last hour. She's determined to present her idea and dismiss mine although I met the requirements that the client had made. Just as I was about to walk out and request her name to be removed from the project, Ace startled us both, "Why not let her present her idea first and then you present yours?"
He stood next to both of the big bosses for our department as he made his suggestion. The new intern eagerly replied before I could, "Yeah let's do that then you can see for yourself that mine is better." I forced a smile as I sighed and said, "Sounds great." I gathered my paperwork and headed back to my office. Ace followed and closed the door behind us. I looked up from behind my desk and asked, "What was that?"
He sat down in the chair in front of my desk and shrugged, "I was trying to help you Nini. You've been arguing over designs all morning. Both of you were on the verge of making a scene."
I scoffed, "I can't help it if I'm right. Her idea is garbage. It's like she didn't do any research on the client nor their expectations."

He nodded, "That girl never does research. She's only here because her uncle is a shareholder of the company, and she wants to make her resume look good."

Irritated I replied, "So if you knew this then why suggest that she present her idea first? Why not just tell her ass to trash the idea. How could you not back me up in there? And in front of our supervisors at that?!"

I flopped down in my chair full of despair as he replied with a smile, "I told you why. You both needed to let it go. Besides your design is great and the client will love it. Plus, I needed you alone so that we could talk about how you've been avoiding somebody for a month that you work with and stay down the street from, and claim is your best friend."

I looked away, "I haven't been avoiding you. You've just been missing me somehow. I mean we're both busy. It's just life really besides we were just together in Los Angeles like a week ago."

He chuckled, "You're right I've been missing you. Plus, it's Friday and somebody has a birthday tomorrow. You got plans?" I shook my head no while continuing to avoid eye contact. He continued, "Good. I'm picking you up tomorrow."

I looked up at him, "Oh no tomorrow isn't good. I have so much to do."

Ace stood up and tapped my desk, "I better be able to find you and you better be ready tomorrow. Bright and early!"

He walked away and I dreaded the thought of having the much needed conversation surrounding Lester's parents' vow renewal that I knew we were going to have tomorrow. The only thing that I had been trying to do was not mess up this friendship again and somehow, I found myself still doing just that. As if that wasn't bad enough, I was still feeling like jumping his bones as he sat in my office. It's safe to say that I've developed feelings and now I needed to figure out how to place them inside of Pandora's Box for good.

The next day Ace was banging on my door like the police at five in the morning. He didn't get a key this time. We managed not to open that can of worms a second time around but the way he banged on my door had me heavily considering giving him another key just to avoid the banging. Ace walked inside rocking full workout attire causing me to stare at him with a frown as I said, "You're taking me to the gym for my birthday? I'm going to be honest with you, I don't want to do this. We can literally order a pizza and hang out here or at your place. Better yet you could cook to save some money."

His smile had become mesmerizing to me at this point. Ace replied, "I'm not telling you where we're going but you are going to need to wear this." He handed me some black gym clothes and reluctantly I went to my room and got dressed. The clothes fit perfectly and when we hit the highway heading to Natchez, I was feeling a tad bit confused, but I stayed silent and enjoyed the ride. As long as we weren't going to the gym then I was cool with whatever he had planned.

After a two-hour drive, we had finally arrived at the Tomahawk Trails. I glared at Ace and was met with a smirk. Buddy was taking me on a nature walk for my birthday. I figured I'd endure this punishment for the way I had pulled back from him. It's not like I had any plans.

Ace went to the trunk of his car, opened it, pulled out two huge bags. He put one on his back and helped me put the other one on my back. We started to walk, and I realized it was really a hike up a small mountain. We stopped here and there because I couldn't walk more than a couple of steps before a spider web, or a bug was attacking my face. It was a great idea, but I was on the verge of full on snobby girl complaining before we eventually made it to the top and he stopped at a clearing in the woods.

It was around noon when he took his bag off of his back and I did the same. With a smile and he asked, "So what do you think?" With a disgusted look on my face, I looked around at the trees surrounding us completely unimpressed until I seen the lake. The sun was shining down on it in the most beautiful way causing me to walk closer and admire the view. This was like a painting out of an art gallery by Bob Ross. It left me speechless. He walked up behind me and held me saying, "Happy Birthday."
His touch was the warmest and yet it sent chills down my spine causing goosebumps to raise on my arms as I uttered, "Wow. I gotta admit this is really cool. Thank you."
We unpacked the bags which contained a tent. One tent. I had hoped there would be two as this was starting to feel more like a set up than a birthday surprise. A camping trip by a lake, my best friend had done it again. He's given me another amazing gift for my birthday. Ace cooked us a well seasoned steak dinner on a cast iron skillet over an open fire while I sat constantly looking over my shoulder, fearing that the wild animals were going to attack us for the food since it was smelling so good but thankfully not one furry little woodland creature attacked us. When we were finished, we sat watching the sun set behind the trees. The way the lake sparkled with the sunset was a view that I wanted to remember forever. It was perfect until he said, "You want to tell me why you left my parent's vow renewal way you did?"
Damn' I thought to myself as I sighed and replied, "I just wanted to clear my head but to be honest Ace, we're lucky that Terica was drunk when she showed up. I want to respect y'all and that means you need to respect y'all too. I appreciate everything you've done for me, and I couldn't ask for a better friend but let's be honest, we almost messed up. If she had seen us, then what?"
Nonchalantly he replied, "Then nothing. I'm single."

Assuming this was because of them, I chuckled with my eyes squinted, "Yeah right. And when did this happen?"

As he nodded his head, he replied, "Two years ago on Christmas."

Taken aback I exclaimed, "Two years ago? Does she know this?"

He laughed and said, "Yes, she knows. She thinks I will forgive her cheating on me with Ken."

My eyes bucked as I said, "Wait she was cheating with Ken?!"

Ace shrugged and replied, "Yeah, she went through my phone and seen a long Merry Christmas message from you which started the biggest argument. She accused us of sleeping together and admitted to stepping out as a way to get back at us. She's been trying to get me to forgive her since Ken went and got Destiny pregnant, but I don't want Terica."

Shame fell upon my face as I replied, "Wow I didn't know my message caused all of that drama. I just wanted to apologize for being paranoid."

Ace nodded and said, "I understood you being paranoid. The accusation hurt but I understood it. I tried to apologize for how I reacted and when I didn't get a reply, I figured you wanted space. It wasn't until I tried to pop up at your place like I always do and seen it was empty that I knew something was wrong. I went by your job, and they hadn't seen or heard from you in weeks."

He paused and looked me in the eyes while saying, "I'm sorry it took me so long to find you."

I smiled, "It wasn't your job to find me but I'm happy that it was you did. I didn't know life could be so crazy until I was in that mess. It made me turn to the only person I had to turn to and that was God. I really don't know how I made it a year in that."

With a smile, Ace continued to say, "I had all the prayer warriors in the church praying for you too. You asked what I had told my mom about you. Well, she always knew about you because she'd

call sometimes when we hung out but when you were miss-ing, I confided in her and told her how I felt about you."
I jokingly ask, "Oh did you express your undying love for me?"
In a serious tone, he replies, "If I did?"
Butterflies filled my stomach from the realization that my best friend had become the love of my life before my very eyes. We continued to talk until we both were too tired to keep our eyes open. When I stood up to retire to the tent, I took a moment to embrace the scenery since tomorrow we'd head back to Jackson, Mississippi.
The sunset was gone, and the night air came in a little cooler than before we arrived. Suddenly, a cool breeze blew past me and gave me goosebumps. Ace noticed me shiver and wrapped his big warm arms around me. It was the most comfort that I had ever felt. His breathing was slow and steady on the back of my neck while the beats of his heart were like the drums of an African love song.
That undeniable chemistry had returned stronger than before. This was my best friend, and he was always going to be my best friend but here I was craving just one kiss. When he whispered, "Are you ready to lay down?"
I quickly replied, "Yes!" not processing his words nor caring about the consequences of my reply.
He chuckled as he walked over to the fire and started putting it out. I walked up behind him and said, "Hey, thank you so much. You are an amazing friend." He smiled and we hugged as if we were about to start our dance from the vow renewal. His embrace once again tantalizing. I pondered at letting him go or not, but I knew I would have to.
Terica or not, he was still somebody that I didn't want to mess over and aside from the constant flirting that he does with every female he sees, I refused to allow pheromones or vibes to mess up a good friendship again. With his arms still around me and his beautiful

dark brown eyes staring into my soul, made it hard to let him go. He started to make his move while I stood there lost, confused, and looking foolish.

As I closed my eyes, Ace leaned in, and his lips planted the sweetest kiss on mine. I instantly melted in his arms, no longer denying him when all I truly wanted was him. He lifted me up and cupped my ass in the most perfect and gentle way ever. The kissing never stopped. If anything, we had become more intense. He walked inside the tent where he kneeled with ease and laid my body down onto our sleeping bags.

When his lips touched my neck, I bit my bottom lip as I moaned out in pleasure. His hands on my thighs slowly tracing up my shirt and back down to my thighs when abruptly he stopped to take in this moment. We stared at each other breathing heavily until he broke the silence, "You are so beautiful. I have wanted you forever, but Imani I don't want to hurt you." I shook my head in response and he smiled, "Nini, I love you. I want to be with you. I want to be your man and show you how a man should love a woman. I have been in love with you since the first day I saw you in the plaza. We can keep going if you want to and I understand if you don't feel the same way. I just wanted you to know before we went any further."

His honesty was everything that I needed as I pictured his adopted parents and how their love seemed to transcend through space and time. I realized he was my forever love. I placed my hands on his face as I smiled and said, "I love you Ace."

That was all Ace needed to hear as he continued in his mission to show me just how much he loved me as we quickly undressed each other. As I laid on my back looking like the goddess that I was in his eyes, he took my left leg and placed it on his shoulder with his head resting on my right leg while he slowly stroked and massaged my clit. I squeezed my breasts as I moaned out with satisfaction for finally giving into my desires. He placed his left hand on my stomach, slightly pressing down causing me to shudder from the quickest orgasm I'd ever had.

With a smile, he placed my leg down and turned me over on my stomach. There was no need for an arch as he held me close to him and pumped in and out slowly while still massaging my clit with his left hand lightly gripping around my neck. My body had never been catered to like this before. As if his only dream was to please me in the most passionate way created.

We rolled over and I sat up, straddling him backwards as I leaned back bouncing to the slow rhythm that he had created with his hands caressing all over my body. I leaned forward, bracing myself with his ankles as if I was riding a motorcycle. He tapped my ass lightly pulling my watering hole to his face so he could swim in my lake. I placed his king sized scepter in my mouth and together we created magic in each other's mouth.

My next orgasm made me shudder so violently that I stopped and stroked his scepter while trying to catch my breath. I rolled over realizing that I had never experienced the best sex of my life until this moment, but Ace was nowhere near done as he had my legs wrapped around his waist, entering me once more. He leaned down and whispered into my ear, "Marry me."

With tears beginning to roll, I gripped my man harder and in between my staggered breaths I managed to say, "Yes."

Insane Infatuation

"Shouldn't have gone down this way. What happened to my master plan? Cause I can't figure out. I could have been a loved child." - Life by K-Ci & Jojo

Destiny

The guard yelled, "Pippins! You've got a visitor."
I walked up to the grey metal door and placed my hands inside the small opening for the guards to cuff me. I walked out wearing my red jumpsuit indicting to the other prisoners that my crime was capital murder. No remorse was on my face as I sashayed my way to the window and sat down in the chair waiting for Chaos to pick up the receiver and speak to me. Tears started to fall as Chaos placed his hand on the glass while picking up the receiver to speak with his once in a lifetime love. Immediately, I lashed out saying, "What the fuck are you crying for when I'm the one in prison?"
He explained with sorrow in his voice, "I just hate to see you like this baby. I should've been there for you more. Is there anything you need? Maybe try an appeal? We can easily say it was postpartum depression and that you weren't in your right mind when you did it."
I scoffed as the events replayed in my mind. It's been seven months since I was sentenced to two consecutive life sentences for the gruesome murder of my daughter. I didn't need anything but a cigarette and a bottle of Jack but that would've given me infractions and taking away my yard time and I couldn't have that.

It was the only time that I could close my eyes and sit back imagining myself on the coast of Puerto Rico sipping Mai Tais with Dustin. I cared nothing about anybody else or that damn baby and I certainly didn't give a shit about Chaos riding in like some captain save a hoe. I rolled my eyes and replied, "You're still too much of a pussy ass nigga for me. Why are you even here?"

Chaos sat up and the tears dried up faster than a drop of rain in the Sahara Desert as he spoke firmly, "I was trying to help you Destiny but since you don't want my help then fuck it. Just know that I've been HIV positive since before we met at *'Scrapin the Coast.'*

My face turned up in disgust as I already knew I had tested positive but believed it came from threesome that I had with Dustin and and some guy he knew. I never said anything because they didn't say anything but I couldn't understand how Niecy or Carlos were still HIV free.

He was lucky that this glass separated us. He was lucky that I was already in prison for murder. He was one lucky son of a bitch. I smiled as I said, "You walked your nasty ass in here to tell me something like this." With a chuckle I pointed my index finger at him as I continued, "I hope you die on that ugly ass bike because I know I'm not first or the last person that you did this to."

Realizing that the conversation was officially dead, Chaos shook his head and tapped on the glass as he stood up saying, "You'll be dead before me."

Before I could say another word, the guard walked up while saying, "Time's up."

Months later, while I laid on my cot with my knees up, sketching the face of my love, an older female prisoner having overheard the whispers of the Infamous Destiny Pip-pins was walking past my cell and stopped to ask, "Did you really feed the baby to the father?"

I darted my eyes at my prison mate and replied, "Nah, he wasn't really her father." I sighed and continued, "That bastard died in a house fire." With a smile, I looked at my prison mate and lied, "I sat back watching the flames after I started it."

The older woman walked on in and sat down on the edge of the bed. Also donning a red jumpsuit as she shared her story, "Damn sexy you don't play no games huh?" She sighed and continued, "My first kill was my father when I was ten years old. He'd just finished beating on my mom and thought he'd have his way with me. I let him have his fun. It hurt but he was going to do whatever he wanted to whether I fought him off or not. When he was done, I went into the kitchen and grabbed the biggest knife we had. Him and my mom were sleeping peacefully like nothing had even happened. I climbed on top of him and stabbed him seventeen times while my mom woke up screaming and calling the police."

I sat up and leaned forward rubbing her back as I asked, "How did it feel?"

She chuckled and said, "It felt amazing. I saw maybe over a million therapists afterwards and all they wanted was for me to express remorse and pain and I didn't have any. I was happy and didn't mind doing it again in a better way. My mom hated me. Called me the fucking devil and performed exorcisms in the form of her beating me in the shower with an extension cord wrapped around a stick. One night I decided to let her meet the devil within me. She was soaking in the tub with her headphones in as she always did, and I tossed the toaster oven in and watched her light up like a Christmas tree."

As I smiled, I whispered, "I bet it was beautiful huh?"

With a smile and her eyes closed, she inhaled as she reminisced and said, "Fucking glorious!"

I took the sketch of Dustin and shared it with my new best friend as I said, "This is the only guy that I've ever truly loved. He knew how to shut up and enjoy the moment for what it is. He was the only guy that accepted all of me and didn't break my heart. I would've turned the world upside down for me if he asked me to. Maybe in another life we could've lived like kings and queens. That's why I made sure to shut up that stupid bitch he thought I didn't know about. He only fucked with her to get back at Nate. She could've just enjoyed having that moment with him but she felt the need to take it a step further on some childish shit, so I drove down to sweet ole Georgia and smothered her after busting her in the mouth with a metal baseball bat." I shrugged my shoulders with a smile and said, "And she didn't say another fucking word."

The older female prisoner caressed my shoulders as she spoke softly, "Who is that?" Tears formed in my eyes as I realized the truth forming in the pits of my stomach. I hated to even say it, but I continued on, "That's Niecy. Mrs. Chanice fucking Love. I never hated somebody so fucking much that I loved them. Dustin told me how she hated me and how she talked about me like a damn dog, but she never lied on me, and she never disrespected me. The nicest bitch I've ever fucking met but crazy as fuck. I fucking adored her evil perfect ass. The bitch is so fucking beautiful that I stayed confused. I didn't know if I wanted to be her or fuck her or somehow do both at the same damn time, but I couldn't be without her. Niecy was my Poison Ivy and if she would've wanted me, I would've been hers with no questions asked but she was so caught up in the bible and wanting love. True love isn't real. It's just what Disney created to make dumbass bitches like her believe that dreams can come true."

I ran my fingers over the sketch of Dustin as my new best friend begin to caress my thigh and ask, "What's his name?"

With a smile I kissed the lips on the sketch and said, "Dustin."

My new best friend nodded and said, "You can call me Dustin, whenever you want to."

I noticed the creepy seductive smile from the corner of my eyes as I sighed and replied, "I'd rather fuck hot curling irons sweetpea."

The female prisoner jumped up and said, "Bitch you're mine now."

I laid back on my cot and looked at the older prisoner and said, "I can't wait to see you choking on those words."

She slammed her fists against the bed just as the prison guard walked up and said, "Hey! You're in the wrong cell again. That's your yard time."

I placed my hands over my lips while giggling like an innocent school as the guard passed me a folded note. Inside of it was a cell phone. I had been making moves from day one and my looks definitely helped me to get shit done. I logged into all of my old social media accounts when suddenly my heart jumped with joy at the news report of Chaos being gunned down in the middle of the street during a shootout.

As I scrolled a bit more there were a bunch of folks saying *'RIP'* to Ken as some woman had run him over repeatedly during a heated argument. I was getting my little cup filled with all of the tea while learning that my mom succumbed to her battle with lupus and Imani's mom had a brain aneurysm and dropped dead in the grocery store.

Just as I was filled with joy, my heart shattered into a billion pieces watching TikToks of the viral couple, Showout King and Katrina Chanice. Tears flowed down my face as I continued to search their accounts, seeing tagged pictures and posts of them at a Golden Warriors game. I screamed and slung the phone across the cell, smashing the screen when I seen a video collage of them loving on each other with multiple dates and kisses that they shared in the snowy mountains of Wisconsin for Niecy's birthday.

After everything I told Niecy about Showout, and she still fell for his bullshit. I never gave a shit about that man and over time I stopped giving a shit about Dustin's ass too. What was so bad with us getting a house and raising our kids together? I gave Niecy all of me! My whole fucking heart and she constantly chose a man over me. I went out of my fucking way to become irresistible to that bitch and she never wanted me. Dustin loved to brag on the threesomes they had and not once did she ever want me. She was my Shug Avery. All she had to do was imagine us together like I had been doing since the first day I met her in Biology class.

My face became flushed, and my body started to heat up. Beads of sweat formed on my forehead as I started to gag from the videos of my woman in love with another man that would only end up breaking her heart. The more I looked, the more I regretted not fucking his ass just to show her that he wasn't shit like the rest of these no good men in Mississippi. I was literally sick to her stomach that she started to hurl up all of her contents.

After days had gone by of me being unable to keep anything down, I was placed in the infirmary. Any time that I tried to eat or drink, I'd violently throw up until I was puking up nothing but stomach acid. After losing entirely too much fluid and weight, I was placed on an IV with potassium filled bags. My levels dropped drastically passed the point of being critically low and nothing was helping me. The images of Niecy's smiling face circled around in my mind like I was in a circus. She seemed so happy and in love with him while she constantly looked as if she was in misery around me. I couldn't understand why I was never enough for this girl. I treated her better than I treated myself and she acted like she couldn't how in love with her that I was.

I was honest when I told her, "Nobody wants Dustin. We all want you."

But all that did was go over her head. Thinking of them only made my health worse causing me to become weaker and weaker. The doctors tried their best to treat the wasting syndrome that I had developed from HIV but eventually I slipped into a coma and died from seeing the love of my life live out her dreams with her true love.

Picture Perfect

"And it's truly my pleasure to share his company. And I know that it's God's gift to breathe the air he breathes." - The Truth by India. Arie

Imani

While standing in front of my full-length mirror that stood in the corner of the master bedroom examining another online purchase that I had finally received in the mail last week, I thought to myself, *'I need to stop ordering so late'* because I always got stuck with the purchase whether I actually liked it or not. It was a white romper that had hints of green, yellow, and blue. It was the cutest fit she seen on FashionNova's website. The back had a see through tail that's open in the front. My original choice was a cute flowy dress, but it's the end of March and it's already too hot to wear anything other than shorts. The goal was to be cute yet comfortable and this outfit had met all of my needs.

Hearing the music start up from the backyard let me know that I was wasting too much time in the mirror. I went downstairs to check on how the setup was coming along, and it was beyond everything that I could've dreamed it would be. There were pretty light green, white, and clear balloons as well as matching streamers that led from the kitchen to the backyard. The food table was looking the bomb.com especially with the beautiful array of fruits on one table and grilled kabobs on another. Niecy startled me when she said, "Girl where is your ribbon?"

I had contemplated pinning the handmade ribbon on my romper but was too busy caressing the basketball size stomach that I had developed over the last eight months thinking back to the day when I took the pregnancy test. Niecy and everybody at Cronix had already begun to tease me about the weight that I was putting on and my hormonal ass snappily confirmed it was just happy weight. The annoyance in my tone of voice only made them tease me more. I had no reason to believe that I was pregnant until of course Aunt Flo didn't come like she was supposed to. There was no denying the pregnancy but even when the test turned positive, I was still in doubt that it was even real.

Granted I had started going to church more and getting in the bible more as well as praying being that I didn't feel worthy of being a mother. Although it was my desire, I continued to meet doubt and guilt from my past troubles. That positive pregnancy test left me feeling terrified, excited, shocked, and perplexed on what I should do next. They told me in church how God is such a forgiving God and how real he is if you just believe and repent. I did all of that thanks to Ace telling me to try to have a little faith in everything that they were saying was the truth. I did but when it all boiled down, I still wasn't in full belief until I felt those first kicks. The realization of actually becoming a mother, left me in tears for days. God saw fit to bless me despite what I had done or even been through.

Being pregnant felt like a miracle to me and I walked in that miracle every day with my head held high until I was five months pregnant, and the doctor discovered a second baby snuggled up behind the first baby five months into the pregnancy. When the ultrasound tech said, "Oh you're having twins." I cried even harder at the fact that this was happening to me. I wondered, *'What did I do to deserve this? I'm not worthy!'*

After that I got deeper in the church, shouting and praising every Sunday the way that I've witnessed others do, even though I used to think it didn't take all of that extraness. The mothers at Word of Life in Flowood covered me and my babies in prayers with blessed oil. I witnessed God's forgiving nature and nobody could convince me otherwise of how real God is. I smiled as I replied, "I got sidetracked when the kicks started up."

Niecy laughed and went upstairs to get the ribbon she had made for me. She's been planning this baby shower since the day that I told her that I was pregnant. Niecy's an undercover craft goddess! Making homemade ribbons, cups, shirts, trays, and whatever else she chooses to do. She walked up to me and pinned the ribbon on my romper while saying, "Listen your ass better not go into labor during this shower. You need to sit down somewhere!"

I smiled while saying, "I can't promise you a thing. Girl with the way my back and feet feel, I'm just about ready to do anything to get these babies out. Besides, does it look like I could stretch any further?!"

She laughed, "See that's why I stopped rubbing your belly. I was afraid you'd pop from being touched." I took Niecy's advice and wobbled to the nearest chair. I hadn't even been walking around long and already my feet had started to swell up. Niecy pulled up an ottoman and said, "You know damn well you need your feet up! You're so hardheaded."

She walked away shaking her head. The girl was acting like she was my mother, doc-tor, and baby daddy all rolled into one with a ribbon on it. It wasn't annoying because I knew that Niecy had genuine love for me and of course like any pregnant woman, I enjoyed the catering for the most part. Together we've been going overboard buying newborn clothes and items.

Niecy literally couldn't walk into a store without going into the newborn section and getting something for both of her baby cousins! She's already nicknamed them *'The Doublemint Twins'* hence the green and white décor for the baby shower. Now the entire Cronix building is awaiting to meet *'The Doublemint Twins.'* The guests started to arrive and that's when Niecy put on her hosting hat.

They were required to put safety pins on from the door and at any time if they said the word *'baby'* or *'twin,'* then they had to give their pin to the person that heard them said the word. I started seeing pins getting jacked left and right. People were taking this so seriously and it was amusing how they were all slipping on the words and trying to act like they said something else. A few people slipped and looked around hoping nobody heard them. My face was starting to ache from the permanent smile that I had plastered on while the babies kicked in joy with every hearty laugh that I made. The funniest moment was when the biggest pin jacker slipped. The entire party reacted in laugher as Niecy jacked her pin. The funniest game to see play out may have been watching the men race to change the baby diaper on the baby dolls. Niecy figured the women would do better in a baby bottle drinking race. These ladies played no games with those baby bottles, had the men cheesing and whispering over in the corner. Whoever invented the guess the size of the belly game is just wrong because I felt so huge when some of the guests had to estimate the size of my belly with toilet paper, but I loved it and certainly loved Niecy for doing such an amazing job on this baby shower.

When the party was over, a few stayed to help clean up which I thought it was so sweet because I certainly wasn't helping. Others had dipped out as soon as Niecy started to thank everybody for coming. My only concern was going to lay down and Niecy agreed. Only problem was that I wanted everybody gone before I went to bed so I sat downstairs eating grapes until they finished cleaning.

Niecy walked up to me saying, "You are always eating grapes. Did you eat anything else?"

I nodded as Niecy sat down near me and with a smile, she said, "Oooo girl my man so damn fine. I might have his baby!"

Niecy looked at me from the corner of her eyes and fell out laughing as I said, "Bitch you need to! It's all I've been praying for! Would've been so cute to been pregnant together."

As I did the pregnant girl rock to get up, Niecy only laughed harder causing me to roll my eyes while heading towards the patio door. She helped me down the stairs of the deck and to the guys. It took no time for Ace to say, "Are you trying to go into labor?"

I quickly dismissed him by saying, "Boy hush! Now what yall out here talking about?"

Ace shook his head, "Every day you sound more and more like Bishop's First Lady."

With a chuckle Lester said, "Hey man don't do my mom like that."

Ace went on to tell us ladies about how him, Lester, and Carlos used to be some bad ass kids jumping off houses, shooting squirrels with BB guns, and playing WWE on the trampoline. The stories that they shared had me, Niecy, and Mion dying from laughter. Lester suggested a game of UNO and that's when I seen for myself just how perfect we all were together. Everybody happy and in love and nobody lusting after the other person's significant other. Nothing but love, laughs, and harmony made this moment feel like heaven on earth.

After maybe two hours, I had Niecy meet me in the kitchen to say, "Why haven't you told Lester the truth yet?"

She looked with a raised eyebrow and said, "What truth?"

Like an over tired toddler, I began to pout, throwing my hands up in aggravation and said, "Ugh! About Dustin molesting your babies when they were two years old. He needs to know that if he's going to marry you and be a father to them. He needs to know about your traumas and how to deal with them. Trust me on this Niecy. It's okay to let your guard down with somebody that truly loves you.... Damn. Now I done peed on myself."

Niecy walked up behind me and looked down and looked back up as if she had seen a ghost as she said, "Imani, that's not pee! I'm pretty sure that your water just broke!"

I chuckled because Niecy's words had my little nerves rattled. I didn't know what that felt like but maybe Niecy was right since she was a mother too. As I looked down at what I thought was pee trickling down my leg to the big puddle on the floor, I looked back up at her while shrugging and saying, "I guess it did break."

Niecy's facial expression was priceless as she replied, "You guess!"

The brothers and Mion walked in smiling as Ace said, "Baby, when are you going to go lay down. It doesn't matter if the house is clean or not. Let me help you upstairs to the room."

Mion calmly interrupted him, "It's a little too late for that. Looks like her water just broke."

Carlos stood frozen and shocked while Lester begins to panic saying, "Well, why the fuck are y'all so calm. We need to get you to a hospital."

Lester shook Ace out of his trance, and we all helped me wobble to the car. Mion grabbed the hospital bag that I had packed that was sitting beside the front entrance of our house and we all traveled to River Oaks.

Chanice

After what seemed like forever, Dr. Brown emerged from behind the double doors of *'Labor and Delivery'* to inform the family of the loss of Imani Walls. During the emergency cesarean she began to experience blood loss which caused her to die on the table before she could ever look into the eyes of her beautiful miracle twins.

Over the next six weeks Ace fell into a depression that everybody tried our best to pull him out of but as time went on, he stopped eating. He stopped going to work causing Lester and I to step up as godparents while trying to help him get through losing the love of his life but seeing Imani's face in the twins only made his depression worse. He locked himself away from the world until one day he just stopped answering his phone.

Everybody wanted to give him space to heal because nobody understood how he had been in love with Imani for years and lost her so suddenly after getting his happily ever after. Since he was an adopted pastor's kid, we believed that he'd turn to God in his time of need or at least to Bishop Walls but that wasn't the case. All Ace wanted was Imani and Imani was gone.

When Lester and I did our weekly wellness check, he had to break the living room window and climb in because Ace was refusing to answer the front door. When he opened the door for me, I quickly threw my hands over my mouth and nose to preventing vomiting from the smell of rotting meat that slapped me in the face when Lester said, "He must've left some food out somewhere."

I walked in hoping to spruce the place up a bit, but nothing was out of order. Only the horrifying smell that filled the air. Lester ran upstairs to the master bedroom where Ace laid in bed, lifeless. He had taken a full bottle of sleeping pills with the intention to never wake up again to a world where Imani didn't exist. After calling the ambulance and the coroner took his body away, we headed back to our house in the beautiful countryside of Terry, MS.

We sat in silence on the couch for what felt like hours as I replayed the last conversation over and over in my head like a cd skipping on my favorite song. Imani understood trauma in a way that I didn't. I forced myself to become my own superhero in a world full of devils.

Despite expressing the emotions, I had accepted the reality of the shitshow I called my life.

Unable to continue being this amazingly perfect superwoman, I leaned down and laid my head into Lester's lap as the tears flowed and the words escaped, "When the girls were four years old, they started wetting the bed. I didn't understand at first until my mom and Meme told me that somebody had been touching on them. The wetting got worse to the point where it would happen as they were standing right in front of me not feeling a thing and then the night terrors started. They'd wake up screaming in the middle of the night. They became irrationally afraid of the dark and I wanted to believe it was just what kids sometimes did."

One of Lester's hands rubbed my head as the other made soothing circles on my back while he listened to my final truth as I continued, "I didn't know who to blame once the lying started. They would hide their panties in the closest and under the bed. They would lie about wetting themselves and all I wanted was for it to stop. I didn't want to blame Dustin. I couldn't allow myself to believe that their own father would do something like that. They were terrified of him, and I thought it was just because he was always so angry about something. I didn't understand why he'd treat them like grown women expecting more from them than what their little minds could produce. It wasn't until a few days before the fires happened that the girls finally confided in me the truth. If I could bring him back just to kill him, I'd do it a million different ways, each being worse than the last. He's lucky that God took him before I could lay my hands on him for what he's done to my babies."

Feeling Lester's arms tighten around me only made me cry harder and once I was ready; he ran me a bubble bath to relax my nerves. He sat on the floor beside the tub with me as we sipped on wine, and he listened to the memories that I never told anybody but God.

When I was done soaking and had dried off, he wrapped my naked body up into his arms and picked me up. With my legs naturally wrapping around his waist, he kissed me passionately as he carried me into the bedroom. When he laid me onto the bed, he softly whispered into my ear, "I'm here now."

Epilogue

THE WIFE OF NOBLE CHARACTER

A wife of noble character who can find? She is worth far more than rubies. Her husband has full confidence in her and lacks nothing of value. She brings him good, not harm, all the days of her life.

She selects wool and flax and works with eager hands. She is like the merchant ships, bringing her food from afar. She gets up while it is still night; she provides food for her family and portions for her female servants. She considers a field and buys it; out of her earnings she plants a vineyard. She sets about her work vigorously; her arms are strong for her tasks. She sees that her trading is profitable, and her lamp does not go out at night. In her hand she holds the distaff and grasps the spindle with her fingers.

She opens her arms to the poor and extends her hands to the needy. When it snows, she has no fear for her household; for all of them are clothed in scarlet. She makes coverings for her bed; she is clothed in fine linen and purple. Her husband is respected at the city gate, where he takes his seat among the elders of the land. She makes linen garments and sells them, and supplies the merchants with sashes. She is clothed with strength and dignity; she can laugh at the days to come. She speaks with wisdom, and faithful instruction is on her tongue.

She watches over the affairs of her household and does not eat the bread of idleness. Her children arise and call her blessed; her husband also, and he praises her: "Many women do noble things, but you surpass them all." Charm is deceptive, and beauty is fleeting; but a woman who fears the LORD is to be praised. Honor her for all that her hands have done, and let her works bring her praise at the city gate.

-Proverbs 31:10-31 (NIV)-

Proverbs 31

"And I want it all, want it all, Nothing is too big or too small, I want it all, want it all, I won't accept impossible, I'll be more than happy to wait, Than to settle today, I want it all
- I Want It All by Melanie Fiona

Katrina Chanice & Showout King

The lights dimmed low with a spotlight on the dance floor where Femme Fatale IV swayed to the beat of *'Giving Him Something He Can Feel'* by En Vogue. We had practiced this dance routine for about a month with me taking the lead, belting out each note as if I had written the lyrics myself. My cares flew out of the window as the crowd ood'd and ahh'd when I started to seduce my Showout King, who was in the middle of the dance floor. Next to him sat Carlos, and two of the groomsmen from Team Flye staring in awe as our beautiful brown selves were winding our hips and flipping our hair creating an undeniable chemistry for everybody watching. Showout adjusted his top button, closed his eyes, and tilted his head back from the touch of my hand caressing his cheek as I slowly jazz strutted behind him.

Bishop Walls eyed his First Lady with seduction as the words echoed from the loudspeaker, *'People out there, can you understand? That I'm giving him something he can feel!'* She blushed with a smirk while shaking her head knowing exactly what her former playboy was thinking. This was one hell of a reception but what could be said against the newlyweds other than, *'Come on now'* or *'Okay sis'* and maybe a few *'I see you bruh!'*

This was the lap dance of the century with the men panting in heat as if they were on stage during the BET awards when *'Cater 2 U'* had Nelly and Terrance Howard struggling to breathe. It wasn't long before some of the guests were up and attempting to give their own little lap dances on the side. We were knocking that performance out of the water and giving inspiration to the masses on how to show a black king some love. Cameras flashed from the phones that were recording the show, while the twins went live on TikTok, giving sneak peeks to the long awaited nuptials of Showout King and Katrina Chanice.

Better known to the world by our alter egos because of our reality show *'The Melanin Midas Empire'* which had become the most watched reality show in the world. Femme Fatale Four and Team Flye were now traveling the world on tour doing shows in London, Barcelona, and Dubai. Already dubbed the flyest couple on the internet, our lap dance became another instant viral sensation causing many celebrities such as Lizzo, Michael B. Jordan, Ed Sheeran, and Drew Barrymore to tune in wishing the happy couple nothing but love, light, and success as we journeyed on as husband and wife.

As soon as I was in front of my husband winding my hips like the Jamaican gyal that I am, the song ended and Showout sat up with his arms around my thick caramel thighs. He lifted me into the air as he stood up saying, "Aight, y'all we gone!" Laughter roared from the crowd while crowns, brown hearts, and Jamaican flags filled the comments. Showout walked off without a second thought revealing the utter shock on my face from the seriousness of my king's intense farewell.

A few assumed it was a joke and actually expected us to return but as Showout and I loaded into an actual horse drawn royal carriage as if I was the black Cinderella heading to Buckingham Palace, all of our guests ran out to us waving and screaming their goodbyes with smiling faces and hearts filled with the purest love that I've ever witnessed.

There were four white horses all donned in a beautiful array of black, gold, and red harnesses and tack as they started to slowly gallop along the cobblestone pathway while I begin to imagine a new life as England's first black king and queen. Our coronation would be for all of the world's wealthiest families to fly out and party with this southern royal queen.

While Meghan Markle and Harry would keep it cute on the sidelines, I'd be on the dance floor popping my royal ass all over my black king as DJ 51/50 spun records that made it impossible for anybody to continue sitting down. With a master mixture of Mozart and Uncle Luke sounding off throughout the castle for every noble and lady in waiting to enjoy. It was nothing to picture the darbuka drums tempting the Arabian royals onto the dance floor as the sensual sounds of a dancehall song flowed out to influence the most epic dance battle to ever be recorded. The greatest televised event in the history of the nations and it was nothing more than a fantasy worth falling asleep and dreaming about.

Seven hours later and we were clinking our glasses together to enjoy our beautiful green, yellow, and red Bob Marley cocktails with mini umbrellas on the inside of them. As we made our way inside of our Hybrid suite, I passed the rainbow colored hookah filled with marijuana to Lester as I innocently batted my big doe eyes with a smirk only meant for trouble. He sighed with an eye roll as he'd vowed to never take a trip on cloud 9 but here we stood in a bud and breakfast in Jamaica all because his love for me outweighed the promises and vows that he made to himself.

He shook his head believing that this one time would only happen here in this villa and never again. Within five minutes the fruity smelling herb had us both giggling and wrestling as if we were eight and eleven years old again. After he picked me up ad tossed me onto the bed, I popped up like a daisy and pulled him down, rolling over on top of him and pinning him like we were Nyla and Simba in our own African safari of love. I tickled him mercilessly as he laughed out loud while trying to regain control.

He had me running off of the bed from his tickles. We had worn ourselves out, breathing hard like we were Usain Bolt having just finished an Olympic game. He sat on the bed eyeing me seductively as I leaned against the wall when he walked up to me and took my hands and held them against his chest as stared into my eyes and said, "There's no me without you. I'm lost without you. Whatever you want, it's yours. Whatever you need, it's yours. I'm yours and you're mine forever."

While lowering himself to his knees, his hands let go of mine and he held onto my thickness as he started to kiss my inner thighs when his hands slowly slid up my oversized forest green Tupac t-shirt that I had changed into, gripping my soft ass when I sighed a moan of pleasure accepting everything he had said.

His words were better than any *'I love yous'* while the thought of living like immortals forever in his arms swept across my mind like a blissful insanity. It was in this moment that I fully understood what Deborah Cox meant when she sung *'That heaven sent to fulfill my needs.'* While my body screamed out for him, he listened attentively and placed one of my legs onto his shoulder, still planting kissing as well as light nibbles on my inner thighs until he came to the center of my garden.

After his feast on love, I was suspended in the air with my legs wrapped around him. Lester didn't waste another second giving his queen all of his love. This was a moment he had dreamed of from the moment we first kissed as kids. Too young to understand what love truly was and yet he knew that one day he would make Chanice Brunner his wife.

This was the song that he sung all through middle school as well as high school. Well into college until life seemed to have had a different plan for him but when we met back up, every emotion that he felt from over twenty years ago came flooding back in and now that he was grown, he wasn't denying his love for the one girl that he's prayed so hard to be with.

After a few hops around the room, he sat on the edge of the bed and leaned back while I turned my back to him and rode him into another galaxy. I turned my head to the side just to ask, "Do you like that?"

He moaned loudly as ever, "Yesss!"

A smile of satisfaction inched across my face because I had him powerless as always. It was his reactions to me that turned me on the most causing my wild girl to emerge and take control. After I bounced a little harder, I slowed down, rolling my body like the waves in an ocean. He moaned out while digging his fingertips into my hips and biting his bottom lip.

Just as I was about to place my hands on the floor, with the thought to place my feet onto the bed, he grabbed my wrists and stood up. It was now him in control as he rammed his mandingo warrior into my wet crevices at full force. I screamed out with pleasure dripping from my words, "Fuuuucccckkkk!"

The sound of my voice moaning out to him only made him ram me harder as he fully knew that I was an amazing gift from God. Electrifying sensations ran through my body as I loved every minute of it. The moment he stopped; my body shook as if there were aftershocks happening from an earthquake producing mini orgasms that I never knew I could experience.

He picked me up and tossed me on the bed just to switch it all up with kisses all over my body while his fingers were swimming in and out of my lady pond. He looked into my eyes as he slowly entered me again and I smiled back from the pleasure of his long deep strokes. My breathing increased causing him to whisper in my ear, "Take all of this dick like a good girl." Hearing those words sent me into overdrive with his strokes still nice and slow. The only words that I managed to say was, "Yes daddy" while squirting the hardest I ever had.

With a victorious smile, he kissed me and moaned, "That's my good girl." He blasted off inside of me hoping to see me pregnant in the upcoming months. Thinking that I'd probably take a nap as always, he laid on his back with *'Knocked Up'* playing on the tv.

I rolled over onto his bare chest and placed light kisses on him. His hands naturally resting on the small of my back as he kissed my forehead and asked, "You good."

My eyes filled with amazement as I asked, "Tutu, are we really married?"

With a chuckle, he replied, "And to think you didn't even remember who I was."

While smiling, I sighed with a wink and said, "I mean I could never forget my first kiss."

He darted his eyes at me and smirked as he stated, "No, I was your first everything!"

As I sat up and straddled him, blocking his view from the flat screen tv, I spoke softly with nothing but love while caressing his chest, "Okay okay. You're the first and the last. The beginning and the end. The Alpha and The Omega."

His smile quickly disappeared as he said in all seriousness, "Don't do that."

While bending down to give him sweet kisses on his neck and nibbles on his earlobe, I continued in a whisper, "Mmmm my King of Kings. My Prince of Peace. I love you, baby."

There was no denying how turned on he was to know that I loved him as if he was God himself. The Messiah returned as the love of my life and yet for so many years, he was considered the ugliest boy that walked the hallways of his high school where no girl dared to ever choose him so of course loving him wasn't even a thought. Skin was too dark. Lips were too big.

He was awkward and learning who he was when it seemed as if everybody around him had already discovered themselves. The only thing that made him attractive as a grown man was having a good paying job and a ring on his left hand. Somehow being unattainable with money was the most attractive thing to these floozies.

Showout embraced me as his true queen as the memories of so many pretty girls snickered and called him every name under the sun except for a child of God and here I was, the most beautiful woman that God had created, loving him unconditionally. I loved kissing his smooth sexy dark skin and completely infatuated with his full soft lips. I smiled with delight and desire every time we were together.

In my eyes, he was the sweetest dark chocolate covered perfection of a God and all I wanted to do was express that to him with every word that I uttered to him. With every single touch that I placed on him. With every luxury item that I gifted to him. With all of sweet nothings that I did with him. With the priceless time that I made for him. Fuck giving him the world.

I wanted to give him heaven. I wanted to create paradise with him. I needed him to know that our love was an eternal burning flame that couldn't be put out. My mission was finally complete..... find a man with a dream. I found a man whose dream was being with me.

Together we rolled over, where he was once again on top and kissing me passionately. He paused for a second to admire the woman that God had blessed him with laying in his arms with love in my eyes for only him as he said softly, "Niecy, I love you."

I smiled and pulled his head to mine, kissing him as my fingers slid amongst his beautiful locs. While into his eyes, I spoke softly, "I'm pregnant."

Tears welled up in his eyes as he slid himself down to my stomach planting kisses of love. This was our happily ever after.

Acknowledgments

To every reader that has enjoyed this story,
Thank You